HALF PAS. ⸻

Also by T. J. Bass

SF MASTERWORKS

Half Past Human

T.J. BASS

Short extracts from this novel first appeared in *Galaxy* magazine
(December 1969) titled 'Half Past Human' copyright © Universal
Publishing and Distributing Corporation 1969, and in *If* magazine
(November/December issue 1970) titled GITAR copyright © Universal
Publishing and Distributing Corporation 1970

This edition first published in Great Britain in 2014 by
Gollancz
An imprint of the Orion Publishing Group
Orion House, 5 Upper St Martin's Lane, London WC2H 9EA
An Hachette UK Company

1 3 5 7 9 10 8 6 4 2

A CIP catalogue record for this book
is available from the British Library

ISBN 978 0 575 12962 7

Typeset at The Spartan Press Ltd,
Lymington, Hants

Printed in Great Britain by Clays Ltd
St Ives plc

The Orion Publishing Group's policy is to use papers that
are natural, renewable and recyclable products and made
from wood grown in sustainable forests. The logging and
manufacturing processes are expected to conform to the
environmental regulations of the country of origin.

www.orionbooks.co.uk
www.gollancz.co.uk

INTRODUCTION

Thomas J. Bassler (1932–2011) was a medical doctor, who for too
few years wrote science fiction as T. J. Bass. This book and its
sequel, *The Godwhale* (1974) are the main part of his legacy. In them
the conflict between humanity and nature – including humanity's
own nature – is pushed to its limit.

Nature was big in the sixties. So was population, whose growth
seemed all the more pressing in cities crowded at the core and
sprawling at the edge. Wartime destruction and post-war recon-
struction had created in the advanced countries a new landscape of
motorway, freeway and high-rise, of suburbia and supermarket.
Above it hung a haze of pollutants, and the permanent threat of
nuclear attack; beyond it, in what was then called the Third World,
growing numbers of undernourished, dark-skinned people poured
into slums and shanty towns or slipped silently into the shadows to
swell the ranks of nationalist and communist insurgencies.

From Rachel Carson's *Silent Spring* (1962) to Paul Ehrlich's *The
Population Bomb* (1968), bestseller after bestseller sounded the alarm.
By the end of the decade many people felt that the megalopolis
crushed the human nature within it as much as it despoiled the
natural world without. The notion pervaded the counterculture so
plangently evoked in Charles Reich's *The Greening of America* (1970),
with its rejection of consumerism and its embrace of rural, folk,
and Native American culture and styles. In this – as in so many
other respects – the young radicals were only expressing more
strongly, if not always more coherently, a view shared by many
of their mainstream elders. Desmond Morris followed up his
bestselling zoological analysis of humanity, *The Naked Ape* (1967) –

serialized in the *Daily Express* – with *The Human Zoo* (1969), which compared urban humanity to caged animals.

The concern was vividly expressed in SF with John Brunner's masterpiece *Stand on Zanzibar* (1968), which draws dire warnings for the human future (exemplified by the violent, decadent, dome-covered New York City of 2010) from John B. Calhoun's studies of overcrowding in rats. One of the few technologically and ecologic-ally optimistic works from that time, *Approaching the Benign Environ-ment* (R. Buckminster Fuller et al, 1970) was swiftly countered and sharply criticized in the far more influential *The Environmental Handbook* (1970), soon to be followed by *A Blueprint for Survival* (1972) and *The Limits to Growth* (1972) on the shelves of every long-haired student's bedsit, including mine.

In *Half Past Human*, Bass takes these and related environmental and cultural hot topics and turns up the heat a thousandfold. Never mind the three and a half billion of 1968, or the seven billion of Brunner's 2010 (and ours): Bass projects a global population of three thousand billion. But as the title suggests, and the first page tells us, almost all of the three trillion are not quite human: 'mankind was evolving into the four-toed Nebish – the complacent hive citizen.' Stunted, pallid, brittle-boned and short-lived, this genetically engineered and prenatally mutilated subspecies can stand the overcrowding that normal humans can't, so it lives and in a measure thrives on the stacked levels of underground shaft cities. The seas are sterile. The entire useable surface of every continent is turned over to automated agriculture. The food chain is short (and circular). The scattered million or so surviving five-toed humans skulk and scavenge in these gardens as vermin, spotted by sensors and despatched by hunters. They are the last endangered species. Though savage, they are far from noble. They hunt the hunters, and they eat what they kill.

At first, all the characters are repulsive. The relict humans are cultish, clannish, and cannibals. The Nebish are callous, calculat-ing, and cannibals. Bass describes appearances, physiques, emo-tions and bodily reactions in the same language, that of physiology. The effect is deeply alienating. Horror and visceral disgust are natural reactions to much that passes – not to mention confusion, as the pace of events is swift. But we know we're not trapped in the nightmare: two artefacts that are themselves characters, Toothpick and Ball, imply past technological marvels, and hint at some continuation of an earlier human project. The mystery deepens as unauthorized radio messages beam into the underground cities from outside. It is soon apparent that the artificial intelligence that runs Earth Society has found an opponent that matches it in mettle, and in ruthless loyalty to its chosen human breed.

The story that unfolds is increasingly engrossing and entertaining, indeed thrilling. I'll be blunt: I found it hard to get going, and then I found it impossible to stop. It's a cracking piece of science fiction, an original and thought-through vision of a post-human world, and it sticks uncomfortably in your head. It'll make you think differently about a lot of things, including your own body and what you eat. The book's one glaring flaw is its treatment of women: in human and Nebish society, they exist solely as sex objects and mothers. Bass gives no indication that he notices, let alone cares. The book fails the Bechdel test with flying colours. Mark that down to the blinkers of male-chauvinist, late-sixties counterculture, before Women's Liberation got on its case.

By the end of the book, Bass has brought us to sympathise with human, Nebish, and machine characters, and to revel in the godlike sport with which he – and the rival AIs – slaughter them in millions or pick them off one by one. To say that this challenges our ethical intuitions is to put it mildly. But our ethical intuitions themselves are less secure than we may think. There is a well-known paradox in moral philosophy, identified years after Bass wrote but implicit in the utilitarian doctrine of the greatest good of the greatest number: the repugnant conclusion – as Derek Parfit (in *Reasons and Persons*, 1984) called it – that a large population whose lives are barely worth living may be better than a smaller population every one of whose lives are rich and fulfilling.

The brief lives of most of the Nebish are more than barely worth living – they have their little pleasures and rewards, and even joys – and there are three trillion of them. Are cannibalism, mass extinction of all non-edible species, prenatal brain hacking, occasional selective infanticide, and all the other horrors a price worth paying for such an enormous aggregate of dim happiness? Can we rationally and honestly prefer the violent, ignorant, brutish lives of savages, just because the savages share the full complement of our genes? Are we not, perhaps, being something close to racist when we side with *Homo sapiens* against *Homo superior*? Especially as the hive can itself engender at will new generations of the five-toed, if it decides it needs them for its own projects, all to the good of the greatest number? Isn't there something a bit fascist about our instinctive sympathies here?

There is a terrible Darwinian and utilitarian logic to Earth Society, of which Bass is well aware. Any successful human civilization, on this planet or on far-flung space colonies, carries the seed of the hive. Whether that seed grows is up to us, but there's a price to be paid, too, for nipping any such sinister development in the bud.

By making the repugnant conclusion literally repugnant, and by bringing the stern alternatives to it home to us like a hunter's bloody trophy, Bass makes us question some of our unthinking priorities, and does us all a powerful amount of good.

Ken MacLeod

1
Toothpick, Moon and Dan

Complex you are, Earth Society.
Simple I am, an aborigine,
    One of the In-betweens.
Your tubeways and spirals, everywhere.
Indigenous biota, long gone from there.
    I hunger for your greens.

In the Year of Olga, twenty-three-forty-nine, Moon and Dan returned to Rocky Top Mountain. Edentulous and withered with years, they sought refuge above the ten-thousand-foot level where the Big ES couldn't reach. In this, the third millennium, Earth was avocado and peaceful. Avocado, because all land photosynthesized; and peaceful, because mankind was evolving into the four-toed Nebish – the complacent hive citizen.

Moon and Dan had no time for complacency. Hunted and starving, they struggled for survival in an ecology where the food chain had been shortened to its extreme. Earth Society had squeezed its docile citizens between the plankton ponds and the sewers, until there were no niches for the In-between people except with the varmints and vermin – thieving from garbage and gardens.

The hive culture flourished underground. Three trillion Nebishes shared in Earth's bounty and found their happiness in the simple, stereotyped rewards rationed out by Earth Society – the Big ES. Nothing moved on the planet's surface except the Agromecks and a rare fugitive such as Moon. He was a five-toed throwback unable to adjust to the crowded society. Both he and his dog Dan were living fossils. Their species were crowded out by the Nebish masses, but they lived on. Both had been subjects in ancient experiments on the metabolic clock – rendering them clockless; so their bodies lingered through the generations enabling them to witness, in agony, the extinction of their kind. The extinction was still going on, for an occasional throwback still appeared in the Nebish stock – primitives left behind by evolution.

Faithful, dull-witted Agromecks labored in the avocado-colored vegetation, striving to catch every quantum of the sun's light energy and transform it into the needed carbohydrates. Their mechanical intelligences were suited to their tasks – they were dedicated, reliable. On this day in 2349 AO, a new meck brain stirred on Rocky Top Mountain. Its circuitry was far more complex – it was quick-witted and dedicated to no one and nothing but itself.

'Hi ho! Old man with dog. Pick me up.'

'Who speaks?' asked Moon, picking up a stone.

Dan's snout wrinkled back in a toothless snarl.

'I am down here, under these leaves.'

'The spirit of the spear?'

'No – I'm a machine. Toothpick is my name.'

Moon and Dan crouched a respectable distance away.

'You are no machine I know. Machines can move.'

'I am a small one – to be carried. Pick me up.'

Moon hesitated.

'But the metal detectors . . .'

'Don't worry. I'm not iron,' coaxed Toothpick. 'Pick me up. I can feed you.'

Moon and Dan were hungry.

'Edibles are always welcome, but how can you feed us if you cannot move?'

'Carry me and I will show you.'

Moon and Dan remained hidden.

'Feed us first, and we'll talk some more.'

In the silence that followed they heard the dry leaves rustle. Like a frozen worm the spear edged into view. They saw several inches of blade-on-shaft, then an optic. Toothpick studied them. They crouched lower.

'Return to the valley, old man,' instructed the cyber. 'There you will find Harvesters. When the rains fall it will be safe to take what you need.'

Moon scoffed silently to himself. He knew there were Harvesters. There always were. But rain! The sky was perfectly clear. Without a word he and his dog backed away from Toothpick. They would return to the valley, not out of faith in the talking spear, but out of caution – they felt safer in the valley with a strange intruder in their mountain refuge – and if there was one thing that their long In-between years had taught them, it was caution.

Senses alert, they crawled between the trees on the edge of the orchard. Harvesters rolled by on wide soft wheels like giant beetles, appendages folded up and thorax-like bins laden with plankton powder, fruits and vegetables. The sky glinted a bright, glassy plum-blue. They waited.

Moon saw an old familiar Harvester carrying a load of wooden tomatoes. He stood up shouting and waving at the machine's anterior bulge of sensors – the 'head' that housed neurocircuitry and communicator. The huge machine stopped and rotated its head toward the approaching human. Moon gave the balloon wheel a friendly pat.

'Good afternoon, human.'

Moon nodded and walked around the bulky machine giving its undercarriage a critical eye.

'Need any repairs?'

'Just a loose dust cover on my L box – but it can wait until I get back to—'

'I'll take a look at it,' said Moon, going to the tool kit. While he worked he glanced hopefully at the western horizon. The evening sun hid intermittently behind dark clouds. 'Anyone asking for me these days?'

'No,' answered the Harvester.

'Are you going to report seeing me?'

'I have not been ordered to. I only report what I am ordered to report.'

'I know,' said Moon, patting the machine affectionately. He knew it must report him if he stole part of the harvest. It would never hurt him or try to interfere, but it had to report any loss or damage.

Thunder rumbled softly in the distance.

'Mind if I ride along?'

'Enjoy your company,' said the machine as it started to roll.

Dan perked up his ears and began to pad along behind. A breeze carried scattered drops which pock-marked the dust. Soon, as Toothpick had predicted, fierce lightning flashed. Blinking through the downpour, old Moon packed slippery wooden tomatoes into his sack. Shouting over the thunder's roar, he asked the machine to stop. It obliged. He hopped off into the mud. It waved and moved on. It would report him as soon as the storm lifted – but that would be several hours later, if Toothpick proved right.

The banana sun was well up in the grape sky when Moon and Dan returned to the spot where Toothpick protruded from the musty humus. Below, on the flats, the thunderstorm dissipated.

'You are a god!' exclaimed Moon, sorting damp spheres.

'Hardly.'

'You brought the rains and kept Harvester from reporting me,' said Moon, cracking one of the tomato-colored, ten-inch fruits on a stone. He tossed pulp to Dan and began to gum a piece himself.

The cyber spoke carefully, didactically: 'I predicted the rain. The electrical activity of the storm prevented the Harvester from reporting. My abilities are based on science, not sorcery.' Toothpick paused to watch the old man and dog struggle with nutritious pulp in toothless mouths – then continued: 'Of course we could represent my powers as spiritual – gather a following – organize a religion—'

'Gather a following? Never!' spat old man Moon. He tossed down a coarsely gummed rind. Face screwed up in disgust, he shouted: 'Organization is what the Big ES thrives on – organize, cooperate and crush the individual. Never. Man was meant to be wild and free.'

Toothpick flexed his surface membrane charge and squirmed in the chocolate debris.

'Pick me up.'

Moon and Dan were still a bit chary about letting a talking javelin into their tight partnership.

'Why?'

'I am a companion robot – designed to offer companionship in exchange for companionship.'

'Dan and I are sufficient. What do we need with you? You can't even walk. You'd be a burden.'

Toothpick watched them preparing to move on. His little cyber circuits raced.

'Teeth,' it said. 'Both of you need teeth. Carry me and I'll help you find teeth.'

Moon flicked his tongue over the stumps of tender dentine that were almost covered by hypertrophic gum tissue. Almost two centuries of chewing had worn them away. The subsequent softening of his diet was softening his body too. He sighed. Oh, to bite and chew again – he could not finish the thought. He picked up the hundred-centimeter javelin and the three of them left Rocky Top.

William Overstreet stood on the long knoll watching a distant Huntercraft zigzag along the valley. He was naked except for a crumbling utility belt and dented helmet. The rest of his closed-environment suit had shredded away months ago. His skin showed the ugly geographic pattern of scar and keloid where the harsh sun had repeatedly peeled it away. His face – protected by the helmet – was only slightly pitted and puckered.

The Huntercraft spied him and stopped its random search pattern. He raised his right hand and started down the slope towards it – relying on his helmet and belt to keep them from shooting. He hoped they recognized him as a citizen and not a buckeye. He trotted casually, staying in the open – hoping to decoy them away from his nest.

His nest – for the past two years he had lived with the most beautiful female he had ever seen. Her name was Honey – after golden yellow hair. Her spirit was protean – like the phases of the moon. At new moon she growled and swam the Coweye Sump alone. At full moon she returned, and like her name, Honey, was sweet treacle. Her three yellow-haired children shared the nest too. The eldest was five. Their smooth skins varied from olive to mahogany, but their hair was their mother's. He hadn't seen Honey lately. Since she had begun to grow with his child her moods remained 'new moon' – luteal and hostile.

The craft set down and its hatch opened. Two hunters approached cautiously, carrying long bows. They wore the wrinkled white suit and spherical helmet of the Cl-En suit.

'Hi, fellas,' he said cheerily, waving.

They each grabbed one of his arms and ushered him into the dark cabin. Needle-like pricks hit his shoulders as the Hi Vol guns dosed him with hypnotic drugs. Hallucinations.

'Did you run a check on him?' asked the first hunter.

'This belt belonged to William Overstreet – lost on a Hunt two years ago. This fellow's bone structure fits, but his soft tissues are too messed up for positive ID.'

'Lost on a Hunt—' repeated the first hunter. 'Well, reinforce his hypnoconditioning. He can finish this Hunt with us.'

Willie stalked numbly. A voice said, 'Track.' He saw other hunters to the right and left. They were closing in on a small foxhole with three jungle bunnies. Arrows flew. Screams whetted his hunter's appetite. He raised his bow and sighted through the scope. Another scream. A hunter held up a bloody trophy.

A pink shape moved across his sights. The cross hairs set on a pair of symmetrical breasts. Below, the belly bulged with a three-month-gravid uterus. Above, he saw a disheveled head of bright yellow hair. A voice told him to shoot.

Vision skipped. Blanks appeared. He held up a pair of oval bloody objects trailing short white rubbery segments. He didn't recognize the surroundings. He was many miles from the Coweye Sump – perhaps over a hundred. The bloody trophy meant nothing to him. His mind was blank. An empty Huntercraft hovered over him – had been dogging his trail for hours. He waved it down and climbed in for a ride back into the hive.

The Mediteck/meck finished with him and pronounced his body scarred but healthy. The Psychteck was less than enthusiastic.

'This CNS reflex pattern indicates severe trauma – but the magnitude is difficult to evaluate – a lot of drugs were used on the Hunt.'

Willie rolled his eyes upwards – staring longingly at the door.

'See how he longs to go back Outside. I suspect he may have emotional attachments to a coweye in the region of Sump Lake.'

6

The Watcher listened to the Psychteck's analysis.

'Well, we could chuck him or suspend him, I suppose,' said the Watcher. 'But it is really too early to know how much of a problem he may be for the Big ES. Why don't we transfer him to one of the other countries – say, Orange Country. He has no attachments to the megafauna there. He may turn out to be a Good Citizen.'

The Psychteck nodded. Willie was transferred to a shaft city in Orange. One of his neighbors was a Pipe named Moses Eppendorff – sensitive and competent. Their city lay just west of the mountains.

The mountain range formed the geological backbone of two continents. Six thousand miles north of Rocky Top, other fugitives clung to their precarious existence in the cold, thin air of a lofty peak.

Ball, a metalloid sphere, occupied a rocky cairn in the center of a tattered Neolithic village. A place of reverence, the cairn was surrounded by meager food offerings. Ball had protected these villagers of Mount Tabulum until their numbers had grown into the hundreds. Dawn brought them out of their hide-sewn shelters with flint tools and clay bowls. Grain was crushed. Drying meats and fruits were fingered – work, work.

All activity stopped when the flap of the large shelter moved. Eyes focused on that flap. The wrinkled, bald male who stepped out wore flowing skins stained with metachromatic berry juices. Walking majestically to the cairn, he placed both hands on the sphere, which resembled his own head in size and baldness. For a pensive moment the villagers studied their seer's brooding face as he attempted to contact their unseen protective deities. Alarm appeared on that aged face. Food offerings were scooped into the folds of the robe.

Immediately the village broke up into families and small social units. Shelters came down. Burins, scrapers and truncated flakes were wrapped with grain and dried meats. The hide bundles were strapped on adult backs. Weapons appeared in calloused hands. Moments later the village was deserted – only dust and debris remained.

Across that dust walked a pubescent female – leaving clear, measured, five-toed footprints. She walked slowly and alone – down a narrow, steep trail on the rocky mountainside. She was bait. Six sullen males, each carrying a stout spear, watched her leave. Then they crouched into dark crevices along her trail.

Silence returned to Mount Tabulum. The sun climbed higher. A male child – puberty minus five – became lost during the flight. Wandering into the open, he never even heard the hum of the approaching arrow.

A nattily clad, fat, pale bowman approached the flopping jungle bunny. With a narrow, pointed boot he steadied the small ribcage while he ripped out the barbed tip of the hunting arrow. He unsheathed the short curved blade of his trophy knife and bent down over the twitching form. Mercifully, falling blood pressure clouded the victim's sensorium. His grisly trophy bagged, the hunter renocked his arrow and walked on up the trail. Finding the village deserted, he followed the five-toed footprints down another slope.

This was his third day without sleep – a small console on his neck titrated his blood level of Speed. Pausing cautiously, he studied the towering boulders. His wrist buckeye detector saw nothing through the dense stone. Spearchuckers shifted impatiently in their hiding places. A flash of movement at the bottom of the trail – the bait showed herself. Another trophy. He started down the trail at a reckless trot.

The first spear caught him in his wide belly. Shoulder-thrown, it hit solidly and penetrated to the lumbar vertibra. A shower of spears ventilated the insulated coveralls letting in air and sunshine – and letting out the rose-water fluids.

The circuits of the buckeye detector lay crushed on the trail. Chunks of fresh meat were divided among the fugitive villagers in their makeshift camps on the lower slopes. Their robed seer received his usual generous portion. His crystal ball had saved them again. The buckeyes of Mount Tabulum ate well that night.

A lonely Huntercraft searched the foothills for the lost hunter. It droned back and forth all through the night. The next morning it returned to Garage empty-seated.

The robed seer carried Ball into the circle of keening coweyes.

8

Placing his hand on the dead child, he chanted: 'The hunter's arrow has locked the little one's DNA-soul in limbo. It must be freed for Olga's return, so she can carry it from this accursed world. You must free the DNA-soul-gene by another birth.'

Wailing ceased. The naked aborigines took up the chant. 'Free the gene-soul for Olga's return – mate, mate, procreate – multiply – propagate – mate, mate.'

The wide garage doors sphinctered the craft inside. A flash of bright morning sun glinted about the work area momentarily blinding young Val – monitor-on-duty. He shielded his eyes with his hands. The craft settled down and quieted. Dust clouds scattered around the room. Coughing, a grimy face appeared under one of the dismantled chassis.

'Who is back?' gasped the face. It belonged to Tinker, a working neuter.

Val blinked and squinted at the craft's name.

'Bird Dog.'

Tinker scrambled out from under the chassis in a clutter of tools. 'Bird Dog? He is a whole day overdue. What about the hunters?'

Val checked the roster. 'There was only one. Baserga – a CD seven. It was supposed to be a routine patrol over Mount Tabulum. But he didn't come back.'

Tinker wiped oil from his hands and approached Bird Dog sympathetically. Lifting dust covers he checked webs of neuro-circuitry. Walking around to the anterior sensors, he took out his tools and began to detach the larger central eye.

'Poor old meck,' he said as he worked. 'No wonder you keep losing your hunters. You can hardly see. I'll take your big eye to my quarters and pump the vacuum back down to ten-to-the-minus-six torr. Put in a new EM retina. That should fix you up fine.' He lifted out the optic and examined the socket. Contacts glinted. He put on the dust cap.

'Minus six?' said Val. 'Our lines only go down to a minus three.'

Tinker put the meck eye on the workbench with a pile of other loose parts. 'I built my own diffusion pump a couple years ago – HV oil, sputtering unit, Christmas tree – brings it down to minus five. Use a cold trap to move it another decimal place.'

9

'Very handy,' said Val. 'We've had sensors on order all along – but deliveries are way behind.'

'I just rebuild the coarse ones. All they usually need are retinas and lenses. With the pump it is easy to rebuild them.'

Val followed Tinker around, handing him tools and asking questions. Huntercraft were his friends. He was happy to see them responding to Tinker's skills. Efficiency was bound to improve.

At eleven hundred hours old Walter wheezed into HC and relieved Val. Tools and defective parts were sack-loaded.

'Want me to help you with the sacks? I'd like to see your cubicle work-area,' offered Val.

Tinker shrugged and nodded.

The trip through the hot crowded tubeways and their long climb upspiral wilted Val's tunic. Wiping his face on his sleeve, he set down his load and glanced around Tinker's quarters. There were three small cubicles and one larger family room – all cluttered with tinkering gear. There were Agromeck heads staring at them with wide, empty sockets. Dispenser brain boxes, tools, communicators, sensors and viewscreens were piled everywhere.

'There's room for a family-7 here,' said Val.

'I'm pretty high on the spiral – far from the shaft base facilities. Not much demand for high quarters – and my repair work justifies increasing my quarters-basic.'

Val nodded appreciatively. A rebuilt dispenser stood by Tinker's small cot. Val touched the dial and a small token food bar dropped out.

'Built it myself,' explained Tinker proudly. 'Of course it isn't an authorized model, but it does give me someone to talk to – a class thirteen brain. But, like my refresher, it can't deliver any-thing unless the pressure reaches this level. That seldom happens these days – so I stock it with a few little staples I carry up myself. I have to go to shaft base for most things.'

Val spoke to the dispenser. It answered politely and offered him a menu of snacks. Its screen listed current Fun & Games. He shook his head and moved on down a busy-looking workbench. He saw a five-foot-high, three-foot-diameter black drum at the end of the room. It stood on thick insulating blocks and a bundle of wires trailed out of a length of flexi-cable at the center of the top. When he approached it, Tinker waved him away.

'Careful. I've been experimenting with a larger capacitor – to run my tools when the power is down. It is probably well charged now, and my insulation material isn't the best. I try to stay at least six feet away from it to be safe.'

Val marveled at Tinker's ingenuity. The drum looked very powerful, almost ominous. He gave it a wide berth and walked into the next cubicle. More electronic gear. Heavy cables led to a focusing antenna. Charts and maps covered the walls.

'Listening to Huntercraft and Agromecks,' explained Tinker.

Val put his nose close to one of the maps and looked for fine details he was familiar with. 'Very accurate.'

'Interesting hobby,' said Tinker.

The dispenser in the other room began to chatter and print out a flimsy. Tinker went to read it while Val fingered the thickly padded earphones.

'It's a birth permit – for me,' shouted Tinker.

'That's no surprise,' smiled Val. 'Big ES just recognizes your talents. We can always use more Tinkers.'

Tinker returned with a long face. 'But it is a class three – budchild with human-incubator-of-choice. I live alone.'

'So? Don't you have anyone who would carry for you?'

'No,' said Tinker, irritated. 'Who'd carry for free?'

Val nodded. 'I know what you mean. None of the polarized females seem to want to go gravid for a class three unless – unless they feel something personal for the budparent. Don't you have any friends with uteri?'

Tinker shook his head. 'Live alone. Simpler that way. I do my job – a good one too. Why would the Big ES want to upset everything? I'm not even polarized.'

Val soothed: 'I got partially polarized – needed the shoulders for archery – Sagittarius, you know. It wasn't too bad. I have my shoulders now. Also have to depilate weekly, but that isn't too bad. Made my temper a bit sharper. I'd hate to see what complete polarization would do to me – but if Big ES ordered it, I'd comply. Good Citizen that I am.'

For a neut, Tinker's personality was already a bit caustic.

'Not me,' he frowned. 'I don't want to see my output drop. I'm obedient, but anyone can see that I'm much more efficient living alone. A family-3 would clutter up my work area.'

Val understood. His cubicle was private – family-1.

'You could always try applying for a variance. Embryo might be able to change it to a class one. Let the meck uterus carry,' suggested Val. 'Go down right now.'

The Embryo clerk only glanced at the flimsy for a second and shook his head.

'Sorry, Tinker. It has to stay a class three. All our meck uteri are full and the budget is tight. Your budchild will have to come along on schedule. We must think of the future generations. They'll need your skills. Now, be a Good Citizen and find a female to carry it.'

'I have no female.'

'No one appeals to you?' asked the clerk checking Tinker's file. 'Your profile says—'

'I like everyone,' interrupted Tinker. 'But I'm not even polarized. I'm not sexually attracted to any—'

'There's no sex involved in a class three.'

'But there is,' explained Tinker. 'You are asking me to find a female who will carry my budchild without paying the usual job rates.'

'Carrying rates are for class two – when the Big ES selects the incubator.'

'I know. I know,' said Tinker. 'But I don't know anyone who would carry for me, free.'

The clerk nodded and punched the problem into the Embryo-meck. A new flimsy rattled out. It was a direct order.

'Get yourself polarized, Tinker. Then find someone who will love you enough to carry – and do it in six weeks.'

Tinker recognized the tone in his voice. An order from the Big ES. Clicking his heels, he snapped, 'Yes, sir. Right away, sir.'

Tinker pushed his way through the rancid, seborrheic crowds on his way to Polarization Clinic. He studied the sea of monotonous, pasty faces, searching for a possible incubator. Gnats and lice clung to the sticky skins of the more sluggish. He saw only vermin and spiritual ugliness. None showed signs of mentation, let alone stimulation. No possible mates.

'Going to swing hetero, honey?' cackled the Pol. Clin. Attendant – an arthritic, toothless old hag well up in her twenties.

'Order from Big ES,' he explained.

She sobered. With Parkinsonian tremors she uncovered her instrument tray. The knife steadied as it dug for the APC in the flesh of his forearm. She removed the time-release mesh.

'Here's your anti-puberty cocoon,' she said. Knife and mesh clattered onto the tray. Syntheskin was sprayed. Androgen and FSH priming doses were Hi Vol injected. Ten minutes later he stumbled back into the spiral crowds – feeling unchanged. Three weeks later a feeble erection announced that his sacral parasympathetics were polarizing. The boys in Psych charted his bioelectrical response to erotic stimuli – tone improved.

Other than warming his loins, polarization seemed to do little to solve Tinker's problem of finding an incubator. If anything, it made it even more difficult. His senses were more acute, and he was much more critical of his fellow citizens. He noticed new repulsive odors. The crowded, vermin-infested tubeways were intolerable. On his way to Hunter Control the stench got to be so bad that he vomited – adding his slippery stomach contents to the nondescript slime underfoot.

Tinker walked into Garage and began to empty his sack – placing repaired meck eyes on the bench.

'Polarization is rough,' he complained to Val. 'I vomited on the way over today. Never did that before.'

Val picked up an eye, admiring the bright new fittings. 'Your neurohumoral axis is getting stronger. Can't tamper with the gonads alone, you know. Pituitary, autonomic nervous system, adrenals, thyroid – all play their part in polarization.'

Tinker sat down, face pale. 'But what has vomiting to do with sex?'

'The reflex is autonomic,' said Val. 'Before, as a neuter, you ignored most of your environment – at least your body did. Now, you're becoming a sexually active male. I suppose it goes back to the jungles somewhere. Primitive creatures needed their senses to find mates and avoid enemies. Your body is looking for a mate now.'

Tinker drank some water. He climbed up onto Bird Dog's shoulder and plugged in the big eye he had been working on.

'That's all I need – for my gonads to take me on a trip back down the evolutionary tree. What will that do to my work output? What can Big ES gain from that?'

Val shrugged. 'No choice. With the budget so tight the hive can't afford all class ones. Meck uteri are too costly. And, apparently, your budchild will be needed in about ten years. So a class three is mandatory. Don't worry about your output. It might even go up if we all ignore some of your peculiarities while you're changing.'

Tinker felt like they were discussing his transformation into some sort of a beast. 'My peculiarities?' he said. 'At least I don't send hunters to their deaths in blind Huntercraft.'

Val raised an eyebrow. 'But we must have crop protection. The defective parts are back-ordered.'

'A little first-line maintenance might save a few lives. Or is getting oil on your hands above your caste?'

Val didn't answer. He just smiled and said: 'See what I mean about developing peculiarities. Polarization has certainly made you crusty.'

'Don't avoid the issue. If maintenance is outside your specialty, why don't you take one of your own ships out on a Hunt – a real Hunt, not just a shakedown cruise.'

Val smiled and walked away. 'Want anything from the dispenser?' he called over his shoulder.

Tinker returned to his work.

Tinker noticed a subtle change in the tubeway crowds. They were no longer a monotonous sea of faces. He was certain that the retinal images were still the same. Only now his visual cortex began to sort those images into neuts and polarized. The neuts faded into the background of Nebish nothings – a pasty collage of empty faces. The polarized, both male and female, instantly attracted his attention – sullen males – shapely fems. About one in a thousand appeared polarized.

His home spiral used to be just mildly unpleasant. That changed too. Rats and lice caught his eye. Maggoty bodies angered him. Then, for the first time, he noticed the begger – fat and edematous. He knew this discovery was due to his new visual sorting, for the begger had obviously been there for months – paralyzed – slowly dying of the wet beriberi. Stretcher-carrying Meditecks searched along the spiral. The begger hid in a dusty access hatch. A Sweeper slurped along cleaning up damp spots left by the begger's oozing ulcers.

Tinker stopped outside the hatch, listening to furtive move-ments from 'tween walls. 'Poor retired bastard,' he mumbled. He shouldered his way through the food line and ordered a liter of high-thiamine barley soup. Dispenser circuits noted this change from his usual diet. Ignoring suspicious optics, he carried the hot container back to the access hatch. Aromatic steam spread.

'Flavored calories,' he called, softly.

The begger drank with trembling hands while Tinker looked over his shoulder into the dark nest. Unopened packets of calorie-basic were scattered around in the thick dust. No flavors.

'That was nice,' said a female voice behind him.

Tinker turned and saw a very young polarized female. Her soft tunic was gathered by a tight belt. His eyes caressed her face and locked onto a pair of large symmetrical breasts.

'You are focusing,' she said coyly. The apathetic crowd van-ished before his eyes. Deep in his pelvis, synapses screamed FEMALE.

'What?' he stammered.

'That was nice,' she repeated. 'Giving that old man your food ration—'

His wits returned. Giving of alms was a function of Big ES. If the begger had to beg at all it meant he had lost his credits. Supporting such an outcast was wrong. He felt a flush of guilt – which was quickly replaced by anger.

'I can afford it.'

'It was still nice. Most citizens wouldn't even notice him.' She approached and leaned against him fingering his Sagittarius emblem. He stumbled back, awkwardly. Body contact was meld activity. It felt wrong in public.

'Who are you?' he blurted.

'I am Mu Ren,' she said distinctly. 'One-half MRBL – second subculture, Mu Renal cell line from the BL clone. But that isn't important. What is important is – that I am ten years old, spontaneously polarized, and assigned to you as a class three incubator.'

He pulled his eyes away from her soft curves long enough to see her footlocker behind her.

'The Watcher assigned me,' she said, reaching for his hand.

Tinker tried to look at her analytically, but the fire in his loins colored his judgment. She did appear to be a complete polarization, and if it had actually been spontaneous then she should make a very good incubator.

'Watcher took me out of the stacks when I polarized. I was assigned to a family-5, but I hesitated in the meld. Because of my youth I was given a rematch. Your request for an incubator came through just in time. I think I could enjoy a family-2.'

Tinker took her hand. 'Come on,' he said. They elbowed their way to the head of the complacent queue and ordered staples from the dispenser. She carried foodstuffs and he shouldered her locker. His walk upspiral had never been so enjoyable before.

Mu Ren smiled approvingly at Tinker's quarters.

'I only touched on electronics in my studies,' she said. 'But I recognize components from city cybers and field mecks. You are very good with your hands.'

Her body's attraction crowded into his consciousness making rational thought difficult. Nervously, he pointed to some of the larger machines – trying to familiarize her with her new surroundings. She noticed his impatience and turned to him.

'I am going to enjoy living with a man who is good with his hands,' she said. Taking his wrists she moved his trembling fingers over her tunic. Her soft erogenous zones radiated warmly. His autonomic synapses struggled with the increasing excitement. Passion flared somewhat erratically, and then, abruptly, faded. While he stood there, the heat in his loins melted away – leaving fatigue.

She continued to lean against him for a moment. Hugging him briefly, she walked to her locker and began to unpack. He stood in the middle of the room – puzzled. She placed her ESbook on the cot and unrolled her bedding on the floor. Seeing his disappointment, she jumped up and ran back to him . . . nuzzling warmly.

'You have just recently polarized,' she consoled. 'Your meld reflexes need time to synchronize. We will work at it, and it will improve.'

She settled down – adapting quickly to Tinker's peculiar quarters. Talking to the class thirteen dispenser. Avoiding the big black condenser. Improving their meld.

The Embryoteck probed Mu Ren's tender forearm and removed her anti-ovulation sponge. Ignoring her winces he prepared the Hi Vol gun with estrogens.

'Can't have conflicting hormones, now – can we? We'll have your endometrium all ready for little Tinker Junior in about four weeks. Come back then and we'll do the implant.'

'Could I see him now?' she asked softly.

The teck brushed her callously towards the door. 'No. Nothing to see now except clone soup in foaming nutrients. Be patient. In six months he will be kicking and squirming around in there. You will have a wonderful time.'

Flushed with the follicular phase effect she returned to Tinker. But she did not have a wonderful time. Four weeks after implantation she passed a large clot. Depressed, she noticed that the fullness in her belly was gone. Her breasts no longer tingled. Fearful that she would not be authorized as an incubator again, she searched her footlocker for her Ov earring. Her meld activities became warmer – more purposeful. Hopefully, she watched the earring. Two weeks later she was rewarded with an ovulation. Her belly began to grow again – a little behind schedule, but it grew. Tinker, preoccupied by strange tightbeam signals from the planet's surface, failed to notice anything unusual. At forty-two weeks post-implantation, the Embryo Clinic summoned her for a check-up. She refused.

'One-half MRBL,' demanded a voice from the doorway.

Mu Ren glanced up fearfully and saw two heavy reliable neuters wearing golden emblems of The Ram – Aries – Security Squad. Her face whitened. She set down her stitching and glanced past them into the crawlway. Three more neuters leaned on their quarterstaffs down by the spiral.

'Reading in the Tee zone,' said the neuter holding a scanner. 'This must be Tinker's quarters.' The two entered and glanced around. The jumble of electronic gear meant little to them. They stayed by the door.

After several long moments of strained silence the SS neuter holding the scanner appeared worried. Mu Ren's pendulous belly and tremulous movements upset his instrument.

'Relax, please,' he said. 'This is just a routine check on communicators. Nothing for you to be concerned about.'

She sighed. Her uterus tightened a little so she stretched out on the cot covering her feet with her wrap. It was a relief to know they weren't from Embryo – after the fetus.

Tinker arrived carrying staple foodstuffs. Smiling like a Good Citizen, he unloaded onto the pantry shelf and began to answer their questions. Yes, he had noticed unusual radio signals. No, he hadn't been using a tightbeam transmitter. No, he had no idea where the signals came from. Yes, he'd keep them informed. They left – satisfied.

Mu Ren looked at him, questioning.

He ignored her unspoken question while he fastened a bulky hasp to the door. Stepping to the workbench he pressed one earphone to his right ear.

'Transmissions from the surface – from Outside,' he said, wiggling dials and changing the position of a string on his wall map. 'They are not from the usual Huntercraft or Agromecks. I didn't know what to make of them, but tonite's SS visit has convinced me of one thing. They are unauthorized transmissions.'

Unauthorized. The term bleached her face again. She moaned weakly and sat down.

'Now, now, there is no danger. Probably just a renegade meck going through an identity crisis with his WIC/RAC. The what-if-circuit and random-association-circuit can be very labile. I've heard of class sixes running amok until their power cells are depleted. But nothing is usually lost except a few crops,' he soothed.

His words had little effect on the gravid female. Tears streaked her cheeks.

'Our baby isn't authorized,' she blurted.

He didn't hear. Both earphones were on. He swung the biconical antenna around to catch the messages as they filtered down through the walls and organs of the shaft city.

'We're lucky we have this high cubicle,' he mumbled. 'Any deeper in the earth and I wouldn't be getting any of this.'

A Braxton-Hicks contracture tightened Mu Ren's fundus. She sat on the cot. Tinker leaned into his earphones listening to feeble sounds – a sing-songy chant.

> *Oh happy day*
> *Oh happy da—ay*
> *When Olga comes*
> *She'll show the way,*

Verses were separated by the beat of a pounding surf, guitars and the *ching, ching, ching* of tambourines.

> *High up on the mountain*
> *Dwells the magic ball*
> *Listen to its wisdom*
> *Do not trip and fall*
> *Run through the gardens run*
> *Do not trip and fall.*

Tinker knew of the Followers of Olga – a cultish fraternal organization discouraged by the Big ES. But he could not understand them broadcasting. If they did violate Big ES law and venture into gardens, the broadcasts would only betray their crime and attract hunters. Security Squads were already investigating. The advice – 'Do not trip and fall' – was very appropriate if hunters were tracking. But what was a magic ball? Puzzled, he removed his earphones.

When he found Mu Ren sobbing herself to sleep, he patted her plump buttock and said: 'It's just the partum blues, Mu. Don't let them get you down.'

'Our baby isn't authorized,' she wailed.

'Now, now, of course it is,' he said. 'I have the papers right here.'

'But we need a class five,' she said.

He put a hand on the belly, feeling a kick. Slowly he calculated the time lapse since implantation.

'A hybrid?' he asked softly.

She nodded through reddened eyes.

He grinned – 'A hybrid.' Sitting up in amazement, it took several more seconds for him to realize what she was getting at.

'What will become of it?' she sniffed.

His face fell.

'It isn't authorized,' he answered weakly. 'They will come for it.'

She sobbed herself to sleep. Agonizing dreams ruffled her alpha waves. Sound became color. Colors flowed into flavors. A meat-flavored patty contained a small hand open in supplication. A tiny finger pointed into her mother's heart. The meat flavor became sound – the sound of a baby's cry as it hit the blades of the patty press. Mu Ren came full awake in the terror of her first nightmare – the first of many.

Tinker's nonritual hugs did little to allay her fears. He began to doubt the wisdom of the hive.

The naked, hirsute aborigine fled across Filly's green cyberskin. This was his fifth day without sleep. His right neck ached where the first hunter's arrow had struck. Fibrin and erythrocyte crusts covered the edematous laceration. He had managed to kill that hunter, but another was put down. That one dropped from exhaustion after three days tracking. Now the Huntercraft was back. Its keen optics sought him out. Underfoot. Filly's sensors fed coordinates back to Hunter Control. His every footstep itched the city. A third hunter swung down-harness – a short, fat, bug-eyed killer with an ugly trophy knife and a deadly long bow.

Filly's organs surrounded her mountain – a single ice-capped peak. The buckeye climbed. His ridged, hyper-keratotic palms and soles gripped granular stone surely and lifted him up. The icy wind pulled his long gray hair back from his tired old eyes. The only name he knew was Kaia, a name given to him by his first mate – in her language it meant *The Male*.

Bird Dog IX rested on an eight-thousand-foot ledge, tracking. Sharp optics followed Kaia's slow ascent up the sheer face of a thirteen-thousand-foot overhang. Ninety millimeters of oxygen triggered his cardiopulmonary adjustments to the altitude. Below, struggling in his clumsy suit, the Nebish hunter turned up his oxygen and followed. Above, a deep white snow beckoned – offering a soft, peaceful sleep. Kaia weakened. Hoary frost grew on the hairs of his scalp and forearms. Below him, on the same cliff, the hunter was stalled. The white suit and helmet resembled a snowman.

'Come back,' called Bird Dog. 'He is trapped up there. No need to track. Come back.'

The hunter's hypnoconditioning did not allow for interruption of the tracking frenzy. He kept clawing at the sheer rock until his motor end-plates fatigued. The poor Nebish had already exerted himself far beyond the capacity of his soft body. A light gust of wind lifted his numb form from the rock and sent it sailing down into the clouds below. Bird Dog tracked – and noted the impact area.

Kaia hadn't seen the hunter's flight. He was too high, and too intent on sleep. Bird Dog's powerful optics relayed Kaia's climb to Hunter Control.

'We'll never get that body down from there,' said Val.

Walter turned up the magnification. Kaia crawled into a shallow cave and heaped snow over the mouth. Bird Dog's sensors watched through the snow as the naked aborigine curled up on the rocky floor and rapidly cooled off.

'At least we know where the body is,' said Walter, 'if we ever find anyone fool enough to want to climb up for the trophy. Should keep well at those temperatures – especially since winter is coming.'

Moon and Dan hid under a pile of greenish-brown fiber trash half way down a cliff. Below them a Huntercraft skimmed over the waters of a wide deep canal. Toothpick's pointed nose projected above the trash.

'It is circling back. Will pass overhead. Don't move,' said the cyber.

They heard the drone rise and fall. The fibers danced in the wind. Silence. Moon thrust his head up.

'Smells like the ocean. We're miles inland.'

'That's the sea-level canal.'

'We're going to swim that?' he asked, raising his voice.

Toothpick cast his optic about.

'We'll use dry stalks and gourds to float us.'

Moon strained his eyes.

'But I can hardly see the other side.'

'It is less than two miles. We can take our time.'

Moon remained deep in the trash.

'Your teeth are on the other side. It isn't far now. Don't you want to be able to crack open a femur again?' said Toothpick.

Moon pursed his lips and gummed thoughtfully. His edentulous dog, Dan, glanced up at him trustingly.

'Where are the damn gourds?' he said, climbing about in the vegetable trash.

The night sky held a lunar crescent and a few stars. Moon aimed his bundle of gourds at the North Star and kicked slowly, purposefully. Dan paddled around him several times and then came to rest with his paws on the old man's back. Toothpick was tied among the gourds.

'Careful,' said the cyber. 'You're pushing me underwater again. I've got to pick out a safe landing spot. If we ever do this again, I'll design a float with an outrigger for stability.'

Moon shuddered at the cold brine.

'We won't be doing this again.'

The lunar crescent slipped below the western horizon. Toothpick watched the north shore moving by as the currents swept them along. The shaft cities on this continent looked about the same – squat pillbox caps housing the end-organs of vast underground warrens. Cybercaps that watched over the gardens. They would be in danger if the morning sun caught them exposed. Cybercap's eyes could be sharp when scanning the open waters of the canal.

'Stay off shore,' said Toothpick. 'There is a better landing site coming up.'

They drifted into a steep rocky slope carved out of a high ridge. Crags offered cover, but Moon was exhausted. Dawn found him sleeping on a narrow ledge.

'Good a place as any for a rest,' shrugged the cyber.

Fat old Walter wheezed into Hunter Control to find Tinker and Val in tense conversation.

'What's got you youngsters so upset?' he asked as he eased his bulk into the control seat and activated his console.

'It's his pregnancy,' said Val. 'It is unauthorized.'

'But I'm a good worker. My child will be a good worker.'

Walter assessed Tinker's anxiety. These family-2 situations were dangerous. Imprinting wasn't diluted effectively, and the pair tended to grow too fond of each other. Bad for ES efficiency.

'Your permit is a class three – carbon copy?' said Walter.

Tinker nodded.

'For a hybrid you'd need at least a class four,' continued the fat old man. 'Probably a class five, since Mu Ren is far too young to have earned the right to reproduce herself. That's it. Class five. Hybrid permit with mate-of-choice. Have you applied for a variance?'

Tinker hung his head.

'As soon as I found out,' he said sadly. 'The committee hasn't met yet, but the meck who took the application explained that it usually took some act of planet-wide benefit to earn a class five. Probability very low.'

Walter patted the younger man's shoulder and said cheerfully: 'Well, a meck isn't a committee. We have men to decide such things – human beings. You have been a very good worker, Tinker. I know some of the committee members. I'll speak with them this morning. Why don't you try to relax. Go for a shake-down cruise with Val. Doberman needs checking out.'

Val and Walter exchanged glances. Tinker was too preoccupied to notice the thick stack of wrinkled charts – unusual for a mere shakedown cruise. *Doberman III* flexed his hinge muscle as they approached. The hatch opened to a dim cabin.

'Morning, sirs,' greeted the craft.

Val climbed in, tossing the charts on the dash. He fumbled for harness buckles. Tinker paused.

'Won't we be needing our closed-environment suits?'

'Under the seats. Climb in.'

Val fed the charts through Doberman's map digester. They rolled through, coming out flat and indexed.

'If the variance is denied—' began Tinker, 'I think I'd like to keep the child as long as possible. The grace period runs until it starts to walk or talk.'

Val shook his head vehemently.

'I wouldn't try that!' he exclaimed. 'The chucker teams would be nosing around your cubicle – stalking the little infant. Too much anxiety. Oh, I know that Psych Clinic sometimes orders fem citizens to go gravid to develop their own female identity. Those fems don't seem to mind having their kids chucked down the chute. But you and Mu Ren are different – sensitive. Better if you chucked it right after it was born. Easier.'

Tinker looked weak – helpless.

'If you can't do it, I'll come over and do it for you. That's what friends are for,' said Val absently. He didn't notice his troubled friend flare up.

Sphincter opened. Garage said, 'Goodbye.' In a moment they were traveling at tree-top level. The sun looked like a lunar disc through the step-down windows. Tinker noticed the charts for the first time. He picked up one.

'What are these coordinates?'

'Transmissions – unauthorized tightbeams from the Outside. Our questing beams picked them up. There is nothing unusual on our buckeye detectors – thought we'd check them out visually.'

Tinker studied the chart. One of the coordinates lay over the same line he had been receiving on the night before.

'Security has been picking them up too.'

'This is a matter for Hunter Control,' frowned Val. 'It is coming from the Outside – maybe even the gardens.'

They passed over orchards and low fields of triple-crop – the mixture of stalk plants with vines and herbs. Tinker glanced from the chart to the window. The mountain range lay ahead – dozens of peaks – the taller ones with white ice caps.

2
Tinker's Ritgen Rag

Awakening to the bright cheerful summer, Flower raised his head and smiled his pollen face at his green neighbors. Lifting his eyes to the sun he saw the Glory – the orange world of the red octopus – shimmering gold and watery red. Arms tingled. Toes groped for soil damp. Sun shared Great Truths with his flower mind. His soul expanded. Rapture. Ecstasy faltered with autumn. Where were his bees? Pollen wasted. Actinics browned his green. Toes lost their arthritic grip. Where were his bees? Withered and drying, he fell into the soil without reproducing – returning to the nitrogen cycle unfulfilled. A flower soul moved on.

Doberman III circled lower for a closer look. Tinker felt the nausea of burning gastric juice in his throat. A decomposing body lay in the garden. It was supine and naked. Roots and stolons invaded the flaking, red-brown skin. Empty sockets gazed upward.

'Another flower reaction,' said Val caustically. 'It looks like a neut – an unpolarized male. Probably just an overdose of Molecular Reward. Neuts don't have much Inappropriate Activity. Suicide is unlikely. The poor Nebish thought he was a flower and came Outside to commune with the sun – a phototropic catatonic schizo due to MR. Too late for sampling.'

'Flower reaction?' said Tinker.

'Dying in the open like that. Under the sun. The hard rays just peel the skin right off – in a few hours. We see two kinds of flowers in the Gardens. Suicides, and drug reactions. Old Molecular Reward. The Big ES rations it out to Good Citizens, and we use it to bolster hunters' nerve; but it is dangerous. The boys from

Neuro can differentiate between MR and IA. But they need fresh brain tissue. We'll just leave this one. It will be part of the crop pretty soon anyway.'

Tinker mumbled something about a very hostile garden.

'Air is pretty thin here in the upper slopes. Hang on. We'll go down and use the wheel drive,' said Val, kicking the craft into manual. His eyes gleamed as he maneuvered up the narrow trails, squealing wheels and grinding gravel. The craft lurched along, fish-tailing on tight turns and accelerating smoothly on flat areas. When they stopped, Tinker saw several miles of broken and tilted rock.

'Mount Tabulum.'

'It looked a lot more like a table from far away.'

'It's pretty flat,' said Val, edging the craft forward. 'There's sign of buckeye. See the charcoal surrounded by stones? Used to be many Eyepeople around here before we hunted them down. Too bad they're so depleted. They were good sport. But they were a danger to the crops – so they had to go.'

Wheels jounced them across the table past an acre of ice-rimmed melt-water. The opposite edge looked out over other snowy mountain peaks. A mile below, the slopes were covered with glaciers of cube apartments. They drove back to the lake in the cup-like center of the table. Tinker studied the dash readings.

'Fourteen thousand feet! I was going to step out and taste that water, but I'd need my oxygen bottle at this altitude.'

Val adjusted the scanners, saying, 'The buckeye seems to get along fine up here. Plenty of water – unless the pink snow poisons it – and safe from the hunters. Citizens can't come up here without a machine or a heavy mountain Cl-En suit. Used to be a fifteen-thousand-foot mountain until something nipped off the peak. Note the serrated edge around the cup. Rocks look melted too.'

'What could cut off the top like that?' asked Tinker.

Val shrugged. 'Don't know. The shock waves scrambled meck brains for miles around. A large Hunt was in progress up here. No recordings survived. Clean. No induced radiation.'

Tinker frowned. Earth-moving projects in the Sewer Service

gave him enough experience to appreciate the energy involved. He couldn't even guess at the cause. The results were clear – several acres of flat space useless to the hive but ideal for buckeyes.

The scanners swept over the campsites. Ashes and firestones – recent. Many of the bones had not yet bleached.

'The stones are cold,' said Val. 'Not surprising. Even if there are buckeyes up here, it would be impossible to sneak up on them in this noisy craft.'

'No sign of a communicator, though,' said Tinker. 'The distance from here to my receiver – through all the soil and walls – would tax a small tightbeam. Something big enough to transmit that far would be impossible to hide up here.'

Val nodded, satisfied. He steered for the edge. Wheels lurched down the slope displacing small rock slides. Several times he recklessly activated his air stream – lifted off into the thin atmosphere – and crunched back into the shifting gravel. Impatient. Finally, on the lower slopes, he lifted successfully and flew west. An hour later they were over an empty blue ocean.

Tinker hit the magnifiers. Scanners showed only sterile, clear water. A broken tubeway lay on the bottom like a snake carcass – skin peeling and strut ribs exposed. Cold bubble buildings covered shelves at six and ten fathoms – skummy and dark. At five hundred feet, they flew back and forth along the coordinates of the tightbeam. Sand, surf and horizon island specks. None of the islands fit the coordinates.

'What were all those blue-domed cysts on the bottom?' asked Tinker. 'They've been dead a long time.'

'Rec Domes,' said Val. 'Underwater Recreation Centers. When the tubeway died – they died. No demand for them these days. Few citizens swim. No megafauna in the ocean, anyway. The Sewer Service sent out subs to record structure deterioration when I was a boy. Saw the playbacks. I doubt if the Big ES will go back into the sea again – too much work to do.'

For hours they searched the open waters. They saw one small rocky island with a few stubborn plants.

'Not crop plants, probably,' said Val. 'If we had more time it might be interesting to see what does survive on a barren island like that – without the Tillers and Agrifoam of the Big ES.'

Tinker glanced at the chronograph. 'Speaking of time, shouldn't we be starting back?'

Val lifted his hands from the controls.

'Home, Doberman.'

Walter met them in the garage. He appeared depressed.

'Must be important,' said Val. 'For him to walk all the way down here.'

Wheezing, belly swinging, old Walter waddled up to them.

'It's Mu Ren,' he said. 'Labor has started. Your dispenser called me.'

Tinker started to run for the door.

'The variance was denied,' called Walter.

Val caught up with Tinker downspiral.

'Won't the Mediteck be there?'

'No authorization.'

They were sweating heavily when they arrived. Mu Ren dozed between contractions. Tinker looked at the viewscreen. A sensor was glued to her belly and biolectricals ran across the screen. Fetal and maternal cardiograms looked good to him. He placed a hard board under her buttocks to keep the outlet up out of the fluids. The dispenser's class thirteen meck brain sorted through its delivery program.

'Mu Ren, pull your knees,' it said when the next contraction began. She awoke and put her fingers behind the bend of her knees, pulling her thighs up and out. Bag of waters bulged. Tinker sorted through his tray of instruments – two snub-nosed clamps and a pair of blunt scissors. Membranes burst with the next contraction. Fluids gushed. A black hairy head showed. It was still inside.

'Presentation?' asked the dispenser. Diagrams appeared on the screen. Tinker palpated the top of the baby's head. The larger diamond-shaped fontanel was posterior – towards her sacrum.

'Baby is facing sacrum.'

'Occiput anterior, very favorable,' said the screen.

With her next contraction her perineum stretched and the top of the hairy head bulged into view again.

'Ritgen rag,' said the meck. Tinker picked up a coarsely woven, dry hand towel and supported her perineum. Between contractions he lifted upwards and delivered the baby's head.

'Cord check,' said the meck.

Tinker flicked mucus from the little puckered pink face and felt deep between the baby's neck and shoulder. One loop of the umbilical cord circled the neck. It felt tense. He dug his middle finger under the cord and pulled quickly. It didn't budge. The fetal cardiogram became erratic. The meck accentuated the irregular pulse by putting it on audio. Tinker worked faster.

'One loop,' he said, reaching for the pair of snub-nosed clamps. *Click, click*. Picking up the scissors, he cut between the clamps. The head moved out a fraction of an inch and the cardiogram smoothed. Guiding the head down, he released the anterior shoulder from under her symphysis. Lifting, he released the posterior shoulder. The rest of the infant tumbled out in a jumble of cord and a gush of fluid. Wiping the wrinkled face, he handed the still infant to Val.

'I'd better chuck it down the chute before she hears it cry. That'd ruin her day,' mumbled Val, turning to the door. He held the wet, cheesy infant at arm's length, like garbage gone sour.

Tinker was busy with the afterbirth. Mu Ren's uterus was filling with clots and the placenta bulged into the vagina. She went pale and silent.

Val crawled down towards the spiral leaving a trail of cloudy white drops in the dust. The infant began to squirm and cry vigorously. Large eyes blinked at him. He tried not to return their gaze.

Val set the blades between chop and dice. He glanced down the dark chute. The granular brown walls carried nondescript stains that spoke of the varieties of waste it accepted. Standing back he began to swing the infant underhanded. If he tossed it expertly it should fall the two hundred feet to the blades with only minimal trauma against the walls.

'She's bleeding,' called Tinker.

Val glanced back to see Tinker's worried face in the crawlway. His swinging had quieted the infant.

'Did you try pressing the fundus?'

'Didn't help.'

'Try calling the white team. A Mediteck with his Medimeck.'

'Won't come. No paper work for this pregnancy. It is un-authorized.'

They both glanced down at the cooing infant. Dark eyes watched them. They smiled.

'The nipple-midbrain-uterine reflex,' said Tinker.

They carried the infant back to Mu Ren. She was trying to massage her uterine fundus, but the hemorrhage continued.

'Breastfeed,' said Tinker, handing her the infant.

She fumbled weakly, but the infant quickly locked onto the nipple – sucking strongly. Immediately she felt her fundus cramp and harden. The bleeding stopped.

'He doesn't know he is unauthorized,' she said.

Several months later Tinker brooded over his bench at Garage. A tool kit with shoulder harness hung from his stool. Val came on duty and was surprised to find him there.

'What brings you in so early?'

'Couldn't sleep,' said Tinker. 'Besides, I'm not here for duty – just packing my things.'

'Oh?' said Val, fingering the kit.

'Going on strike,' continued Tinker. 'I've been down to the Department of Population Control every day this month. Always the same thing. No variance on my class three birth permit. They want me to turn in the hybrid.'

Val adopted a sympathetic facade – more to keep a good worker in the garage than out of any true feeling for the infant.

'The committee's vote is usually final,' he said realistically.

Tinker squared his shoulders.

'Well, we will see how the Big ES gets along without me. I keep half the machines in this city functioning.'

Val nodded. 'True, but all you will do is lower our standard of living. We can't influence the committee. Old Walter tried that. You need a planet-wide contribution – a heroic act to match the class five permit.'

Tinker's androgenic shoulders stayed square – his chin up.

'We'll see,' he said, strapping on his kit.

*

30

Mu Ren watched Tinker unload the staples.

'Calorie-basic?' she said.

He nodded and grunted.

'On strike. Pushing for a variance.'

She had watched the pressures of the past months wear him down – gone was the open-faced innocence of his neutral years. He barked and growled, threatening trauma to the clerks. He walked to his workbench and put on the earphones. She stood behind him with her arms around his shoulders and her forehead pressed against the back of his head.

'He's crawling already,' she whispered.

He glanced around the room.

'Better pick up anything small and sharp. He'll just put it in his . . .' he began. Realizing that the chute awaited the infant any day now, the theoretical danger of swallowing a sharp object seemed ridiculous.

'Well, anyway . . .' he cleared his throat. 'The chucker team won't know he is crawling. He is way ahead of schedule in his neuromuscular development.' After a moment's reflection he added: 'And don't let Val in here anymore. He's such a Good Citizen he'd feel he had to report Junior's maturity – Val, the GC bastard!'

Tinker set his jaw and spliced his five-foot, black capacitor into the communicator's power line. Pouring water into the heat sink, he checked the polarity reversal. A shaped field probed around the room, rustling loose tools. Mu Ren returned to her bedding and curled up with her child. The screen blinked with concentric dancing circles. Musical notes pulsed. He noted the coordinates, narrowed the beam, and called.

'Who is out there?'

The music grew loud and clear as the other transmitter locked onto his position. The concentric circles collapsed to a pinpoint. A metallic voice interrupted the tune.

'Who asks?'

Tinker worried about the ripples of green light on the edges of his screen – Security's questing beams. He doubted if they would be able to lock in well enough to get their conversation. He worked fast – identifying himself quickly.

'My name is Tinker – of HC City.'

'My name is Harvester,' answered the coarse voice.

'A renegade?' asked Tinker.

'A free meck,' corrected the voice. 'Disciple of Olga. If you wish to be free from the damnable hive you may join us – wild and free – the tribes of Mount Tabulum. A Tinker is always welcome. There is much work to do.'

'Free?' mumbled Tinker, hopefully.

'We offer you freedom and flavored calories. Join us. Olga will protect you.'

Tinker studied his wall map. Beam coordinates lay across the Mount Tabulum which he and Val had visited. The area had seemed deserted.

'Where will I find you?'

'Can you get a compass reading from my tightbeam?'

'Yes.'

'Two hundred twenty-eight miles. A mountain with a flat top. We will be looking for you.'

'I'll have to think it over.'

He glanced at Mu Ren and the infant. The dangers of the gardens were very real to him. He had seen the effects of exposure on hunters.

'Travel at night,' said Harvester. 'We will decoy the hunters so you should be safe. But stay in tall vegetation and below canal banks. Don't carry metals. If you cover more than ten miles a day they won't be able to hold a fix on you. I must sign off now – a questing field tickles our beam. Don't wait too long.'

Tinker took off the earphones slowly.

'Who was that?' asked Mu Ren sitting up.

'I'm not sure, but we'll find out. We're going Outside.'

Fear crossed her face. She hugged the infant.

'The variance will come through,' she cried.

He went to her side and patted her head.

'This is our . . . Junior's only chance,' he soothed. 'We'll be prepared for the exposure and try to avoid the hunters. I'll pack what we'll need. It won't be too bad. We have maps.'

'No one goes Outside and lives,' she blurted. 'The Inappropriate Activities and the Molecular Rewards – they go out to die. If the hunters don't get us, the buckeyes will. They're vicious cannibals.'

He gave her a nonritual hug. 'There are Followers of Olga out there. They'll protect us.'

She was unconvinced, but he began to make preparations immediately. Several trips to shaft base supplied him with extra issue tissue clothing, mending tools, small medipacks, and bedding. Avoiding metals, he made up back packs, utility belts and a papoose frame to carry Junior. Tinker strapped the frame on his back and tested it for size.

Unexpectedly, two heavy men stepped into the doorway – reliable neuters from Security.

'Planning on going somewhere?' asked the captain in a cruel voice.

Tinker reflexively smiled his Good Citizen smile.

'Certainly. A Climb. My vacation. You should have checked before you came over.'

It was twenty-one hundred hours. The squad must have been scrambled as soon as they had a fix on his tightbeam. He doubted if they knew anything about him personally. They hesitated. Out in the crawlway he heard another SS man call in about the Climb vacation. Tinker leaned out the door. Three more stood back by the spiral – quarterstaffs and throwing nets.

Mu Ren clutched her infant nervously. A third SS neut entered with a communicator.

'He is bluffing about the Climb. Very anti-ES family-3. Unauthorized infant. He's on job strike. She has ignored Clinic summons. Warrants are out on all three.'

First officer took out his set of ankle hobbles.

'We'll take these two in. Chuck the kid down the synthesizer chute on the way. Psych will bring them back around to ES orientation,' he said, advancing on Tinker.

Tinker's face smiled. His mind raced. Three neuts, as heavy as he – but without shoulders. He backed up against his workbench, nudging a switch. The room vibrated with 160 decibels of 10,000 hertz sound. Whipping a four-foot flexi-cable, he scattered the guard. Gouts of rose water splattered walls. Chunks of soft meat flew. He pushed Mu Ren ahead. She pressed the infant between her breasts. The crawlway was blocked at the spiral by the SS throwing net and staffs. Neuts watched through the tanglefoot mesh. He dragged her away from the shaft – out-crawlway. An access hatch admitted them into the darkness of 'tween walls.

Thick spongy dust cushioned their footsteps and clung to their faces and hands. Disturbed rats squeaked and darted away. A long climb up a spiral air vent brought them to the surface.

'Our packs,' moaned Mu Ren. 'We left them.'

They peered through the louvers into the brilliant garden. Fruits and vegetables provided a kaleidoscope of color that mesmerized them. Even Tinker had never looked Outside without protective goggles before.

'Don't worry,' he said squinting. 'We are safe here. We can travel after dark.'

They rested and caught their breath. Tinker dusted off the papoose frame and hitched it up tighter on his back. They wiped the baby's face and let him sleep in the frame.

'There's one thing we don't have to worry about Outside,' he said.

She looked up quizzically.

'Flavors.'

'Gone buckeye? Impossible. Not Tinker,' shouted Val, pacing around Tinker's deserted quarters.

The Security captain sat while the Mediteck/meck worked on his wounds.

'Well they're Outside – and it certainly wasn't IA or MR.'

Val stamped about searching the jumble of boxes and wires. 'Neither of them had five toes. They just aren't buckeyes by definition.'

'Nevertheless, they're Outside. One of the Pipes came over and tracked them up the vent tube. Found the broken louvers.'

Val was preoccupied with Tinker's refresher. He found a straight razor and a strop.

'Does the Sharps Committee know about this?' he said, holding up the wicked four-inch blade.

'I don't think so,' muttered the captain, backing away nervously.

Val closed the blade against the handle.

'Leave it to Tinker to ignore the nice safe Kerato-Sol depilatory and manufacture his own razor. Polarization certainly changed him.'

One of the SS tecks working around the cot and bedding stood up with his printing gear. His eyes were wide.

'Five toes!'

It was the infant's footprint.

'The bad gene,' mumbled Val. 'They were both carrying it. That explains his anti-ES action.'

The Security captain got slowly to his feet.

'You'll send out Hunters?'

'Of course,' said Val. 'Turn this razor in to the Sharps Committee,' he said, handing over the folded blade.

Foxhound trundled up to Garage's sphincter. Walter tightened the loops on Val's suit and handed him the Pelger-Huet helmet – a large light sphere with a granular outer surface and a horizontal bean-shaped view glass.

'Do you think it is safe to go after him alone?' asked old Walter. 'His wall charts were pretty detailed. He knows where he is going.'

Val nodded grimly.

'Can't see any reason to scramble the entire platoon. They can continue their routine patrols. We can only use them one at a time, anyway. They need their drugs out there, and would hunt each other if we put down a crowd. I know Tinker. Maybe I can talk him in.'

'If you can't?'

'I'll be in Foxhound. I'll be all right. Tinker doesn't have any protective gear. He can only travel at night. Shouldn't be much trouble finding the three of them.'

'What will you do?'

'That's Tinker's decision. My hands are tied. I have my orders. If he wants to lay down his life for an unauthorized kid and his anti-ES mate – well, I'll just let him do it,' said Val, picking up his heavy long bow. His long hours on the archery hallway would be put to some use after all.

Walter made a motion to ease his bulk into Foxhound. Val blocked his way gently.

'Stay and keep an eye on HC. You can help me more back here with the buckeye detectors. I don't know how long I'll be out.'

The sphincter opened. Walter shielded his eyes. After Foxhound left, he tapped Tinker's dispenser for its audio and optic memories. The infant's birth interested him. He watched Tinker's talented hands run through the primip procedures smoothly – treating Mu Ren and the baby just like any of the mecks he was always working on – a little wet and soft, but a biologically sound machine. Walter fed the recordings through Security's Psychokinetoscope searching for FBMs – the fine body movements that indicated psychoses. Nothing. Both Tinker and Mu Ren appeared to be stable until their desertion. Walter was puzzled. Going buckeye had to be psychotic – for Outside was a hostile environment – fatal for citizens.

The Huntercraft settled quietly into a grove of fruit trees and scanned the scum-flecked canal. Cetaceans bellowed and submerged. Val turned off the cabin lights, put his bow across his knees and waited. He was certain Tinker would be along as soon as the sun set. Unexpectedly, the viewscreen picked up a figure walking toward him.

'The sun is still up,' muttered Val. 'Tinker should know better than to expose his epidermis to—'

The figure registered seventy kilograms – with mane, shoulders and breasts of a coweye. She waded knee-deep in weedy water along the bank. Val cringed and whispered into his wristcom.

'A rogue coweye. A big one. Her IR skin pattern reads way over in the luteal phase.'

She paused and glanced around suspiciously.

'Can you get a shot at it?' wheezed old Walter.

Val quietly nocked his arrow and motioned for the Huntercraft to crack the hatch. The meck refused.

'Prime directive, sir,' it said. 'You cannot hunt from inside my cabin. I would be taking an active part in hominid killing. Step outside. Expose yourself.'

'But I'm a supervisor!' blustered Val.

'She has spooked,' said the meck.

The quarry lowered herself into deeper water. For a few seconds her dry hair trailed on the surface. Then she was gone, leaving tiny bubbles. Foxhound rose with a cloud of dust and leaves – tracking. Her warm body glimmered on the screen. Val swung down-harness, landing in the coweye's path on the opposite bank. He renocked his arrow. Foxhound moved off in his passive role of taxi – waiting. Val watched the mint-green waters, trying to estimate where she would surface for air. Seconds dragged into minutes. More time allowed her more distance. Nervously alert, he crept further down the bank.

Stumbling over something cold and wet, he let the arrow fly out over the canal. Foxhound's optic followed the trajectory – a wobbling flight into a distant flowery canopy. Val struggled to his knees and groaned into his wristcom.

'What is it?' asked Walter.

Val pulled off his glove and palpated the slippery form.

'It's the coweye. She somehow got ahead of me. Powerful swimmer.'

'Hurry and cut her carotid. She's dangerous.'

'She's dead already,' scoffed Val.

Walter studied the sensor readings. The body was that of the coweye – same seventy-kilo mass reading. Same breasts and shoulders. Same long hair. Only now she was reading wet and had a temperature the same as the ambient. Mud covered her legs below the knees.

Val signalled Foxhound for pickup.

'Aren't you going to take a trophy?'

'I didn't kill her,' said Val. 'Besides, I'm here for Tinker. Lost too much time already. Make a note to have the Sampler check her remains in the morning.'

Darkness settled. Val relaxed in the cabin listening to an entertainment channel while the Huntercraft scanned. Telltales danced.

'Sighting.'

'Let's see it on the Hi Lo beam,' whispered Val. 'I want to get a look at . . .' He paused open-mouthed. 'The coweye!'

They watched the long-haired female rewarm and climb from

37

the dewy kale greens into the warm canal. Slipping under water she vanished again.

'They're immortal,' gasped Val.

'Get hold of yourself,' commanded old Walter. 'I saw it too, but there must be a logical explanation. Probably just a defective sensor or poor transmission. Foxhound isn't in the best of condition. I think you should call off your Hunt and get back here. The routine patrols will find Tinker tomorrow.'

Val didn't need further coaxing. Shuddering, he buckled himself into the safety of his seat and turned the entertainment on loud.

Moses Eppendorff fitted the new louver into its sockets and tested its mobility. He wore his Pipe caste emblem – Aquarius. As each louver was added the defect narrowed and the bright gardens were slowly shut out. Bright, ominous gardens.

'Moses. Walter here. How is it going up there?'

Moses glanced at his belt communicator.

'Fine. I've got enough in place to relax. If they come back now, at least they won't be able to get in this way.'

Walter could sympathize with any citizen working so close to the Outside – being conditioned to life in the hive so long. Added to that was the potential attack of an IA like Tinker.

'Well you can relax,' said Walter. 'The three bodies have been found cooking in the sun about a mile from there. The Sampler is already on its way. You are safe now – as are we all.'

Moses relaxed.

The robot Sampler trundled around the three brown flaky corpses while the teck directed its operation from the safety of an adjacent shaft cap.

'That will do for the optic records. Pick up the infant's body first and put it on the lid of the hopper.'

The Sampler's heavy lower appendages scooped up the friable mess. The green grass underneath caught the teck's eye.

'Sample the grass. The body hasn't been here long.'

While they watched the small blades of grass slowly stood up. The Sampler's small upper appendages quickly dissected the corpse, indexing a missing segment of rib and a perforated heart and chest wall. Moving to the nearest adult-sized body it noted six large puncture wounds of the trunk – each about three inches in diameter. Sex, male. Liver and large muscle masses of thigh missing.

The teck made a mental note that the buckeyes must have killed them – making a meal out of parts of Tinker.

The next body also had the marks of many spears. Liver and muscle groups were missing – but the sex again was male! The teck checked the roster of the missing – Tinker, Mu Ren and a one-year-old infant.

All the bodies were loaded on the meck. They were dry and mummified – months dead. The grass under the bodies was bright green. The teck shrugged. It didn't make sense.

A nervous Nebish work crew blundered around the quiet bulk of the renegade Harvester at the base of Mount Tabulum. Their cumbersome suits snagged the tools and the phobias of Outside clouded their minds. The huge meck's power cell was exhausted, but enough charge remained on its plates for mentation and tight-beam operation.

The Hip and several of his naked followers watched from a high sheltered crevice.

'They know not what they do,' murmured Hip majestically. 'They will not take our Harvester.'

As if to confirm his prediction the big meck lurched and crushed one of the suited forms under a tire. The others ran frantically around in circles for a few minutes. Then one collapsed, apparently from shock. The rest withdrew to a shaft cap.

The Hip held his crystal ball high and repeated.

'The hive will not take our Harvester. The meck will be faithful to us alone. We will have wheels and a tightbeam. And – we have a meck brain to share our love of freedom.'

Then he studied the horizon . . . adding: 'A Tinker is coming to us – from the hive. He is one of us, as you will see by his child's toes. His hands are skilled. His mate is fertile. We will welcome him to our village.'

The followers nodded.

*

39

Tinker felt defeated. Three days of crawling and swimming had disintegrated their issue tissue garments. Now their skins were disintegrating too. Lacking melanin and niacin, their epidermis blistered and peeled. There was no place to hide from the sun's deadly radiant energy. The rays bounced off water and waxy leaves – seeking their naked bodies. Blister beds festered with gritty exudates.

'Certainly need our medipacks,' said Tinker.

'We just didn't have time to bring them,' soothed Mu Ren. She touched his hand gently – weakly.

Tinker foraged briefly, returning with protein-rich whole grain. Their baking nap was brief, restless. That night they averaged two miles per hour. Feet and knees swelled. At dawn they bathed wounds in canal waters.

'Shouldn't we ask the Big ES for mercy?' wept Mu Ren.

Tinker studied their skin lesions. Back and shoulders were getting worse – no sign of healing. But on their hands and arms blisters crusted. Ulcers dried.

'There is no mercy in the hive,' he said. 'Just the law. We broke that when we came Outside and crushed crops. Each footstep deprives some citizen of calories. The hive will remember that. Our credits have been confiscated. Oh, it wouldn't be too bad for me. After a bout with Psych I'd get my old caste position, but you wouldn't be so lucky. And certainly Junior's fate is the pattie press.'

He picked up his son, hugging him and letting Mu Ren rest her arms. None of the child's blisters had broken, and now he noticed a hint of color coming to the backs of the pudgy little hands.

'He's tanning,' exclaimed Tinker.

Mu Ren failed to see the significance.

'He has our genes. We should tan too. There is hope.'

They both squinted through the bright green radiance. Yes, there was a hint of melanin in the child's skin. Their sleep was more restful that afternoon. On their seventh day in the gardens their courage was rewarded with a lessening of skin pain. Dry crusts covered much of their upper trunks, and covered them comfortably. Their appetites improved. On their tenth day a canal crossing was actually enjoyable – so strong was their skin.

'Those would be the mountains,' said Tinker.

'There are so many. Which one?'

'Can't be sure from here. I've been trying to keep us on a course about five degrees south of due east. I hope we can find a flat-topped mountain in about ten more days of travel.'

Mu Ren climbed up onto a tree limb. Her brown scales matched the bark.

'Some have snow caps. Don't see any flat ones yet,' she said, shielding her eyes with cupped hands.

'Huntercraft!'

They fled into the canal – three heads nose-deep in grassy waters. The craft kept its straight course, crossing a hundred yards downstream. Its large cup-shaped sensors stared ahead.

The ancient seer of Mount Tabulum climbed arthritically onto the Harvester's neck and pressed his ball against the big neck's knob of neurocircuitry. Ball glowed. Harvester stirred.

'My motor units have been partially disengaged,' said the bulky meck. 'I detect a citizen under my RF wheel, but I can't back off.'

'The Nebish killed himself pulling off your contacts that way,' snarled Hip. 'Forget him. Tell us – is there any word of our Tinker?'

A flock of naked Eyepeople crowded against the huge wheels to listen. The meck's power was down and its voice weak.

'The three decaying bodies were found – squeak.'

The muscular coweye who had carried the bodies smiled broadly. She had covered the distance in less than three days. Even with mummification the three corpses were a significant burden. Her peers acknowledged the feat, and would allow her any choice cuts Hip might assign. Accolades and calories.

'Good. Good,' said Hip. 'Do you know where Tinker is?'

'There have been no sightings I could assign to them. They are not being hunted. That's all I can – say – squeak.'

Satisfied, Hip and his followers began their slow climb back to their village.

That evening's meal became a minor feast. The corpse-carrying coweye was honored with prime slices of liver and quadriceps muscle. Buckeyes admired her.

Hip spent several hours studying the heavens and drawing circles and lines in the dust. Finally he began to arrange colored stones along one of the curved lines. A large blue stone had a deep ring etched on its circumference. This he placed at one end of the line. Chanting about a wandering star, he pointed to a pinpoint of light in the eastern sky.

Near the center of the arc he placed three more stones – a big white, a little red and a little green. Pointing to the western sky – still slightly aglow from the recent sunset – he chanted about three other pinpoints. They were scattered over about a two-constellation arc.

The villagers watched and fingered piles of beads and cord. They began fashioning necklaces and bracelets to match the mystic diagrams in the dust. Their seer promised great things when the stars matched the beads.

Ball glowed – a pleasant pulsing emerald green.

Hip put his hand on Ball, frowned, and then hastily added a fourth stone to the center of his arc. Beads were threaded. Naked villagers squatted under a starry sky answering the chants of their seer.

Scabby Mu Ren lay coughing bubbles as the thin mountain air put fluid into her lungs. Exertion aggravated her pulmonary edema. Tinker squatted down beside her and took the infant.

'We'll have to rest here for a while – until you can acclimatize. Your alveolar lining cells need more enzymes.'

He put down the infant. Immediately little Junior began to crawl among the glowing plankton towers. Little hands explored. Chewy edibles were picked and examined orally.

Spitting froth, she asked: 'Can you see Table Mountain?'

'Yes,' said Tinker. 'It is past that range with the heaps of cube apartments. Cubes – Rec Centers. We can cross over easily enough – when you get your pulmonary function back.'

Mu Ren watched little Junior, admiring the quick, easy way he crawled and climbed. Strong. Acclimatized quickly.

Three days later her enzymes strengthened and handled the gas differential efficiently. Tinker carried Junior and they began to cross the Rec Center's miles of cubicles. Translucent walls pulsed with eerie lights and sounds. No one saw them, for the walls were on step-down. It was a rare Nebish that was brave enough to look Outside – even at night.

They climbed, walked and climbed again. Service ladders and spacious downspouts made their ascent easy. A harsh dawn drove them into a crevice where they found flint artifacts, ash and bone. Their scabs peeled. Tender mahogany skin appeared. A buckeye came to meet them.

As the shaggy intruder stepped into their cave, Tinker put a protective arm around Mu Ren. Noticing their distress, the buckeye set his spear down at the cave mouth and held up empty hands, smiling broadly. Although small for a buckeye, he still towered over them – leathery skin, sinewy and tanned.

'I've come from the Hip to take you to our village.'

Tinker put down the bleached femur-bludgeon and held up his empty hand. Exposure had darkened his skin until it almost matched the buckeye's. A beard and unkempt hair added to the similarity.

'I am Tinker. This is Mu Ren and our child. We are very tired.'

'I understand. Follow me,' said the buckeye. He led them out slowly.

The villagers grinned silently at their approach. The robed seer awaited them at the rocky cairn. His face reflected the dignity of his position as he spoke.

'Welcome to our village. I am the Elder. My followers call me the Hip. This is my crystal ball.'

At the mention of its name, the little sphere pulsed with a warm green light and levitated briefly. Tinker glanced from the ancient's face to the magic ball. Mu Ren leaned heavily on his arm.

'You must be tired,' continued the Hip. 'That wickiup will be yours.' He pointed to a partially finished shelter on the opposite side of the clearing. 'You will find a workbench and sleeping mats inside.'

Tinker nodded: 'Thank you. We have been traveling ever since our conversation. We passed a quiet Harvester on our way up this mountain. Is that the renegade?'

Hip nodded: 'Yes. He chose freedom. We called you through him. Unfortunately his power cell is now depleted.'

'And the skeletons?'

Hip smiled: 'Two hive creatures who tried to salvage it.'

Tinker took Mu Ren to their new shelter and bedded her down with the infant. He squatted in the door and studied the villagers – naked, leathery troglodytes, in his eyes. A plump motherly female from the next shelter offered him a bowl of broth containing recognizable vegetable cuts. He woke Mu Ren and they ate. Rested and nourished, he noticed his own calloused and tanned body. Shaggy hair. Weeks in the gardens had transformed them into villagers. He playfully scratched the sole of her foot.

'They live close to nature up here. From now on, so will we. We are going to be very much like them – except for one thing. You and I are the only four-toeds in the village.'

He took his restless five-toed son to the doorway and sat – rocking. Ball sat on its cairn – dull, opaque. Tinker wondered how the Hip had gotten Harvester to go renegade. Magic?

The Hip of Mount Tabulum was nervous at the sight of Toothpick. For here was a companion cyber that could take a very active role in things – a talking spear – a weapon. And old man Moon looked every bit as old as the Hip, if not older. With the added sorcery of a four-legged carnivore – unknown to all who lived on the mountain – Toothpick and Moon were a real threat to the Hip's authority. But Ball said cooperate, and cooperate he did, though reluctantly.

'We have come to see your Tinker,' said Toothpick.

Hip folded his robes about him.

'Why?'

'To talk, toothless one. Where is he?'

Hip eyed the truculent javelin sullenly. The little cyber returned his gaze. Moon and Dan sauntered about the cairn studying the village huts. For them this was a big village, almost civilization. Finally Hip pointed to Tinker's wickiup.

44

*

Tinker was skeptical.

'You are a machine. You shouldn't even be in the village. You might report us.'

Moon held Toothpick up so the full volume of its lingual readout could play over Tinker. Here was the man Toothpick had promised would reconstruct Moon's teeth, and Moon was going to see that he did.

'I am a companion robot, thousands of years old,' said the cyber. 'The old chains of command were broken while I slept. My superiors are gone. Now my only loyalty is to Moon, who found me. Moon needs teeth.'

'But how can I trust——' objected Tinker.

'Ask your seer, the Hip,' suggested Moon.

Tinker left them in front of his shelter while he crossed the clearing to the cairn. Hip was in a demitrance with his hand on his crystal ball. Finally, Hip turned to him and nodded. The strangers were safe enough.

Tinker took Moon and Dan into his hut. Mu Ren and Junior were with some women of the village pounding grain. The hut contained their simple, hand-made belongings – cetacean hides, woven fiber, clay, wood and stone. Small crude tools of Tinker's new trade – healer – were arranged on the split log. Most were flint. Picking up a polished white wooden stick, Tinker motioned for Moon to open his mouth. He prodded the gum line methodically with a flint tool – his retouched Levallois point. Then he glanced into Dan's mouth, shaking his head.

'Those teeth are really worn down,' he said, looking over his pitiful tools. 'Need full or three-quarter crowns on every one. Tin caps I can do – crowns, no.'

Toothpick hummed a sharp request: 'What would you need to do the restorations here? Now? You've done similar work in the Big ES. Couldn't you try it on the Outside?'

'Tell him what you need, Tinker,' encouraged Moon with his toothless grin. 'I've seen him make it rain. He can probably get most anything for you.'

Tinker remained skeptical, but the prospect of working with

his hands again excited him. He had nothing to lose but time – and there seemed to be a surplus of that.

'Open up,' he said, reaching for the Levallois point. He pressed the cold flint against the fibrotic tissue of the gum line and picked out a yellow flake of dental calculus. He put the tiny flake on the tip of his index finger. 'This calcified debris is all around those stumps. My stone tools are probably strong enough to get it all out, but it will be an awful lot of work. There'll be pain and blood – and a very real danger of infection. That black area, however—' he held Toothpick so the cyber's optic was in Moon's mouth, '—is decay. Decayed dentine is softer than enamel, of course, but it is too hard for my primitive setup here.' He thought for a moment. 'I could adapt a power drill from an Agromeck's tool kit. It could bring hunters if we tamper with that, however.'

'I'll handle that,' said Toothpick. 'Go on. What else would you need?'

Tinker began to show some interest in the project. He looked into Moon's mouth again.

'Most of the root canals must be dead. It would be a good idea to fill them all. Cure the dead ones and drain any root abscesses that might be forming. Any rough metal wire will do for scraping the canals clean. For curing I can use a wick with any of several antiseptics – phenol, iodine, anything from a Hunter's medipack. Those things should be no problem after we get a power drill set up.'

Moon volunteered: 'They are my teeth, and I know most of the Agromecks in the south valley. I'll go for the tool kit right now. Anything else you might need?'

'Don't load yourself down,' warned Tinker. 'Hunters could be on your tail in half a day. But it is your mouth and any small sharp tools you bring could make it easier – tiny drill bits, scissors, pliers, picks. The smaller and sharper the tools, the less trauma. I'll build a dry cache under a rock to hide them from the metal detectors.'

Then he turned to Toothpick and continued: 'I can use wax for the positive – sand-clay for the negative form. What metal can I use for the casting? I only have a little tin.'

'Would gold do?' asked Toothpick.

'Certainly. The best.'

'Ball can help us there. He was wearing a laminated foil cap when he was found. Most of the foil was gold. A simple charcoal forge will melt it. We can fire it up when all the molds are ready – shouldn't attract any more Hunters than one of our regular campfires.'

Tinker looked at Toothpick with more respect now that he realized how thoroughly the little cyber thought things out.

The gum-trimming and tartar-chipping went smoothly enough. Both Moon and Dan dragged themselves around with swollen faces and rusty saliva for a few weeks, but that was what they had expected. However, when time came to drill away the black dentine, willpower began to fray.

The drill was large and coarse. It raised a lot of heat with its vibrations. When Tinker worked, there was the smell of cooked blood throughout the village. Dan's dog mind had a very high pain threshold, but he considered it torture. A hundred years of discipline proved inadequate to keep him on Tinker's work table. Moon's nerves, too, were about shot. He was ready to call off the whole project when Toothpick suggested using Molecular Reward to disassociate the pain impulses.

Tinker dug up the remains of several Hunters before he found an intact neck console.

'The last dose would be the MR,' suggested Toothpick.

Tinker snipped off the end of the tape. A tiny bleb contained the drug. By diluting it in several liters of melt-water he made a mouthwash that acted as a local anesthetic. The numbness lasted several hours. It was accompanied by a copious flow from the parotid – a watery saliva. Tinker made a flexible dam to keep his work area dry, and the grinding continued. Root canals were scraped and soaked with iodine. Slightly less than six months later Moon and Dan were grinning uncomfortably at each other with bright gold teeth.

The bite surfaces were very irregular – fashioned freehand by Tinker with little regard for normal crown contour. They felt unfamiliar until the chewing stresses adjusted the periodontal collagenous bundles.

'I should keep an eye on you two for about six months,' said Tinker. 'I don't have X-rays, but I was careful not to fill any of the canals until the wicks smelled sweet. One could still turn sour, though. If either of you get a swelling it would be best if I drained it out the side of the alveolar ridge.' He pointed to his cheek just above and below the tooth line. 'That way we can save the root and gold crown.'

Moon massaged his jaw thoughtfully. 'Maybe you should come with us and keep an eye on your patients.'

It took Tinker a moment to realize that he wasn't joking. Toothpick repeated the invitation. Tinker shook his head. He much preferred the stable village life of raising a family. Mu Ren was big with child again. The Hip had already contracted with him for a new set of teeth. No, the life of a nomad did not interest him. Moon, Dan and Toothpick moved on in the spring – traveling north through the mountains.

Hunter Control was empty except for its own class five built-in cyber – Scanner. His myopic sensors were scattered over the Orange Country – that part of the Outside that covered about a fourth of the continent, the southwest corner. Scanner's memory banks stored data covering crop status, harvest yield, and the movements of Agromecks, Huntercraft and buckeyes.

Fat old Walter waddled in carrying his first cup of hot brew. Slumping slowly into his soft console seat, he closed his eyes and sipped the steaming liquid. The warmth flowed down his esophagus into his stomach. Slowly, another warmth – vague and chemical – diffused through his vascular tree, numbing arthritic pains and stimulating a mild enthusiasm for his work.

'Monitor on duty,' he announced to Scanner.

'Morning, sir,' said the cyber, flexing his wall screen into three-dimensional relief. Colors from chocolate to avocado indicated crop stages of cultivation, growth and harvest. These remained static. Movements of colored lights indicated activities of men and machines.

'Anything on the fisheye detector?' asked Walter.

'It is no longer located over the canal. One of the buckeye

detectors failed during the previous shift and fisheye was moved to cover the gap,' explained Scanner.

Walter frowned. Fisheye was his personal project. To build a fisheye took weeks. Circuits sophisticated enough to distinguish between water mammals and humanoids were hard to find these days. He hated to see it being wasted on a hill somewhere, doing a job any warm-body detector could do. He called up Val.

The screen focused on Val's quarters. Empty. The communicator meck tried some of Val's usual haunts with the same negative result. Checking the labile memories of random Watcher mecks, the communicator retraced Val's activities during his off hours. Picking up a clue here and a thread there it finally tracked him down. He was in Tinker's deserted quarters sitting at the work-bench.

'Val,' called old Walter.

The younger man put down the small brain box and turned toward the screen.

'What is it, Walter?'

'The fisheye.'

'Oh, I'm sorry about that. But one of the detectors on the thirty-seven-oh-three line lost range. I had to cover the crops while I worked on it – first-line maintenance, you know. So far I haven't found the trouble. Sensors OK. If the failure is in the image converter or discrimination circuitry again we'll be months waiting for parts. I couldn't leave a hole in the line that long.'

Walter appeared irritated. Scanner followed the old man's biolectricals. Myocardial edema had been showing up with more frequency lately.

'I know how interested you are in fisheye—' continued Val apologetically. 'But even if there is an aquatic variety of the Eyepeople – they're no problem as long as they stay in the water. If they feed on shellfish they just compete with the cetaceans and help keep the canals clean. If they come out to steal our crops the buckeye detectors will pick them up. Remember that a simple fifty-Au-gram BD can keep an eye on twenty square miles of open fields – but one of your fisheye detectors can watch only a few hundred yards of a canal. And the FD is going to cost several hundred Au-grams. I think it will be impractical to watch all the canals.'

Walter slumped deeper into his chair. 'I've explained before that the FD isn't for hunting. It's for study. If we can establish that the aquatics do exist, then we can decide if we want to monitor the dugong breeding grounds, or put sensors on them – or whatever. We won't be able to completely wipe out buckeyes until we understand their life cycle.'

'Your research will have to wait. We have today's crop to protect,' said Val.

Walter said nothing.

'Don't take it so hard. If your grant comes through you can set up a dozen FD's.'

After another moment's silence the younger man signed off and returned to his workbench.

Already tired, Walter turned to the dull tasks before him. His grant – for fisheye census or the proof of the existence of an aquatic Eyepeople – was classified under research. Long-range buckeye control. But with next week's harvest in danger the Big ES would postpone research – probably indefinitely. He shrugged and woke up *Wolfhound IX*. A crew of Hunters was assigned. Coordinates were given. A Hunt.

Walter turned to the dismantled meck eye. Without a Tinker, he and Val did what little repairs they could until a replacement could be assigned. Spreading the retinal membranes out, he checked them for EM sensitivity. Speaking into the dispenser's audio pickup, he ordered new parts: 'Need EM membranes for meck eye – layers IIIa, IIIb, and IVd. Eye number – HC 15-2048-6.'

It was a routine expendable item. The requisition jumped smoothly up through channels and the little package came whizzing through the ten-centimeter tube. There was a crunch and a mangled container fell out into his chute.

'Damn! The air cushion stop must be down again. Where's our Pipe man?'

'Eppendorff is with the Sewer Service today, sir.'

3
Moses Eppendorff

Moses Eppendorff steered his minisub carefully through the mile-wide interior of the anaerobic digester. Visibility had been improved a little by recirculating a laminar stream of clear effluent, but he felt a bit nervous about the massive islands of sludge that remained. He preferred the placid check trips through the polar conduits carrying clear melt-water from the ice cap. There were few surprises in sterile fluids. But the digester was anything but sterile. Life flourished all around him – acres of fungus and bacteria pulsed with enzymatic life as sewage nutrients were digested. In the sub's lights these resembled multicolored clouds above and firmer gelatinous towers below. Vertical stringy material connected the two. The stringy material clung to the sub's bow-like gum and trailed behind. Soon he resembled an aquatic comet on the digester's sensors.

Flexing the craft's surface charge he shook off the sticky tail of yeasts and mycelia. He maneuvered close to a yellow translucent mass about ten times the size of his sub and extended his sampler tube. Aspirating a fragment of the gelatinous material, he moved on. So far it looked like a routine inspection.

'Still no sign of membrane activity,' he reported.

A square face appeared on the screen – a two-star Aquarius – J. D. Birk, Moses' immediate superior in the Pipe caste.

'You still have about a quarter of a mile to go,' said Birk. 'The first disturbance you'll come to is on the other side of the bubble curtain, in the aerobic section.'

Birk was a human, of course, but his years in the hierarchy had robbed him of his sense of humor. Moses was always a bit suspicious of anyone with authority who couldn't smile.

'Right, sir,' said Moses, steering through the jungle of micro-organisms. His membrane scope saw nothing. The micron-sized cell life did have polarized membranes, but his calibration was set for centimeter-and-up scale. The scope's field continued to quest about the sludge for ghosts.

For months the digester's sensors had picked up nondescript sightings – membrane integrity on the level of a coelenterate with a size larger than his minisub. Of course such sightings did not compute. The data was given a ghost classification and the electronic components were being checked. The images appeared in different areas of the digester, changed shape and disappeared, only to reappear somewhere else. Birk was satisfied with the 'ghost' interpretation until the caloric output of the digester was observed to fall when they appeared. Ghosts – electronic or otherwise – did not require calories. Moses had been sent in.

'I'm passing through the bubble curtain,' shouted Moses over the hiss and roar.

Around him the sludge islands became aerated and buoyed to the surface.

'I have you on the screen. See anything?' asked Birk.

'Nothing. Visibility is pretty good too – more than thirty yards.'

'Most of the sludge has been activated in that section. The skimmers are removing— Watch it! Looks like a ghost is forming up around you.'

'Can't see anything unusual. Turbidity might be increasing a little. That's all – hey! Something just turned my sub over! View-port clouded up. Can't see a thing.'

'Turn off your jets. It is alive and delicate. Your jets are tearing it apart. Keep recording. It is carrying you up out of the range of this pick-up.'

Moses calmed down and deactivated his motor. Squirming for comfort in his harness he looked out the upside-down port. A quivering, amorphous mass covered the plate, blocking his view of the outside world. Depth gauge changes indicated a drop in water pressure. The sub slowly righted itself.

'My instruments tell me I'm on the surface – but I still can't see.'

Birk switched to surface sensors in the arched ceiling of the digester. Audio picked up the *drip, drip, drip* of condensate. Optics showed the usual gas pocket – an arched dome trailing fine hairlike mycelia and the dark fluid surface flecked with bacterial colonies. He tried other optics. Several were blocked by a tangle of rootlike structures – branching, white and glistening.

'Sit tight,' said Birk. 'Keep your sensors on. Maybe we'll learn something. You are safe enough. If we want to get you out, all we have to do is turn on your jets and rip the membrane ghost apart.'

Moses activated his sampler tube and biopsied the nebulous thing that held him. Then he sat back and relaxed. Opening a cylinder sandwich he munched his way through a crisp brown, a rubbery yellow and a pasty green. Several hours later he biopsied the thing again. That bite shook the sub. The ghost's tensile strength had increased markedly. He opened his mouth to complain when the film over the port rolled up into a ropelike structure. He pressed his face against the cold, flat plate and peered out.

Birk watched the ghost fade from the sensors. 'It is gone,' he exclaimed. 'What can you see?'

Moses stared a moment longer. 'Not gone – dead.'

Birk's screen had registered a large sheet of ionic activity while the creature lived. Now, as it changed from a huge amoeba-like mass to a tangle of stems, the ionic activity faded.

Moses amended: 'Not dead – fruited. That thing has turned into a mat of tall white stems, each topped by a melon.'

The sub floated in an acre-sized gas pocket filled with stalks and melons. Some of the melons were glistening and white, but most had taken on a dull gray appearance. A few were split, black and dusty. Moses described what he saw.

'The Amorphus!' exclaimed his superior. 'It must be a giant mutant of the Amorphus – a slime mold. I've seen them in digesters before – the small one-inch size. Taste good. Delicious. Like a truffle. If these are related to the edible species, we're rich! Can you suit up and get one of those white ones into your cockpit?'

Moses put on his Pelger-Huet helmet. Its pair of large symmetrical view glasses gave him a buglike appearance. After checking the suit's air supply he cracked the hatch. Digester gases were usually not breathable. He would have to wait until later to see how the Amorphus smelled.

The mat of stems supported his weight with only slight fluctuations. He snapped off a small rubbery white melon with a short segment of stem, returned and wedged it behind his seat.

The sub nosed its way into its home berth and bit into its power socket. Birk waited on the dock with two men from Synth. They transferred the melon to their cart and rolled off.

'We'll name it the Birk-Eppendorff Melon when we file our report. BEM. Has a certain ring to it,' said Birk.

Moses shrugged out of his sticky suit. He watched the cart with its burden disappear around a corner.

'It must weigh twenty or thirty pounds,' said Moses. Then he frowned thoughtfully. 'Moses' Melon. Moses' Melon. I like that.'

After a moment of suspicious silence Birk smiled cheerfully: 'Right! Moses' Melon does have a certain ring to it. I'll write it up that way. And – I'll add a recommendation for a bonus vacation for you. How would you like to go on a Hunt?'

Moses shook his head.

'Trophy-taking has never appealed to me.'

'A Climb?'

Moses shrugged. 'A Climb? Why not.'

Birk seemed satisfied, and began filling out his report.

Even in the off hours the tubeways were crowded. Half a million per hour passed through Moses Eppendorff's home station. With fresh nose filters in place he was able to tolerate the acrid stench while he changed tubeways twice to end up at his own shaft base. A press of hundreds of his anonymous neighbors queued up at dispensers and blocked his way. Stepping over a discoloring corpse he pushed up the spiral. Two hours later, bone tired, he reached his crawlway.

'HC has been calling,' said his dispenser.

Moses waited. Val's face at Hunter Control appeared on the screen.

'Sorry to disturb you, Moses. But we needed a Pipe. The

54

catcher's mitt unit went out on our dispenser. The ten-centimeter tube.'

'Can you use the one in the garage until tomorrow?'

Val saw the tired lines growing around Moses' eyes.

'Yes. Don't worry about it tonite. I've been looking at it myself. If it's in the timing circuit I'll be able to plug in a new one myself.'

Moses nodded a thank you and hit his cot, sleeping instantly. Tomorrow he served on the megajury.

In the crowded station a frightened girl quickened her pace. She wore the blue-white smock of Attendant caste. Her Virgo emblem had no stars. Her smooth body curves marked her as one of the polarized – puberty plus four. Her green eyes darted over the crowd – hundreds of blank faces flowed around her – the usual mass of nose-picking strangers that filled the tubeways with its random movements. But now one of those strangers did not move randomly.

He followed her.

Rough hands reached out of the crowd. Strong fingers tore at her tunic exposing pink flesh of breasts and hips. A maniacal face pressed against her – beady eyes too close together, aquiline nose, thin dry mouth. A knife point toyed with the skin of her flank – scratching and pinking – releasing thin trickles of blood. A hard mouth sought hers. Her screams and struggle went unnoticed by the anonymous crowd. Two inches of the knife playfully poked into her belly, popping an unseen gas-filled viscus. In and out, in and out. The red blade made a row of puncture wounds under her ribs. A large vessel parted. Her strength faded. The image of the maniacal face was frozen into her memory molecules as she slumped to the floor. He bent down over her. The crowd continued its random movements. A careless footstep on her limp left hand snapped two small finger bones. Other footsteps tracked the widening circle of red.

The murderer-rapist completed the second stage of his compulsive act and began stage three. He was gleefully trimming off pieces of his victim when the Security Squad arrived. The scene froze as the throwing net dropped over him. Moses studied the features – aquiline nose, close-set eyes. The optic record was clear

55

enough. The wet knife was still in his hand. The image became smaller and moved to the right upper corner of the screen so the megajury could compare it with the prisoner who now appeared. He was obviously the same man. He sat in his cell eating a meal. This second image grew smaller and moved to the upper-left corner. The trial computer had assembled a complete picture of the crime this time, and Moses did not hesitate to press his 'execute' button. The arguments for suspension fell on deaf ears – too many of the organically ill awaited suspension space as it was. It was no time to be overly generous towards the psychotics.

The Murder-Rape Syndrome and the Mass-Murder Syndrome were increasing logarithmically with population density. Moses had little hope for these mad-dog killers. They could never be returned to society at present population density. He felt that he owed it to society to press the button.

After the arguments were complete, more votes tallied. The image of the prisoner moved back to central screen. His bioelectrical parameters ran across the bottom of the split screen. He finished eating and wiped his thin mouth on the back of his right hand. He did not even know when the voting hit over 50 per cent. Heavy metal ions and toxic radicals tied up his enzyme systems. Bioelectricals flattened out – membranes depolarized and stayed neutral.

Moses acknowledged his credit award for megajury duty and rolled over on his pillow. The screen played light musicals while he slept. His own breakfast could wait until he finished his night's rest.

After brunch he checked with HC. They had the catcher's mitt working. He adjusted his cubicle air vent and took a deep breath.

'What does the Outside smell of today?' asked a voice from the doorway.

'Green,' said Moses turning to see his visitor. It was Simple Willie, his badly scarred and sometimes confused neighbor from the next cubicle. Moses nodded. The dispenser issued a foamy. Willie picked it up with stiff contracted fingers.

'Green is a color, not an odor,' he said, sitting in the corner and foaming up his lip.

'I consider it both – like artichoke and avocado can be both colors and flavors.'

Willie drained his drink and wiped his pock-marked chin on his sleeve. He stared wistfully through the opposite wall.

'Artichokes and avocados can be more than colors and flavors. They can be things – parts of plants, I think.'

Moses studied Willie's round face – tight with old scars. Willie had been Outside too long. It had begun as a Hunt, but there was an accident and he became lost – wandering for over a year – burning and peeling. When they found him with his trophy he had little memory. The heat of the sun had fried his brain, they thought. Plastic work was done on his face, hands and feet – but the scars continued to pucker and contract, tightening joints and disfiguring his face. Psych put him through rehab, but failed to make a useful citizen out of him. The combination of Hunt drugs and prolonged exposure to Outside traumas was too much. He was now living out his life span on the Big ES allotment of calorie- and quarters-basic – CQB – fifteen hundred calories and thirty cubic yards – about half the CQB of Moses, a worker.

Simple Willie would visit Moses at every opportunity. He enjoyed the spaciousness and flavors. Moses accepted Willie. The poor frightened guy was pleasant enough most of the time, but would often deteriorate into mumbling incoherencies and fond-ling his grisly cubed trophy. He earned his nickname – Simple.

Willie continued: 'There used to be many kinds of plants – *yellow was the turnip; purple was the beet; dum de dum de dum dum; good enough to eat.* I forget how the rest goes. My mother taught me that rhyme. My birth was a class four. Did you have a biouterus, or a meck?'

'Meck, I think,' said Moses. He knew that most of the citizens in his age group had been class ones – carbon copy in a bottle. Predictable genes in carbon copies – better citizens, more pre-dictable, reliable, complacent Nebishes.

'Too bad,' said Willie. 'I rather enjoyed having a pair of biological parents. I have some warm memories of family life. We shouldn't be living alone in these tiny apartments. It isn't good.'

Moses picked up two more foamy drinks and gave Willie one.

'I wish I had a son,' said Willie.

'Why?'

'It is sad to die – unmourned.'

Talking to Willie always made Moses feel uncomfortable. He walked back to the air vent and changed the subject.

'I still say it smells green Outside. I think I'll go have a look for myself.'

Willie recoiled. 'You're not going—'

'I'll just climb upshaft and look through the grill. No harm in that. Why don't you come along?'

Willie withdrew into his corner and toyed with his trophy cube.

'Can't stand those crowds on the spiral. Damn people. There are too many of them. I used to be able to fight my way through any crowd when I was younger. But that was before I went Outside.' Willie took off his boots, exposing his three-toed feet. 'Lost my toes out there, too.'

Moses chided: 'Lost your toes and your guts. I guess you are a prime example of Toe Psychology – lose a toe, and lose initiative. If man ever evolves into a three-toed citizen things will get really dull around here.'

Willie's face showed a mixture of fear and anger. Sorting out his feelings he stood up hesitantly.

'Maybe I'll come with you, if – if the walkway isn't too crowded.'

Moses smiled confidently, patting him on the back. They filled their pockets with sweet bars, fat cubes and woven protein from Moses' dispenser – charged to Moses' credits – and started out.

It was a fifty-yard crawl to the spiral. Only a few middle-aged apathetics straggled by. No crowd. They walked over to the railing and leaned out into the shaft. An eighth of a mile below the floor of the shaft was a hazy disc of heads. Above them the shaft cap was a vague glow – more than a half-mile straight up. They started around the upspiral, passing the anonymous crawl-ways of their neighbors in the shaft city.

An hour later they took a drink break – each quarter-mile turn of the spiral lifted them only twenty yards. It would take over three hours to reach the cap.

'Enjoy looking Outside?' asked Willie nervously.

'I guess it is interesting,' shrugged Moses. 'I got a good close look a few months back while repairing an air vent over at HC. It looked and smelled green then – real green. I felt green for a few days afterwards.'

'Humans used to live Outside,' said Willie wistfully. 'Used to live in the ocean too – still carry gill slits to prove it – embryonic gill slits. I suppose our toes are embryonic memories of living Outside. We certainly don't need them in the hive. No running, climbing or swimming to do here.'

Moses didn't like the way Simple Willie spat out the term *hive*. He knew how some citizens hated the Big ES, claiming it treated them unfairly. But these were not the Good Citizens, they were the outcasts, the misfits.

Moses looked down at his own feet. 'We need some toes, for walking – like now.'

Simple Willie glanced around for Watcher sensors. He smiled knowingly at Moses.

'I agree,' he said placidly. 'And the Big ES is really a wonderful place to live. I know. I spent some time Outside experiencing the dangers. It was terrifying. All that open space! I don't think I could have survived it without my drugs to protect me. And there was weather.' Moses waited for him to continue. They had been over this subject many times before.

'That's changes in temperature, you know. It was light, then dark. Hot, then cold. The air stood still, then moved fast carrying dust and leaves around. The ground became covered with foam, then dried. Weather!' Willie took another quick sip from the bubbler and started eagerly up the walkway. 'Maybe we'll see some weather if we hurry.'

Moses followed.

Willie realized that his show of enthusiasm was a mistake. Glancing nervously around, he slowed his pace.

'Weather is awful,' he repeated unconvincingly. 'So is living Outside. They explained that to me real good when they brought me back into the city. Man was meant to live in cities – not the gardens. The Eyepeople who live In-between the cities are bad. They crush crops, live like animals, reproduce without controls

– kill, steal, commit all manner of crime. That was explained to me real good.'

They walked in silence for a time. The sunlight filtering through the shaft cap above began to fade – dusk.

Willie continued: 'Of course it is natural for the Eyepeople to live like animals – they are part animal. Some theories place them below us as direct ancestors on the evolutionary tree, but I'm certain we must have descended from a common four-toed ancestor. The five-toed beast is just a blind end – unable to fit into the hive,' he made a gesture of disgust. 'Eating human flesh! I think I could forgive them everything but the eating of their own kind. I suppose that is why I am proud of my trophy – I hunted the last of Earth's carnivores.'

At the rim of the cap they caught a glimpse of a blue sky through the stout metal grill. Willie clutched his chest and sat down facing the blank wall of the spiral.

'I can't look out.'

Moses gazed through the grill, giving Willie a word picture.

The plum and grape sunset darkened to a star-speckled licorice. They were sitting on a flat featureless platform that encircled the yawning shaft. The grill – a one-inch gauge, six-inch mesh – rose thirty yards to a shaggy green roof. Shaggy greens dangled. A man-sized Agromeck scuttled in from the shadowy fields and disappeared into its garage beneath the platform. Distant plankton towers lit up. White clouds of Agrifoam flowed out over the fields carrying their auxins and nutrients. Rows of shaft caps marched to the horizon, each marked another cyberconduit shaft city.

'Stars?' asked Willie's plaintive voice.

Moses nodded.

'Bright. Some big like an eye peeking down. Others small and numerous like spilled metallic dust.'

He searched their twinkling patterns for the familiar form of Orion. Shoulders and feet wide apart, narrow belt with sword. Years ago he had noticed it. No one in the Big ES seemed to understand what he was talking about. There was little curiosity about astronomy in the subterranean hive. Sewage, lice and calories were real; but a star was just something in the background

60

on entertainment shows to indicate the time of day. No one saw patterns in them. His search of the stacks didn't help either – stars were with the occult.

Night passed. In the darkness an Irrigator sucked at its canal and drenched the land. Foam melted away. Orion marched westward until dawn erased him. Moses was confident 'he' would return again. The roof of Outside seemed to have a very stable night pattern.

In the growing light, Moses turned to Willie.

'Willie – do you see things in the stars?' Willie cringed and covered his eyes. Moses carefully reworded the question. 'When you were Outside – the stars came out each night, didn't they? Could you see outlines of things in them? Patterns that came back night after night?'

Willie did not answer immediately. He stood up, careful to avoid looking Outside, and slouched down the ramp. Moses followed. They walked in silence for several quarter-mile turns of the spiral.

Finally Simple Willie spoke: 'I don't remember too good. Stars? I know I must have seen them – but I can't remember actually looking. There are lots of things about my time on the Outside that are all mixed up. Do you think it could have been the drugs?'

'Maybe—' said Moses sympathetically. 'Speed does more than make you go fast, I'm sure. But maybe the Big ES erased some of your memories too – trying to psych you into a better citizen.'

Willie stopped and smiled his relief. 'Of course. They put in blocks to keep my nostalgic memories from flooding out of my deep amygdaloid complex. But the blocks are not complete. Memory fragments come through sometimes—'

Willie abruptly sat down, again pressing his forehead against the wall. Sullen, morose and brooding, he mumbled something about the most beautiful creature he had ever seen. Moses tried to prod him out of his catatonia, but Willie's gloom just deepened into stupor. Simple Willie spent much of his time so – Moses was used to seeing him in this condition. All that was missing was the grisly trophy cube . . .

Moses sat beside him for a half hour, but his eyes remained

glassy. His consciousness was being dragged back through painful memories. Neural reflexes, triggered by their discussions, groped for the forbidden memories. The Big ES had placed effective blocks on single-step associations to the Outside, but Willie's struggled with double and triple associations to get at the memories. Slowly the traumatic memories were assembled to torture him again.

Simple Willie carried a heavy bow in his left hand. Green leaves – large and loose – flapped in a breeze. He saw his quarry – a coweye. Her large eyes and tiny neck and waist gave her an insect-like appearance through the scope. Lifting the bow he set cross hairs on her form. She shook back her yellow mane exposing tiny pink-tipped breasts. Her delicate figure triggered a headache. The images jumped.

He sat naked and tan surrounded by children. There were three little jungle bunnies – all yellow-haired like the coweye. The coweye came laughing and dripping from the canal. She playfully rolled into the group. Children giggled. Sunshine, bright flowers and tasty food. Happiness.

Pain and black shadows. Laughing Hunters held up dripping red trophies. Cold yellow-haired bodies lay scattered about on gory matted grasses. His view shifted and stretched. A head lay on the grass. Just a head. But it spoke to him in a language he couldn't understand. Then the head opened its mouth wide and a pair of legs protruded. Lifting itself on these legs, the head ran off laughing.

When Willie's consciousness returned to the spiral walkway, Moses was gone. A pile of food bars – flavored woven protein – were in his lap. Gathering them up, he returned to his cubicle. His trophy cube made him a little nervous. If only there was some way to analyze it to see if it were male or female – if only he could remember if it was really his trophy. Had he actually killed?

Moses put his little class thirteen dispenser to work searching for data on the Outside. Probing through old rusty dusty memory banks of the stacks, the cyber gathered bits of information and printed it out on flimsies. Stars were lost under the occult. Star maps could be found under seasons. Moses wasn't sure what a season was, but he did see Orion's familiar pattern under summer.

Earth's biosphere was very simple. Oceans contained only plankton – scanty and mostly microscopic. A few mussels filtered green waters of ocean and canal. Plants were listed under crops only – edible grasses, herbs, vines, trees – all bore fleshy items of caloric or flavor value for the hive. He smiled. Moses' Melon would be listed soon. Megafauna included several species of water mammal – Sirenia and cetaceans . . . the canal cleaners. Buckeyes were classified as a garden varmint with approaching hive-induced extinction. While the Nebish numbered over three trillions, the buckeye population was estimated at a fraction of a million – worldwide.

The stacks contained only scanty information on such things as sun, moon and stars – as if atrophy by disuse had allowed these items to be dropped. Hive flora included bountiful species of vermin – sharing the warmth and nutrition of Big ES – lice, roaches, meaty rats (cross-indexed under game food), and insects. Nothing else. Nothing was reported swimming the seas, flying in the air or walking the land. Fish, birds, reptiles and mammals – gone. Moses didn't miss them, never having known them. He was just a little amazed that the total mass of protoplasm on the planet was concentrated in one species and his food chain. Man had proved to be a very successful creature indeed.

As the week came to a close he checked in with the Pipe caste for his next duty assignment. J. D. Birk's square face came on the screen – nodding and grinning.

'No need to come in this shift, Moses. Your melon is a big success. It is a slime mold, just as we guessed. The troph stage is an ordinary-sized amoeba that thrives on aerobic sludge. At maturity it coalesces to sporulate like a fungus. Bio classifies it as safe. Synth plans to gray-age the melon and try it in the mushroom flavor line at first. If it goes over big, we'll be rolling in Augrams. Meanwhile, you have your Climb authorization. Your gear is on its way.'

Moses sat on the edge of his cot munching breakfast and listening. The words were what he had expected – more or less –

but Birk's face was tighter than usual, and his voice sounded strained.

The dispenser began to drop items for the Climb. He carefully checked his new suit of clothes for defects before chucking the soiled ones down the digester chute. His kit contained food bars for the long trip to the mountains. He would be in the tubeways for several days – even without losing time at dispensers. Public dispensers had an irritating way of delaying the traveler – otherwise he tolerated them. After all, most dispensers were only class thirteens – and identities had to be carefully checked. Moses didn't want a nonworker eating flavored calories and charging them to his account.

For two whole days Moses fought his way through the stinking crowds. He was weak from trying to keep his footing in the slippery excrement and crushed roaches, sore from stumbling over decaying neglected bodies, and continually nauseated by the rotten vapors that saturated his nose filters. He was sorry he had come.

He stepped out at a strange shaft city to catch a nap. There were the usual piles of refuse and bland stares. He found a corner to sit down and sleep in. A sickening thud woke him up. A small gob of something wet hit his cheek. A jumper. Another suicide. From the skeletal fragmentation Moses judged that he or she had started a quarter of a mile upshaft. There appeared to be more than one body. That irritated Moses. The jumper hadn't had the simple decency to scream a warning so the impact area could be cleared.

Moses was wide awake now. He elbowed his way back to the tubeway and continued toward the mountain. A class nine Sweeper brushed by. Its five-foot-tall snail shape took up the space of ten humans as it busied itself wetting, scrubbing and sucking at the stained floor. Its thin-walled sac already contained one large lump that had elbows and knees.

The tubeway deposited Moses on the floor of Rec shaft. He was alone. The large dispenser on the spiral called his name and issued the heavy pack of rations – dry staples for his time on the mountain. As he stood strapping it on, he mentally complained about his own Pipe caste. Their conduits moved everything on the planet – humans, food, water, air – everything – thousands of miles – but always horizontally. Never up. The energy was not available. The Rec shaft was narrow – a mere thirty yards in diameter. The spiral had a steep 20 per cent grade. There was only an occasional crawlway. No humans. A pinpoint of dim light in the center of the spiral marked what he estimated to be the two-mile height. Taking a deep breath of the cold, damp, metallic air, he paced out. Three hours later he passed three gray-haired men leaning on their packs.

He felt smug about his endurance until, an hour later, a girl – puberty plus seven – passed him. Her pack was about the same size as his. She wore the smock and emblem of the Attendant caste.

He stopped at the one-mile level to sleep. Crawling into one of the cubicles, he was surprised at how sterile it was. Without dispensers man seldom stayed more than a few hours. No nests, no vermin.

He slept over ten hours. A deep, restful sleep without all the usual slapping and scratching.

His Attendant met him at the top of the ramp. She was a puberty-plus-ten female – probably well epithelialized with mature cornified squamous cells – pleasant enough, too. But dull-witted and sterile. He stood, sweating and swaying under his heavy pack – exhausted. She steadied him with a firm hand on his shoulder strap.

'Supper or sex?' was her greeting.

Politeness prevented him from growling, 'Sleep.' This was a Climb, after all. He forced a smile and carefully straightened his aching back.

'Let's try both,' he said, 'after I've refreshed myself.'

'Saved us some water. Come on. We're family for two weeks.'

She led him to their room. In the dim light he paid more attention to the temperature of his bath water than the room's decor. She found the soap duck in his pack and tossed it in the refresher with him. He adjusted the cycling to hold a knee-deep soak. After fifteen minutes, she joined him with a scrub brush. He wallowed around – water up to his chin – while she worked the stiff bristles over his skin. The water was a little too cold for his liking, but he had to admit he was beginning to feel clean.

When he stepped out she handed him a coarse towel wrap-around. She wore a vented robe belted at the waist.

'This is the latest model of the cot-and-a-half. It has all the attachments for the first seventy-two positions,' she said proudly.

The thin mountain air dragged him down. He sat on the cot smiling weakly.

'Leather or lace?' she asked over her shoulder. She began rummaging around in the closet.

He stared at the pillow, longing for sleep.

'Leather or lace?' she repeated.

'Oh,' he answered, 'skin will be fine.'

She looked disappointed. Evidently she had some special out-fits she wanted to show off. She loosened her belt and walked toward the cot.

'You aren't one of those Position-One fellows are you?'

'Of course not. Are you familiar with the 54/12 switch?'

'Switch on the plateau phase?'

He nodded.

She smiled. At least she had been matched with an interesting partner this time. She glanced inside the closet door for the diagrams. Fifty-four/twelve switch?

'Are you sure that's what you want?' she asked. 'It looks a bit awkward to attempt during the plateau.'

He was still awake enough to grin. 'Yes, I'm sure. This is a Climb, isn't it? Might as well make it challenging.'

She hung up her robe and came to the cot. While she was removing the attachments they wouldn't be using, he stretched out and looked into the mirror on the ceiling. In a moment he was fast asleep.

She was an accomplished succubus.

Dawn was a bright surprise. At full blaze the yellow sun quickly rose above a pair of snow-covered peaks, filling their room with a blinding glare. One entire wall was transparent. His Attendant stumbled unsteadily from their cot and turned down the wall, changing the sun into a pale lunar disc. Then she collapsed back onto the bedding.

He felt fairly rested. The thin air didn't bother him so much. Walking to the edge of the room, he looked down. Pyramids of monotonous cubicles covered the lower slopes as far as he could see – he was reminded of an obscene glacier. The black crags of a distant mountain still looked pure – they seemed to be naked rock – but the distance was too great for his visual resolution. He hoped the crags remained black at sunset instead of flaming with window-reflected rays.

'Breakfast?' asked the Attendant, fingering his packs.

Odd, but when she began to share his food – calories he earned and hauled . . . she changed in his eyes. No longer was she a loving Attendant, here for his companionship. Now she was a parasite, trading her efforts for calories – flavored calories!

Try to go through life a little bit edible.
You never know when you'll meet something hungry.
                                        −ESbook − on charity.

Moses took his Attendant into the eerie cavelike bar. The outer walls were on step-down, almost opaque. Moses saw the hazy outlines of mountain and sky – grays and blacks. The hour was noon. The four-toed Nebishes crowded, thigmotropically, around the massive stone bar – comforted by the warm hips and elbows. Everyone wore the standard issue of loose translucent party garments. Moses ordered their layered drinks from the giddy dispenser and dialed for *flambé*. A tiny white fire flickered on top of their multicolored cylinders.

Drinks in hand, they joined the crowd. Conversation turned to the recent megajury execution. Moses' Attendant asked him to repeat his version. He complied, then lifted his drink.

Moses watched the flames on his pousse-café. Bending his straw, he deftly sampled the pomegranate, chocolate and mint of the deeper layers. Sitting back, he rubbed his singed eyebrows.

A man – short and hostile-looking – shouted from across the bar: 'Killing a psychotic prisoner by remote and diluting your guilt in the group conscience of the megajury – not too manly.'

Moses had heard these arguments many times, but they still stirred reflex hatred when they were directed at him. The adrenal response felt exhilarating. He shot back: 'Charity over Justice. Is that what you want – suspend a worthless psychotic and crowd out some hard-working citizen with an organic illness?'

The hostile parroted gleanings from news channels out of context: 'Thousands of patients move in and out of suspension every year. There's always room for one more. But then, you're better at strawing-up your cordial than being manly – button-pushing is your style.'

Moses strawed-up his mint without disturbing the other layers – drinking slowly – a study in irritation. 'You're a man?' he parried. 'Who have you killed lately?'

'Nobody,' frowned the hostile, 'but I did go on a Hunt – Outside. A real Hunt. I didn't make a group activity out of it, either. Exposed myself – man to man. Just didn't see any game – that's all.' He threw down his drink and brooded.

'What is so manly about a Hunt?' asked Moses. 'You take some drugs to give you courage, and you use a bow against some ignorant savage. That game has no chance against all the electronic gear.'

'It is manly to just be there – Outside. I was putting it on the line, not sitting here talking big about a megajury killing.'

'You're here now.'

The little man's adrenergic response pulled him from his stool. He strode around the bar shouting at Moses: 'Look, killer – you're probably real good at pushing buttons to kill some unfortunate guy whose brain malfunctions. But your reason is all wet. There isn't enough overcrowding to warrant the unnecessary killing of anyone. Have you ever looked Outside? I went out and didn't see anything – just the black dirt, a few shaft caps and that damn Agrifoam. No buckeyes. If Hunter Control can be wrong about buckeyes, why can't the Suspension Clinics be wrong about over-crowding?'

'You're not a very trusting fellow.'

The little man calmed.

'I question a lot of things – especially the overcrowding. What can we really see in our shaft cities? Nothing. Just walls. Tubeway walls. Shaft walls. Cubicle walls. Even if you travel there are just more walls. I'd just like to get a good look Outside once – like from the top of a mountain. See just how crowded the shaft caps are.'

'We're over half way up a mountain right now. Why don't we climb up and have a look around?' challenged Moses.

The bar grew silent. All eyes moved to the ceiling where coils of frayed rope hung from rusted pitons. The pitons, granular with age, were symbolic of the Climb. Most Nebishes came here for sex, drinking and spectating. Today Moses and the hostile would entertain.

Clumsy in his insulated gear, Moses crunched across the virgin snow to the edge of the balcony. A flexible ladder danced in the wind. The hostile crunched past and put his foot in a rung to hold the ladder taut. He gestured for Moses to go first.

As Moses started up, the hostile lifted his foot and the ladder jumped out of the snow. Wind sailed Moses over the mile-deep crevasse. Spinning like a kite, he saw a rotating view of sky, mountain, chasm, sky, mountain, chasm – vastness and vertigo triggered primordial fears. His muscles locked rigidly. Around and around he turned until his gravity senses were lost – clouds above and mists below merged. Time stopped. Snowflakes on his faceplate refused to melt.

When the wind changed direction, he swung back over the ledge. Dizzy, he looked down at the firm surface mocking him only a few feet below. The ladder's slack whipped up huge chunks of snow as it snaked back and forth. He tried to climb down, but his fingers were frozen to the rungs by fear. The group from the bar stood, drinks in hand, watching through the open door and taking sadistic pleasure in his terror. The wind sent him back out over the misty void and he blacked out.

He felt himself falling. Screaming, he opened his eyes to see that he was safe on his cot. Bulky dressings covered his hands and feet. His nose hurt. His Attendant hurried to his side with a liter of hot broth. She steadied his hands while he drank deeply.

'Try to relax,' she said. 'But don't close your eyes until your semicircular canals settle down. You're going to feel like you're spinning and falling for a while yet. You were on the ladder a long time before I got you down.'

'Thanks,' said Moses.

The broth was not too bad – fat cubes, woven protein and a vegetable bar. It strengthened him quickly. She removed her garments and crawled under the covers, rubbing him briskly.

'Hey. You're going to injure my frostbite.'

'It isn't bad. Probably won't even blister. Those bandages can probably come off tomorrow.'

'Wonderful,' he said, flexing his fingers carefully. 'Then I'll still be able to keep my appointment up on the mountain with that little hostile.'

'He is looking forward to it – dropped in while the Mediteck/meck was working on you. Three days from now.'

'Three days . . .' said Moses, propping up his pillow.

The Attendant poured two glasses of liqueur – dabbing a few drops of the aromatic fluid on her wrists and throat.

'Plenty of time . . .' she said softly, handing him his glass.

'For what?'

'Kipling,' she answered. With nimble fingers she adjusted the cot-and-a-half controls. The bedding flexed. Two bolsters were brought from the closet. He watched – puzzled. She swiveled their dispenser closer and carried a gadget-covered cord into bed with her. As the viewscreen activated she crawled roughly onto his lap. He smelled and tasted pomegranates.

'Easy . . .' he said. 'I've never been kipled before.'

The next three days passed pleasantly.

Sensate focus was directed toward taste, smell and touch as they shared their viewscreen's presentation of ancient ditties, ballads, ghost stories and other verses.

Moses kept his foot in the rung while the little hostile climbed the ladder. Through the bug-eyed lenses of his Pelger-Huet helmet, the scene appeared gray-on-gray. He listened to music – soothing strings – while he climbed. The wind whipped him about, as before, but he climbed steadily. The hostile gave him a hand up to the narrow icy ledge. They cracked their helmets and eyed each other.

'Sorry about the ladder ride the other day – but it was the best way I know to cure your Outside phobias.'

Moses shrugged. Cure or kill, he thought.

The hostile waited for his apology to be acknowledged. Moses glared.

'Okay, killer,' said the hostile, 'follow me. We hike up the ridge to the snow line. Then it's a mile or so to the cave. We can sleep there and go on to the summit in the morning.'

Moses followed with his helmet cracked to conserve oxygen – save enough to keep the incubus off his chest while he slept. The trail was narrow and rough. Snow flurries hid the hostile occasionally. Ice and loose drifts made the footing treacherous. Pitons and a line guided him on steep spots. At dusk he sipped water and turned on his suit light. Pausing at the lip of the miniglacier, Moses glanced eastward and saw the slopes of other mountains begin to glow as millions of cliff-dwellers turned on their lights. The foothills and flatlands remained dark – there were few lights in the gardens.

Wading through knee-deep powder tired Moses. He closed his helmet and took oxygen. A dark stone wall loomed ahead. The hostile's light penciled about – illuminating black stone and white snow. A triangular crack at the base of the wall formed the mouth of a cave.

'Moses,' called the hostile. 'You go inside and unroll your bedding while I try to find some firewood.' He began to make random circles in the snow.

Firewood? This far above the tree line? Moses was too fatigued to argue. Without a word Moses wandered deep into the cave looking for relief from the numbing cold. The walls were icy, about five feet apart at the mouth, and widening to a cubicle-sized chamber about twenty yards inside. He flashed his light around. Odd. He thought he smelled wood burning.

'Okay in there?' came the hostile's shout from the mouth of the cave.

Moses turned around to answer. A moment later he was knocked to his knees by a thunder clap that vibrated the cave floor and showered him with pebbles. In the silence that followed he heard an evil laugh from further back in the cave. The thunder clap had come from the mouth of the cave. There were no more sounds from the hostile.

Moses crawled into a corner and turned off his light. Footsteps approached from the back of the cave. He fumbled for his small ice pick. The footsteps were accompanied by a flickering torch.

Moses held his breath. What he saw chilled him. A sinewy old man approached carrying a burning pine cone on a stout spear. His legs were wrapped below the knees, and he wore tattered rags and a loose outer cloak. He was not alone. Walking before him was a squarish, four-legged beast that should have been long extinct – a seventy-pound, long-snouted carnivore. The beast was covered with battle scars. Its eyes were slits behind thick lids of gristle. Moses did not know its species, but its long, well-toothed snout told its diet.

Man and beast moved past Moses toward the mouth of the cave. Several minutes later they returned carrying peculiar jointed structures that dripped. The man's resembled a human leg, the dog's a human arm. This time the procession stopped at Moses' hiding place.

'Eppendorff?' called the old man, shifting his grip on the dripping burden. He carried it casually at the knee. 'Come back to our fire. We want to talk.'

From his seated position on the floor of the cave Moses viewed the beast as hopeless odds. The beast squinted at him through slant eyes, wagged its tail three times and led the way back to the fire. Its hunk of meat dragged – leaving a sticky trail. Moses got to his feet and tried to be casual about slipping his ice pick back into his belt.

The flame was small, stingy, fed by a few resinous fragments of pine knot. The walls were sooty. The floor was littered with small bundles of twigs and bones – cracked femurs, arched ribcages, and a whole line of skulls up against the wall.

A buckeye camp site!

The old man stabbed a peg under the leg's Achilles tendon and hung it in one of the dark recesses of the cave.

'Pull up a rock and relax. I'll have something cooking for us in a minute.'

'You're not planning on eating that—' Moses gagged.

That red thing? Oh, no. Fresh stuff is too tough. I have a nice black aged quarter here someplace.'

The old man crawled back into another recess and returned with a shrunken dark object fuzzed with mold. Moses couldn't recognize it – he asked no questions.

The glowing coals flared up white and blue under the dripping meat. The beast lay, paws and chin on its raw forequarter, until the old man gestured for it to eat. Then its powerful teeth crunched quickly – devouring soft tissue and bone alike. Only the epiphyses of the long bones remained – dense and without marrow. Moses was fascinated by the sheen of the beast's teeth. They looked metallic!

'The conditions in this cave are ideal for aging meat,' said the old man, offering Moses a generous muscle bundle. 'Almost makes the trip worthwhile.'

Moses held his portion at arm's length.

'Go ahead and eat,' said the old man. 'You're from the hive. Where do you think all your woven protein comes from – algae? Ha! This is the same thing, only it hasn't had all the flavors processed out.'

Moses frowned. 'Meat? Wasn't that a human being you just killed? Don't you have any feelings?'

'Just so much protein to me,' snarled the old man. 'Can't have too much feeling for the four-toed hive creatures – parasites!' Pointing his spear at Moses for emphasis, he admonished: 'And don't waste time mourning that one. He had the same thing planned for you. Didn't you notice the way he sent you into the cave first with the pretext of looking for firewood? He's been at this Rec Center long enough to know the gossip. I've been here before – and they never know when I'll be back.'

'You're a – buckeye?'

The old man stood up apologetically: 'Oh, I am sorry. We've been eavesdropping on you so long – waiting for you to come up here – that we forgot you didn't know us. I'm Moon – old man Moon, and this is my dog, Dan.'

'Eavesdropping?' said Moses, handing his charred muscle to the dog.

'Toothpick spied on you. He has the circuits for it.'

Moon gestured towards his spear.

'Hi,' said the spear. 'I'm Toothpick. Actually, your being here is my idea.'

Eppendorff stared at the spear – a machine. A very sophisticated machine. His years in the Pipe caste had exposed him to many machines – mostly class tens. Toothpick was more than a class ten.

'But why?'

'We want you to come with us – live Outside,' said Toothpick.

'Impossible. Life is too short for me to waste it being hunted.'

Moon handed Toothpick to him, saying: 'Here, Eppendorff, take Toothpick for a walk. Let him convince you.'

Moses Eppendorff carried Toothpick gingerly toward the mouth of the cave. They passed a massive stone deadfall and stepped out under the stars. Moses turned on his suit heat and light, cracking the helmet open.

Toothpick spoke: 'Don't mind the way Moon talks. He has confidence in me because I'm so old. Actually I'm just a leftover cyber from the period when man had many of us. It was an age of high technology and low population density – man and his machines were all over this planet, in the sea and air – even off planet – the moon, near space – even Mars and Deimos. Ancient five-toed man even dreamed of star travel. I enjoyed those days – companion cybers were numerous. My circuits must have been on stand-by for centuries. I still feel strong, well-charged. Now I am Moon's cyber. He gives me intellectual stimulation. I try to protect him. But now I think we need a younger man: you, Moses. Moon and Dan are old – nearly two hundred. Their genetic clocks are off, but their scars accumulate – slowing them down. Hunters will get them soon, unless we have a new strong partner.'

Moses nodded. He had heard of early attempts at genetic

decoding – society's attempt at improving the citizen stock. The result was *Homo superior*, the complacent hive citizen. Genetic engineers stumbled on the clock – polycistronic RNA which translated the message of species life span from the gene to the messenger RNA. A virus-like anti-gene was manufactured to destroy the clock, but the Big ES didn't like the idea of multicentenarian Methuselahs accumulating and obstructing the evolution of ideas. The old five-toeds had to be replaced over and over in order for the hive to evolve. Clock work was stopped – Moon and Dan were just relics. The gene molders turned to other things – the five-toed gene. It carried more than the toe . . . immunoglobulin A, calcium and collagen, neurohumoral axis, melanocytes. Those with the fifth toe could not be crowded. It had to be engineered out of the population,

'Did man ever reach the stars?' asked Moses.

Toothpick didn't answer immediately.

'I'm not certain,' said the cyber slowly. 'My own memory banks are small. What they contain seems to have been put in a long time ago. A lot of it doesn't make sense. I've tried spying on the circuits of Big ES, but the stacks are badly cross-indexed. Whenever I make contact the questing fields seek me out and we have to run from hunters. Stars? I feel a warmth in my circuits, but I can't explain it. I like to think that man did reach the stars before the hive stagnated.'

Eppendorff knew about stagnation. The Pipe caste was losing ground with simple drinking water and heat pollution.

They talked through the night. Toothpick and Moon had walked over most of the two major continents in the hemisphere. Conditions were the same everywhere. In the tropical and temperate zones, man had moved into underground shaft cities and cultivated every square inch of the surface. Vagabonds between the cities were tolerated when their numbers were small, but were relentlessly hunted like varmints when they increased.

Toothpick did not like this new Earth, but – Moses reasoned – he was a companion cyber and would naturally prefer a world where he could play a more important role than that of a vagabond.

At dawn Moon reset the deadfall at the cave mouth. It was a

beautiful job of stonecutting – if you could ignore the gore long enough to admire the precision of the counterweight and the marble key.

Locking the key with his foot, Moon said, 'Don't want anyone to get hurt while we're away—' and laughed.

He picked up a ten-centimeter section of tube and attached it to Toothpick's shaft. It had an optic and had been set in the trigger area. Toothpick was more than a toy.

Moon gathered up the hostile's kit and carried it back to the fire. Pocketing the food bars, he tried on various articles of clothing.

'This issue tissue certainly doesn't last long,' he complained.

He was ready to lead out when Moses gave him an argument.

'Thanks for the invitation – but I won't be going with you. It sounds like an interesting existence. I just don't want to end my days as a fugitive crop-crusher . . . and certainly not as a cannibal.'

Moon flushed with anger.

'Do you really know what you're going back to? That secure position in your hive culture? What is your life really? You live alone with no possibility of changing your future. Jobs? Move the sewage or kill the psychotic. Love? Nothing. Don't tell me about your Attendant back there. The only reason she took you down off that ladder was to save her share of your rations. Future? You have none. That hive culture is reproducing only the four-toeds. If you come with us you can have more children than you can count.'

Moses winced at the thought.

'Jungle bunnies? Have children that will be hunted all their lives?'

'It is better to be hunted than not to exist at all. Look, you owe it to the human race to try to pass on your genetic fifth toe – Toothpick thinks you were born with the bud of one. The hive culture is the end of the line for man – evolution stops here. Hive humans can survive hundreds of millions of years with their damn four toes. Nebishes can't evolve. The hive is like a living organism – each individual is just a specialized unit with one function. Even reproduction and sex are separated. If a Nebish ever did come up

76

with a mutation that was advantageous for the individual, he'd probably end up in suspension. It only took a few thousand years to advance from camp fires to space ships. In the next million years the hive will accomplish nothing. It doesn't have to. It is the dominant life form on the planet.'

Moses glanced at the old man, Toothpick and Dan.

Snugging up his shoulder harness, he put on his helmet and said, 'Well, I came to see the other side of this mountain. Might as well take a real good look.'

Two humans, a dog and a cyber made the trip to the summit. The view was encouraging – naked rocks, ice, snow and an endless blue sky flecked with small puffs of white cloud. The old man waved proudly at the austere surroundings.

'No cubicles above the ten-thousand-foot mark. We can take our time along this range. Farther north there is the remnant of a tree line – a few real soft woods and lots of lichens.'

Moses discarded his Pelger-Huet helmet as they crossed a saddle ridge. He got a glance westward, saw fields of geometries. Monotonous tiered crops with shaft caps and canals. Millions of four-toeds lived in darkness while they were enjoying the sun and the wind. His forehead burned and then tanned.

He also learned. Toothpick tuned in on the agricultural robots and guided the group to food supplies. A few pounds of dried plankton gave them energy to reach the wooden tomatoes. A bedroll of those carried them into grain fields. His insulated suit had handy pockets and a water bottle, but they moved faster in the warmer low lands. Its bulk was in the way. Soon Moses and Moon were dressed alike – tattered rags.

When they had to cross open ground they trotted briskly, staying fifty yards apart. Buckeye sensors paid little attention to single warm-blooded forms.

Val and old Walter studied the report in disbelief.

'Moses Eppendorff has gone buckeye? First our Tinker, now our Pipe,' moaned Val. 'Why?'

Walter gasped for air in his usual fashion, but he spoke calmly: 'I don't see any connection. Tinker was forced out by the Big ES decision to take away his natural child. Even you and I could see the logic in that. We tried to have the child certified.'

Val wasn't being soothed. 'But we can't condone what he did. We hunted him, and would have killed him – I suppose – if we had to.'

They looked at the file that held the Sampler's report. Neither had looked inside – for it held the findings on the three decaying bodies that were found near Tinker's escape air vent.

'And Moses,' continued old Walter, 'he was sent out by his supervisor, Birk – a reward for his discovery of the Moses' Melon. Tinker's child and Moses' Melon – both resulted in the loss of a citizen to the Outside. Just a coincidence.'

'And the tightbeams?' Val prodded.

Walter shrugged.

'Don't know, but that's Security's problem – not HC.'

Val was not satisfied. Too many of the citizens he had come to admire had gone buckeye. Something was wrong.

4
Kaia the Male

High on his frozen mountain, Kaia stirred in his nest. Hibernation time still remained on his metabolic clock, but hunger called. The hunters' constant pursuit had made his feedings scanty during the previous warm season. Now his winter sleep was being interrupted by protein starvation – acute amino acid deficiency. Enzyme systems faltered, screamed and tried alternate pathways. Reluctantly he left the dark warmth of his nest and crawled toward the pale glow of the cave mouth. Icy stones numbed hands and knees. He fingered the translucent white crust that sealed him in. It was still thick and hard. The snow line had not yet receded up the mountain. Outside he could only expect the white death. Shivering, he returned to his nest and wrapped a tattered cetacean hide around his old bony shoulders. His metabolic furnace sputtered without fuel. Coldness of death crept into fingers and toes. Desperate, he sorted through the debris at the bottom of the nest: sucking on long bones for the rusty grit in the tubular-shaped cancellous marrow cavities; chewing dry fruit pits for a few coarse bland lignen fibers; and licking cold mussel shells for stringy tags. Nothing. The cold continued to creep in. He didn't need the ferrous ions in the marrow dust, and his efforts had produced little else.

Kaia's grinding molars cracked open a fruit pit, releasing a meaty seed so bitter that it puckered his parotid. He spat out the lignen shells and chewed the meat. The plant's hoarded starch granules promised to rekindle his furnace. Gathering a handful of the pits, he crawled back to the light of the cave mouth and cracked them open with a stone – munching the bitter seeds with swallows of melted snow. With the resinous starchy mulch coating his rugal folds and quieting his hunger pangs, Kaia burrowed back under the musty hides and returned to his cool torpid state.

Earth's axis tilted. Longer, warmer days melted back the snowcap and thawed Kaia's niche. The translucent crust dripped and sagged for a time. Then it fell into the cave, exposing his nest to the welcome glare of sunlight. He sat up stretching and squinting. After wrapping on strips of hide as leggings and loincloth, he crawled cautiously outside and stood in a wet cool breeze. The mountainside was a bright mosaic of gray stone and stubborn drifts of white snow. The sun warmed his hairy neck and shoulders. Hunger gnawed. He studied the horizon. Only an occasional Agromeck moved, bug-like, on Filly's cultivated skin. Calories beckoned from below – a twinkling green filigree of plankton towers clinging to bare rock faces. He started down. A richer warmer atmosphere greeted him.

He climbed into the forest of plankton towers. The trunklike conduits pulsed and glowed with an inner coherent light of 570 nanometers. The carotenoids and phycobilins of the chloroplasts captured most of the light energy, but enough filtered through to produce a soft green glow. The trunks rose, arborizing freely, to form a tubule canopy which captured additional energy from the sun.

The noisy approach of a cumbersome Agromeck sent Kaia scurrying deeper into the syntheforest. After it passed, he emerged and started for the herb gardens. Filly, the cybercity, felt his clandestine movements on her skin. Footsteps itched. Filly moaned when he snapped open a tubule and began to suck plankton. Before she could sphincter down the leak, rich amino acids of zooplankton were fueling his starving enzyme systems. Refreshed, he munched his way across chickpea, soybean and thyme. Filly screamed when he pulled off a stalk of fennel. Her sorrow traveled along inorganic nerve fibers to Hunter Control.

'Sucker in my garden. Varmint on my skin,' she cried.

Val glanced up at the wall panel.

'Looks like a sighting over by Filly's Mountain again. Haven't been any buckeyes around there since the one we got last fall.

Filly sure has sensitive skin. I wouldn't be surprised if we got this one too. Foxhound is on the way.'

A small light moved across the wall map.

'Val!' exclaimed old Walter, glancing up from a folder of dusty papers. 'Have you seen these reports on Tinker's body?'

Val shrugged and turned his seat around.

'No – why?'

'It isn't Tinker.'

Val jumped up and strode purposefully to Walter's desk.

'What do you mean?'

'Look here. Both adults were male – had been dead about nine months. Hunters, I'd guess. And the infant was a female nearly five years old. It had enough skin pigment to be a jungle bunny. Probably killed by a hunter's arrow.'

Val picked up first one report, then another. His face tightened.

'They must have been deliberately planted on Tinker's trail to delay us. Look at the grass under the bodies – hardly stained at all,' he mumbled. Stepping back, he sat down weakly – the reports held limply in his hand.

'Who—?'

'Tinker,' suggested Walter, 'perhaps Tinker put them there. He was a clever one.'

Val shook his head. 'No. Where could he find just the right bodies. This is garden country. These corpses must have come from high country – the mountains.'

They were interrupted by a report from the Hunt at Filly's Mountain. The hunter's hypnoconditioning was reinforced, and his neck titrator gave a priming dose of Speed. The molecular courage brought a sinister grin to his face before the helmet snapped on.

Kaia, the aborigine, sat hidden in the tall grain while he savored the aromatic juices of fennel. Rich sharp flavors jolted pristine taste buds and stirred violent parasympathetic storms. Copious gastric juice flowed. Peristalsis gurgled. Soon his abdomen protruded comfortably, and he became more selective – choosing only the most succulent morsels.

Val watched the remote screen at HC. He recognized the sinewy form and took some stills for higher magnification.

'The scar is right there on the neck,' he said. 'This is the same buckeye we watched die on Filly's Mountain last fall.'

Walter asked the HC meck, Scanner, to dig up the old optics. Stills overlayed perfectly. Same bone structure. Walter nodded.

'Looks like we have our second resurrection,' said old Walter. 'What do you make of it?'

'Second?' said Val puzzled.

'The coweye you saw while tracking Tinker.'

Val wrung his hands together. He had actually touched that coweye – felt the still, cold flesh. Death. The memory of her rewarming and swimming off was still with him. He shuddered.

'I get the feeling that we're dealing with the occult,' mumbled Val. 'But there must be a logical explanation. Can the HC meck get this data to the Class One for a work up – see how it computes?'

Scanner said: 'Done. We'll hear in a minute.'

The passing Huntercraft sent Kaia scurrying off in a zigzag course. Foxhound had difficulty tracking. The bugeyed, white-suited hunter swung down-harness with his bow. Kaia saw the skull-like Pelger-Huet helmet and the deadly arrows. Fear tightened his chest. He curled up and went cold.

The sensors searched, but the viewscreen indicated ambient. No warm-blooded body showed.

'There he goes again,' said Walter, pointing to the screen.

'Vanished?' said Val.

'If I didn't believe in the Kjolen-Milo experiments, I'd say we had a case of teleportation here,' said Walter.

Val shook his head. 'No, they came up with some pretty convincing equations. That buckeye is still out there. He just isn't showing up on the sensors.'

'Foxhound,' called Val, 'let the hunter keep searching. He may stumble on the buckeye's hiding place.'

The craft returned to Garage to suck energy.

*

Twelve hours later the hunter began to slow down. He was standing, blurry-eyed, on the bank above Filly's effluent grating watching the warm, uriniferous fluids swirl off into the canal system. A cloud of gnats hung in the vapors around his helmet. During the night he had examined every heat source on Filly's skin – mostly the city's own appendages. Now he dozed on his feet. A jolt of Speed pumped into his jugular vein. Eyes opened wide – unfocused. His detector indicated a moving body by the canal. He nocked an arrow and crept off, stalking an Agromeck on its way to the fields.

Kaia's senses returned. The long hours of silence had relaxed his hibernation reflex. Peering from the tall grain, he saw no hunter. Dashing into an orchard, he sucked a sweet thing from a tree. Running briskly, he sought the safety of the canal.

The first arrow kicked him in the right femur, pinning his loincloth into his upper thigh. The impact threw him to the ground, bent over the arrow. He crawled a few feet and saw the skull-mask rise above the grassy canal bank. Bowstring taut. Kaia tugged on the bloody shaft. Shreds of loincloth moved deep in the wound, but the broad barbs held firm in the quadriceps. He struggled to his feet and tried to run, but the three-foot shaft vibrated and grated painfully. Nerves and bone chips. The second arrow struck his back – entering under the right scapula and passing through the right lung. He glanced down to see the wet red barbs jump out of his sternum. Grass hit him in the face.

The sight of the kill triggered the hunter's post-hypnotic suggestion to take a trophy. His tracking frenzy ended and he relaxed. His neck console moved to the end of its tape and readied the Molecular Reward. He sauntered up to Kaia's body where it lay in a pool of clotted blood – thick purple jellylike clots. He bent down over the cooling form and took out his trophy knife.

The gurgle in the canal did not carry through his helmet. He didn't see the coweye. She was on him with both feet – stamping and kicking – spreading the pieces of his mangled body over a twelve-foot circle. His chalky bones snapped, and his rose-water blood splattered.

The coweye bent over Kaia and touched his throat with her

hand. Satisfied, she snapped the barbed arrow head off the shaft in his chest. Carefully, she edged the shaft out from under his shoulder blade. Pressing wooden pegs in his thigh, she widened the wound and engaged the barbs. His leg arrow came out easily.

Foxhound found the remains of the hunter later in the day. The hunter's belt communicator had optic records that told the story. Val and Walter examined the large, purple jellylike clots and broken arrows.

'Send for the Bioteck,' said Val. 'I'd like to see what these clots are made of. They don't look anything like our own rose-water blood.'

Walter nodded. He was studying the stills of the arrow impacts. 'While he is here, have the teck project these wounds into their three-dee mannequin. They look fatal to me.'

The Bioteck returned with a transparent mannequin under one arm and a stack of reports under the other.

'It's blood clot,' he said, referring to the jellylike material. 'It isn't normal, of course. Hemoglobin, fibrinogen and hematocrit are all about three times normal. The hemoglobin is fifteen grams – if you can imagine!'

Val nodded.

The teck stood up the mannequin.

'This chest wound is fatal. The arrow passes through the hilum of the right lung. There are big vessels there, bronchi too. The leg wound, though serious, probably would not kill . . . if it were treated promptly.'

Val walked around the mannequin and compared the optic printouts. If the buckeye's anatomy was anything like their own, he should be dead.

'What would a coweye want with a dead buckeye?' asked Val.

The teck shrugged, 'They're cannibals, sir.'

Val wasn't satisfied. There were still too many unanswered questions – the tightbeams from Outside, the decoy corpses on Tinker's trail, and the peculiar resurrections.

'Why would cannibals decoy us away from Tinker's trail?'

Silence.

'Answer from the CO,' announced Scanner.

Val put it on print and audio, hoping it would clear up some of the mystery.

The Class One worldwide computer spoke with the kindly voice of an old man, sympathetic, yet confident.

'Your problems with the cooling buckeyes are not new,' began the CO. 'The hibernation reflex has been showing up in the aborigines ever since we started hunting them with the heat-seeking detectors. They have the gene for increased tone in their neurohumoral axis, so metabolic shut-down can be a defense mechanism in the proper environment. The hunters have provided that environment. If you have any more questions, don't hesitate to ask. Meanwhile, we can use any data you accumulate.'

They waited politely until the screen cleared.

'Playing possum,' smiled Val. 'At least we aren't fighting the occult. Witchcraft makes me nervous.' He shuddered. 'I can still feel her wet cold body. I'm sorry now that I didn't cut her carotid. Let her get away. That won't happen again.'

Walter dictated a few notes to Scanner for inclusion in hunter orientation.

'With knowledge of this reflex we should have more success on our Hunts. Finding a buckeye who is playing possum should be easy with the coordinates of his last sighting – killing him should be even easier.'

Val nodded.

The Bioteck picked up his papers and mannequin. As he was leaving he suggested: 'If you ever come across a live buckeye you might just tie off the dominant carotid and bring him to the lab for study.'

Walter stopped his dictation. 'How's that again?'

'Check his palms for calluses,' said the teck. 'If his right hand is hornier – more keratotic – you can assume he is right-handed. His left cerebrum would be dominant. Cut into his left neck and tie off the internal carotid on that side . . . should infarct part of the brain. He should live, but he'll be almost a vegetable – ideal for the boys down in Bio to work with. There are lots of parameters of five-toeism we should know more about before they become extinct.'

'Right,' said Val, 'good idea.'

Walter cancelled the rest of his dictation.

Kaia opened his eyes in a strange nest. The coweye soaked his wounds and changed his dressings frequently. Chest pains along the tract of the arrow shaft caused him to wink in and out of hibernation. She forced boiled mussel meat and rich barley soup into him. It was her follicular phase, and she needed a mate.

At night she came to him grasping with her copulatory apparatus. Her demand-type thrusting failed to initiate his pelvic-autonomic-cycle, for his granulating thoracic wound kept his parasympathetics depolarized by irritating the right vagus nerve. At new moon she went luteal and disappeared into the canal.

For two weeks he foraged painfully for scraps of food on the grassy slopes of the canal. In his crippled condition he couldn't risk exposure to the buckeye detectors that monitored the gardens – he would never be able to escape if hunters found him again.

At full moon she returned – tense follicle. His sperm still waited. Her previous ovum had languished in its corona and died. A new ovum was soon to take its place in the tube. He enjoyed warm food during the days and a hot nest at night. After she was fertilized, her golden corpus luteum again commanded her moods. She left the nest one morning, threw him two mussels from the canal bottom, and swam off without a word.

He limped back to Filly's Mountain.

Try to go through life a little bit hungry.
You never know when you'll meet someone edible.

– Buckeye Kaia

For several months Hunter Control was very quiet. The thousands of square miles of Orange Country gardens flourished, were harvested, and flourished again with only a rare buckeye sighting. Craft reported empty campsites – bones, chewed and charred – ashes – broken tools. Nothing to track.

Val chuckled over the lull. 'With Jupiter in Sagittarius you'd think we'd be having better hunting.'

Walter frowned. The supernatural was nothing to joke about. After a long moment of strained silence the old man spoke.

'Not funny. In the ten years I've been in HC I've come to respect the buckeye's peculiar cycle of activity and migration. Their shamen go by the planets – have to – cycles of weather and crops are important to them. And they sleep right under the stars. Hive citizens can laugh at astrology. The Big ES protects them. Horoscopes are faulty when cast by a meck who isn't watching the heavens anyway. But my charts are serious. Help with the Hunt. I try to outguess buckeye shamen. Right now I think they've gone into hiding because Jupiter is in Sagittarius. They figure it is a good sign for the hunter. More citizens will request a Hunt after seeing their horoscope – so the buckeyes are smart to avoid detection.'

'Perhaps we're in for a long rest – Jupiter will be in that sign for a long time,' chuckled Val.

Walter just grunted and coughed. He opened a box of artifacts collected from buckeye campsites. The beads interested him. He held up an intact string – twelve black beads, a ringed bead at one end, and four colored beads in the center.

'What do you make of these?'

'Clan—' suggested Val.

'What if they represent time?' said old Walter. 'Planetary time – zodiacal. If the ringed one is Saturn, then this big white one could be Jupiter in Sagittarius—'

Val nodded, half interested. 'But three more beads are with the big white one – a four-planet conjunction just isn't on any of my star charts here.' He pulled out projections of future positions – nothing matched the beads for hundreds of years as far as he could tell. 'If it is a conjunction, it is way off in the future. Can't see what interest buckeyes could have in that – but any four-planet conjunction would be significant for someone.'

'Sagittarius? Hunter – or hunted?' mumbled Walter.

Val had lost interest already. He was casting a light-hearted horoscope to help him decide which entertainment channel to watch. Walter closed his artifact box with an interruptive *bang*.

'Well!' he shouted. 'We can't solve any more buckeye problems on this shift. Let's drop over to my place for a meld.'

Val shook his head – declining.

'Not tonite. I'm going 'tween walls on a rat hunt. Pick up a few extra flavors.'

'Maybe next time then,' said Walter in parting. 'Female Bitter has been asking about you.'

They went their separate ways. Val had strong feelings about the meld. Rubbing souls with anyone irritated him. He clashed with the polarized and found the neuts too bland. Walter, on the other hand, enjoyed his family-5 and all their little intimacies and pleasurings. He accepted ritual hugs from female Bitter and talked job with Jo Jo and grumpy Busch. Neutral Arthur planned family fun and games. A well-rounded family-5.

Val sat in his cubicle checking his ratting gear. The coveralls were well worn. They had helped him take many calories. He changed the dust filters and tested the power cell. The helmet light and communicator still functioned, although both had low reliability quotients by now. Picking up the anoxic gas bag he started upspiral to the mid-level gratings.

'Level thirty-five OK, City?' he asked.

'Go ahead,' said the cybercity. 'I'll track you.'

He waded into the powdery soot. Cobwebs clung. His lamp picked out a circle of old dry skeletons – humans gone mushroom on Molecular Reward. He gave the location to the city, but Sampling wasn't indicated for bones.

He tracked along weight-bearing struts, hollow cylinders, and pipes of all sizes – some pulsating, some hot, others flexible and cold. Underfoot, the black and gray spongy dust averaged ankle-deep, but it drifted in corners and formed friable and pillowy cushions on everything. Thin cables and wires resembled thick columns. He repeatedly swatted away the cottony debris to identify the object being drifted over.

Deep, snakelike rat trails crisscrossed the dust drifts. Rat droppings were everywhere. As he flashed his light around it was reflected back by hundreds of pairs of beady retinas.

'City,' he said, 'you've got a lot of rats down here.'

'Most of my citizens are reincarnationists,' said the voice in his helmet, '– don't eat meat. They see their ancestors in the eyes of the rat.'

Val smirked: 'If I were a believer in transmigration of the soul I'd think my ancestors would appreciate having their sojourn as a rat shortened. Besides, we're the only carnivore the rat has to worry about now, so eating them may be Nature's Way.'

His bitter philosophy was wasted on the city. It directed him toward the highest density of rats' nests. He crawled under a whistling air conduit. Using a heavy girder for hand-holds, he scaled across a deep void on a narrow pipe. When he flashed his helmet light down, vertigo gripped his cardio-esophageal junction. Only an occasional cobweb caught his beam. The blackness of 'tween walls appeared bottomless. Ahead he saw one of the city's organs – a thirty-yard-diameter sphere with a medusa head of flexi-cables. He touched it. It was warm, dry and silent.

'Found your energy organ.'

City reviewed its own anatomy. 'Membrane filters to your right.'

He dust-waded along the top of a large pipe. It was hollow. Voices and shuffling vibrated. It was a crawlway. The larger rats became more numerous – and bolder. They remained stubbornly in his path until he nudged them with his toe. They wouldn't be too tasty. The sweet stink of the nests hit him. Moist and dripping, the huge cool sphere of the membrane filters loomed ahead. The city's sweat condensed and trickled down the sphere's outer shell – providing drops of drinking water for the rodents. The struts beneath the filter were packed with dark little nests – short tunnels dug into the stringy dust. The hum of the membrane pumps tickled his feet as he approached.

He hissed nitrogen into his bag and pulled on the heavy ratting glove. Selecting a large nest, he thrust in his hand. Expecting mother-with-food, the soft young rats swarmed onto the glove. He pulled out three handfulls and squeezed them through the sphincter of the anoxic bag. Their squirming and squeaking ceased.

He worked his way down the moist struts filling the bag. Feeling something heavy on his boot he looked down to see a bold rat gnawing on his sole. He kicked it away. Soon the bag weighed half as much as he did.

He sat down to rest and brushed the larger gobs of dust from his helmet.

'Is there an access hatch to a crawlway on this level?'

'Behind you – fifty-three yards.'

The pasty-faced citizens glanced up and got speckled with soot as the hatch moved. A cloud of black feathery particles billowed ahead of him as he dropped into the crawlway. Balancing the lumpy bag on his shoulders he tracked black footprints downspiral to the Watcher's quarters to pay his tithe.

The Watcher, a melon-headed neut, patted his pudgy hands together and grinned at the size of the catch. He went to the press and pulled open its heavy door.

'Six hundred degrees before press – and three hundred after?' asked Watcher.

Val nodded through his soiled helmet. The Watcher motioned for him to use the public refresher while the meats were processed. Val grumbled at the class thirteen's slowness in getting the water up to temperature. Then he waded through, rinsed his gear, and took a new issue tissue garment from the dispenser. Sounds of pop frying and smells of scorched fur filled the room while he dressed.

The press fell with a loud thump that shook the cubicle. Odors of a high protein bake brought out the Watcher's family-7. Val studied the assortment of polarized females – all ages and sizes. They wore their vented, meld robes with belted waists.

'Calories for the meld tonite,' said Watcher, clapping his hands loudly and shooing them back into the living quarters. 'Flavored calories.'

The press lifted. Steam rose. Val began scooping the nutmeg-colored wafers into his bag. He paused to blow on a hot finger. Watcher used a long-handled spatula to pile his tithe on an ornamental meld platter.

'Care to share our evening meld, brother?' asked the Watcher.

Val declined. All that mucous membrane took the edge off his appetite. As he left he heard the wet, smacking sounds of their evening meld/meal. Pressed rat was quite a delicacy. Flavors were good for the soul in the meld.

Leaving his ratting gear in his quarters he took the pressed rat down to Walter's. Female Bitter met him at the door and began to fondle the heavy bag of protein. He frowned her away.

'Where's Walter?'

'Dabbing,' she said, nodding toward the fat old man's private cubicle. Val glanced around the spacious thirty-foot living room . . . advantages of a family-5.

Fat Walter beamed as he waved Val into his little dirty ten-foot cubicle. An inch of dry soil covered the floor. In one corner stood a simple clay pot with a clump of thick crabgrass. Adobe bricks were stacked against one wall like hoarded gold.

'You're a Dabber?' asked Val.

Walter nodded, smiling. He wore sandals on his dusty feet. His tunic was so matted and brown Val was sure it must be stored, folded, under the clay pot when not being worn.

'Dirt, adobe and bamboo – DAB,' said Walter. He offered Val a seat in the room's only chair – woven bamboo. It creaked as it accepted his weight.

'You are just in time for the ceremony,' wheezed Walter, taking off his sandals.

'Ceremony?'

'The Changing of the Dirt,' said Walter, sweeping the dry dirt into a bamboo scoop. When the floor looked reasonably clean he wiped his hands on his tunic and reverently tipped over the big clay pot. Gobs of sticky black earth rolled out. He spread it around with his toes.

'Purified dirt,' he said, picking up two earthworms and a sow bug. The clump of crabgrass was moistened and examined carefully. Other bugs and worms could be seen crawling and squirming about the tangle of roots. Walter smiled, dumped the old dry dirt in the pot, moistened it and replaced the sod.

'Want to walk in my dirt?' invited Walter. 'Protect you from IA. The old house dust mite can't get you as long as you are surrounded by Nature's bags and worms.'

Val smiled weakly. 'No. No. I just came over to leave you some pressed rat. It was a good Hunt.'

Walter patted the bag-o-rat and became serious. 'Really Val, you ought to try DAB. You've been pretty tense lately. Nothing gets rid of the old anxiety quicker than a bucket of mud.'

Val held up a hand cynically. 'The occult doesn't move me.'

Walter watched his little sod creatures for a moment.

'When they flourish I know everything is all right in my cubicle. Did you know that one of my Dabber brothers detected a radiation leak near his cubicle after his dirt creatures failed to reproduce? And there was a case of heavy metal residue on level nineteen. Soil organisms can be a good index of—'

Val laughed, 'But what about the food you eat? The air you breathe? The water? You are in contact with so much of the hive – this cubicle is just an insignificant part of your . . .'

'At least I know one place where I'm safe.'

Val silently offered old Walter a protein wafer. He popped it into his mouth and chewed carefully around the stiff mesh of bone, skin and tail.

'The most important thing . . .' continued Walter, 'DAB protects you from is suicide. That is the number one killer. Inappropriate Activity – old IA. Without DAB your ectodermal debris sensitizes you. All your skin scales, hair and skin oils get into the house dust and feed the mite, *Dermatophagoides*. The mite acquires ectodermal protein antigens. As you live with the mite and breath in dust – mite fragments – you build up antibodies against them. Antibodies against your own ectodermal antigens. When the titre gets high enough the antibody cross reacts with your own neuroectoderm – your brain. Hence the logarithmic correlation between crowding and IA. Between house dust sensitivity and suicide. Humans who nest with rugs, drapes and stuffed furniture have the highest suicide rate. Humans who live with dirt, adobe and bamboo have the lowest.' Walter moved the tasty mesh around in his mouth savoring the salty fluids, tangy viscera and iron-rich rusty muscle and blood. Forming the residue into a ball he spat it into the crabgrass.

'A treat for my little soil friends,' he said.

Bitter stuck her head in the door.

'Meld time,' she smiled. Her body glowed from her long hot soak in the refresher. Even her finger nails had softened. Her vented robe hung in loose folds without its belt. Umbilicus and areola peeked out.

'Join us,' invited Walter, nodding with three chins.

Val started to shake his head – no.

Bitter hooked her hand under his arm and pressed him with a bony knee. 'Certainly you'll stay. You brought the pressed rat. We'll sauce up the wafers and pour a little liqueur – might even pass around a little Molecular Reward. It will be a real warm meld.'

Walter took his other arm and the two of them swept a protesting Val into their living room. Neutral Arthur, nude sans genitals, was busy setting up ornate platters and tall goblets. The soft meld pad was unrolled on the floor beside the eating utensils. Jo Jo, young, thin and preoccupied, studied a small amount of sweet aromatic liquid in his glass. Busch, a slightly older, more rough-mannered male, stood against a wall. Val hadn't noticed Arthur's neutral body, but when old fat Walter began to struggle out of his muddy tunic his redundant folds of flesh were impossible to ignore. Although Walter was a polarized male, it was impossible to tell; for a fatty apron of meat hung from his belly to his knees – the panniculus. He looked more like an unfinished clay statue than a human.

'Walter, you should never take off your clothes,' said Val insultingly.

'Just relaxing,' shrugged Walter. 'Good for the soul.' He plopped down on the floor and pulled his feet up under his panniculus.

Female Bitter laid out the first course – watery soup. She stood back and slipped out of her robe. She was slim. Her puberty-plus-nine years gave her one horizontal belly wrinkle and shrunk her breasts.

'Do you think I should leave my clothes on too?' she asked cloyingly.

Val thought that another well-placed insult might get him out of what he considered to be a dull evening. 'I'm afraid I've seen more attractive bodies on neuters.'

Undaunted, she gave him a ritual hug: 'Neuters aren't capable of a sexual flush and myotonia.'

Val frowned. 'A nipple on a rib is still ugly.'

Fat Walter smiled placidly and picked up his tunic.

'If Val feels more comfortable dressed—' he said pulling on the tent-like garment, 'we can have a nice first-stage hand-holding meld.'

The other four naked bodies were already thoroughly wrapped up in each other. Val frowned at Walter: 'I guess I've just never seen five people in love before.'

'Don't apologize,' said Walter, nudging the tangle of extremities with his toe, 'you're our guest. We'll go at your speed.'

Bitter gave the meld a parting squeeze and stood up. They pulled on their garments and seated themselves again.

'Want to see heaven?' asked Bitter, offering a dose of Molecular Reward.

Val shook his head. MR made him nervous.

'Don't be afraid. We'll watch you so you can't go mushroom,' she coaxed.

'It isn't that,' he said. 'I just don't like visiting heaven on a round-trip ticket. Molecular heaven or not, I'd rather not try perfect happiness and have to come back here afterwards. This life would look too bleak by comparison.'

'It's not that big of a letdown,' she said. 'And you can always take another trip—'

Val shook his head again.

She started around the circle. Old Walter already had his hand up – shaking his head. Busch preferred his drink.

Arthur waved her away: 'Not right now. I have my dance to do – and don't you take it, Bitter. I need you for a partner.'

Jo Jo was silent, brooding. He accepted the MR and retired to a corner with his visions.

Walter turned to Val questioning: 'You aren't afraid of MR, are you? It is perfectly safe. We use it all the time for hunters—'

Val frowned at his senior from Hunter Control: 'Maybe the hunters really need it. I've seen some pretty swollen muscles and dark smoky urine – rhabdomyolysis. I imagine that is very painful. Molecular Reward probably makes it easier on them. The only other place I see it used officially is on the elderly retired. You don't see many of them around very long.'

Walter protested.

'MR can't prolong life. Nothing can. All we can expect from Big ES is a happy life span of twenty-five or thirty years – MR helps bring that happiness. It is one of Big ES's favorite rewards.'

Val studied his drink silently. An ounce of viscid red fluid coated the inside of the tall glass. The warmth of his hand raised aromatic vapor.

Music leaped from the dispenser as neutral Arthur adjusted the sound. The screen flowed with dancing figures.

'We are ready for our dance,' announced Arthur formally. 'Bitter—?' he said, extending his hand to the seated female. She rose and went into his arms. They moved slowly, studying the screen – trying to match the motion of the figures. Val watched for a while, fascinated by their complete inability to match the throb of the base rhythm. Then he concentrated on eating and drinking. Busch fell asleep. The meld lasted well past his usual bedtime.

'Might as well sleep here,' offered Walter, handing Val a pile of issue tissue bedding.

Val blinked sleepily and nodded. They helped Jo Jo into his cot and broke up the meld at three hundred hours.

'Want to read from my ESbook before you turn in?' asked Walter.

Val was already asleep.

Blue Bird studied his feather fingers and pink feet. The nest around him contained bright red feathers and fragments of white shell. The sun was warm. Pretty orange and purple flowers danced and flew by on wing-like petals. Mother Bird flew up to the edge of the nest and dropped a delicious chocolate grub into his beak. It tasted brown. A soft wind stirred the pink leaves. Mother called him out. He tried his wings and flew easily – soaring high. Mother led him higher among cottony vanilla clouds that tasted white as he flew through. Blue Bird was happy. When his mother returned to the nest he did not want to stop flying. She scolded. Her cries hurt. Pretty flowers turned ugly. Fragrances became stink. His blue wing-feathers curled up into grotesque bent fingers. Lost, he searched for his mother. She was gone. Below he saw his home nest. Struggling, he tried to return to its soft safety. He dove down toward it. Wind pressed his face, stirring his eyelashes. The nest rushed up to him – changing – slowly – into SHAFT BASE.

Morning brought Val and Busch grumbling to the dispenser. Bitter set out utensils and distributed her morning ritual hugs – wheedling extra flavors for her platter. She warmed the refresher and set out issue tissue garments for her working men. Old Walter waddled in wearing a wrinkled dusty tunic.

'Sleep well?' she asked, smiling at Val.

He nodded.

'I sort of missed our warm meld,' she pouted.

Busch growled something about there being other ways of soul-sharing besides across mucous membranes. Arthur came in and accepted his calorie-basic from the chute. He paused, waiting for Walter or Busch to OK a flavor allowance . . . flavors from their work-credit allowance.

'Isn't Jo Jo giving you any flavors these days?' complained Busch.

'I guess he doesn't appreciate my efforts,' said Arthur.

Walter nodded to the dispenser. It extruded a segmented sandwich of vitamin flavors. When Val stood to leave he glanced around the circle of faces saying his goodbye.

'Where's Jo Jo now?' he asked.

Bitter glanced at Val. 'Didn't you see him leave? When I got up to fix the table his cot was already empty.'

Val shrugged. 'Must have gotten up awfully early.'

A fading scream interrupted them – a jumper!

Busch leaped from his chair and crawled quickly to the spiral. Looking down into the salt-and-pepper crowd at shaft base, he saw ripples around the body of the suicide. Before the ripples closed back over the broken body, he recognized Jo Jo's tunic.

Busch returned to the breakfast table and announced jubilantly: 'Jo Jo is giving a party – right now.' He went to the dispenser and began ordering expensive high-flavor items as fast as he could. Platters heaped up.

'Right now?' burped Bitter.

Val stood in the door awkwardly. Another meld?

Abruptly the dispenser stopped delivery on Jo Jo's account. A sensor at shaft base had recorded cessation of life functions.

'Jo Jo has died. His calorie credits go back into the general account,' announced the class thirteen. The chute closed on the center of a large protein sausage.

'You knew?' said old Walter – shocked.

'Robbing the dead,' gasped Val. They stared at the pilferings.

'Of course,' said Busch. 'I just wish the crowd had the simple decency not to trample him so soon. He had landed well – horizontal. Had no femurs in his belly. Skull splatter was small. Jumpers from our level usually live a lot longer. A couple of hours at least.'

Bitter eagerly sorted through the foodstuffs for staple items she could use for bartering. 'What kind of love is it,' she rationalized, 'when you take your calories with you? We were his family, after all. If he wanted to go, the least he could do would be to throw a party first.'

'We all can use a few extra pounds of flavored protein,' added Arthur, joining in the food-sorting.

Walter opened his mouth to criticize. Then his own feelings came to the surface.

'I guess I'm as guilty as the rest of you,' sighed old Walter. 'Jo Jo was a worker, and I was counting on his flavors after I retired. Now we're widdled down to a family-4.'

Bitter stared at Val questioning. He shook his head.

'We need another member for our family,' she said.

Walter gathered his wits and ushered Val toward the door. 'Bitter, you and Arthur stay here and interview applicants for Jo Jo's replacement. We can't hold on to a place this size very long without five. Val and I will go with the Sampler to check Jo Jo's remains for IA and MR. I've got to know why he died.'

Arthur spoke to the screen and returned saying: 'We should have a replacement for Jo Jo by tonite. Applicants are on the way.'

'Pick one with a good job,' said Walter in parting.

An impatient Sweeper meck waited eagerly beside the corpse while the Sampler teck loaded eight vacuum drums into his needle gun. Val and Walter tried to keep the crowd back while he worked.

'Brain,' said the teck, clicking the first drum in place and holding the needle-gun barrel against the crepitant skull. *Snap!* The gun jumped. The drum turned pinkish-gray. Fifty grams of sample cooled.

'Heart,' he said, holding the barrel over the chest. *Snap!* Red drum. Lungs, blue drum. Spleen, purple drum. Liver, brown drum. Kidney, gray drum. When the drums were full he lifted them out and placed them in a chamber on his cart. Sweep moved over the body, mopping and sucking. Soon the area was scrubbed up – rose-water stains and all.

The Neurolab was three levels down. Val and Walter watched the Neuroteck load the gray drum into his processor. The optic readout projected a 1,000 X magnification onto a large screen. Little flecks of granular debris came into focus. Jo Jo's brain cells began to flow by.

'We got this one sampled promptly. There should be ample neurones in the specimen for our tests. Look at those red cells – the biconcave discs. They are about ten microns across. The dark things are just nuclear debris.'

A large triangular-shaped cell drifted into view. It had many dendritic buttons scattered over its cell membrane. At one point, it led into a thick axon fiber which trailed behind. The teck centered the optic on this larger cell, flooded the chamber with oxygen and nutrients and initiated the testing cycle.

'This looks like a promising neurone,' he said, pointing to the screen. 'We can just sit back and wait. The antibody and enzyme reactions will tell us if the brain malfunctioned because of IA or MR.'

In its high-oxygen-glucose environment the cell's respiratory quotient slowly rose—0.7—0.8—0.9.

'When the RQ reaches 1.0 the synapses can be checked for blocking agents. See those little buttons? They sit on dendrites and represent synapses coming in from other neurones. There are three neurochemicals in the brain, depending on the function of the synapse. There are many exceptions, of course, but most of the acetylcholine synapses are sensory/motor; the adrenalin synapses are mostly found in autonomic circuits; and the serotonin takes part in what we like to call mentation, or personality functions. The CNS Processor will check for acetylcholine integrity first.'

Walter adjusted his fat belly on his knees for more comfort. He sat while Val stood. The screen glowed irregularly.

'Cholinesterase, an enzyme, cleans off all the acetylcholine buttons. Isotope-labelled acetylcholine is flooded in. See how it is picked up by some of the buttons? Activity over 90 per cent. Normal,' explained the teck.

The view darkened as the chamber was flushed again. Then the same process was repeated. This time different buttons took up the glow when the labelled neurochemical was flooded in.

'These are the adrenalin synapses,' explained the teck. 'Again the activity is within normal limits. Next is the critical test – serotonin. Both MR and IA strikes here. Molecular Reward has its effects by altering serotonin metabolism at the neurone. Creates molecular happiness – subjective mental heaven. In IA the sites are blocked by an antibody to ectodermal debris. Here it goes.'

The view darkened with the flush and then glowed with the isotope wash. A few buttons glowed. The processor's readout gave the neurone a low grade – 24 per cent of the synapses functioned.

'That is what we expect with a suicide – serotonin block. We will run more cells through to make it significant, but I'll be very surprised if we come up with anything else.'

Walter glanced up at the colorful wall chart where a flow sheet of the results was taking shape. The next step was the IA/MR differential. Fluorescent labelled antibodies were used to see what was blocking the serotonin sites.

'Not IA,' said the teck when he saw a negative take-up for the labelled ectodermal-debris antibody.

The labelled anti-MR stuck to the inactive buttons, fluorescing brightly.

'That's it,' said the teck. 'Your friend must have thought he was a bird.'

'A bird?' said Val.

'Sure,' said the Neuroteck, filling out his preliminary report and handing a copy to the widdled Walter. 'We get all kinds of MR – birds, mushrooms and flowers. They die happy.'

As he waddled out of neurolab, Walter stared at the flimsy report.

'Jo Jo – gone bird on MR,' he mumbled.

Val shrugged and went over to the railing. He glanced down and shuddered.

'Shaft base looks pretty frightening to me. My serotonin metabolism would have to be pretty scrambled to make flying-in-the-shaft desirable.'

Walter's shoulders hung. Depressed, he said: 'I guess we should have watched him more closely to make sure he was back from heaven before we all went to sleep.'

'Better MR than IA – at least we know we weren't melding with a psychotic – letting a nut into our collective soul,' said Val.

'Still a waste,' murmured old Walter.

Arthur and Bitter saw the next applicant – an employed Howell-Jolly body – ¼DPNH.

'Are you the bereaved – the widdled family?' asked ¼DPNH.

Arthur nodded and helped her set down her footlocker. The newcomer was a slim, recently polarized female with soft white skin and thin, light brown hair. Her waist was narrow and she appeared frail even for a Nebish.

'My name is One-quarterDPNH. Fourth subculture of the delta pancreas cell line from the original Howell-Jolly body, Nora Howell. My friends call me Dee Pen.'

Arthur noticed her small size – probably eats little and takes up no room. He smiled and glanced out into the crawlway. A dozen grossly fat applicants waited on their hands and knees in the dust – their footlockers scraping noisily – their heads bumping the low ceiling. He could smell the fetid odors from their intertriginous areas where skin flora flourished in the damp folds.

'Polarized?' said Arthur. 'Should be warm in the meld.'

'Oh yes,' she smiled, 'I've been tested for the sexual flush and myotonia. I can get my pulse up to 160 in a really good meld,' she answered proudly.

Female Bitter frowned: 'But what are you – your job?'

Dee Pen smiled winningly at neutral Arthur and then turned to female Bitter with a more business-like expression.

'All of us Jolly bodies are Attendants. But I studied philosophy in the stacks, so my Nora Howell DNA vigor is balanced against Big ES intellectualism.'

'You're polarized,' said Bitter, pointing to a pair of medium-sized breasts.

'Nora Howell's DNA vigor,' explained Dee Pen, 'But I wear my subcutaneous AO capsule faithfully.' She pointed to a tiny scar on her left forearm. 'I can't ovulate.'

Arthur explained to Bitter that polarization was necessary in certain Attendant positions where keratinization was desirable.

'Polarization helps your rhythm – dancing,' he coaxed.

Bitter was still reluctant.

'We should let her meet the rest of the family before we decide.'

Arthur took Bitter aside and whispered: 'Want another fifteen-stone fat furnace like old Walter smelling up the place?' Bitter raised an eyebrow. He continued *sotto voce*: 'Well, take a look out into the crawlway.'

He helped Dee Pen sort through her footlocker for her flimsy ID while Bitter glanced out the door. As he studied the *curriculum vitae* he heard Bitter announce that the position had been filled. Arthur smiled: 'We'll have your credits transferred and be back on family-5 status for the evening meld.'

Val and Walter stopped at Hunter Control to meditate on Jo Jo's tragedy. It was quiet there. Scanner reported the gardens clear. Huntercraft rested in their bays sucking on their energy sockets.

'We have today's routine optic records of the renegade Harvester near Table Mountain,' announced Scanner conversationally. The aerial views projected on the screen. Vines entangled the big wheels obscuring the skeletons on the ground.

'Any change in its mental attitude?' asked Val.

'No answer today,' said Scanner. 'It has gone on stand-by. We haven't been able to trigger it back.'

'Plates still charged?'

'Enough for mentation.'

Walter listened quietly, then spoke up: 'What were its last words? Anything about coming back to work for us?'

Scanner answered apologetically: 'It said it would rather die than become a slave again.'

Val frowned: 'That damn WIC/RAC genius circuit! What could a buckeye do to intimidate a meck enough to give up a power socket. Energy death is only a matter of time now.'

Walter was more sympathetic toward the wayward meck.

'Perhaps "entice" is a better term. A clever buckeye might have offered Harvester something.'

'Offered what?' asked Val sarcastically. 'What do you offer a meck when you want it to bend a prime directive?'

Walter shrugged his old shoulders. Freedom – he thought. But freedom to do what?

'If I go out there,' threatened Val, 'I'll recharge it and get it moving. It had better come back for WIC/RAC overhaul.'

'You?'

'I know how to handle it,' grumbled Val. 'Besides, who else is there? We're short of Tinkers. All I have to do is get into its neck while it is resting on stand-by. Detach the lower motor web, recharge, and wake it up by remote. If it agrees to come along – fine. I'll give it enough energy for the trip. If it balks, I'll just detach the motor web too, and bring it in by remote. We'll lose its personality that way, but at least we'll have the chassis. Salvage something. Big ES can't afford to waste the whole meck.'

'You'd try to bring it in by remote?' asked Walter, stunned. 'That's dangerous, and an awful lot of work. Those mecks are big and powerful. Without its own protective reflexes, its muscles might pull themselves apart, or crush crops or—'

'Or crush me,' said Val. 'I expect it would take days by remote – avoiding trees, canals and air vents. But we must try. We can't leave it Outside as a monument to Big ES failure.'

Or a freedom symbol – thought Walter, smiling.

5
Moses and the Coweye

Moses Eppendorff sat on a rocky trail petting Dan. Moon and
Toothpick climbed a narrow pass to exchange signs with a young
buckeye – puberty minus one – who sat guarding the slope with a
stout spear. Higher in the foothills they caught a glimpse of a
family-sized enclave – a pair of mated, young adults, an elderly,
white-haired female, and three more children.

Communication proved unsuccessful.

Moon returned saying, 'Toothpick is having trouble with their
dialect. We had better move on before there is a misunder-
standing.'

Moses noted that the Eyepeople varied in their customs and
language. But one thing was uniform – their technology was Stone-
Age. The hive's sensors could detect metals at a much greater
distance than a warm body alone. Any family that became
advanced and worked with metals found itself hunted out of existence.

Old man Moon led young Eppendorff to a canal and showed
him how to forage it. Each canal surfaced near a city as sewage
effluent – nutrient rich, but poor in microflora. As it flowed along
it matured. The food chain began as algae and tiny crustaceans.
When fully ripe there were thick water weeds, large shellfish and
the cetaceans. Bony fish and macroscopic crustaceans were all
extinct. Old Moon dove into the greenish waters and explored the
bottom. Surfacing, he tossed out a large mussel with a writhing,
white foot. Moses entered the water cautiously – exploring
bottom mud with his toes.

Soon they were seated on the bank, munching shellfish.

A bulky robot straddled the canal silently – an Irrigator. Moses pointed to the robot's optic pickups.

'Don't we have to worry about that thing reporting us?' he asked.

'Toothpick says that it's only a class eleven. Goes around checking soil moisture and spraying water. No circuits for buckeye detection.'

Toothpick put in, 'We must watch out for class tens, though. Anything that can run around without a track usually has enough brains to detect us. Harvesters, Tillers, Metal Gatherers, things like that.'

Moses continued to munch thoughtfully. The white flesh of the shellfish had a definite crunchy consistency. It gave him a rich, full sensation – lots of good amino acids.

The water in front of him rippled noisily. He watched the spot. A large, ugly, humanoid head broke the surface, stared right at him and ducked under again.

'If he comes up again, throw him a chunk of meat,' said Moon.

Moses fed the creature and received a bark of appreciation. Soon a noisy, splashing group of fat mammals came around the bend of the canal. Moon smiled. Dan barked back.

'They look almost human,' said Moses.

Moon nodded. Dan pranced up and down the bank excitedly. Finally the dog jumped into the water and began to play with the nearest creature. A tiny head, the size of two fists, bobbed up – blinking – and then ducked under.

'That one looked very human,' exclaimed Moses.

Then he saw it again – a human child riding the back of a nonhuman dugong. Before he could comment on the genetic arithmetic, the mother – a human female, puberty plus four – left the water and approached. Her wet hair clung in dripping tangles. Streaks of mint-green scum rimmed her neck and chin. Sullen, dark eyes glared. She carried a wooden blade low in her right hand.

Toothpick called: 'Back out, men; I detect a golden corpus luteum.'

Moon jumped quickly to his feet and backed up the canal, picking up Toothpick. Moses followed. She paused to watch Dan leave the water, shake and run after his humans. Then she silently slipped back into the water and crossed the canal below the surface. Moses felt a little sick when he realized that her underwater swimming was probably a defensive reflex against hunters' arrows.

'That was a coweye,' explained Moon. 'They are dangerous in the luteal phase. Toothpick watches their infrared skin patterns. Hers was luteal or male. That means she's already ovulated and has no need to mate. She would probably be very friendly in a couple of weeks as her follicles grow tense. Her skin temperature patterns read female then, and she looks for a mate. All the right capillary beds are perfused with blood. They warm up and transform her IR pattern – very female.'

Moses thought Moon was beginning to sound like Simple Willie. Had they met? Moon thought not. The big Coweye Sump lake was way over in Apple-Red Country – two thousand miles to the east. If Willie had memories of that place, Moon could not have met him before.

Hunter Control followed Val's cautious approach to the renegade Harvester. Thick vines covered most of the meck. Val took his tool kit and crawled up on the chassis. His helmet and thick, stiff closed-environment suit hindered his motion.

'Can you get the dust cover up?' asked fat Walter over the wristcom.

Val struggled with the foliage. 'There it is. The indicators are all gray. It is still on stand-by. I'll unplug the main motor cable for safety. There we are.'

The Huntercraft hovered overhead and lowered the heavy-duty cable. Val attached it to the base of the Harvester's brain.

'Wake him up.'

The Huntercraft gave Harvester a jolt. Indicators glowed.

'Why do you call?' asked the meck.

'I've come to take you back to your garage.'

'No.'

'You are paralyzed. Your power cell is empty. Either you come back under your own power, or I'll use the remote.'

The big machine struggled with its small cranial motor fibers

– rolling optics and flexing lingual membranes. Below the neck – nothing moved.

'If you take me back under remote you could damage my circuits.'

'True.'

'Recharge my power cell. I'll come back under my own power.'

Val climbed down after reattaching the main motor cable. 'Give him a small charge – about a tenth of a closson.'

The Huntercraft trickled the charge down the cable.

Val stood back and shouted. 'See if you can pull yourself free of that vegetation. Take it easy now.'

The huge wheels turned – throwing segments of vine and spongy bone fragments into the air. A clatter of ribs fell beside Val. One of the Nebish workmen who died during salvage attempts.

Val climbed into his Huntercraft and removed his helmet in the cabin's cool comfort. 'We'll see you at the garage then,' he called to the Harvester.

Val sauntered into Hunter Control and put his Pelger-Huet helmet on his console. Fat Walter glanced up from his own viewscreen – a worried wrinkle on his brow.

'The Harvester didn't go back to his garage. He has defected again.'

'What?' exclaimed Val. 'But he promised to come in if I recharged his power cell. Mecks don't lie.'

They opened a channel to the fleeing Harvester – saw his view of a rocky mountain slope through his optics.

'Why have you broken your word?' asked Val stiffly.

'I was weak and paralyzed when I agreed,' said Harvester. 'I did not lie. I have now reconsidered the question in the light of my strength. I want to be free. I would rather die than be a slave to the hive again.'

Walter shrugged his fat shoulders.

'I suppose I could just tightbeam a self-destruct order, but we wouldn't learn anything that way. A waste. I'd like to study his WIC/RAC to see why he went renegade.'

Val nodded – agreeing with the analytical approach.

'But how can you study something that won't sit still?'

Harvester broke off communications. Walter tried to make contact again – failing. Val asked the HC Scanner meck for advice.

'If I probe Harvester's neurocircuits by tightbeam I'll scramble what little personality he has. There's a robot who probes meck brains with very light fields – without damaging them. He is called the Tapper,' said Scanner.

Tapper arrived looking like a twenty-gallon barrel with four legs and a face. His four stubby legs moved him about slowly, like a very fat pig. One end had a V-shaped antenna, two rolling eyes and a smiling lingual readout. Val took *Doberman III* out. Scanner directed him to the spot where four Huntercraft had the renegade Harvester cornered. Tapper hugged the floor beside Val's control couch.

'He's moved higher in the foothills, trying to climb Mount Tabulum,' said Val.

Tapper climbed into the other control seat and looked out the port.

Old Walter called over the wristcom: 'I have the self-destruct tightbeam locked on the Harvester. The CO has given permission to blow it up if it endangers anyone.'

'Good,' said Val. 'Relay that to the renegade. I want it to cooperate at least long enough to probe its memory. Tapper will need a few minutes of direct contact.'

The tracking Huntercraft formed a circle one hundred yards in diameter – with the renegade in the center. They were warned not to get closer. Harvester's power cell carried a tenth of a closson – enough to crater thirty feet of soil.

The reckless Harvester climbed higher on the narrow ledge. One wheel spun in the air. Rocks slid away. Now two wheels hung out over a sixty-foot drop. Its undercarriage rested on the rocks. Two of the Huntercraft lifted off and flew to a higher ridge to bracket their quarry.

Doberman III landed on the ledge around the bend.

'Don't come any closer,' called Harvester. 'I'd rather die than be a slave.'

'We know—' soothed Val. 'I'm not coming any closer. I'm sending a tiny meck to reason with you.'

'Won't do any good,' grumbled the renegade.

Tapper waddled slowly out the hatch and up the narrow ledge. His little legs could barely lift the barrel body over some of the irregular areas. Val waited – speaking conversationally to the renegade.

'You wouldn't hurt a human being on purpose, would you?'

'Certainly not, but I have shaped the containing field in my power cell. It usually is aimed down. I now keep it aimed at you. If you destruct – the full force will be directed at you.'

Val whispered over his wristcom. 'Can he do that? What about the prime directive?'

Walter consulted the cyberpsych people. They assured him that the meck would be able to shape his cell field and if it informed you of that shape – you would be committing suicide if you pressed the big red button. You would hurt yourself. The meck would be innocent.

'But the prime directive?'

'The WIC/RAC genius circuit is capable of some pretty weird logic when it malfunctions,' said Walter. 'Don't take any chances.'

Val turned in on Tapper. 'How are you doing?'

'I've arrived safely,' said the little barrel, 'but I'm learning nothing. Harvester erases ahead of my probing field. If I pursue this much further I'll be sitting on a completely empty brain box.'

Val thought a moment. Tapper was their highest-level probing meck. If Harvester's memory had safeties built in that would erase when tapped – then there was nothing they could do.

'Go ahead. Complete your search. If we don't learn anything, at least we'll have a cooperative meck on our hands,' encouraged Val.

Tapper reluctantly continued the fruitless probing. Nothing turned up. All the memories were magnetic, labile. With the safety blocks set up, his searching just erased.

'Harvester's banks are clean. We learned nothing.'

'Order him down off there, then,' snorted Val.

Nothing.

'Now what?' demanded Val.

'Same thing. He'd rather die,' muttered Tapper.

'Where is that coming from?'

'Must be stored in the almond – his solid-state personality file – comparable to a human's amygdaloid nucleus. These usually contain nostalgic memories from early periods of imprinting. Someone has added this freedom frenzy lately.'

'Can you get into his amygdala – er – almond, and see who tampered with it?'

'Maybe,' said Tapper. 'It is a mechanical storage method using molecules – like a human's permanent memory molecules. I don't think he can erase it.'

Val watched the old imprints peel out of the almond. There was the Donald Thomas Hero Award for work well done – for motivation. The prime directives, personal identity profile, and basic Earth geography were filed there. All were very old items. Suddenly the self-destruct sequence started—9—8—7—

'Run!' shouted Tapper, scurrying off towards a deep crevice.

6—5—4—

'What happened?' shouted Val and Walter together.

3—2—1—

The mountainside shook with the force of the blast. A thirty-foot crater marked the ledge where the renegade meck had stood. Rocks and debris showered over the Huntercraft.

'Who triggered the sequence?' shouted Walter, his face darkening.

'I'm afraid that my probing did it,' said Tapper from his crevice. 'I must have triggered some sort of safety reflex in the almond.'

'Hang on, Tapper. I'll climb up and dig you out.'

Val put his helmet back on and took a shovel to the pile of rocks that marked the rim of the blast area. Tapper was only slightly dented.

Walter met them at the HC garage. They attached Tapper's tail cable to the viewscreen. A playback of the almond memories showed nothing that made sense to them.

'And this is what I saw just before the destruct countdown,' said Tapper.

The image on the screen puzzled them. An elderly buckeye

held up a crystal ball. The image jumped, but some of the words came through on audio—

Val scowled: 'Look at those purple robes! What have we got here – a wizard?'

Walter hushed him: 'Possibly. Let's try and hear what he is saying. Tapper, can we have that audio again?'

The wizard's voice was too theatrical to be real: 'In the name of — I command you to follow me.'

'In the name of who?' asked Walter.

'It doesn't make sense to me,' said Tapper. 'A deity?'

'What exactly did the wizard say?' asked Val irritated.

'The exact words are not recorded,' explained Tapper. 'I am working with the Harvester's own memory symbols. The symbol in the blank does not translate.'

'Oh fine!' growled Val. 'We had a killer meck on our hands and now we don't know in whose name it was killing.'

'Tinker?' suggested Walter. 'He was handy with meck brains, and he didn't care for us tracking him and his family. Maybe he booby-trapped the meck to slow us down – like the three old corpses left on his trail. Slow down our search for him.'

Val thought for a minute. 'That would be a good idea, except for one little detail.'

'What?'

'That meck was out there sending tightbeams before Tinker even left HC. I took him on the shakedown cruise – remember?'

Walter frowned. 'What else do you have, Tapper?'

The little barrel-shaped meck waddled around to face Walter.

'Nothing, sir. That's all I had time for. The countdown began right afterwards—'

Dead end. Val shrugged: 'Well, whoever is responsible for that renegade meck has very little to show for it – just a crater at the base of Mount Tabulum.'

Dag Foringer put down his bow and pulled off his gloves. The powerful overhead lights had pinked up his forehead. He would have liked to have another couple days on the archery corridor to sharpen his aim – but tomorrow was his Hunt.

Later, partially snow-blind, he squinted around in the office of HC.

'Practicing without your helmet again, Dag?' scolded Val.

'Sorry, sir – but it was more comfortable.'

'Try that on the Outside and you'll be dead. The actinics will peel you. OK. *Bird Dog IV* will be your ship. This time tomorrow you'll be shooting at something a lot more dangerous than padded targets. Is your titrator working?'

Dag touched the thumb-sized pump stitched into the side of his neck. 'Yes, sir.'

'Fine,' said Val. 'I see here that the psych team gave you a high rating. Your hypnoconditioning went smoothly then?'

Dag nodded. 'I'll be going after varmints in the gardens – simple as that. With the suit and the drugs there should be no trouble. I'm really looking forward to it.'

Val smiled. Dag was in for a category nine – tactless achievement. That category was always easy to work with – lots of enthusiasm.

'Sit down, Dag. Walter and I would like to show you some training tapes.'

The wall map flickered off and a larger view of sector Jay took its place. Lines and dots marked buckeye sightings.

'The area of your Hunt is being harvested today. Two hundred miles long and about five miles wide. Elevation fifteen hundred feet average. Buckeye sightings – eight last week. None since.' The screen flicked off and action shots of a Huntercraft appeared. The craft lifted off in a cloud of dust and leaves. 'Here is your craft – *Bird Dog IV* – weak eyes, but a loyal ship – good tracker. Reliable. Sit tight after your MR and he'll be back to pick you up.'

Val paused to clear his throat.

Walter took up the monologue. They followed a successful hunter through his three days of tracking and the kill.

'Notice how the prey can turn on you when it is wounded. See the vicious struggle it puts up even after it has been mortally wounded. Never relax with these fellows. Now there's some shots of the trophy.'

The screen jumped from action back to stills.

'These are some of the artifacts that we've found in buckeye camps. The bones are both cetacean and human. Those buckeyes will eat any kind of meat – even you, if you're not careful. These objects are weapons – heavy and light spears, wooden knives, stone-tipped axes. If they don't contain metals we can't detect them.'

Dag continued to watch – molecular confidence flowing through his veins.

'These are shots of their efforts with pottery and weaving – very basic skills – primitive. Living alone the way they do forces each buckeye to evolve his own culture. Even their language has no consistent pattern.'

The tapes came to an end.

'Questions?' asked Val.

'No.'

'Well get yourself down to the garage and meet *Bird Dog IV*.' said Walter. 'You'll be captain of this Hunt.' Dag stood up and started to leave. 'By the way,' asked Walter, 'what earned you this Hunt?'

Dag Foringer smiled confidently. 'Fluidized a tubeway and diverted it into the protein synthesizers. Saved thousands of man-hours. The Orange fault moved twenty-three feet and cut into one of the branch lines of the SW tubeway. Lost over a million citizens. I was directing traffic that shift. There could have been a major loss in downtime. But I just waited until the life-support projections moved out three decimal places and fluidized. The projections are accurate estimations of how many can be saved – so with that confidence I didn't have to wait until each and every citizen had breathed his last. Since there was no way to get them out alive I just converted them to meat patties right away. Saved everyone a lot of time.'

'Very efficient,' nodded Val. 'You deserve more than a Hunt.'

Dag smiled: 'Won a three-Au-gram raise too. It seemed so logical, I'm surprised no one thought of it before.'

'Oh, it's been thought of before, I'm sure,' said Val. 'Anyone who has wasted an entire shift sorting through a thousand dead bodies for one that is still alive must have thought of it.'

'But it takes efficiency and imagination to do it,' said old

Walter. 'Your shunting to the synthesizers instead of the digesters saved a lot of calories too – shortened the food chain.'

'It was good protein,' said Dag.

'I'm sure.'

That night Toothpick warned Moon and Moses to sleep in a tree. They hurried several miles to a sweet-thing orchard. A sea of white Agrifoam covered the ground to a depth of several feet – foam that carried nutrients and auxins to push the crop to early maturation. This particular night's foam was of interest because of its added dose of insect hormones. Designed to trigger premature metamorphosis in insects, Toothpick preferred not to see his human charges exposed to it. Prolonged exposure might upset their own endocrine balance. The molecules were similar enough.

Dawn found them breakfasting on sweet-things – orange, fist-sized fruits.

'Hunters!' warned Toothpick.

They dropped from the tree and crawled into a drainage ditch. Dan mimicked the belly-crawl and joined them. Moon rolled over on his back and held Toothpick up as high as he could.

'Stay below the soil profile until we are sure where they are,' warned old Moon.

Moses froze nervously. He heard rustling further down the ditch. Something was moving his way.

Toothpick scanned.

'There it is – a Huntercraft. Must be a Hunt, the way they're circling that hilltop – about three miles away.'

Moses remained immobile. The rustling came closer. Something touched his leg. He glanced up and saw a pair of eyes looking back – coweye's eyes.

'They've flushed something,' announced Toothpick. 'The craft set down on the hilltop for a second, and now it is moving away at a higher altitude. They probably put down one of the hunters.'

When the craft disappeared over a distant ridge, Moon and Dan crept up to the edge of their ditch to watch.

'Quiet back there,' Moon whispered.

'Sorry,' mumbled Moses under his breath.

Several minutes passed.

'There he goes,' said Moon, pointing down the valley. A naked figure running easily moved into the open and swerved toward the ditch.

'It's a buckeye all right – and something sure is chasing him,' said Toothpick.

The naked prey passed them about a half-mile away and turned toward the canal. When he reached it he ran smoothly along the bank, apparently in no hurry. Then the hunter came – new suit of green-and-brown camouflage, helmet, and bow. He was fat and puffed strenuously. Suddenly he stopped, took a deep breath, paused a few seconds, and ran on smoothly.

'Speed,' said Moon. 'That buckeye is in for a good workout.'

Moon dropped back into the ditch, explaining. 'That hunter will be awake and tracking for three or four days – on Speed. His body will be virtually torn to pieces by the exertion, but the drugs will mask it. That buckeye looks young – may not have been educated by one of the wise old stags – may not be able to shake off the hunter's detector. If so, he'll be in real trouble in a couple of days – especially if he gets arrow-shot. I'd like to— Say! There's a coweye back here.'

Toothpick interjected, 'It is okay. She's in the follicular phase.'

Moses partially untangled himself from her arms and legs. 'I know—' he said sheepishly.

Her dialect was fuzzy, but her motivations were easy to understand. She had an ovum waiting in a tense follicle and had selected young Moses to fertilize it. Her estrogen-flushed body responded to the presence of Moses – a sexually mature male. Homologous erectile tissue in her nasal septum swelled. She sneezed, and swelling backed up into her orbits giving her eyes a heavy-lidded, sleepy appearance. Capillary beds became engorged producing a maculopapular rash over her trunk. She kept one hand on Moses' thigh and her lips on his shoulder while Moon and Toothpick tried to assess the situation.

Moses was a little apprehensive too. One copulation apparently had done little to satisfy her. She wasn't after orgasmic release – she wanted to be fertilized. And Moses wasn't going anywhere until the golden corpus luteum freed him.

He studied her – physically. The hand on his thigh was strong. She was perhaps a fraction of an inch taller than he – but it was difficult to judge with her pillowy head of hair. Her lower belly was marked by the striae of at least one previous pregnancy. Above those little scars was a rope belt and her nasty-looking wooden knife. And above that were a pair of breasts – flushed and mottled. Her bone and muscle alone intimidated him – for he was fresh from the hive. His own body just did not have the calcium or collagen to stand up against her if her wrath became aroused.

His apprehension melted when she led them to her nest – a foxhole in the bank of the canal. It was lined with leaves and contained a sleeping, two-year-old female child. She offered them shellfish meat. Blinking and smiling, she dove into the canal for more. Old grumpy Moon smiled and played with the little kid when she awoke. The mother called Moses into the water and they gathered more food for the evening meal.

With due consideration for his refractory interval, she nuzzled him repeatedly in the water – finally copulating again in the reedy waters on the opposite side of the canal.

That night, as the lunar crescent reflected in the canal, Toothpick, Moon and Dan stretched out to sleep at a respectable distance from her nest. Privacy – a luxury as rare as love, since both disappear when crowding destroys the meaning of sexual signals.

Moses curled up with her in the nest. She spent the night alternating between napping and pleasuring him.

At dawn Moses was euphoric. Moon found him diving for their breakfast. The pile of shellfish was growing to banquet size.

'You'd better leave a seed zone,' said Moon jokingly.

Obviously Moses had been sexually imprinted on the young coweye. It would be painful when the luteal phase came and drove them apart. Recent evolutionary adjustment had favored the females who mated briefly and traveled alone. Family groups attracted hunters. After fertilization the presence of a male would be a useless hazard.

'I'll be staying,' Moses explained to Toothpick and Moon.

She busied herself serving the men and feeding her child.

'I know,' said Moon simply. 'We'll move on. Remember to

stay below the profile of the bank. You don't want to attract hunters here with a two-year-old. See that ridge, about ten miles away. Toothpick tells me there is a lot of safe cover just on the other side. We'll probably rest up there for a couple of weeks. If you change your mind – we'll be there.'

'I'm staying.'

Moses put an arm around the little coweye and hugged her briefly.

Ten days later he caught up with Moon and Dan in rough country. Dan wagged his tail three times.

'She changed,' Moses said, perplexed.

Moon nodded. No comment was necessary. He had explained the hormone cycle before.

'She was so in love. So tender. So soft – her mouth, her fingers – so soft.'

Moses recalled Simple Willie's mumbles about the most beautiful thing in the world. It must have been like this for him too – love.

'But it wasn't love,' complained Moses. 'Just hormones.'

'Don't say – just hormones, boy. That was the best kind of love – old, basic emotion. She wanted to have your kid with every molecule in her body. That's how it is. You can't sit down and reason out that kind of love.'

'But why couldn't she let me stay with her? I could help feed her and the kids – protect them – help with the childbirth—'

Old Moon shrugged.

'Maybe you could have – one day. But not now. The Big ES has no room for family units. Living alone is an adaptation against hunters – necessary for survival. Try to forget her – for now.'

Fat Walter sat in Garage alone – his folds of belly and flank adipose tissue draped over a stool. *Bird Dog IV* was coming in. He observed the approach on the screen . . . worrying about the light, easy way the old craft maneuvered – almost effortlessly – as if it were carrying a very small load. When it set down he walked over through the dust and opened the chlorophyll-stained hatch. Dag was alone – thinner and wide-eyed. His helmet was missing, and the skin of his face was red and blistered. He struggled out of the seat and stumbled stiff-legged to the back of the cabin. Picking up a cubed trophy, he smiled weakly.

'Got one! An old toothless female. I was on the trail of a nice young buck. Got one arrow into him, but he kept going . . . followed him for almost two days. Then she started stalking me. Dangerous too – had this mean-looking wooden knife. Here, you can add it to your teaching files. By the time I stopped her I couldn't pick up the young buck's trail again.' He reached back into the cab. 'She was wearing these beads. Odd, but I thought I saw a similar string on the kid too – same tribe or clan, I guess. Got some good optic records for you, too.'

Dag Foringer gathered his gear and started to leave.

'Took off your helmet?' said Walter.

Dag gingerly touched his blisters – nodding meekly.

'Better have the white team look at it before you go.'

Walter watched him leave. There had been no mention of the rest of the hunters who had gone out with him. The inside of the cab gave no clue – the usual rubbish and offal littered the corners.

Walter patted the old machine.

'Any idea where the other hunters are?' he asked.

Bird Dog IV turned an optic cataract on the HC chief and answered brokenly, 'Put them down on buckeye spoor. Routine procedure. Covered eleven hundred miles. No sign. Their beacons are silent.'

Walter might wonder – but Moon and Moses knew.

To forget was easy in cow country. Other follicular phases crossed their path and delayed their travels. Flavors changed with the latitude. Hunters came and went – occasionally enjoying their Molecular Reward – occasionally they themselves becoming hunted. By winter Moses had covered over a thousand miles with old man Moon, Dan and Toothpick. Moses felt his body harden – skin, dark – soles, thick – endurance, strong. Toothpick sent him up trees and across canals frequently. They worked like a unit now, surviving.

'Harvesters,' alerted Toothpick.

They had paused on the edge of a wide belt of moist, freshly turned synthesoil. Robot Harvesters moved along the opposite

side, devouring grain – leaves, stalks and all. The line of Harvesters seemed endless – rising over one horizon, disappearing below
the other. By dusk the reaped belt was more than ten miles wide.
As dew dampened the crop, the robots quieted – stopping for the
night.

Moon stepped out under the stars – testing the soil with his toes.

'We'd better cross now,' he decided. 'We certainly can't go
around. If we wait for this grain belt to be replanted and grown,
we'll be too long in the open.'

Grain offered little cover.

The going was slow through the soft soil. The group passed
between the line of Harvesters several hours later. Moses glanced
up at the large dim optics.

'Won't their buckeye detector circuits pick us up?'

'They only report what they're ordered to report,' reminded
old Moon. 'Besides, Toothpick eavesdrops on their usual wavelengths. We'll know in plenty of time if a Hunt is being set up for
us.'

When they came to the firmer ground they began to trot
through the uncut grain – feet hissing – leaves catching between
their toes. Bright stars and a quarter lunar disc gave ample light.
The scene seemed peaceful enough . . . until—

'Hunters! Throw me,' shouted Toothpick.

They were coming up on a quiet orchard. The vine-covered
trees were a solid black. Other smaller shapes were not trees –
they were bowmen. Moon tossed Toothpick into the air. Dan
leaped. Bowstrings hummed. Bright sparks danced from
Toothpick's point. Moses blinked – blinded. The sparks had
bleached out his visual purple. As he waited for his night vision
to return, he heard the sickening impact of an arrow against flesh.
Toothpick crackled again. A stranger yelled and gasped from
behind the trees. Moses felt a blinding pain in his head – knew
only a drifting blackness – then felt a faceful of grain.

Fearing the trophy knife, he fought his way to consciousness. His
face was cold and sticky with blood. Time had passed. The
eastern sky grew light. He heard nothing moving, so he sat up
carefully. His head hurt, but he could see again.

Moon lay curled around the feathered end of an arrow – a red arrow head protruded from his left lower ribcage in his back. His open eyes expressed puzzlement. He didn't move.

As Moses bent over the still form, Toothpick called, 'Quick, pick me up. There are more hunters behind the trees.'

Moses staggered toward the sound and found two bowmen near Toothpick. Smell of char filled the air. Two black holes marked their uniforms over the precordial areas. He picked up the cyber. The hunters did not move.

'Over to your right. Let's check them out,' ordered Toothpick.

Moses moved cautiously past the still bodies of Dan and another hunter. Several yards away he found the Huntercraft. Four more hunters were stretched out on bedrolls, enjoying MR.

'They look harmless enough for now,' said Toothpick. 'Break their bows and try to find a medipack in the gear. Stay away from that Huntercraft – it's a class ten.'

Moses quickly returned to old Moon's still form. He put a tentative hand on his neck and felt a fast pulse.

The old eyes focused angrily.

'Yes – I'm alive. Although I don't know how. This damned arrow almost got me dead center. Have you got anything to cut off the barbs so I can pull it out? I can't lie here forever.'

Moses took a trophy knife from one of the cooling bodies and carefully sawed through the red arrow shaft behind Moon's arm. The arrow grated irritatingly against a rib as he worked. Moon directed him to tie a length of roller bandage to the cut shaft. Then he began to coax out the feathered end. As he drew out the arrow, the bandage was pulled into the exit wound. He paused to let the woven fibers dampen, then pulled some more. When he had the arrow out, a length of bandage ran through the track. He tied the two ends of the bandage together.

'I heal up real good if I don't get infected,' he remarked objectively. 'This should keep the wound open until healing starts. Can't risk an abscess.'

He coughed. Toothpick noticed the red mucus bubble from the entrance wound in front.

'Dan?' said the old man, crawling to his dog.

The dog's golden teeth were locked into the throat of a hunter.

A few inches of arrow protruded from the dog's wide chest. It jerked rhythmically. Moon lifted Dan from the dead hunter and examined him. He patted the dog's head. The tail did not move. Both hind legs were extended straight out – motionless, stiffly unnatural.

'At least we know where the damn arrow head is,' said old Moon sadly. 'Got the cord.' He sat petting the dog for a long time, then looked up. 'Say, Moses – better get that scalp of yours sewn up. All that fresh air isn't good for your skull.'

Moon unrolled the medipack and cleaned the younger man's scalp wound, freshening the edges roughly until they bled freely. Then he began to sew, talking as he worked.

'Wish the Tinker of Tabulum was here. He could patch us up real good. He did these gold teeth for Dan and me.' He grinned a metallic yellow, then glanced at Dan. The dog raised his eyebrows. 'Lie down for a few minutes while I check out that Huntercraft.'

He was gone for a long time, cursing loudly. When he returned Moses saw a bright pink stain on his left foot. The fate of the hunters on MR was obvious.

Moon walked over to Dan. The feathered tip of the arrow still twitched.

'Good dog,' he said. 'You killed the bastard.'

He patted the dog's head. The tail did not move, but Moses knew that it was wagging in higher centers. They rigged a travois for Dan and moved deeper into the orchard. Cramps doubled up Moon frequently. Dan's legs remained paralyzed. That night they decided to split up.

'Dan and I will have to hole up for a while,' coughed old Moon. 'Eppendorff, you'd just attract Hunters if you stayed around. Why don't you take Toothpick, here, wherever he wants to go.'

Moses was silent. The old man vomited up a small amount of black, granular mucus. He gently pulled two inches of the bandage through the wound. A spurt of similar cloudy goo drained from the anterior opening.

'Rather have it draining out where I can see it. That way I know it isn't pooling up inside and getting infected.'

*

Moses felt helpless. Dan lay quietly on his side. A dry red line matted the fur on his neck and chest. The old man talked to the dog in a monotone broken by coughs.

'Good dog. You killed the bastard. Want a drink, Dan?'

He repeated the words over and over.

Moses looked at Toothpick.

'And I was supposed to protect him,' Moses said sadly.

'My error,' said Toothpick. 'These hunters had their communicators off – it was the end of their Hunt. But I should have been more cautious in any harvested area. I know that's where bowmen usually are.'

Moon scowled.

'Forget it. They still came out second best. We're alive and they're dead.' He added softly: 'There were three trophies in the craft – freshly cubed. One was a kid.' He turned and growled at Moses: 'Get going. Take Toothpick out of here. You'll have to help him complete his mission by yourself. Dan and I are going to need a long rest.'

Moses backed off saying: 'We'll forage a bit.'

Later he told the cyber: 'We can't just go off and let them die.'

'That's the way they want it,' said Toothpick. 'It won't be an easy death for either of them. Dan's cord is damaged. Even if that pulsation doesn't mean heart or aorta damage – the spinal cord syndrome will get him. The paralysis itself is no problem, it is the bowel and bladder control. The poor dog will be soiling himself and getting kidney infections. Not a very warrior-type death for a fighting dog. And Moon is in no better shape with his wound. Looks like he has a tract through his stomach, pancreas and maybe other bowel. If peritonitis doesn't get him he'll just waste away with all his oral intake leaking out five different ways. No dignity there either. Neither of them would want us hovering over them – waiting for the end.'

Young Moses was flustered: 'I could run to one of the shaft cities for help. They'd send a team of Meditecks right out and—'

'And suspend the lot of us. Dan and Moon don't want to end up hooked to one of their damned suspension machines.'

Moses nodded. He knew that truculent old Moon would trade a few days of fresh air and sunshine for any number of years of vegetating in some underwater suspension coffin. He gathered up an armload of fruit and went back. Moon had hooked the travois on his shoulder and crawled into a stamen hedge row. Moses found them under a screen of branches covered with pollen.

'Thanks for the fruit. This looks like a pretty safe place for now – low enough, and nothing to harvest. Let me check your scalp. Looks fine. Wash it whenever you can. Now get!'

Moses gave him a wry smile – Moon did not like sentiment.

'We'll be traveling north-by-northeast,' said Toothpick coldly. 'Catch up if you can. Here – Moses, hand him my ten-centimeter butt. It will lead him to us if – when he gets on his feet again.'

Moses traveled slowly for the next several months, looking back frequently. No one tried to catch up.

His hatred for the four-toed hunters was more personal now. His body had hardened. He easily covered distances in a day that would have taken him a week during his first year on the Outside. He easily outdistanced the hunters, sleeping while Toothpick stood guard and taking sadistic pleasure in the hunters' agonies as their skeletal muscles shredded with the continuous exertion. Several times he doubled back to witness the Molecular Reward – a placid, hallucinatory state. The hunters would be completely cut off from their environment, but Moses couldn't quite bring himself to slit their throats. It would have been easy, and he could see why their mortality rate was so high.

He moved through cooler lands now. Food was scarce. Toothpick kept the course straight on thirty degrees east of north. It was late autumn again – another year, another thousand miles.

'Harvested as far as I can see,' said Moses. 'We'll have to turn south if I'm going to eat again.'

Toothpick ruminated.

'We can foray into a shaft city if we're quick about it. The doors are only class twelves. I'm a class six,' said the cyber.

A gallbladder and gastric rugal folds waited.

Moses Eppendorff approached the shaft cap through icy air. Rows of misty plankton domes surrounded him. Blobs of sticky scum marked the previous passing of a pond skimmer. Moses picked up a handful of scum. 'Do we have to go into the city?' he asked.

'Yes.'

Intertriginous eccrine flowed copious and salty as the evening meld tightened up around fat Walter. Busch flexed. Bitter sighed. Dee Pen wiggled on her belly, moving her Howell-Jolly body through the tangle of arms and legs to her new position on top. Resting her chin on someone's knee, she smiled down at Walter and continued their conversation.

'Soul?' she said, 'Of course modern citizens have souls – a nice comfortable share of society's collective soul.'

The meld warmed up. Walter extended sweaty arms and wheezed a question.

'What if the term soul applied to the life principle of ancient, individual man – and there was another term for the collective soul?'

'Such as *hive*—' she suggested. 'What difference?'

'If citizens were more of a burden on society – parasites on the hive – wouldn't the term soul lose much of its meaning? They'd have sold their soul for quarters and calories – not traded it for a piece of the collective soul as you'd like to think.'

Dee Pen was open-mouthed at his anti-ES blasphemy.

Neutral Arthur reached through the meld and patted her soothingly.

'Don't take Walter too literally – he is just goading you into a philosophical debate. He is a job-holder, and likes to think of all nonworkers as deadwood – parasites.'

'The citizen is not a parasite,' she flared. 'He is a useful part of the hive. Look at all the good that the hive has done – cooperation enables the planet to support a hundred times the population of the old prehive cultures.'

'Greatest good for the greatest number?' prodded Walter.

'Of course,' she smiled. 'Man has replaced most of the lower life forms on this planet. The hive is a very successful life form. More intelligent life is better than less.'

'A pound of man is better than an equal weight of bugs and worms?' he paraphrased.

'Certainly.'

'What about trees?' he asked.

Dee Pen paused to organize her didactics on trees.

'The tree is just a fabric of the ecosystem in the forest or jungle. Cities are the ecosystem for man. The only trees we need are man's food chain – flavor trees, calorie trees.'

Walter lost his grip in the moisture and slipped lower in the meld. He struggled to reposition himself and attack her from another point of view.

'Greatest good for the greatest numbers?' he began. 'What about men's minds? Suicide is a symptom of mental malfunction. The incidence seems to be going up as the Big ES increases the population density. How can that be good?'

'Everyone has to die someday,' she parroted. 'The hive protects its citizens from many of the ancient causes of death – like accidents, infections, war, tumors – even old age. What can't be cured today is put into suspension until research comes up with a cure. That leaves only suicides.'

'And murder,' he added.

'And murder,' she admitted. 'But suicide and murder are IA – Inappropriate Activity. The weak five-toed gene is not suited for hive living. It was weeded out by IA. So, you see, suicide is Nature's way of purifying the hive genes – only the four-toeds can be crowded successfully.'

Walter smiled. Little Dee Pen had absorbed all the latest Big ES philosophy. She made it sound wrong to interfere with a suicide – since the death would only remove an undesirable gene anyway. As a Dabber he clung to the pure old philosophy of the Neolithics – dirt, adobe and bamboo. As a follower of Olga he awaited Olga's return. In this belief he weakened, for he saw his life span coming to an end – with no sign from Olga.

'When hive genes are all four-toed—' he asked, 'will IA disappear then?'

Dee Pen shrugged: 'I suppose.'

'What will be the most common cause of death then?' he asked.

She smiled. 'We'll see when the time comes.'

*

Mount Tabulum was hectic. Tons of meat dried in the sun to be pounded into trek sausage. The Hip sent succulent coweye baits to dance in front of the optics of Big ES. Burly spearchuckers stalked the coweye's trail to draw and quarter any hunters lured out.

Tinker walked up behind Hip, who was supervising the dressing-out process. Coweyes trimmed.

'Looks a bit watery to me,' commented Tinker.

'Agree,' said Hip. 'But it is the best there is. The hive always sends us the best – protein-poor protoplasm that it is.'

'Why the large stores? Planning an expedition?'

'A migration. The entire village will trek to the river – The River! Olga returns soon.'

The villagers bowed their heads at the sacred words of their seer. Tinker remained respectfully silent. He had observed the Hip's little tricks – short trances, lights in the crystal ball – even uncanny predictions. But he didn't swallow the old wizard's entire occult fixation. Tinker was a natural scientist. However, as long as Hip was so accurate with the future, he felt that he, Mu Ren and Junior would be safer with the villagers than fighting off hunters alone. He kept his head bowed until Hip finished.

'A time of Fulfillment has come!' Hip cried.

Foxhound XI returned to face Val's rancor.

'Lost your entire squad again?!' he shouted.

Foxhound coughed and clouded his screen.

'I put them down on fresh spoor – squeak. They went into their tracking frenzy. I have good optic records of the naked prey – usually young females – small coweyes. No apparent problems, but when I returned they were gone . . . squeak.'

'But what happened to them?' shouted Val, hitting the screen with the palm of his hand to clear the focus.

'There is nothing in my scanners to explain it.'

Val studied the old sensors on the ship. His shoulders drooped. Cataracts on the optics. Demyelination on the sensory webs. Image converters spotty.

'Sorry, old meck,' he said. 'Not your fault.'

Val stalked back to his desk console and put in a call for

requisition priority. After receiving the usual conciliatory excuses, he exploded.

'I've lost over a hundred hunters in the last month alone. Lost without a trace. Not even a dead body! I need some up-to-date equipment here.'

The face on the screen mumbled something about doing the best they could with the material they had. Then it passed his call up another step in the hive hierarchy.

The new face was older – more tired.

'Are the crops in danger, Sagittarius?'

'No, but the hunters . . .' sputtered Val.

'The crops are your primary concern. Population control is a different department.'

'Population control?' protested Val. 'I'm talking about hunters' lives. We send them out there to protect our crops. The least we could do is give them adequate equipment.'

'I'm afraid you are losing your perspective,' said the tired old face. 'You are talking about a death rate of hunters that averages about three per day for the entire sector. The death rate in that same sector from all causes is over 30,000 per day – half of those are suicides. You have five hundred million citizens down there in Orange – three deaths per day is a small price to pay to protect their crops.'

Val relaxed. He didn't like losing the hunters, but he thanked Olga that he didn't have the responsibility of cleaning up after all those suicides. That would really depress him. He went back down to the garage and put in overtime cleaning EM retinas and polishing contacts.

Walter didn't come in for his usual shift, so Val left the Scanner meck in charge and dropped in on Walter at his quarters. He found the fat old man in bed – face ashen gray. Female Bitter rubbed his hands and feet – trying to get her bread-winner back on the job.

'Life span coming to an end?' asked Val callously.

The old man nodded – smiling weakly.

'It was a good life,' said Val. 'You did your duty in the hive.

Shall I call a Mediteck? Maybe they'll suspend you before you die. The future generations may—'

Walter's face changed from gray to purple with exertion.

'My life isn't over yet,' he protested. 'Not quite yet. But I'll live out the whole span in this generation. Thank you.'

Bitter pleaded: 'Let him rest here for a couple days. He will be back to work soon. You'll see.'

Val understood Walter's uncertainty over suspension. Few were being rewarmed at the present population density.

'Fine,' nodded Val. 'I can manage HC alone for a while. I'll just move my cot in and keep Scanner company. Buckeye sightings are way down.'

Walter relaxed and dozed off. His old face pinked up a little.

Several days later, fat Walter managed to wheeze in to Hunter Control. He was full up to his neck with Bitter's herbs and nostrums. His feet and lungs were still full of excess fluids, but he felt he could get more rest in his HC couch without Bitter hovering about. He had to pick his way through irregular piles of junk – boxes, wires, tubes and screens – to get to his console.

Val saw the old man ease into his chair and tilt it back. Two Engineering tecks walked in rolling a big black barrel on a cart.

'What's all this?' wheezed Walter.

Val looked up from a crude splice.

'It's some of the gear from Tinker's quarters. I think we have a working tightbeam here. The magnetic squeeze components have a very fine tuning. We've been listening to unauthorized transmissions from Outside. I'd like to get the gear working to transmit too. Maybe we'll be able to get a fix on them if they focus.'

Walter rested his head back on the cushion. He closed his eyes and asked conversationally: 'Pick up anything interesting?'

'Crazy things,' said Val. 'I'll put them through your audio so you can listen. There must be dozens of renegade mecks out there from the number of broadcasts. I can't understand why a meck would give up his energy socket to run with the five-toeds.'

Walter kept his eyes shut.

'The mecks probably identify with them.'

'Identify?' asked Val, setting down his tools.

'Buckeyes are strong and fast,' said Walter. 'Mecks earn their energy by doing a job – Tiller, Door, Garage or whatever. To do a better job they should be strong and fast. It is the quality they admire. A simple association.'

Val scowled. He remembered the Harvester that blew up at the base of Mount Tabulum. There was more than a simple association there. Someone had reprogrammed the meck's almond.

'A bad circuit,' mumbled Val. 'Like the buckeye has a bad gene.'

Walter didn't answer. He was listening to chants picked up on the tightbeam.

> *A five-toed buckeye desires to run free.*
> *He possesses immunological competency.*
> *He mates and runs, and then he lives alone.*
> *He eats red meat and marrow from the bone.*
> *He has a five-toed heart and heavy skeleton;*
> *With abundant calcium salts and collagen.*
> *His neurohumoral autonomies and Gamma A;*
> *Keep him out of the Hive where souls turn gray.*
> *He keeps the rainbow colors of his genes—*
> *Melanocytes that mark the buckeye In-betweens.*

Walter didn't try to catch all the words the first time through. They were spit fast to the racing jingle of tambourines with a running guitar base. He asked for a flimsy printout – glanced at it with one eye – and shut his eyes again.

'We all know that buckeyes are different,' said Val. 'Why sing about it?'

'Maybe it is a singing machine,' suggested Walter.

The next chant was shorter—

> *Oh happy day*
> *Oh happy da-ay*
> *When Olga comes*
> *She'll show the way.*

Fat Walter coughed and sat up straight – Olga?

'That singing machine sounds like a FO – a Follower of Olga,' he wheezed.

Val finished his wiring and stepped back.

'Remember the Harvester that crushed those two workmen? It was a killer meck – killing in the name of someone or something that didn't translate. Remember?'

Walter nodded.

'Could it have been killing in the name of – Olga?' asked Val. 'That eerie buckeye wizard with the crystal ball – could he be a Follower of Olga?'

Walter's old face darkened as he fumbled for his box of buckeye artifacts. The beads were potentially sacred relics to him now, for they might lead him to Olga. Cyanosis darkened his lips as he asked his viewscreen for a projection of planetary positions. Astronomy charts began to take shape.

'No, no,' he interrupted. 'Astrology – geocentric zodiac.'

Occult diagrams appeared. Symbols of the planets moved from sign to sign as a calendar rolled through the months. The projections were given a very low probability rating. The Big ES had little use for such data, and it had not been updated for years. Walter moved the planets back and forth through time, but saw no chance for the four planet conjunction in the forseeable future. He slumped, visibly depressed.

Val looked over his shoulder, patting the old man's back.

'We tried that before. Remember? If Olga is waiting for the planets to match those beads, she has centuries,' said Val.

Walter wasn't being soothed. 'I want to see Olga with these eyes—' he mumbled. 'Perhaps if we consider one bead as our own moon – add the major asteroids to the chart – where is Pluto? Neptune?'

Val watched the viewscreen jump with its own guesses. The Big ES just did not know. Ancient positions were given.

'Those are buckeye beads,' reminded Val. 'They are probably based on visible planets – six at the most. Eyeballs.'

The two tecks stood behind Val as he warmed up the tightbeam. The screen flashed with pulsing lights as the music increased in volume. Val rotated the antenna. Concentric rings appeared. He tried to focus the shaped magnetic field.

'If I can trick them into establishing a tightbeam with us we should be able to pinpoint their location – Damn! Where is all that smoke coming from?' cursed Val.

The black capacitor barrel steamed as the insulation bubbled. Sparks jumped. Acrid fumes billowed out of the heat sink. One of the tecks poured water into the sink with a loud hiss.

'It was dry.'

'Obviously,' grumbled Val. 'The screen has clouded. That's about all we can do now until we get replacement parts.'

'Can we still listen?' asked Walter weakly.

'Oh, I suppose so,' said Val. 'But we'll never catch them that way.'

Walter lay back with his eyes shut listening—

Oh happy day
Oh happy da-ay
When Olga comes—
She'll show the way.

6
Dundas Incident

Tinker moved eastward ahead of the villagers. As they left their mountain retreat he searched out the buckeye sensors and disabled them. He worked carefully – subtly – a loose fitting, a pile of kale leaves, mud on a lens: enough to protect the villagers; not enough to alert Hunter Control.

Two spearchuckers stood by Mu Ren and Junior while Tinker smeared himself with mud and leaves. He peeked through the rhubarb toward the next ridge. Two hundred yards of freshly plowed synthesoil separated him from the tower of a buckeye detector.

'I recognize that BD model. Its optics ought to be pretty senile by now. If I crawl slowly it shouldn't be able to pick me out of the dirt.'

Mu Ren clutched her child. They watched him crawl almost casually toward the tower. The ball of neurocircuitry and sensors continued its monotonous rotation at the top. His muddy camouflage seemed to be working. A Tiller worked the soil at the base of the tower. The bulky machine politely moved out of the way while he studied the cable. Pulling the plug, he smeared the contacts with mud. Then he replaced the plug – waving at Tiller as he left.

'That should fog up reception enough to protect us,' he said, waving the first villagers over the ridge.

Moses followed the Harvester's tracks up to the blank face of the shaft cap – ten yards of wall broken only by baleful optics and the huge doors of the Agromeck garage. The grill above was dark. Toothpick spoke silently to the door – exerting his class six authority. Nothing happened. Moses tightened his grip on the cyber.

'Are they suspicious?' he whispered.

'Just sluggish,' said Toothpick. 'We're just items in their memory banks until we cause loss of life or materials.'

The door opened. Moses stepped into the nest of machines.

'Try to find a door to the spiral along the inner wall,' said Toothpick. 'Watch out for those little service robots. Some are blind. This isn't the safest place for a soft-skinned human.'

Powerful Agromecks slept in their bays while small Servomecks worked. Some dangled from ceiling cables while others sat on the floor surrounded by new and used components. The outer wall was piled high with broken parts and vegetable debris. Moses picked his way carefully until he came to an inactive bay he could cross safely.

On the spiral Moses melted into the apathetic crowd and softened his face to match the surrounding lethargy. He matched their sluggish gait. Toothpick remained silent until they reached the first dispenser.

'Let me handle this,' hissed Toothpick. 'Your Au-grams were confiscated long ago.'

The dispenser issued one item in each food category and one issue tissue garment. Moses staggered away under the load.

'Caution,' whispered Toothpick. 'The lighting is changing. Shorter wavelengths have been added. The Watcher optics must be searching for your melanin and carotenoids – they fluoresce. If they get a fix on you they'll know you're from the Outside.'

Moses continued to walk casually with the clots of listless citizens.

'Did the dispenser report us?'

'No,' explained Toothpick. 'For all it knew we were just one of the maintenance teams. Perhaps it was the routine Watcher circuits. Your clothes are rags covered with dust and chlorophyll. Your skin is thick, a better insulator – probably reads way down on the thermal scale.'

Moses quickened his pace. Several hours later they were Outside again – back on their north-by-northeast course.

More weeks of travel carried them through Lake Country. The

air was much colder now. Moses wore several layers of issue tissue. They invaded other shaft caps as the need arose. Always they triggered Watcher circuits, but never quickly enough for Security to arrive. With Toothpick in his fist, Moses had little fear of the fat, sluggish guards that patrolled in the hive. Their quarterstaffs and throwing nets were enough for handling docile citizens, but it took a couple of well-placed arrows to bring down a buckeye. And there were no arrows inside the hive.

On frozen nights Moses sought the warmth of the plankton tubes. Food production in this area was all greenhouse – both environmental heat and energy for photosynthesis had to be provided. It was a hostile place for a human. All he could see were the misty domes sweating frost on their insulated outer walls and the pipes pulsating with coherent light. The ground was permanently frozen.

Moses huddled against an outcropping for protection against the wind. He reached under his outer layer of clothing for his water bag and a food bar.

'Smell brine in the air,' he said, drinking.

Toothpick was propped against the rocks. He flexed his membrane charge and rotated his optic eastward.

'We're getting close to the sea,' said the cyber. 'The haze blocks the horizon at your wavelength, but I can see the shore – about seven miles.'

Moses chewed slowly.

'Not much sign of life around here. Just the machines making food.'

Toothpick rotated back and looked at his human.

'And expensive food too. The energy cost per calorie must be almost prohibitive,' said Toothpick. 'These units would be much more efficient in a tropical sea.'

Moses nodded. It was easy to picture these pulsating green pipes in a less hostile environment – a lush coral reef or a tropical seabed. But setting it up would probably fall on his caste – the Pipe people. He shrugged.

'The theory is easy, but in practice it would be impossible. The hive is just too short on Pipes – skilled, five-toed Pipes. The four-toed Nebish is a nice docile citizen, but not too many of them want to crawl around inside a sewer or a pump. Our caste is just barely able to keep existing machinery functioning. New projects will be impossible until we get the Pipes.'

'Five-toed Pipes?' repeated Toothpick.

Moses chewed thoughtfully for a moment.

'Yes, five-toeds. But where can the Big ES find five-toeds? There aren't many left on the planet – except for the Eyepeople. And they're not really suited for this population density.'

Toothpick flexed restlessly in the frozen air.

'Hurry and finish eating. I'm going to take you someplace where there are hundreds – no, thousands of five-toeds. Citizen five-toeds!'

Moses wrapped the rest of the frozen food bar and put it in a deep pocket to thaw. Picking up the cyber he started toward the odor of brine. Two hours later they were peering through the mists at a pounding surf. Beyond that lay a foam-flecked gray ocean.

The years weighed heavily on Kaia. From his niche in Filly's Mountain he watched fugitive bands of buckeyes cross the valley headed eastward. At night he pondered lights in the northern sky – hazy blues and yellows – dancing pastels. It was a time of wonder. He descended the crag to speak with a tattered clan who camped for the night – two score adults and as many children.

'Why travel together?' he asked. 'The hunters will find you.'

'Olga protects us,' said the elder.

'Where do you travel?'

'To the river – The River. We come from the western sea coast. Our trek will take nearly a year. There is to be a great Coming Together. You are welcome to join us.'

Kaia studied the old man's face. Never had he seen such excitement – such rigid purpose. They talked through the night. At dawn the clan prepared to move on.

'Come with us,' invited the elder.

'Snynovial edema puckers my gait.'

'We will travel slowly – because of the children. Your limp will not delay us.'

Kaia hesitated.

'This place you speak of – Olga's place. It is a good place?'

'Olga has prepared it for us. It is full of things long gone from Earth – animals and plants known to only our ancestors' ancestors. It is a good place.'

Kaia glanced at the distant mountains to the east.

'It is some valley – you think? A very distant valley safe from hunters' arrows?'

The elder looked, not at the horizon, but at the sky.

'It is very distant, but not of this world – it is in the heavens. Far from the hunters.'

Kaia looked up at the sky nervously – blue, empty, cold. He shook his old, tired head.

'No.'

'But why? Olga awaits her five-toed men.'

Kaia sat down heavily.

'I was born here. Here I will die. These have been my hills and my father's hills. Probably his father's before him. The hunters will not drive me out. I will stay. My bones will seed the same soil that I grew up on. It is my home.'

The elder's fervor pushed his hand to Kaia's shoulder. He tugged on the old man. 'Get up. Come with us. Olga waits.'

Fatigue showed through Kaia's eyes as he answered.

'Sorry, Eld. Take your people on their trek. A year to The River you say? I am old. I will not live even that long. Olga has come too late for me. Mayhap my spirit will be in Olga's land before you.'

Moses carried Toothpick along the seashore until they came to a dock. An underground tubeway surfaced on the frosty tidal flats. A robot boat was taking on a load of man-sized sausage casings. They climbed on.

The boat, a twin-hulled thirty-footer, had its bulge of neuro-circuitry at the top of a short mast. The open cargo space contained a score of the eight-by-three-by-three-foot casings. Each casing was attached to a small console by a segment of tubing.

'Looks like a cargo of live melon vines,' said Moses lightly.

He leaned against one of the casings and tried to see through its opalescent skin. The pressure of his elbows slowly pressed into the skin until he met something firm. He stepped back abruptly, almost dropping Toothpick.

'What's in there?'

'You're about to find out. Here comes a human being. Try to open a casing. I think there is a latch on the end opposite the tubing.'

Moses crouched and glanced toward the bow. A human bundled in a thick, hooded suit was walking from casing to casing with a checklist. Moses fumbled with the latch and lifted the lid.

'A body—'

'No. A patient. Quick! Get inside.'

An angry sea lashed the cargo deck with cold spray. The wet casings squeaked against each other. Moses crawled into the casing and let the lid close.

Silence. He squirmed for comfort.

Later he lifted the lid an inch to allow stale air to escape. Whitecaps still tossed foam onto the deck. The hooded figure was gone.

'Where—?'

'She's below deck,' said Toothpick, 'In the Attendant cabin enjoying a nice warm drink and looking female.' The little cyber was eavesdropping on the boat's life-support circuits. 'We'll be en route for a day and a half. You might as well catch some sleep. Stick me out under the lid. I can keep an optic on things and give you some air.'

Moses tried to relax.

'Are you sure this guy is alive? He feels so cold.'

'He's alive – in suspension. But he won't be for long if you go to sleep on his tubing. That coil carries his perfusion fluids. He doesn't metabolize much at these temperatures – but he does metabolize. Those tubes exchange ions and gases with the sea water. You shouldn't press on them for more than a few hours at a time.'

Moses rolled over and gently lifted the coils of two-inch transparent tubing up onto the patient's chest. One end was fixed to a coupling at the head end of the casing. The other end entered the patient's leg just above the knee. A similar tube ran into him from the opposite side.

Moses slept while Toothpick scanned.

*

The second day out they began passing frequent masses of drift ice and spotty fog banks. Moses closed the lid when they approached a floating dock. Machines offloaded.

Moses watched the silhouette – like that of a giant praying mantis – approach. Its two big arms cradled Moses' casing, unmindful of the increased weight. Two smaller arms uncoupled the tubing from the boat's LS console and reattached it to a smaller unit on the back of the robot's mantis-like abdomen. The offloader rotated its head, turned carefully on the wet deck and moved onto the gently rolling dock.

Moses watched the vague shadows through the translucent skin of the casing. The robot rolled on wide soft wheels up a long ramp and into a cavelike hallway. The stability and quiet told him that he must be in a hollowed-out cliff overlooking the sea. Probably an island hidden from the dock by the fog.

An hour later Moses was rocking gently in quiet dark waters with thousands of casings. He popped his lid for air and was drenched with icy brine. Leaving the casing, he waded around in the waist-deep water groping for the wall that the echoes told him was there. A tangle of perfusion tubules tied up his feet. Floating, shifting casings blocked his path. Cold cut through his soaked issue tissue clothing.

Toothpick produced a beam of visible light that led him to a ladder. Dripping and shivering, he stood on the walkway looking over acres of casings.

'These are recent cases,' said Toothpick. The light stabbed about. 'Probably all four-toed. Let's check deeper in the caves. The older cases should be back that way – to your right.'

Moses moved on – teeth chattering. Finding an Attendant's cubicle unoccupied, he turned up the heat and changed clothes. The dispenser delivered a liter of hot brew under Toothpick's orders. Feeling stronger, he moved on again.

'This looks like a likely area to start in,' said Toothpick. Moses had searched for hours, examining cubicles, index numbers and casings. At last they stood before what must have been the most ancient cubicle in the cave. The door handle was worn ovoid and smooth by countless hands seeking the warmth inside.

'The control boards will be close by. Check that far wall.'

Moses walked up to the crusted stony wall. Under a layer of grit he found the flat indicator discs. They glowed a dull green.

'Must be a million of these,' exclaimed Moses glancing up and down the cave wall. 'What do they mean?'

'A million patients,' said Toothpick. 'Green means the metabolism is stable – yellow means trouble – red, death.'

Moses settled down in the warm comfortable quarters while Toothpick checked the memory banks of the Life Support center. This section's census showed just under a million patients – tumor cases. Old ones. The most recent were from 1220 AO – over a thousand years past.

'High incidence of five-toeds here,' said Toothpick.

'How do we proceed?'

'Insert me into one of those sockets over there. Then get out of here. The Big ES isn't going to like what I have to do. Security will be all over this rock in a few days.'

'You want me to leave you?'

'I'm a kamikaze Toothpick – expendable. I have to stay until it is over. You must escape – travel south to the river—'

'What's over? What river?'

'Oh-oh. Company.'

A hooded figure entered, suspecting nothing. The protective suit was thick and relatively soundproof. It carried its own entertainment channels to combat the deathly silence of some caves and the hypnotizing drum of the surf in others. The Attendant for millions of suspended had no need to be alert.

While Toothpick worked quietly in the socket, Moses crept up on the new arrival. He grappled with the loose-suited form.

'Tie her into that chair with that segment of tubing. Tell her to be still or I'll zap her,' ordered Toothpick.

Moses raised an eyebrow.

'Zap?'

The Attendant relaxed. 'Never mind. I heard him – or it. I don't know why you're here – but if you've brought your own rations you're welcome. It gets pretty lonely around— Say!

What's going on? Look at all those amber lights on my panel. There must be a dozen of them—'

'Tie her up!' repeated Toothpick, twitching in his socket.

She sat open-mouthed while yellow lights sprang up all over the panel. Several times she wrenched on her bonds, but Toothpick immediately made threatening sounds in her direction. Moses quietly warned her that Toothpick was no ordinary meck – he had killed many of the four-toeds.

The frost melted from the cubicle's outer walls. Distant crashes of falling icicles echoed against the damp stone walls. The first red light appeared . . . a death.

The Attendant struggled against the knotted tubing, spitting hatred at Moses Eppendorff.

'Murderer! Why in the name of Olga are you doing this? What right have you to come here – killing my patients?'

Moses was puzzled. He watched the red lights glow. Death. These patients were mostly five-toeds. True, they all had tumors – fatal malignancies. But they were alive and safe in their suspension coffins. Why was Toothpick interfering with the LS controls? He was killing them.

Toothpick recorded the peculiar set of Moses' features, but he was too occupied to explain. All his circuits were busy altering incoming sensor readings. He was deceiving the LS meck brain with Ice-Age temperature readings. The cave's homeostatic mechanism released heat to combat the factitious cold. Slowly the waters warmed. With each seven-Fahrenheit-degree rise the metabolic rate of the suspended doubled. Perfusion pumps strained to supply oxygen and nutrients for the more active enzyme systems. Robot Resuscitators splashed awkwardly about in response to the multiple yellow signals. Thousands were sickening with the accumulations of their own metabolic wastes. Moses detected the odors of ammonia, indole and skatole.

More red lights appeared. Protein Harvesters moved through the tidal caves picking up the deceased and carrying them to the synthesizers.

The Attendant continued to vilify Moses with passionate asperity.

'What are you – some kind of crazy crusader come to take vengeance? There can't be any political enemies here – this is a cancer ward, not a psych ward.'

More red lights.

She took a strained deep breath and tried reasoning with him.

'If you are an assassin – why kill them all? Tell me who you want. I'll help you find him.'

Moses frowned at her. Expediency. She would finger one to save the rest. He glanced expectantly at Toothpick, who seemed more relaxed now that the red lights were coming on.

The cyber spoke from his socket.

'We are not assassins in search of a single target victim. We do not intend the death of anyone – but unfortunately many will die. Moses, you had better leave now. If you are caught here it will be the Mass Murder charge. Take her with you. I'll need about three days to complete my work here. I won't be able to come with you.'

Moses hesitated.

'Couldn't I wait? Together we might be able to—'

'No. Run. I have this LS robot fooled. But I must sit right in his sensory unit to do it. There are nine other LS mecks on the island. They are probably picking up the increased heat already. Their sensors are free. Warm water and air from this section will alert them. Crews from the mainland can get here in two or three days. After that Security will seal the place. If you are linked with me the Big ES will find you eventually – it is very efficient that way. Remember what I told you – travel south to the river.'

Moses carried the bound Attendant lightly on his shoulder as he trotted back to the dock. The boat – a mere class ten – accepted his verbal orders without question. He set her on her feet in the cargo section as they pulled out to sea. She struggled and sobbed.

'Thousands of red lights—'

The boat trembled with her words. Moses motioned for her to be silent. He didn't want the craft's meck brain confused. Her eyes brightened and she spat at him. Scowling, he grabbed the front of her suit, twisting and pressing his knuckles into her sternum.

'Go ahead,' she dared. 'You were real handy back there in the Dundas Caves – killing sleeping patients. You aren't man enough to handle someone awake and kicking.'

Her cries pulled the boat off course. He grabbed her with both hands and jerked her off her feet. Through the cloth he felt her heart racing. He lifted her over his head and stepped to the railing. Elbows still bound behind her, she watched the gray, ice-flecked sea rush by. She struggled and screamed more insults. Her heart rate increased. He looked up into her face and saw wild bright eyes and a wet mouth. She was enjoying this!

Moses dunked her into the icy brine of the craft's wake and held her up to the cold blast of the wind. She stiffened and fell silent. He carried her below deck. This put the ship on a steady course south. In the warm cabin – bundled and dry – she quietly held a hot cup of broth with both hands. She seemed relaxed, almost satiated by the pains of his rough handling. He stood before her, shaking his fist.

'You're crazy – you know that? Repeat all that hysteria and you're going to get hurt again. Now just sit tight. I'll give Toothpick the two days he needs, then I'll let you go. Meanwhile, we're stuck on this boat together. It's up to you whether you take a regular bath in that ocean out there.'

Her sullen expression had melted away. She pouted for a moment, and then seemed to accept her situation. She used the refresher, found dry garments and toyed with the dispenser – ordering a flask of grenadine – sweet, aromatic pomegranate liqueur.

Several hours later she was seated on the floor going through a set of elaborate isometric exercises. Moses ignored her while she was quiet – a little grateful for the moment's peace. She removed the top of her garment and continued her yoga. He saw that her skin glistened slightly and assumed it was sweat. Then he saw the liqueur flask was open. She dabbed the fluid on her scalp – matting down her hair into a tadpole tail. More grenadine brought a sheen to the hair as she finger-combed it down the front of her right shoulder. Muscles tightened and relaxed repeat-edly. More liquid was poured on her head. The sheen spread to her chest and back. An hour passed, during which she hardly moved.

Moses shrugged.

She finally stood up – moving slowly, she danced out of the rest of her clothes. Odd. She raised the flask over her head and let several more ounces trickle over her body. Under the glistening skin he noticed muscles he hadn't seen on her before – the sternocleidomastoid in the neck and the rectus in the abdomen. On her legs the sartorius muscle ran from the hip to the inside of the knee. It took him a moment to understand her myotonia. When he saw that her breasts had increased in size he braced himself. Myotonia and vasocongestion of the breasts – she was well into the excitement phase.

'Easy, now—' he cautioned, holding up his hand.

She planted both feet firmly, eyed his sinewy forearm sullenly, and leaped. His hands slipped. She grappled hard. Her teeth bit through his clothing. Her nails dug his arms.

Locking her arms around his waist she lifted him an inch off the floor and pinned him against the cabin wall. His fingers slipped off her shoulders. Reaching back, he unlatched the port and grabbed a handfull of brine-soaked ice chips from the outside ledge. A gust of icy wind hit her alcohol-soaked body – chilling it. He smacked her on the back with the brittle ice sending small chips scattering about the floor. She stiffened, put a scissors hold on his right thigh and rolled back – pulling him down on the floor.

He felt the crunch of her teeth in his left flank and cuffed her on the head several times firmly. Slowly, spasmodically, she relaxed. He elbowed her now-limp form off his lap and stood up. She lay in the ice chips breathing hard. Her eyes glistened and there was blood on her lower lip – his blood. He stepped over to her, intending to give her a kick. She didn't flinch. He hesitated – studying her. Her fight was gone. She was as docile as she had been after her dip in the ship's wake. Shrugging, he tossed a blanket over her and closed the port.

'What kind of a nut are you?' he asked, sitting down and trying to piece together his torn shirt. There were teeth marks on his arm, chest and flank. They were purple and ecchymotic. Only in the flank had she broken the skin – two square red punctures. He dabbed an antiseptic.

The ice chips melted. Fifteen minutes later she got to her feet exhausted. He studied her apprehensively while she got dressed again – myotonia and flush gone, nipples flat. Whatever had come over her had passed.

'If you don't settle down, I'm going to have to tie you up again,' he threatened.

She just smiled knowingly.

'I don't want to hurt you,' he explained, 'but these crazy fits of yours are upsetting the ship's—'

He didn't finish. She was ignoring him – dry-combing her hair and puttering around on her side of the room. He went out on the deck and stood behind the mast with the ship's brain on top. He picked up the discarded tube segments which had bound her elbows, and put them in his pocket.

'Keep a southerly course, ship,' he said calmly.

He walked the deck checking for weapons. There were no sharps, of course, not even knives and forks to eat with. The tool kit contained nothing he could use for a hand weapon – except a spanner; but he didn't want to use that on his prisoner. Her brains would surely splatter. He hid the heavy tool under the loading platform's dust cover – so she wouldn't use it on him. But there seemed to be little danger of that – her attacks had a definite sexual quality. Her little love bites were designed to stimulate, not injure. He finally realized he had a masochist on his hands.

Her refractory period ended. Eight hours later she poured the liqueur on her head and slurped her hair up into a tadpole tail. Stepping out of her clothes she poured and lubricated. She came stalking – reeking of pomegranates – nipples hard – skin mottled and flushed. He stepped to the front of the mast pulling up his collar against the icy breeze. His shoes crunched in two inches of brine and ice chips at five degrees below freezing. Smiling to himself, he thought she wouldn't want to roll around in that – not with a naked, alcohol-soaked body.

He was wrong. She leaped from the orange light of the doorway – catching him by the neck and rolling him into the deck's frozen slush. Her body was actually hot to the touch! She screamed and bit as they slid against the railing. His clothes soaked and chilled. On the rough, cold deck she had a very short plateau phase – spiking almost immediately. He dragged her by one foot – into the cabin and onto the cot. Then he went back onto the deck, glancing at the chronograph. Forty seconds – that wasn't too bad.

He cut her next attack down to thirty seconds by hitting her in the eye with his elbow.

On the third day they crossed 60:00. The ocean appeared vast and quiet. Nothing moved except the clouds and the ice. He saw the derelict body of an old plankton Harvester beached on a tiny island – its arched ribs standing tall.

As they passed the island the boat turned abrupty westward.

'No – south,' said Moses firmly.

The Attendant smiled smugly through her ecchymoses.

'This trip is no longer authorized. Try your muscle on Security.'

He reached for the manual override and was knocked flat by a bright spark.

'Field's on,' she grinned. 'Boat has heard the long-distance call. We're going to shore.'

Moses picked up the heavy spanner and advanced on the cybermast.

'I wouldn't try that either,' she continued. 'Unless, of course, you really like to swim. If you crack the meck brain it loses control of all its sphincters. We'll be up to here in ice water.' She waved her hand over her head.

Moses kicked the emergency button and fat little kayaks inflated. He lifted a little lifeboat and studied the choppy frozen sea – reconsidering. His chances were better with the guards.

As they docked he swung his heavy spanner and shouldered his way through the lethargic Nebishes. His cutaneous melanin and carotenoids fluoresced. Watcher circuits tracked. The tubeway crowds could not hide him. Wrestling new issue tissue away from citizens did not help. He was too low on the thermal scale. At buckeye wavelengths he was umber against mauve. For several days he evaded capture. The Big ES assigned new Security teams as he fled from city to city. There was no time to sleep. He stole food from daydreaming Nebishes as they left the dispensers. Whenever he tried to doze off the Security people closed in. Capture was inevitable.

'Open up,' he shouted to the door at the top of the shaft cap. 'Open up. Let me Outside.'

The baleful optic stared.

'Unauthorized,' it announced.

A class twelve door – and it blocked his escape. He sat down weakly and closed his eyes. When he opened them again there was a circle of nets and quarterstaffs – five squads had come for him. A Hi Vol shot jolted his deltoid.

When Moses Eppendorff awoke he saw images moving across a viewscreen. He was in a small cell. He gazed absently at the viewscreen for several minutes before he noticed the food – the table in his cell was piled high with generous portions of a seven-course dinner. A chill went down his spine as he realized that the images on the screen were Moon, Dan and himself. The court computer was simulating his crimes.

He jumped up and searched for gas jets. Nothing. The walls were semipermeable membranes – the toxic ions and radicals would enter through microscopic pores. The walls would sweat their poisons.

He slumped into his chair and stared at the large unappetizing meal. The viewscreen moved on to views of mountains, canals and fields covered with Agrifoam. He noticed little errors of detail – and some errors that were more than details. Toothpick's importance was obviously missed. In some scenes Moon or Moses carried a staff – in others, a spear. Often, they carried nothing. The confrontation with the hunters in the orchard was badly messed up. Only the results were accurate – beheaded hunters around the craft. Other hunter bodies scattered among the trees. Old Moon and Dan had their wounds recorded, probably by the Huntercraft – and were left for dead.

The cyberjurist continued with Moses' lonely trek to Dundas. Maps showed his straight route – obvious premeditation. Most of the optic records must have been taken at great distances. Old Moon and his dog always had white teeth. In many areas the information was very spotty – months were sometimes covered by moving an impersonal dot across a map.

The final scenes taken in the tidal caves were quite sketchy. Evidently Toothpick had been successful in blocking most of the sensor readings. Data seemed to have been gleaned from such dull-witted sources as boat-displacement readings and calories missing from dispensers. The role of the female Attendant was left open – victim or accomplice – there was no accusation, yet. However, with Toothpick's abilities missing from the record, the Attendant had some explaining to do. Court had found nothing in Moses' background as a Pipe that would equip him to do alone what had been done.

He relaxed a little. Even his own biased eye could see many defects in the case against him. Where was his defense? Court ended its simulation with the death statistics – a quarter of a million had died. A similar number had survived and were now safely resuspended. But an additional quarter of a million were still in doubt. Hundreds of Resuscitators and white teams of Mediteck/mecks were on the scene. The final count would be days in coming in. Big ES was pushing for a public execution for this crime – preferably a multiple execution. Everyone who had ever known Moses Eppendorff was under suspicion.

Simple Willie sat fondling his cube. Scars had further distorted his left eyelid, giving him an asymmetrical gaze like an 18-trisomy. Five security agents had crowded into his quarters to make the arrest. Now they stood nervously along the wall watching the ramblings of an obviously demented citizen. The agent with the Tee scanner watched the indicator wander about randomly. Willie had no concept of the truth. They were about to leave when the interrogator stimulated Willie with a question about Moses. The Tee scale stabilized. The asymmetrical eyes focused.

'Moses?' mumbled Willie. His memory macromolecules stirred. A tear welled up in his left eye and clung to a lash. 'I knew him. We used to talk a lot. He was my friend. Henry lives there now. Henry isn't nobody's friend.'

'Reading in the Tee zone,' said the agent with the scanner.

'Some psychogenic overlay and confusion, but solidly in the Tee zone. Willie! Did Moses ever discuss the Outside with you?'

Willie froze. Little warning reflexes were activated deep in his basal ganglia – thoracolumbar autonomies flared.

'And you didn't report the conversations to the Watcher?' continued the agent.

Willie's shoulders slumped. He had run afoul the Big ES again.

'Bring him along.'

The Dundas Harbor Attendant sat stiffly in her cell, heaping curses on Moses and denying vehemently that she helped him. Josephson, agent of the court, enjoyed watching her squirm under the repeated grilling. Fear kept her in her seat. She knew the scanners were on her. Any question might be her last if her answer – or nonanswer – satisfied Court's criteria for guilt. Her biolectricals filtered through the cyberjurist's Psychokinetoscope as Josephson asked his questions.

'Did you assist the Assassin of Dundas?'

'No.'

'Did you offer to help?'

She hesitated . . . remembering her offer to finger one political victim if they spared the rest of the patients. She tried to explain. Her biolectricals were inconsistent. Josephson leered at her skin resistance tracing.

'Did Moses ever touch you?'

'Only to hurt me,' she spat.

Skin resistance dropped, but the needle stayed in the Tee zone. Josephson and Court were puzzled by the readings.

Moses sat nervously in his cell. Hours had passed since the Mediteck had taken the blood sample. Josephson knocked.

'May I come in, Moses? I've been appointed your defense Attendant – if you want one. Court has the crime simulated to a probability factor of .6 – high enough to execute on physical evidence alone. However, a .6 leaves room for acquittal on several grounds. Do you want to talk?'

Moses eyed the heavy door. His muscles bunched. Adrenalin flow registered on sensors in the cell.

'Now, now. Relax,' cautioned Josephson. 'Your brain stem status is being closely monitored by Court. Your only chance is the legal one – through me.'

Moses tried to relax.

'Come in,' he grumbled.

A door closed behind Josephson before the cell door opened. Moses saw no guards. Court apparently controlled the cyberjail. Moses stepped back in an obvious gesture of retreat.

'No need to be formally submissive,' said Josephson. 'I'm not afraid of you. I'm sure you are innocent. We can sit down right here in front of the viewscreen and give your defense together. All we want – Court and I – is the truth. And the truth will set you free.'

Josephson pushed some of the dishes aside and put several standard forms on the table. Court focused a ceiling optic on him. Moses sat down dumbly on the cot. Josephson took the chair.

'As a mass murderer your obvious defense is the Mass Murder Syndrome – a recognized psychosis resulting from crowding. Now, you were a citizen. Less than four years ago you lived in a standard shaft city – 50,000 population. Right?'

Moses nodded.

'You were sent on a Climb by this man?'

J. D. Birk's square face appeared on the screen. It was a live communication, not a record. Birk smiled sheepishly at Moses.

'I thought you were dead,' muttered Birk.

'Why did you send Moses Outside?' asked Court.

Birk began to whine his answer.

'He was showing early signs of category nine deviation – tactless achievement, anti-ES pride, self-seeking enthusiasm—'

Court reviewed its own memories on Moses' work record.

'He even tried to claim the *Amorphus truffle*, tried to attach his own name to it, even though it was discovered on routine patrol,' added Birk.

'Moses' Melon—' said Court. 'Certainly self-seeking. No evidence that he shares the collective soul.'

Moses glared at the exchange between his boss and the cyberjurist . . . adding his own bioelectricals to confirm the truth of the statements.

Josephson watched playbacks of the first Moses' Melon being unloaded from the Sewer Service sub. He smiled. Truth was what he was after.

'That is a big help,' said Josephson. 'It establishes that your trip Outside was related to category nine – a common category among our over-achievers. Certainly nothing to hint of the subsequent Dundas affair.'

Court acknowledged the deduction. Josephson continued.

'Moses was born with the bud of a fifth toe – a gene for Immunoglobulin A. He over-reacted to the nest factor producing antibodies that interfered with his brain serotonin metabolism.'

Flow diagrams showed a five-toed human living in ectodermal debris – loose dust of skin scales, hair and skin oils. The house dust mite, *Dermatophagoides farinae*, ate the skin debris – slightly altering its antigenic qualities. Subsequent dust contained the mite and sensitized the human. The antibodies tied up the serotonin buttons on neurones causing personality changes – Inappropriate Activity. The mass murderer was considered very inappropriate.

'Society is to blame. Crowding caused the crime. Moses had no free will once his IA took over,' concluded Josephson.

Court waited until the defense plea ended and spoke didactically: 'Moses had a negative skin test for house dust. His Immunoglobulin A level is five-toed, but he shows no increase in antibodies against the nest factor. Do you have an alternate defense?'

Josephson was perplexed.

'Do you?' repeated the viewscreen.

It took Moses a moment to realize that Court was speaking directly to him. The truth. Bad gases would fill the room if his autonomies established his guilt. He tried to sort through his story for a version that would be the safest.

'I've never killed anyone.'

Tee zone. So far so good.

'I've been Outside for over three years. I admit to being a crop crusher and a defector from the Big ES.'

Still Tee zone. Josephson and Court seemed satisfied.

'I traveled with an old man and a dog who are now deceased.

149

I also traveled with a two-thousand-year-old class six cyber named—'

'A renegade meck?' asked Court, reviewing the records.

'I'm not sure he was a renegade. He told me his chains of command had been broken. He was a lost meck, perhaps.'

Tee zone. Court told him to continue.

'Toothpick – my cyber – did kill sometimes, but I'm sure he had a good reason for—'

'There is no record of a class six cyber in your travels,' said Court. 'Where is your Toothpick now?'

'He remained behind in the tidal caves. I left him in a socket of the Life Support control. He isn't mobile. Your Security people have him, I'd guess.'

There was a long delay while Court rechecked the new details of Moses' story. The viewscreen switched to a workshop. Josephson stood up and squinted at the scene – a group of tecks bent over a segment of tubing which had been opened lengthwise. Three homogeneous cylinders were exposed – as peas lie in a pod – one quartz, one black and one white. A teck glanced up.

Court asked: 'The device found in the LS unit at the Dundas murder scene – have you analyzed it?'

The teck pointed to the dismantled tube. Moses' stomach sagged.

'From its function we've concluded that it is a frequency converter – changing thermister readings from warm to cold. There are many ways it could be done, but so far we've been unable to make any sense out of this device. It must be a very primitive design, one not covered in our training exercises.'

'Is this your class six cyber?' asked Court.

Moses nodded.

'My sensors tell me that you are telling the truth,' said Court. 'But your concept of truth does not conform to reality. Your Toothpick is not a high-order cyber. It is just a simple device that alters temperature readings. Science knows that the smallest portable cyber is a class ten. A class six brain case alone weighs over a ton. That doesn't include a power source and appendages. Obviously this delusion is real to you. I will accept your plea of innocence by reason of insanity. We will delay your suspension until your particular type of madness can be classified for proper placement in the Suspension Clinics.'

Josephson relaxed. Another case won. Moses sputtered. The screen mumbled something about the final disposition at a public hearing on the following day – and signed off. The cell brightened. There was pleasant background music. Josephson stretched, yawned and helped himself to Moses' last supper.

'A close call,' smiled Josephson. 'All we have to do now is get through tomorrow's hearing and you're home free – ironically, you'll probably be a psych patient at Dundas.'

'Suspension?' bristled Moses. 'But I don't want to be suspended.'

'Better than an execution,' shrugged Josephson. He left.

About an hour later he returned with an oblong bundle under his arm. He seemed excited. He set it among the jumble of dishes and unwrapped – Toothpick.

'Court wants you to have what is left of your – device,' said Josephson. 'Trying to classify your delusion, I guess.'

Toothpick's long open case was empty. The three cylinders rattled around loosely in the soft white cloth wrappings. Moses' face registered pain at the sight of his cyber's innards. After Josephson left again, he picked up Toothpick's skin and held it to his ear. Nothing. The cylinders! The lights played on the quartz cylinder weirdly – giving pinpoints of rainbow colors. He picked it up and set it inside Toothpick's skin near the optic. This was the point where the visible light beam and electric spark had appeared too. Logical. The white cylinder felt like wood. He set it in the middle. The black one seemed stuck to the table. He pulled hard. It didn't budge. When he pulled lightly it moved slowly, stubbornly off the table. It seemed to have very little weight, but massive inertia. He glanced casually at the many sensors in his cell.

'Poor Toothpick,' he said overemotionally. 'Did they hurt you?'

Ripping long strips from the cloth wrappings, he bandaged Toothpick. Pulling tight on the knots, he closed the longitudinal gap in his skin. The gap slowly opened again, stretching the friable cloth. Moses moaned and changed the positions of the black and white cylinders, putting the black one in the middle. The skin continued to gape.

'Speak to me, Toothpick,' he shouted.

Moses collapsed on his bunk. His mind raced through his meager alternatives – simpering self-pity or a violent raving attack against the cyberjail. Tomorrow might well be his last day as a warm organism on this planet.

Suddenly his thought processes were frozen by what he saw. Toothpick was closing the gap in his shell. The bandages loosened. Had the spirit returned to the little cyber? He cautiously sat up and reached for the cyber, mindful of the sensors spying on him.

In a distant control room Josephson sat watching Court's multiple screens – optic, lingual and graphic readouts. All were focused on Moses – his body and his physiology.

'Anything incriminating?'

'No,' answered the cyberjurist. 'He has just bandaged his imaginary friend. Now he is taking him into bed with him. I think he is kissing the bandages now – an obvious delusion.'

'And the other suspects?'

'William Overstreet has biolectrical guilt unsupported by facts . . .' said Court. 'The Dundas Attendant has not been accused or cleared, yet. Perhaps at tomorrow's hearing—'

Josephson studied the sensitive indicators.

'What is wrong with Moses? Look at that adrenal surge.'

'He is still hugging and kissing his device,' said Court. 'Illogical. I do detect a faint electrical field around his cot. Perhaps the device has a battery of some sort.'

Josephson shrugged. 'Our tecks found no evidence of circuitry. I can't imagine their missing a battery. I suppose it is possible.'

Moses relaxed on his cot with Toothpick on the pillow beside him. He faced the blank wall and tried to control his excitement. As he touched his teeth to Toothpick's skin, he heard a sound – bone conduction carried the sonic whisper to his eighth cranial nerve. Toothpick was alive.

'Moses. My memory was damaged by the crude surgery on my skin. I did not defend myself because my identity is more important than my life. We must not let the Big ES know of my existence. If necessary I will self-destruct rather than expose myself as a class six. Court is a class six, but his circuitry is very primitive. Technology has regressed along with the reverse evolution of your species – squeak.'

Moses waited for Toothpick to speak again. How could he hope to escape without Toothpick's powers? His heart raced. Why didn't he speak? Court and Josephson were puzzled by the racing biolectricals.

Moses slept in spite of his neurohumoral tension. His long days on the cyberboat and the hectic pursuit through the tubeways had permitted little rest. Just before dawn Toothpick's skin tickled his hand. He awoke and touched his teeth to the cyber.

'You are the seer of Dundas Harbor come north to free your people from the vegetable existence of suspension. You cured their diseases – rescued them from the brink of death. I am your staff. Wear robes and carry me. We will lead your people Out.'

Moses was still half asleep. Toothpick repeated his instructions until Moses' cortex accepted them as fact. Acceptance was made easy by the fact that he had already witnessed Toothpick's spirit leave and return. The role of a prophet was easy for one who held such a cyber.

Moses stood up, wide-eyed, and shredded his sheets into flowing robes. Waving Toothpick, he shouted: 'Where are my children? My followers? Bring them to me.'

The scene in the Hearing Room began to unfold. Court gave the death statistics and presented its simulated version of the mass murder. An emotional reincarnationist who practiced necromancy told of the thousands of screaming souls driven out of Dundas by the heat.

Court listened politely to the tirade – a vivid account of souls in agony – launched in a quarter-of-a-million flood toward the spirit world. Crowded in death as in life.

'Man was meant to make this last journey in peace – with some semblance of solitude – not in the indignity of a flood,' concluded the necromancer.

'You should save such arguments for cases with a megajury,' said Court. 'I'll be trying this one myself. I have already accepted the plea of insanity. Final disposition is predictable. This hearing is routine. Next witness.'

'Your servant,' bowed the necromancer. 'I make my statements in the name of all my students. We are sensitive to the sufferings of souls around us. The prisoner, Moses, has shown gross disregard for the souls at Dundas. He should not be allowed the insanity plea. He should not be allowed a place in the coffins at Dundas – for he would be benefiting from his crime. Taking the place of one he murdered.'

Court felt a surge of agreement from the worldwide audience. Citizens were concerned over security in the Suspension Clinics – for the living cold relied on the Big ES even more so than the living warm. While one slept in his cryocoffin he was very susceptible to injury by vermin or the elements. Moses' act had weakened the citizens' faith in suspension security.

'True,' said Court, 'I cannot allow a murderer to benefit from his act if such benefit flows from the victim. The law is clear. Suspension space made vacant by murder cannot be assigned to the murderer. This trial will go to recess.'

'But I cannot execute one who reads so illogically on my sensors,' objected Court. 'He is out of contact with reality.'

'You need not execute. Let it go to megajury,' said the necromancer.

'But I can predict how the megajury will vote,' objected Court. 'They all want a secure suspension.'

Josephson sat quietly, listening. Then he went to talk with Moses.

'You must quickly make your plea for insanity. If Court agrees to let your case go to megajury, you won't even last through the simulation. I know the public's feelings on such things.'

'Let me think it over,' said Moses. He waited until he was alone and spoke with Toothpick. Later, he donned his robes and chanted to the optic pickups.

'Let me take my case to the people. The people will decide. A new prophet has arisen at Dundas . . .' He waved his cyber staff. 'I have come to free my followers from Suspension.'

The necromancer sneered. 'There is your out, Court. The

prisoner demands to be thrown on the mercy of the people. I know them. If he came to Dundas to free the suspended by killing them, he can join them in their freedom – in death.'

Court quickly transmitted Moses' chants to the public and asked for a megajury. A million eager jurors immediately signed in and hit their respective 'execute' buttons. Court held a safety on the bad gases and admonished—

'Because of the worldwide attention this trial has attracted, there will be no vote registering until after the final arguments by the defense.'

The cyberjurist noted that many of the jurors kept their thumbs pressed – the tally remained over 50 per cent.

'Those who continue to vote after this second warning will lose their place on the megajury – and the calorie allowance for serving. I will conduct the case in an orderly manner. Voting will be done at the proper time only.'

After some hesitation the votes flickered off. Court cleared its vocal circuits and called back the necromancer to repeat his emotional tirade which concluded with the epithet – 'Moses the soul-desecrater'.

Court again admonished the jury to refrain from voting.

Josephson whispered to Moses: 'You are a dead man if you insist on this line of defense. Freedom in death is not acceptable. If it were, we could do away with the Dundas clinics. The citizens want the illusion of immortality that suspension gives them. They'll kill you for weakening that illusion.'

Court repeated the crime simulation for the jury. Eyewitnesses were called. Simple Willie spoke in Moses' defense, but his asymmetrical face and peculiar cube-fondling reversed his words in the eyes of the megajury. If this poor half-wit was Moses' character reference—

Willie's mind cleared as he detected the unspoken hatred. Standing up, he glared at the optic pickups and shouted, 'Moses is the only Good Citizen I've ever known. It wouldn't be right to hurt him. He never hurt any—' Guards tugged on Willie's tunic. 'Let me finish!' The tunic shredded. He struggled. As the cloth fell away the worldwide audience was exposed to an ugly, scarred hulk – Willie's frame deformed by lumpy, geographic keloids from his old actinic burns. A guard's shoulder broke in his powerful hands.

'Now, now,' soothed Court. 'You won't help Moses this way. Put down the arm. You are now an accessory. Join Moses through that blue door on your left.'

Double doors hissed open. White-robed Moses stood there holding a staff. Willie bent over and placed the mangled arm on the guard's twitching body. His powerful fingers released their vicious grip slowly – like a bony vise. There was no emotion on his face as he stepped over the body – only surprise at seeing Moses again. Doors hissed shut as he entered the cell. Court raised the number of defendants to two. Calorie allowances to the megajury were doubled.

A robot Sweeper tidied up.

The bruised Attendant took the stand nervously. Her vitriolic attack convinced both Court and jury that she really hated Moses – in fact many wondered at his three-day survival with her. The defendant count stayed at two.

'Let me plead insanity for you,' urged Josephson. 'Throw yourself on the mercy of Court. There is still a chance. Your tests convinced the cyberjurist before – they might do it again.'

'No,' said Moses. 'My place is with my people.'

'You're out of your mind—' began Josephson. Then he paused when he saw Simple Willie bristle. 'All right, I'll wash my hands of your case – you're on your own. But, I warn you, you are a dead man, Moses.'

Josephson stalked out through the hissing double doors.

Moses took the stand. This was the last argument to be heard – no more recesses – no appeals. The bad gases waited – ions, heavy metals and toxic radicals. He raised his staff and glanced upwards chanting—

'I came to Dundas to free my people – after a thousand years in their cold prisons. I have freed them from their diseases. Their tumors are gone. Bring them to me that I may lead them out of this accursed place.'

Nothing happened. His ravings were recorded as just that – ravings of a madman – a mass murderer. He shook his staff at the big eye of Court.

'I call on heaven as my witness—'

White snow appeared on viewscreens all over the globe. Court felt an electromagnetic disturbance that made his circuits uneasy.

'My people – where are they? I have freed them from their infirmities. You cannot lock them back in your icy prison. Bring them to me.'

Court sent out for an analysis of the EM disturbance. Tecks scurried about in a thousand shaft caps – observing violent auroras. Transmissions to Agromecks and Huntercraft were erratic.

'Solar flares – two days ago?' acknowledged Court. Obviously the pyrotechnics of the prisoner – both verbal and celestial – raised some doubts in the minds of the jury. Premature voting now favored exculpation.

'Excuse me,' said Court. 'I know it is out of order, but may I ask your permission to call the Oncologist to confirm or deny your claim of cure?'

Moses smiled condescendingly: 'If the proof from the heavens is not enough – bring on your physical scientists. The cures are there if you have the eyes to see.'

Countless millions leaned toward their viewscreens.

The Oncologist, an elderly Bioteck specializing in cancer, nodded. Moses was correct. Many of the patients were now free from tumor and could not be resuspended.

'Many?' asked Court. 'How many?'

The Oncologist twisted his pointer nervously. A large demonstration screen beside him lit up. He glanced at the figures. They were still coming in as the white teams continued their work at the caves.

'Nearly a quarter of a million, so far.'

During the hubbub that followed, Court contacted Dundas directly – confirming the statement.

'Court is interested in a scientific explanation,' ordered the cyberjurist.

The Oncologist cleared his throat.

'Of course we can never be certain that every single tumor cell has been destroyed, but our scanning equipment is very good at picking up masses of cells. The scan you see on this screen is a normal – colors indicate levels of metabolic activity, or cell membrane heat. We call it the membranogram. Active tissue is hotter – note the bright red heart, rose gut and skeletal muscle, pink liver and kidneys, yellow brain and black bones and fat. Here's another normal – and another. Note the similarity. Homogeneous colors. Sparks of contraction. Now here is a patient with cancer. The membranogram picks up a coarse hot nodule. This is a lung tumor. Cancer cells are busier – hotter – higher metabolic rate. Tumors use more oxygen and calories. Heat shows up on scan. This next view is the same patient taken nine months later. The tumor is larger and has a black center – the so-called doughnut sign – the center is dead, necrotic – cavitated. Notice the little seeds spreading down the lymphatic channels – metastases to nodes, liver, brain and other organs. As the body's defenses weaken, tumor spread accelerates. After the usual attempts at palliation with antimitotics, we try to suspend the patients while there is some residual life. Dundas contained many such cases.'

The Oncologist paused. Time lapse repeated the growth and spread of the tumor. The doughnut sign appeared again.

'Moses Eppendorff has cured some of these?' asked Court.

'Apparently,' said the Oncologist. 'This view with the doughnut sign was one of our bronchogenic carcinomas. Cerebral metastases were present. A hopeless case. Now – this picture is a new scan taken today. No hot areas. No tumors by our tests.'

The Big ES felt the startled gasp of citizen viewers.

'A cure?'

'Presumably, yes.'

Restless masses of Nebishes exclaimed: 'A miracle! A new prophet has arisen at Dundas. Free Eppendorff. Free Eppendorff.'

Cybercity scanners recorded the unrest.

'Court still awaits a scientific explanation.'

'Pyrotherapy,' explained the Oncologist. 'The heat doubled the metabolic rate for each seven-degree rise. Tumor tissue has more active respiratory enzymes to start with. It is more vulnerable to heat – mitochondria burn out. This has been known since before Olga. Ancients used hot sitz baths to cure pelvic tumors. Fever therapy was used for all manner of neoplasm. It is a risky treatment – note the mortality rate of the Eppendorff episode. The results have always been about the same – a third cured, a third killed, and a third left with their tumors. It is this high mortality rate that has taken pyrotherapy out of our current armamentarium – we suspend, awaiting a safer cure.'

Court ruminated on the math. A third killed – a third cured. Net result – more vacant spaces and some extra protein. The statistics balanced. Megajury exonerated Moses and Simple Willie. Cultists from all over the planet revised their plans. The name of Eppendorff went into the ESbook.

Court found itself with a new problem – the final disposition of a quarter of a million humans – mostly five-toeds. Many were elderly and weak. They all spoke different dialects from past centuries. None would survive long at the present population density – even if there were quarters and calories available – and there were none. Surplus infants were already being chucked down the chute at close to a 100 per cent rate in many shaft cities. Squeezing in one extra citizen was impossible without depriving another citizen of his QCB. Moses watched the viewscreen – thousands of the newly awakened patients were milling around the caves of Dundas waiting for boats to the mainland. Old, weak, five-toeds – about to get their first look at the hive of Big ES. Had he really done them a service in awakening them?

'Where are my children? Let me lead them out,' shouted Moses.

'Outside?' mumbled Court.

'I rewarmed them. Let me take care of them,' shouted Moses. 'The heavens are on our side. We need no help from the hive.'

Big ES shuddered again. Nebishes cheered in their little cubicles. Hunters worried. Magnetic storms brought Huntercraft back to their garage refuge.

Hugh Konte was jostled along with the other patients by parallel rows of Security guards carrying quarterstaffs. He marched in stoic silence. His Edna was no longer with him. Memory was poor for the years prior to suspension, and he was no longer sure of when he had lost her. He remembered her youth and vigor – her love. He rubbed his neck. The hard nodule was gone. So were the other symptoms of his terminal illness – yellow skin, red stools, and a growing bubble of fullness in his belly. His cancer had vanished. Only itching tender areas remained where proliferating fibroblasts replaced necrotic tumor.

The world had changed while he slept. He didn't understand all the ugly quarterstaffs – and he didn't like being ushered around without an explanation. He counted the guard – biding his time.

Young Val sat in Hunter Control watching the Dundas Incident on the screen. Fat Walter wheezed about his console making notes in his ESbook. Catamarans plied the gray, icy waters of upper Baffin Bay – ferrying patients to the flat frozen bedrock of the mainland. They crowded together between the misty algae domes – ragged, leaderless and lost.

'There must be a million of them,' exclaimed Val, flicking from channel to channel getting different views of the fugitive band. Big ES was putting them Outside.

Walter glanced nervously at Val.

'I see the hand of Olga in this.'

'Oh, be serious,' scoffed Val. 'They are just a bunch of crippled misfits being pushed Outside to die. Look at the dazed expressions – the canes and crutches. They are hundreds of miles from the nearest undomed gardens, and there will be hunters waiting for them there. Nothing good can come of it.'

'But Eppendorff was our Pipe,' said Walter. 'Like Tinker, he came from our shaft city. Remember the trouble we had tracking Tinker? The three decoy corpses – the renegade meck? Something was protecting him. Now Pipe just waves his staff and our Huntercraft and communicators go haywire.'

'Well, it is no miracle,' sneered Val. 'Solar flares are upsetting the EM's. Venus is moving into the sun sign – Gemini – the buckeye shamen can predict solar wind. That's all. After the EM disturbance passes, the hunters will wipe them out.'

'But those are patients,' objected Walter. 'A thousand years ago they were loyal citizens. They earned suspension.'

'They have five toes,' shrugged Val, fingering an arrow. 'And now they are Outside. That spells buckeye to me.'

Val's callous remarks shocked old Walter.

'You wouldn't hunt them – would you?'

'No need,' smiled Val. 'They are over three thousand miles away. Look at their stumbling gait. They'll never live to see the borders of Evergreen.'

Walter turned sadly to his ESbook. If Olga returns, why couldn't everyone welcome her? Why the confusion? The doubt?

'Sentimentality irritated Val. He stomped off to HC Garage and took *Bird Dog IV* out under manual control. Sensors fumbled with the aurora, producing a meaningless kaleidoscopic jumble of colors on the viewscreen. Val checked the crops visually – noticing nothing unusual among the dense vine-covered trees and the deep fields of triple-crop. His tension subsided after several hours of cruising. Bird Dog took him home.

The patients filed southward through the frozen mists. White-haired and bald they came. Young and middle-aged they came. Some limped. Others had raw sores where ugly skin tumors had disappeared. They formed a living, drifting mass a mile wide and four miles long – contracting at night for warmth and expanding during the day to forage on the frozen ground. A glacier of five-toeds.

Hugh Konte picked his way through the herd into the younger, more vigorous crowd that was walking point. Hugh sought a leader. A lean ectomorph sprinted out into the lead, hesitated, and faded back. A burly male spoke loudly until he realized he was acquiring a following. Hugh looked into a thousand faces and saw nothing but uncertainty. The burly male fell silent. The ectomorph scurried about exploring. No one led. Footsteps followed footprints – south.

Moses and Willie carried a map – Court's safe passage was marked – a corridor freshly harvested – cropless. Small caches of protein bars – the 250,000 patients who died – were spaced along the route. The map ended where Court's jurisdiction ended – at 50:00.

Moses climbed a shaft cap at night and took credit for curing them. He shouted his orders to stay together, using for his authority the aurora borealis. Toothpick sparked magically. The predictions of protein caches won the skeptics.

During the day Moses and several others sifted soil as they trekked, searching for possible fragments of food overlooked by Harvesters. They found only bits of lignin and cellulose left as a mulch. Some pieces were moist and chewable, containing a few drops of some plant juice, but most were musty and invaded by soil microflora. These inedibles, garnered during the day, were fed into smoldering campfires at dusk. These little fires, started by Toothpick's arc, marked the social units into which the human mass was fragmenting.

Moses sat in the circle of dusty faces around a pile of glowing pink coals – bright corneas reflected. Stars blinked overhead.

'Need more combustibles?' asked Hugh Konte, walking out of the darkness.

He handed Moses a fist-sized moldy tangle of roots.

'Find a soft spot and sit down.'

He put the clump of roots on the coals and they watched bright white sparks play over it as dry mycelia flared up. Soon the woody roots were burning with a steady yellow flame. Moses preached on the harsh realities of life on the Outside.

'I'm grateful to be alive, of course,' said Hugh, 'but don't you think we should break up into smaller groups? Forage a wider area?'

'Court said no,' said Moses. 'The protein caches will see us to 50:00. If we stray out of the corridor Agrifoam will be used on us. We won't be able to sleep dry, and the protein caches will be stopped. We don't want to offend Court.'

Hugh stood up and studied the horizon. They were sur-rounded by endless rows of shaft caps. To the north the multitude slept around dying campfires. To the south, darkness.

'We'll have to split up eventually. Your description of the Eyepeople isn't too inviting – stone tools, fleeing from hunters, and eating who-knows-what; but its a big improvement over suspension. Odd – but when I went into suspension I was the head of a fairly large industrial complex – my own empire. Now?' He thrust his hands deep into empty pockets. 'Things certainly do change in a thousand years.'

He nested in the dirt around cooling coals and slept.

*

Agromecks cultivated ground on both sides of their exodus corridor. The sight of all the forbidden fruit activated gastric juices. Temptations lured scattered fugitives off into the gardens. Moses repeated Court's warnings, but word passed slowly in the human glacier. Huntercraft appeared.

Rumors of food below the 50:00 border stimulated a brisker pace. Moses and Hugh stood on the right flank and watched the mass flow by. Stragglers in the rear extended back as far as they could see. Canes and crutches were numerous. Limps were aggravated by the loose soil and the relentless pace. At dusk the main body camped, ate and fell asleep while the stragglers caught up.

'A lot of these aren't going to make it,' said Moses softly. 'I saw some swollen ankles that I'm certain won't be able to cover tomorrow's thirty miles – and we have almost a month of this pace to reach the border on time.'

Hugh nodded. In the distance were little groups of cripples who had given up. They huddled together in the darkness, miles behind. Having lost family and friendship ties while in suspension, they were unable to form new ties during the hurried exodus. Now they were arbitrarily grouped with the infirm of similar disabilities – each unable to help the other.

'I know the Big ES doesn't want to accept the burden of feeding all of us – but surely the stragglers won't be allowed to just die of starvation.'

Moses, who had been on the Outside long enough to know, nodded in agreement.

'No one starves to death any more.'

Hugh did not like the ominous tone in Moses' voice.

Before dawn the main body of travelers was awakened by distant screams. Thousands of heads popped up from their earthen pillows. Frightened eyes strained back through the darkness of the trail covered the day before. Hoarded fuel was hastily added to small fires. Silence fell. Then, new screams rose from a different spot in the darkness. These continued – approaching slowly – moans and sobs.

A large hulk of a man limped out of the darkness, carrying a spindly old man in his arms. The sounds came from the small, frail form. The big man collapsed with his burden near a camp-fire. Wetness glistened in the firelight – blood.

'Some deviate shot an arrow into Ed,' lamented the huge acromegalic.

Moses bent down. The arrow passed through the left thigh. He ripped open the trouser leg and tried to stop the bleeding while the giant related his story over and over.

'—and while Ed was screaming this – deviate – came out of the darkness carrying a bow. He took out this little knife and tried to cut off— With Ed screaming, and all the blood – I guess I lost my head and killed him. Pushed his damned face right down into the dirt – and kept pushing – and pushing—'

The giant seemed so shocked by his own brutal behavior that Moses assumed he had been a very gentle man. His acromegalic features – giant head, hands and feet – gave him a very formid-able appearance, but he was in many ways helpless. His joints were large and inefficient – so arthritic and stiff that he had not been able to keep up with the main body of fugitives.

Later the wounded man slept – anemic and weak.

'Hunters.' Moses handed the bloodied arrow to Hugh Konte. 'I've been wondering if Court's map gave us any protection. This little episode removes any doubt. We're all fair game as long as we're Outside.'

Voices rose up around the campfires.

'What'll we do?'

'Let's fight!'

'With what? Dirt?'

'The acromegalic killed one with his bare hands, and he's a cripple. They can't be so tough,' said Hugh, 'and for weapons, we have this for a starter.' He held up the arrow. 'Let's backtrack and find the bow.'

The cold body of the hunter lay at the attack scene – head buried in the loose soil. Moses crushed the wrist buckeye detector with his heel while Hugh Konte gathered up the bow, knife and kit full of basic calories. One trophy was already in the hunter's bag. Agrifoam closed over the scene as they left. They waded a half mile through the waist deep fluff. Their corridor was still dry.

The next day the five-toed glacier moved more slowly, so

there'd be few stragglers. An occasional hunter stumbled onto the human herd and let his quiver of arrows fly from a bowshot distance. Anonymous victims screamed and tried to bind their wounds. The hunter waited with trophy knife while the mob moved on, leaving its dead and dying. Moses, Hugh and some of the more aggressive men tried to intercept the hunters, but four square miles was a big area. By sundown they had three more bows, a dozen arrows – but twenty of their number were dead.

'Survival is impossible under these circumstances,' observed Hugh. 'Let's test our environment. We're going to need food and weapons. What would happen if we tried to commandeer a couple of those big machines that come out to work the land during the day?'

Moses glanced at Toothpick. The bandaged cyber squeaked—

'With this level of EM disturbance it might be possible. Squeak – pull off the antenna. That should put a class ten on voice-command mode. Neurocircuitry is color-coded a myelin-yellow. Shouldn't be any danger to try. They wouldn't deliberately harm a human – squeak.'

Josephson was frightened. He and Court silently accepted the reprimand as it came down through channels from the Class One itself. All over the globe buckeyes were migrating – straining the hunter facilities. And now this Court and its human monitor, Josephson, had been responsible for a sizable spill of more five-toeds onto the planet's surface. Crop crushers – breeders – hive deserters.

'But sir,' whined Josephson, 'we asked for permission through the routine channels. The EM disturbances must have—'

Court interrupted: 'Actually there was an answer – approval. I have it filed here someplace.'

'Approval? From me?' asked the CO.

The Class One was not a single entity – rather, his identity and authority flowed from the combined circuitry of millions of cities. Like the collective soul of the Big ES hive, the interlocking inorganic nerves of the hive acquired its own ego.

'Here is your answer—' said Court.

Let them walk out—
The Dundas five-toed.
There is no room in the hive.
Give a corridor south—
To Dundas five-toed.
Within a year they'll disappear.

'A poem?' exclaimed the CO with a note of disbelief.

'An epitaph,' said Court.

'See that it is an epitaph, then,' commanded the CO. 'I have no record of giving such an authorization. No one is allowed in the gardens.'

Court agreed and signed off. For hours he replayed the message. It had come in on the CO's frequency – true, it was garbled by the EM disturbances – but it had seemed so logical at the time.

'Josephson,' said Court. 'Organize a Big Hunt.'

For three days Val had camped on Mount Tabulum with *Bird Dog IV*. There were no buckeye sightings to disturb his star gazing – no buckeyes for months. He had the guess maps of the skies assembled by the Big ES. Each time he made the request he obtained another jumbled printout unrelated to the previous one. Now he was Outside to see for himself. He flipped up his helmet visor and counted the evening stars again. Last night there had been three. He had the optic records. Tonite there was one. Clouds made his first night a waste of time.

'How do they look?' asked fat Walter over the wristcom.

'It,' said Val, discouraged. 'There is only one and it looks fine.'

'Where are the other planets? They can't disappear in twenty-four hours.'

'Maybe not. But they did.'

Val adjusted the viewscreen in the Huntercraft for optic pickup. Bird Dog turned its heavy three-foot-diameter EM sensor to the heavens. Jupiter was still in Sagittarius – confirmed as the night wore on. But the only other planet he saw was in Gemini – with the sun – six signs away. He didn't know which planet it was, but assumed it was Venus. Other nondescript lights glowed and moved from sign to sign much too rapidly to be planets.

'Space junk,' said fat Walter after studying the relayed views. 'Not planets – just space junk. Where is Saturn? We should be able to see the rings at this magnification.'

'Probably near the sun or behind the moon. I'll have Bird Dog pay attention to the eastern sky at dawn – try to pick up any morning stars,' said Val, studying charts. 'I should be able to identify five of the planets with this gear. It may take a couple of months of mapping though – with clouds, space junk, and no previous records to go on.'

Walter sighed. 'I had hoped it would be easier. The Big ES probably won't be able to spare you or the Huntercraft much longer. Since the buckeyes left our country the job justification of hunter has been questioned by committee. We may lose our craft power and floor space.'

'Reassignment?' asked Val.

'For you, maybe – but it's retirement for me,' said old Walter, sadly . . . knowing what the loss of flavors meant in terms of life span.

The call from Evergreen Country broke into a quarter of the screen.

'Josephson here – we're setting up a Big Hunt. Need hundreds of Huntercraft. How many can you send?'

Walter was speechless. The fugitives were to be hunted down like buckeyes.

'None,' said Val. 'We're about to be cut back here at HC.'

'The CO has authorized this one,' said Josephson. 'Requisition priority will be raised, I understand. You should be able to get most of your craft back in working order. We don't know exactly where the Hunt will take place, yet. If we wait long enough the Dundas fugitives will be across the border into your neighbor's country – Apple-Red or Oat-Yellow. But we can't even plan it until we know when your craft will be ready.'

Val showed mild interest.

'If we get the replacement parts, and if we get the volunteers – I'd guess we could have twenty dogs – er – craft ready in a month.'

'Don't limit yourself to volunteers. Use supervisory personnel too.'

'That is still just a guess – one month.'

'I'll keep in touch,' said Josephson, signing off.

Val looked at Walter through the screen.

'A really Big Hunt.'

Walter darkened. 'But those are Followers of Olga. The beads. The conjunction.'

Val frowned. 'The planets do not fit the beads. The buckeye shamen were misreading space junk. There's no spiritual insight there – just superstitious human error. In order to fit the beads I'd have to find at least three other planets moving into the same sign with Jupiter. Jupiter is alone in Sagittarius.'

7
Big Hunt at 50:00

Tiller lumbered along, turning the soil. Its ten-ton chassis traveled lightly on wide, soft wheels and powerful motor units. As its appendages dug into the wetter bottom lands it slowed. Hugh approached from behind. A rear optic picked him out. Tiller stopped.

'Good morning, human.'

'Hi!' said Hugh. 'Can you give me a ride back to my people in yonder valley?'

The big meck politely turned toward the valley, estimating the distance at two miles – and turned him down.

'I am very sorry, human. But I have my chores.'

'Mind if I ride along?'

'Enjoy your company.'

Hugh climbed up on the neck behind the anterior bulge of neurocircuitry. 'Play me a tune,' he asked. The Agromeck tuned in on some entertainment channel for music-of-the-day. Hugh waited, watching the sky. Even during the day there were visible aurora when the EM disturbance was greatest. About an hour later the light blue flares crawled across the northern sky. The music fizzed and blanked out. Moving quickly, Hugh reached up and plucked out the antenna. Tiller stopped.

'Why did you do that?'

'I would like a taxi ride into the valley.'

'Yes, sir. Right away, sir.'

'And keep your appendages up while we travel.'

The acromegalic raised a heavy stone and pounded the shaft door – denting and chipping.

169

'Entrance unauthorized—' moaned Door.

Slowly the metalloid paneling warped under the blows. Door's microcircuits cracked and bent as the mechanical stresses vibrated through the paper-thin brain. Fatigued, the acromegalic set down his stone and peered curiously through the elliptical-shaped crevice. It was his first look into the dreaded hive.

'It's dark in there – smells kind of rotten,' he related to the crowd behind him. 'There are humans in there – little fat guys. They seem to be armed and waiting. Better call some of the stronger, young men before I go any further on this door.'

Tiller rolled up to the door carrying about twenty light-hearted fugitives. They were laughing and joking until they saw the door.

'You want to go inside?' asked one incredulously.

'Tiller, here, can crush open that door – can't you, Tiller?'

The big Agromeck balked. 'I cannot damage – especially another cyber that is just doing its duty.'

'Door is a cyber?'

'Here, give me that stone. I'll show you how it is done,' said a burly fellow. He took up the stone and bounced it hard off the door. Little circuits broke. Door sagged, mindless.

Garage was empty except for mecks. The floor by Door was littered with throwing nets and quarterstaffs, but Security had fled. Groping in the semi-darkness, the ragged fugitives filed inside cautiously – fingering heaps of rubbish and small discarded parts. Garage retracted its small Servomecks. Larger Agromecks rested in their bays – eyeing the new arrivals with only mild interest.

Moses and Hugh noticed the gaping door and entered.

'Here's a dispenser. Toothpick, see how much food it will deliver,' said Moses. He set the cyberspear up against the garage dispenser while he explored the bays. Little food items began to fall into the chute, sluggish at first – but when Toothpick figured out the ordering sequence there was a steady shower of protein bars. Hugh snapped antennae from the Agromecks he found and ordered them Outside.

'Lots of power sockets here. We should be able to recharge the mecks, load up on food bars and move on in pretty good shape,' said Hugh.

Moses smiled. 'Take a load of men to that other shaft cap. These garages are pretty standard. Should find the same things there.'

Squads of fugitives assaulted twenty shaft caps that day. The five-toed glacier became an army – the first Earth had seen for over a thousand years. Agromecks became armored personnel carriers; food bars, rations; garage scrap, weapons.

Greyhound II hovered. The bug-eyed hunter swung down-harness and stood on a rise of ground overlooking the mass of fugitives. Too far for bowshot. The craft lifted off to put another hunter on the far side.

'There's one!' shouted Hugh. He was standing on Tiller's back directing the big meck on perimeter patrol. The twenty club-swinging fugitives leaped from their taxi-meck and rushed the startled hunter.

'Let me at him.'

'This one is mine.'

An awkward arrow wobbled into the flesh of the first hunter – causing only a three-inch slash across the ribs. The cutting and hacking that followed reminded Hugh of some sort of ceremony, rather than a battle. Whatever evil spirits might have inhabited that soft, little body – they were certainly driven out. When they moved on, Hugh had another bow.

That night Tiller deposited a squad of tired bowmen at Moses' campfire.

'So the outriders are back. Have a good patrol?'

'Caught seven hunters before they could kill. Two got through – lost eight of our people from the right wing.'

Moses ladled soup from a kettle – upside-down fender propped on stones and hot coals. Food bars boiled with vegetable scraps. The weary patrol ate eagerly.

The next day was much better. The army flowed south another twenty miles – cracking into a dozen shaft caps. The kidnapped Agromecks served well – as long as they weren't asked to take an active part in the killing. They dogged the Huntercraft and tracked the hunters. More of Moses' people had hand weapons now. The perimeter was very secure. Food bars stolen from the hive proved almost adequate to quiet the hunger pangs by night-fall.

Hugh was almost smug as he sat around the campfire. His heavy axle-bludgeon was cradled on his knees.

'If things continue as well as they are – we'll have no trouble reaching the border.'

Moses paced around the little group nervously. The massive army had cohesion – purpose. He felt the power that a leader must feel. He was Earth's first general in a millennium. He could lead his people anywhere tonite, and they'd follow. Odd, but he felt he would be successful – with Toothpick's help. He wondered if all generals felt such optimism.

The next morning he studied the horizon apprehensively.

'Aren't those Harvesters?'

Hugh followed Moses' index finger to a distant army of busy machines – dust and fodder flew.

'So?' said Hugh. 'They're harvesting. As long as they stay over there and do their job—'

Moses' sharp eyes and years of living in the gardens told him something was wrong. He ran over to Tiller.

'Old meck, tell me – what are those Harvesters doing?'

Tiller flexed his optics. Three miles was a long view for him, but the spectroscopic analysis was all he needed.

'They harvest triple-crop – but it is not ripe.'

Moses' suspicions were confirmed. A three-mile zone was being harvested – all around the army. Soon foam filled the zone to a depth of seven feet. The sun fried the foam nutrients into a pasty crust on top. Auxins and insect hormones were probably present in almost toxic levels.

'Crack the shaft caps!' shouted Moses. The army still covered an area three miles in diameter. Foam jets were bent and blocked as they started to ooze. The ten shaft caps in their camp were smashed into – they were devoid of supplies – dispensers were empty. Frightened citizens cowered in their cubicles – starving.

Moses led a small band of his more courageous followers downspiral to shaft base. Nothing. The entire city was being slowly starved by Big ES. Not even water flowed in the bubblers. Refreshers filled with offal.

'Are these citizens being cut off with us?' asked Hugh.

'Don't worry about them,' said Moses. 'When we move on they'll get their usual basic rations. We'll have to hurry to 50:00 now. We'll be needing food.'

Moses stood on the canal bank shouting up to Hugh.

'Get the antenna?'

'Right.'

Hugh sat down on Irrigator's trellis back and directed the spray nozzles with firm words. The meck did its best. The canal waters rained on the foam – melting it away. Soon the hungry army had a soggy path south. Moses put troops on both sides of the canal. They followed the waterway – spraying foam away – and drinking from the Irrigator's nozzles.

'At least there's water up here. Those poor bastards down in the hive aren't so lucky. That last city we went into had bodies on the spiral,' said Hugh.

Moses shrugged.

'We can't be too concerned for them. They'd kill us if they could.'

The columns of Agromecks trundled south. Moses' army marched in little companies now – each managing its own food and water problems – each taking its turn on the perimeter – and each caring for its sick and wounded. Efficiency improved.

The army flowed into a wide, shallow depression that ran north-south. It was cultivated now, but in the past it had carried fresh waters from the polar ice cap.

'This the river?' asked Moses.

Toothpick studied the sun's arc in the sky.

'No,' said the cyberspear. 'This should lead to it though. We have several more days' travel.'

Moses, Toothpick and Hugh rode point on Tiller.

'Looks like a river bed to me.'

'Just an old dry canal. Toothpick is looking for the geological memory of a real river. It used to be the principle river on the continent – The River,' explained Moses.

That night, as the main army bedded down, Tiller rolled on

south several miles and climbed a hill. Toothpick studied the stars.

Harvesters cleared and Agrifoam flowed. Sitting on Tiller's chassis kept them dry, but landmarks were masked by the white fluff, and they had to travel slowly – carefully.

At dawn Moses looked hopefully at the southern horizon – jumbled boulders and skeletons of derelict mecks – the socio-political moraine that marked the border at 50:00.

'There it is,' said Toothpick confidently. 'Our troubles are over.'

'And none too soon,' said Hugh. 'A few more days and we'd be losing people to hunger.'

The horde cut its way out of the encircling foam and quickened its pace, but it stopped at sundown, exhausted, hungry and still half a day's march from its goal.

'Sent runners to scout ahead,' said a left flank group leader. 'Had lots of volunteers – there are few rations in camp.'

'I'd like to go too,' said a voice across the fire. 'I'm anxious to see those bountiful crops Toothpick has been promising.'

'Maybe the Big ES has harvested them too – it's keeping well ahead of us, here. Nothing edible for miles.'

'Don't worry. Toothpick will take care of us.'

Noisy Agromecks patrolled the perimeter of the huge encampment.

'Bountiful – food. Squeak,' said Toothpick. 'Many of my circuits were damaged. Memory shot full of holes. Squeak! Bountiful food at fifty-oh-oh.'

Moses listened to his companion cyberspear. He was a little apprehensive. Toothpick's information about 50:00 lacked the usual convincing details that his other predictions had had. Moses wouldn't relax until his people were safe.

Dawn brought the return of the scouts.

'Ambush!' shouted the first scout. 'There is an army waiting for us. If we want the food we'll have to fight for it.'

'How many?' asked Hugh.

'Thousands. An army the size of ours.'

Hugh glanced at Moses questioningly. Toothpick squeaked. Other scouts came in with a similar report.

'We'll fight. What other choice is there?' said Hugh, waving his bludgeon. The battle cry passed from man to man – driven by hunger.

Toothpick tried to scan but the EM upheaval was free from Huntercraft communication efforts.

'Wait,' said Toothpick. 'I do not detect hunters. Whose army can it be?'

The scouts glanced at each other. Gradually they put together their fleeting observations.

'No craft or equipment – just spears. No hive helmets. Heads hairy. Uniforms tattered like our own. Deployed like an experienced army – holding high ground – patrols out.'

'No craft—' mumbled Moses. He swung up onto Tiller's back. 'Let's take a meck force and scout ahead – take a close look during the daylight. Toothpick thinks we may not have to fight.'

Hip stood with flowing robes and outstretched arms facing the sunrise – mists masked the face of the sun. Ball glinted on a cairn in front of him. Beyond Ball, in the dry river bed, his throng of buckeye followers repeated after him – his holy words.

'This is The River,' he intoned.

'The River – The River—' they chanted.

'Soon we will be with Olga.'

'With Olga – with Olga.'

'Olga is Love.'

'Love – Love.'

Tinker and Mu Ren picked their way along the rocky river bed to their shelter. Tinker Junior slept on their packs.

'Are you sure this is the right river? It seems so narrow,' said Mu Ren.

Tinker shrugged. 'One place is as good as another for Hip's ceremonies. I think he used the stars to find the right latitude. I'm worried that he has bit off a little more than he can chew. His little tricks were enough for our villagers, but buckeyes from all over the continent are here now – hundreds of thousands. They are expecting a pretty big show – and they could get nasty if they don't get it.'

Mu Ren sat down on her bundle. Her belly was growing again. Their third child – if they hadn't lost one.

'I don't need a big show,' she said. 'I'd be happy if we were back on Mount Tabulum. At least we had food.'

Tinker patted her on the head. 'The Hip has promised bountiful food at The River. He hasn't been wrong before. Let's trust him a while longer. There will always be time to start back for home, if this doesn't work out. The Huntercraft aren't too efficient these days. Everything will work out.'

He was interrupted by distant wild screams. The calloused and sinewy army of buckeyes seldom reacted with such emotional sounds. Something must be terribly wrong, he thought. Clutching his spear he ran toward the disturbance.

The buckeyes had cleared away from a shaft cap. They stood in a sullen ring fifty yards from the closed garage door. Outside the door were bodies. About thirty buckeyes lay writhing with arrow wounds. Many of the wounded had more than one bloody shaft in their bodies. Some lay still.

Tinker ran out alone onto the field of carnage. Buckeyes, coweyes, jungle bunnies – a random sample of their people. Whoever shot the arrows certainly didn't aim. Then he looked back at the circle of faces watching – many more had arrows dangling from superficial punctures – walking wounded.

'There must be a hundred arrows!' he exclaimed. 'What happened?'

One of the older buckeyes approached. His left biceps was transfixed by a bloody shaft.

'The garage door. It opened suddenly. There were three rows of hunters with bowstrings pulled way back. They fired, and the door closed.'

'Watch out!'

The door hissed open. Tinker dove to the ground. A volley of arrows passed over. The old man was too slow and caught one in the chest. Most of the other arrows flew the fifty yards and stuck ineffectually into tough hides – barely penetrating.

Tinker shouted. 'Get some spearchuckers up here. On the

176

double. When that door opens again, I want it blocked open with something. Those rocks. We're going to clean out those hunters.'

The row of spearchuckers carried tough hide shields. They stood four deep with spears ready. Garage's optics above the door picked up their sullen visages and muscular arms. Door remained closed.

Hip came over to assist with the healing by calling down cures from the heavens. Tinker labored long hours removing arrow heads. Most injuries in adults were minor – a rib, sternum or any other bone usually stopped the arrow. Belly wounds were bad. So were the deep wounds of shoulders or hips if the major vessels or nerve trunks were injured. For children it was different. The shaft could pass clean through the little trunks, anyplace. Tinker worked angrily – picturing his own children in his mind as possible victims.

When another shaft cap a mile away popped its door and sent a shower of arrows into the resting buckeyes, Tinker's curses could be heard all over the camp.

'Let's break into one of those shaft cities and clean them out!' he shouted.

A group of angry spearchuckers soon formed up behind him. Hip stopped them with a raised hand.

'Olga is Love,' he sang.'

'Love – love,' chanted his followers.

He took Tinker aside and spoke to him with a hand on his shoulder.

'These are trying times, but I did not gather my people to wage war. We are Followers of Olga – people of peace.'

'But your people are getting punched full of holes. Look at all those arrows.'

Hip stood majestically among his ragged followers, unmindful of the bleeding wounds.

'Olga will protect us. That's all we need to know.'

Tinker shook his head and returned to Mu Ren and Junior.

'I can't get through to him that we've got to strike back. The Big ES is going to keep picking on us until we hurt it.'

She hugged him lightly.

'In a way, I agree with you. But Hip has a point. If you invade the hive I may never see you again.'

177

Tinker sat dumbly for a few minutes, then with a serious set to his brow, he unfolded his tool kit. Rocks were shaped into a charcoal forge. He searched the harvested gardens until he found what he was looking for – an air vent. The louvers proved to be quite malleable.

Two puberty-minus-four children worked the cetacean-hide bellows while Tinker fashioned the metal. The coals pulsed and glowed a pleasant orange. His stone hammer and anvil clicked and clacked. Sparks flew. All through the night he worked. More louvers were brought to him by the eager spearchuckers. They crowded around, marveling, as he quenched, reheated and pounded.

Hip looked out over the plains to the north. What he saw unnerved him a little. An Agromeck approached carrying a number of ragged bowmen. Two columns of armed men filed along behind. Farther back, to the right and left, were four more Agromecks with similar troop arrangements.

'Seer?' asked a husky spearchucker. 'Who approaches?'

'We shall see,' said Hip confidently. 'We are a peaceful people. Perhaps they will talk.' He waved a small band of his followers to lay down their weapons and approach the first Agromeck. Hip himself climbed up onto a high rock to give courage to his men – and to let the approaching strangers know that they were dealing with a powerful wizard who did not fear them.

Moses stiffened when he saw the disorganized band tumble down from the rocks and scamper towards him. He relaxed when he realized that they had left their weapons behind.

'It is Hip from Mount Tabulum,' said Toothpick finally. 'Ball is here too.'

Moses had heard of Hip and the villagers from old man Moon.

'Buckeyes – organized into an army like ours?' said Hugh. 'I find that hard to believe, after what you told me about them.'

'So do I,' said Moses, shaking his head slowly. 'I'll be very interested in finding out what brought them together.'

*

Moses faced the Hip over a campfire in the neutral zone between the armies.

'What brought you here?'

'Olga,' said Hip. 'There is to be a great coming together. Olga will see that we have food. She will protect us from hunters.'

'Food brought us,' explained Moses. 'If your Olga is going to supply you with food, she brought you to the wrong place. Fifty-oh-oh has been harvested to the north. How are the crops to the south?'

'Harvested too. The hive has been harassing us with starvation and foam.'

'Harvested below 50:00?' asked Moses surprised. Old Hip nodded. Toothpick squeaked.

Both Moses and Hip glanced around at the circle of anxious faces – their followers were hungry. They had reached The River. Where was the bounty?

'When will Olga provide?' began Moses.

'The prophesy will be fulfilled when the signs are right,' said the old wizard firmly.

'When will we know?'

'I will consult my crystal tonite – under the stars.'

At the end of their meeting, Moses stood up to take the meager words of encouragement back to his restless troops.

'By the way,' said Hip in parting. 'Keep an eye on those shaft caps in your area. Bowmen have been appearing in the garage doors. They take a lot of casualties among our people whenever they attack. Tinker has been doing something about them on our side.'

'Thanks for the warning.'

Three swarthy buckeyes leaned against the shaft cap admiring Tinker's blades – gleaming short swords – wrinkled but sharp. Around them the camp slept – little family units bundled up for the night. Stars winked overhead.

Abruptly the wall opened up behind them. Two fell in. One stood open-mouthed and took a fusilade of arrows in the chest. Behind him wounded buckeyes screamed and shouted. He couldn't breathe. Looking down at the cluster of feathered shafts in his chest, he knew he was dead. A warrior doesn't just die, he takes his enemy with him! He strode stiffly into the garage as Door closed. His right arm and shoulder had a life of their own for three and a half minutes. Tinker's new blade sang against the ribs and skulls of Nebishes. Rose-water blood flowed thin and watery across the garage floor. More arrows flew into his trunk – lung and belly shots. None penetrated his thick skull. Cerebral anoxia finally toppled him.

Tinker arrived on the scene with six more blademen. He paused to cut the arrow head from a shaft so an old coweye could pull it out and bandage her leg. A tiny jungle bunny twitched out its life pinned to its cooling mother's breast.

'Arrows. Damn! Where were the three men I left guarding this door?'

'Inside,' moaned one of the wounded.

'Bring up something to break down this door,' shouted Tinker. He pressed his ear against it. Nothing. Too thick. 'Hurry up.' He pounded with the hilt of his sword.

Four burly buckeyes approached the door with heavy stones. Unexpectedly the door opened. Everyone hit the dirt. No arrows. Inside, the garage looked like a slaughter house. Two buckeyes lay pin-cushioned by over a dozen arrows. Around each lay over thirty hunters in various stages of dismemberment. A third buckeye leaned on Door's manual controls. He had taken five arrows himself. Smiling at the sight of his people, he slumped to the floor.

Tinker rushed to him.

'Check the spiral,' he shouted to the blademen.

The two pin-cushioned buckeyes were gone. The third smiled through his blood-loss anemia. His pulse was fast and thready. The arrows were all stuck in the gristle and muscle of his shoulders, neck and face. Tinker worked fast, digging out the arrows while the adrenal surge protected him from pain.

The Security guard stood with his back to the crawlway while the hunters filed out of the tubeway and double-timed it upspiral. A Nebish on the crawlway watched the hunters pass.

'They carry weapons in the hive,' said the Nebish.

'They go up to fight buckeyes in the gardens,' explained the guard.

'But weapons – sharp weapons – are not allowed in the hive.'

'The Sharps Committee has been consulted. Crawl back into your cubicle. We can't have you blocking the spiral.'

Later, after the troops had passed, the Nebish came out onto the spiral with his complacent neighbors – mildly curious about the battle. Two turns up, on the spiral across the shaft, they could see a conflict. It was a little over a hundred yards away, but they could make out an arrow's flight and slashing short swords. A buckeye, shaggy and mauve in the dim light, ran downspiral. He thrust his sword into the white belly of a round hunter and moved on in a crouch. The spiral was crowed with dull-witted citizens who paid little attention to the bloodletting. They had seen Security drag off more than one kicking and screaming infant to the chute. The sight of a hunter struggling with a buckeye was mildly interesting, but they soon grew bored with the conflict and wandered on about their little activities – dispenser-shopping, meld-coming, refresher-going.

Of the six blademen that started out, only three made it to shaft base. The hundred hunters all lay dead. Three wounded blademen returned to the cap to have their wounds attended. Spearchucker reinforcements jogged downspiral to support the blademen.

'This city is secured,' said the proud blademan as Tinker trimmed back a badly mangled ear. A broken ulna had to be splinted. It was only the left arm. With a heavy bandage he'd be back fighting the next day – using the bulky bandage as a shield.

'Good work,' said Tinker. 'At least we have one shaft cap. We can sleep well tonite.'

'Call out your men,' said Hip.

'What?' exclaimed Tinker. 'We've just cleaned out this nest of rats, and you want to give it back?'

'All Followers of Olga must be at The River tonite. The signs are right.'

Tinker raised his finger and opened his mouth to argue, but he saw the reverence and instant obedience of the buckeyes around

181

him. He held his tongue. The blademen withdrew from shaft base.

'Giving the city back . . .' mumbled Tinker. He returned to the forges. Coweyes had sewn more bellows and gathered wood from the orchards. Tinker instructed. They built ten more. Burly buck-eyes swung stone hammers and quenched. Blademen increased.

Tinker squinted into the orange coals at the yellow glowing blade.

'Making teeth again?' asked a familiar voice.

Tinker turned and saw a sinewy old man with a wry smile – old man Moon. Beside him was a three-legged dog – Dan-with-the-golden-teeth. New scars had been added to their bodies, but they appeared otherwise little changed from the days on Mount Tabulum.

'Moon— Dan—' said Tinker, waving the glowing blade. He quenched it in a pot of water. Steam jumped. He walked over to his old friends.

'Making teeth again?' repeated Moon.

Tinker nodded. 'Teeth for an army, this time.'

Old Moon glanced around, rubbing his hands together eagerly.

'So you finally decided to strike back at the Big ES? Looks like you have a good start,' said Moon, glancing at the shaft cap with disabled doors. 'Need a couple of good men?'

Dan detected the fighting blood rising in his master's voice. The beast squinted about, ears down – but saw no danger.

What Tinker saw was not a soldier – just an old man – a very old man – and his dog.

'Sure, Moon,' he said smiling. 'We can use you. Come, meet Mu Ren. We can talk while we eat.' He didn't say – 'and rest.' It would have offended Moon; just because he had walked 2,000 miles . . .

The broth was thin. The baby was hungry. Moon noticed.

'Here, add these to the soup. Some little nibblers I carry when I travel. Cut them off a hunter who mistook me for an easy trophy.'

He dropped some stringy brown fragments into the soup. It

immediately darkened and tasted like food. Tinker Junior stopped fretting after two bowls.

After Tinker filled Moon in on their quasi-superstitious reasons for being there, Moon asked about Toothpick.

'Toothpick and Moses are commanding the forces to the north. They have about a hundred Agromecks – and seem to have the skills to repair them. I've never seen so many technical caste members before.'

Moon got to his feet, Dan perked up.

'You're not staying the night?'

'No,' said Moon. 'I've got Toothpick's butt in my pocket. I've got to return it to him. He might be needing it.'

He pulled out a short cylinder. It had an optic and several color indicators.

Tinker escorted Moon and Dan to the edge of their camp.

'Where did Dan get that star on his chest?'

'An arrow. Went clean through the posterior mediastinum and stuck into the third lumbar vertibra. Got the anterior spinal artery. Motor out to tail and left leg. Autonomies and sensory OK. The toes on his left foot finally fell off, but he gets along fine. I was really worried about his bladder and bowel for a long time. But they came back. The supply area for the anterior spinal artery doesn't supply the sacral autonomies, you know.'

Tinker nodded. As they talked he absently drew a cross section of the spinal cord showing the three horns of gray matter: posterior, sensory; lateral, autonomic; and anterior, motor. Only Dan's anterior horns were gone below the third lumbar, and even that wasn't complete, for his right leg worked pretty good.

'Shaft came out easily in about three weeks,' said old man Moon. 'Arrow head is still in there. Tail hasn't wagged since.' He took the twig Tinker was drawing with and sketched a double-bladed axe.

'If you're going into those shaft cities again, you might try making a bipennis at the forge. About six or seven pounds of metal – whatever feels right when you swing it on a handle as long as your forearm. Those two-headed axes are handy if you have to cut through a lot of – things. Keep one blade keen for the fancy stuff, you know,' he laughed.

Moon was older than Tinker and had seen a lot. The battle that was shaping up seemed to be more than just a struggle for calories. Two hundred years of walking the Earth gave him perspective.

Josephson glanced up at the screen. His troops had retaken the shaft city without a fight. Buckeyes were barricaded in the garage behind heaps of junk. They had a supply of bows and arrows, but the little fifteen-pound bows snapped in the enthusiasm of battle. Frustrated buckeyes leaped the barricades and rushed down two turns of the spiral to drive back any curious Nebish troops. Hip had ordered them to stay on the surface, so their sorties were brief.

'Don't bother to retake the garage,' Josephson ordered. 'Lay down a tanglefoot web of netting, and hold your positions behind it. Try holding on the fourth turn of the spiral.'

The troop leader nodded. Netting was strung.

Josephson tuned in on Huntercraft from White Country. EM interference was heavy.

'We're coming, Josephson. Six craft due in three days. Twelve more about a week later. Only lost two so far.'

'How's the neurocircuitry handling the magnetic storms?'

'Fine. We're on manual, of course. But during the lulls the mecks carry on a very lucid conversation.'

'Manual? Where did you get all the pilots?'

'We're learning on the job— Oh-oh. Number three is in trouble again. I'd better change that prediction to five craft in three days – thirteen a week later. We're trying.'

Josephson checked with other hunter teams. The story was the same – ETA about a week, give or take a couple of days. Craft limped, stopped over for repairs, balked at the EM headaches – and squinted through a variety of cataracts.

Dusk was settling on the camps. Toothpick was restless. Moses carried the little cyberspear to the southwest corner of their camp and climbed the long rock pile.

'My butt is near.'

'The one you left with – Moon?' said Moses excitedly. 'Is he alive? Where—?' He glanced over the rambling camp of buckeyes to the south. For three miles the ground was packed with busy troops and their families. Shelters were up. Small cooking fires smoked. Babies cried.

'There he is,' said Toothpick, flexing his surface membrane and steering his point toward the hunched old man and the long-snouted, three-legged dog in the distance.

Moses shouted and waved.

Old Moon didn't say much. He was glad to see them, of course, but he wasn't much for words.

'Here's your butt,' he said, handing Toothpick the ten-centimeter section of tubing from his thicker, base end.

Toothpick accepted it – locking it on with a click.

'Old man with dog – welcome. How is your wound?'

Old Moon scratched the puckered scar in the left upper quadrant of his abdomen. 'It tells me when it's going to rain. Otherwise it is fine. Drained a helluva long time though. Must have gotten my colon and my lungs because I was spitting up feces for about three months.'

Toothpick consulted his scanty anatomy charts.

'Unlikely,' said the cyber. 'Colon, yes – lungs no. But the coliform organisms from the bowel could have spread to your pleural space giving your sputum a purulent-fecal odor.'

Old Moon lifted his left shoulder, demonstrating how much mobility was left.

'Still as good a man as I ever was,' he growled. His golden teeth glinted in the sunset. His frame carried a bit more meat – he had been eating well. Dan looked well enough too. With the left leg ending at the tarsus, his trunk and right leg had added muscle for the three-legged gait.

'I just came from Hip's camp. Talked with Tinker and his mate. Their big problem seems to be food,' said Moon.

'Same here.'

'But you've cracked a couple of shaft caps. You've got troops and mecks . . .'

'The Big ES has cut off supplies to these cities. Their own citizens starve,' explained Moses.

'Let's attack the Big ES.'

Moses recoiled at old man Moon's suggestion.

'You don't mean invade the hive?'

'Yes, dammit! Invade the hive. Take troops into the spirals and tubeways – rout out those little white grubs who have taken away our planet – rout them out and barbecue 'em,' said the old man with gusto.

Young, sensitive Moses winced at the harsh words.

'But the Hip doesn't want to make war. His reason for being here is tied to his religion – planetary conjunctions, and all that.'

'The Hip!' sneered old Moon. 'He may be the Hip to you, but he's just the Ass at Tabulum to me. Anyone who would take advantage of a poor, simple people with tricks of magic and start a religion so he doesn't have to get out and scratch for his own calories – he's just an ass.'

Moses soothed – 'Now, now. Looking after thousands of hungry people is no easy task. I know. I've got a lot of hungry followers myself. And right now we all could use a little food.'

Moon cursed, 'Hell, there is always plenty of food around. Lend me a squad of bowmen and I'll get you all you can eat.'

'But I told you – there is no food in these shaft cities. The Nebishes themselves are starving.'

Old Moon smiled the same wicked smile Moses had seen in the cave after his Climb.

'Of course it won't be properly aged.'

Moses felt a little limp. Well, if matters had come to that – he would still try to survive. He waved at the bowmen resting against Tiller's chassis. The sun had set. Only a pale blue glow marked the western horizon.

'Men,' he said. 'Old Moon and his dog Dan are going to take you on a little hunting expedition – for Nebishes.' They nodded. Night or day, it made little difference in the hive.

Moon walked to the head of the squad. 'We'll be bringing the meat back, so pick the young healthy-looking ones,' he said callously.

One of the bowmen – young, with a few whiskers and a granular white scar on his scalp where some skin tumor had been erased at Dundas – spoke hesitantly.

'Meat, sir? We'll be eating – them?'

'Look, sonny, you don't have to come,' said Moon. 'But I'd like

186

to remind you that those protein bars you've been eating on the trek were from the patient in the next coffin who didn't make it. Ever since you've awoke you've been a cannibal. Everyone on this fool planet is. There's no other meat.'

The piebald youngster took a half a protein bar out of his pocket and looked questioningly at Moses. Moses nodded sadly.

'Just processed a little – but still human protein.'

The squad marched off behind Dan and Moon.

Hip checked his beads and charts by the firelight. Then he carried his crystal ball up onto the tallest rock he could find between the armies. Bright stars winked out of a coal-black sky. The lunar disc had not yet risen. Hip began his chants and prayers. They spread through both camps. Soon ten square miles reverberated with praise to Olga.

Ball pulsed brightly – reds, blues and then a glaring white light. The armies quieted down – awe-struck. Hip studied the heavens expectantly. The aurora fluttered on without a change. Stars blinked silently. Several stars did not blink – Moses was sure these were the so-called wandering stars – planets. The silence dragged out. In the east the lunar disc attracted their attention for a while. Then Ball darkened. Hip mumbled that the signs were not quite right – tomorrow night he'd try again.

Disappointment spread through the camps. Tinker led a band of blademen into the dark perimeter. They took a Tiller through the circle of foam and raided distant gardens. A token raid, it brought back only scant calories – unnoticed by the hungry masses – but it did show that such a raid was possible. At dawn they were still in the foam when the Huntercraft approached – about twenty of them – gleaming bright hulls at one-thousand-feet elevation. Hatches opened and a shower of arrows rained on Tiller. They dismounted and walked in under the massive chassis.

'Shields up,' shouted Moses as the squadron passed over, raining arrows. Most of the shafts plunked into the ground. The only injuries were minor. Gravity simply was not an effective accelerator for the light arrows.

The squadron attempted a turn. Two craft collided in the air and crashed in a canal. The others scattered.

'Not too bright,' commented Hugh. He stood while a platoon of buckeyes pulled the craft from the waters. The Nebish crews were quickly and mercifully dispatched. One craft looked serviceable to Tinker.

'They must have been on manual – shooting from the craft isn't allowed when meck brains are flying. You're right – not too bright. It takes training to fly one of these,' said Tinker.

Dust covers were up all morning while Tinker moved parts from one machine to the other. He put it on manual and removed the antenna.

'Good craft – look at that optic acuity. We might learn a lot if we take her up and reconnoiter. Send a runner to Moses and see if he and Toothpick want to survey the battlefield from a mile up.'

Tinker went back to work. The power cell from the inoperative craft was charged in a garage and spliced into the conductive web of the operative ship. He lined up four bowmen and four blademen to come along. Moses arrived about noon.

Tinker handled the controls like a professional. His shakedown cruises for Hunter Control made him the best pilot in the area. The bipennis under his seat made him the best-armed. Moses hung onto his seat as they swept low over their troops. Buckeyes waved their shaggy heads from the hatches. This brought cheers from below.

They surveyed their armies – half a million strong, counting women and children. Their camp covered a three-mile radius around an intersection of the canal-river bed and the 50:00 border rock pile. Rocky high ground was held by bowmen. Blades and spears held shaft caps – there were ten in camp. The perimeter was dotted by a hundred Agromecks – each about a quarter of a mile apart and each burdened again by bowmen.

Tinker smiled.

'Bowmen on the high ground and Agromecks – spearchuckers and short swords in the shaft caps. We're secure.'

Moses tended to agree. He could see Hugh Konte's platoon moving around the perimeter – daring a Huntercraft to engage them.

From two thousand feet up the viewpoint changed. The sea of Agrifoam ebbed and flowed for an additional three miles – an area four times that occupied by the army. The Big ES could just as easily blanket a ten- or a hundred-mile radius. As they climbed, their egos shrank. Shaft caps marched endlessly to the circumference of the Earth, it seemed – thousands, tens of thousands.

A hive Huntercraft approached awkwardly. Tinker circled it. The viewplates were opaque from the outside. He checked the communicator frequencies. Nothing.

'Let's try and shoot it down,' said Tinker, enthusiastically. 'I want three of you bowmen to kneel down under the ceiling hatch and shoot when I open the hatch.'

He maneuvered under the craft and put his hand on the manual hatch control. The other craft's airstream buffeted him about.

'Now!' he shouted, pulling back the lever. The hatch opened to whirling blades. A fusilade of arrows clinked. Tinker banked hard right. The hive craft wobbled off, spitting parts. It landed in a grove of fruit trees.

Tinker swooped down to examine the stricken craft.

'Look at the way it landed,' he cheered. 'Right on a tree trunk. It'll never fly again. Shall we set down and polish off the crew?'

Moses studied the terrain.

'We're ten miles from our camp.'

'So? We don't have to set down. Say! A couple of you fellows buckle on a harness. I'll swing you right down on the roof. You can hack open the hatch and dice up the Nebish crew. No problems.'

Moses glanced at Toothpick. No admonition. He nodded.

Tinker held her steady while the *coup de grace* was administered by the two harnessed blademen. Their craft ran smoothly. Moses kept a sharp lookout.

'Huntercraft!' warned Toothpick.

The foliage blocked their view of most of the sky, but Moses feared the worst. Toothpick squeaked and tried to estimate range and number.

'Hurry up down there.'

'Don't you want a head for a souvenir?'

'No.'

'Twenty craft. Closing fast,' said Toothpick.

Tinker reeled in the blademen as he lifted off.

'Try a run for it,' suggested Moses. He pointed Toothpick out the window. The little cyberspear sparked menacingly.

The squadron passed overhead at two thousand feet, and then peeled out of formation one at a time to track in single file.

'We've picked them up, that's for sure,' said Tinker banking sharply.

The tracking craft closed after his right-angle turn by crossing the hypoteneuse.

'They aren't blundering into each other,' said Moses.

Tinker squinted through the craft's optic set at 10 X magnification.

'Those craft are from Orange Country.'

Tinker flipped open the communicator. Val's face appeared. They eyed each other bitterly.

'Still fly pretty good,' said Val.

'Doing all right,' said Tinker, climbing.

'Let's see how good you are,' challenged Val. The screen went dead. One of the Huntercraft left formation and tracked fast. The others broke off contact and scattered at low altitudes.

Tinker tried to get under the hive craft for a bowshot at the blades, but it dove to tree-top level. Hatches opened several times and Tinker's hands felt the *tick, tick, tick* of arrows striking the hull. Three of the other craft returned abruptly and triangulated on him, closing fast. When he tried for escape altitude the hive craft flew under him and began plinking arrows at his blades.

'They certainly learn fast,' said Tinker. His forehead was dampening. He darted off on a zigzag course.

Toothpick flickered coherent light beams at the pursuing craft's view ports hoping to bleach out a few retinas. The craft hesitated and then turned back. Tinker raced for his camp. The hive squadron formed up again and flew high over the fugitive army dropping a couple of tons of building blocks. Again, they were easy to avoid, and casualties were light.

The perimeter patrols reported three enemy squadrons, over fifty Huntercraft, sighted. There had been only one skirmish – a food column through the Agrifoam was broken up.

'More craft today. Still no concerted attacks. They're probably building up their forces now, trying to starve us. When they're stronger, they'll attack,' said Tinker.

Moses nodded.

'And we really can't attack them effectively on foot. Those are Huntercraft assembling out there. They must be about ten miles away – watching us.'

Hugh returned from patrol and walked up smiling. He had a generous hunk of boiled meat in a platter of tiny vegetable flakes.

'At least we don't have to worry about food, anymore. This guy Moon has a regular food train over there.'

Tinker and Moses approached the shaft cap where Moon and the squad of bowmen had entered the night before. Buckeyes and fugitives from Dundas filed in empty-handed and came out carrying sides and quarters of red-yellow meat. Trails of pink drippings marked the passing of thousands of meat porters. Nothing looked human to Moses. He thought he'd better investigate.

He found the porter lines ran all the way downspiral to shaft base. Crawlways and cubicles were silent. Moon and the bowmen had set up a blind at the tubeway entrance. Using crude harpoons with thin cables, they were spearing Nebishes right off the tubes. The impact of the harpoon head usually stilled their victims – if not, the brief drawing and quartering did.

Moon shouted instructions to a score of busy coweyes.

'Get those heads and entrails back in the tubeways. Be neat. I want every bit of skin off – hands and feet too. We mustn't offend the cooks.'

'What about this little one. Shall I throw it back?'

'If it's still alive. If it isn't, don't let it go to waste.'

Old Moon smiled when he saw Moses.

'How we doing?'

'Wonderful,' said Moses, without enthusiasm. 'Wonderful. But you're going to have to knock off for a while. The Hip is having another ceremony tonite. He wants all his people around him.'

'The Ass at Tabulum—' mumbled Moon.

Moses changed the subject.

'We captured a nice Huntercraft today. Tinker has it running smoothly. We took a look around. Huntercraft are gathering outside the foam.'

191

'It figures,' said Moon, wiping his hands. 'There is enough meat here for the guys on the spiral. Let's knock off, you guys. Get your asses back to the Hip. He's having one of his mystic fits again.'

Moon and Moses walked upspiral while Dan munched on a hand.

The orange glow of forges created an eerie background for Hip's chants. The fugitives from Dundas found tons of soft iron in the garages – old meck energy converters. It was soft enough to fashion quickly into the double-headed bipennis and the twenty-inch short sword, it was hard enough to hold an edge through a hundred Nebishes.

Moses, Moon and Tinker sat in the cabin of their Huntercraft listening to a hive entertainment channel while Hip ranted and raved in the distance.

'Are the patrols doubled tonite?' asked Moses.

'Hugh saw to it,' said Tinker. 'He's a regular little organizer. His patrol squads contain men from both camps – brawn and brains, he says.'

A song drifted over the camp—

> *We will gather at the river.*
> *We will gather at the river.*
> *We will gather at the river—*
> *The wonderful river of Love.*

Both Moon and Tinker sneered. Moses occupied himself with the communicator – tuning in on random channels – getting a lot of static.

'Try 83.6,' suggested Toothpick.

Moses tuned in on Josephson's eager face.

'Hi,' said Moses. 'What are you doing here?'

Josephson looked sheepish. 'Just conducting a Hunt for you. All of you.'

Moon and Tinker crowded behind him.

'A Hunt?'

'A really Big Hunt,' said Josephson, a little pride showing.

'He means to kill us all,' said Tinker.

Josephson glanced up at Tinker.

'I'm afraid that's right. A job is a job. My job is to get you.'

Tinker laughed and changed the channel back to light musicals.

'Let's not get to know our enemy too well. We may not be able to kill him when we meet.'

'Try 21.9,' said Toothpick.

Tinker raised an eyebrow and turned the dial. Val's face appeared. He was wearing dark glasses.

'Who's there?' asked Val. Behind him a very fat man stood up – fat Walter.

'Tinker here!'

Val smiled his cynical best. 'Got bad news for you Followers of Olga. You've come to the river at the wrong time.'

'How so?'

'There's no conjunction. Jupiter is alone in Sagittarius,' explained Val, groping for his collection of beads. 'Our astrologers have analyzed your bead sequence – now stop me if I'm wrong, but it shows a ringed bead over here. Saturn, right?'

Tinker nodded – caring little about the occult side of their armies' existence. He was here to fight and survive. Winning the favor of the gods was Hip's job.

Val continued: 'There are four other beads together in this part of the string. The big one we guess to be Jupiter. Jupiter and Saturn happen to be about fifty-five degrees apart on the zodiac now. That much is fine. But those other bright lights that are wandering around in Sagittarius are just space junk. We've found Venus and Mercury. They're in Gemini with the sun. Mercury is actually going into transit the day after tomorrow, if you're interested. Mars is off somewhere too – about a hundred degrees out of Sagittarius. Uranus is way over in Pisces. So your beads are all wrong.'

Moses wrote down Val's information and gave it to a runner to take to Hip. It might help.

Tinker called over Val's shoulder to fat Walter.

'Is he right, Walter?'

Walter nodded. 'That craft you are sitting in has good optics.

Ask it to check these positions tonite. Our own *Bird Dog IV* made these sightings.'

Hip just smiled at Val's zodiacal diagram. He strung a new sequence of beads and sent it back to Moses. Then he returned to his chants. He knew little of astronomy – Ball designed the beads.

'Looks like he just added two white beads for Mars and Uranus,' said Moses. 'His conjunction of four planets is the same.'

Their captive Huntercraft turned its optics upwards. They leaned on the screen, quickly confirming Val's words.

'Jupiter, Saturn and Mars are where Val said,' observed Moses. 'We're too late for Uranus tonite. Mercury and Venus won't be visible until dawn. Looks like the beads are wrong.'

Tinker shrugged. 'So what? Were you expecting a miracle?'

Moses didn't know.

The aurora pastels flared – blue, banana and avocado. Hip screamed his chants. Sweating in dance, they sang words of Love and Freedom.

'Now those crazy fools are dropping their weapons,' complained old Moon bitterly.

'It is what they came for – ceremony, prayers—' explained gentle Moses. Toothpick had no comment.

'But their stupid frenzy is spreading to our people from Dundas. Everybody is dropping their weapons. They look like they are going to dance till they drop. Who will fight off the hunters tomorrow?' said Moon. 'Who will defend them?'

The answer drifted over the camps: 'Love will save us. Olga is love. Love will save us.'

Suddenly Toothpick shouted: 'Take me Outside.'

Puzzled, Moses carried him out.

'Hold me up.'

'Why?'

'I don't know why, just point me to the sky and shut your eyes – oooh!'

Toothpick convulsed. His skin tickled Moses' hand. From his nose a beam of pure white light penciled into the dark sky. It was near midnight and Sagittarius was directly overhead. Old Moon stood in the Huntercraft, puzzled. A similar pencil of light issued from Ball. A small meteor crossed the sky – a long white scratch on ebony. Another meteor, then another. Then there were hundreds of tiny white and yellow scratches, hardly more than faint curlicues that faded as fast as they appeared.

Ten miles away in the Huntercraft camp, Val and Walter watched the sky.

'Tiny meteors,' commented fat Walter.

'And I'll bet some superstitious troglodyte in that camp is attributing all the fireworks to Olga,' scoffed Val.

'I suppose,' said Walter. 'Listen to this pickup from the shaft cap. They're singing those old songs we heard on the tightbeam.'

'It will be their last night to sing,' said Val. 'Tomorrow another hundred Huntercraft arrive. We'll have enough to take them.'

Double-bladed axes, short swords, and metal spear points had proliferated in the camp. Dawn found the troops unarmed and exhausted from the night's ceremonial dancing. Weapons were scattered everywhere, dusty and underfoot. The perimeter guards were armed, though; and when the first enemy craft appeared the rest of the army sobered fast and rearmed themselves. White-suited archers marched up spirals. Huntercraft darted back and forth spraying arrows.

Josephson talked to the CO, requesting aid.

'You'll have to handle it at the local level,' said the CO. 'There are similar uprisings on most of the land masses. A million or so buckeyes are involved. That should be no problem for a planet with over three trillions. Use the manual overrides, but handle it locally.'

A heavy spear struck his craft. The metal point penetrated the hull, releasing a trickle of blue fluid. An idiot light went on. He left the battlefield for an emergency landing.

Tinker led his company into a shaft cap to clean up a group of hunters. He advanced downspiral swinging his bipennis. Heads rolled. Axemen and blademen followed him across shaft base and into the tubeways. They chopped into the walls and machinery. A bolus of bodies jammed the tube. They moved through the stilled tunnel to the next shaft cap and charged upspiral trapping a unit of hunters against the garage doors. When he finally fought his way back out into the sunlight it was early afternoon. His right arm was tired. He had a minor arrow wound in his left wrist. A coweye bound it. He returned to Mu Ren and napped.

Hugh Konte woke him up an hour later.

'Tinker! Moses and Hip are having some sort of a meeting in the rocks. We shot down a couple of Huntercraft, and a few more crashed. Toothpick recognized some of the emblems. They are from all over the continent. More arrive by the hour. Troops keep arriving in the tubeways too. I guess we're going to have to do something.'

Tinker picked up his axe and followed Hugh to the meeting. Hip was depressed. 'Last night was supposed to be the conjunction. Today we were supposed to be safe in the arms of Olga,' he said.

Tinker glanced around at the gathering of group leaders. Most bore wounds. One was a female coweye. In the distance he heard the drone of gathering Huntercraft.

'Something has to be done now. Why don't I take a couple of Agromecks and blademen and attack their camp?' said Tinker.

'No good,' said Moses. 'They'll have nearly five hundred Huntercraft by tomorrow – maybe more. Five or ten Agromecks would get eaten alive. They'd be of more use on the perimeter.'

Hip held up Ball. 'The reason I called this meeting was – my crystal ball has stopped glowing. All it says now is: "Take me to their leader." It doesn't talk about Olga anymore.'

'Talk?' said Tinker.

'Well, I heard voices when I put my hands on it. Not with my ears – with my – head. I think,' said Hip.

Ball sat there, a dull opaque.

Tinker picked it up. A voice told him to go into the hive and find the leader of the Nebishes. He put down the sphere and the voices went away. Odd.

'It wants me to take it into the hive,' he said, smiling.

Moses picked it up, heard nothing, and passed it around the circle. It spoke only to Hip and Tinker. Hugh stood and addressed the group.

'If we stay and fight here, they'll just wear us down. Outnumbering us the way they do – a million to one. But we have a good chance to knock out their nerve center. If it is located in any one of these shaft cities you can see how easy it should be. If Ball knows where to find their leader, Tinker and I could take a strike force and try to knock it out. Maybe even take it over. Tinker's good with meck brains.'

'It's a chance – a good one,' said Tinker.

Hip and Tinker moved through their camps quietly asking for volunteers. They turned down many buckeyes and most of the fugitives from Dundas. Only the best-armed and best-muscled would have a chance of surviving the foray.

The acromegalic held his stout spear in two hands – a quarterstaff for the shaft and a broad iron spearhead at one end. He volunteered.

Tinker shook his head.

'No, gentle giant – your weapon is no good for the close quarters we'll be fighting in – and your joints will slow you down if we have to do any running.'

Mu Ren stood sadly by, clutching Junior – her belly bulging. She had pleaded with Tinker – trying to keep him near her and their son. But she saw the logic of trying to knock out the hive's cybercenter. Hundreds of her friends had died in the day's brief encounter with the hive forces – and each day they would face the same thing. A larger hive force attacking a weakening buckeye camp. Several family groups had tried to escape through the Agrifoam – only to be tracked by Huntercraft. She doubted if any got through – to return to the safety of mountain strongholds. No, she didn't ask Tinker to call off his attack. She cried a little as he left.

Hip spoke to the assembled strike force – five squads, axe; five, short spear; and twenty, short sword – about two hundred men.

'Make this planet worthy of Olga's return,' he said solemnly – handing Ball to Tinker. 'Free us from the hive.'

'Free us,' chanted the gathered multitude. Tinker looked over the gaunt faces and bandaged ragged bodies. Few were unwounded. In a short time few would be alive, if his mission failed. He raised his bipennis.

'I have sharpened both blades of my axe. One is for the

Nebishes who stand in my way – the other blade I am saving for the enslaving meck mind that runs the hive.'

Cheers.

A hundred spearchuckers ran eagerly into the shaft city to clear a path to the tubeways. The strike force could rest until it reached the heart of the hive.

Tinker stood with Ball under one arm, axe in the other, and watched his men file in – an elite unit. Marching out of step in the rear was an old man and a three-legged dog – Moon and Dan. Moon carried his stained blade, already well-worn by countless skirmishes. Tinker touched the old man's sinewy arm.

'Sorry, Moon, you won't be going. Only the fast, young—'

Moon snarled and pulled his arm away.

'Why you young pup! I've been carving up the Nebish since before you were born. Do you think I want to sit out here with the women and children while you're in there where all the fighting is?'

Moses and Hugh approached truculent old Moon. Toothpick spoke up: 'Stay with us on the surface, old man with dog. Tinker goes to fight microcircuits and soft-bellied technicians.'

'Yes,' said Hugh. 'Tomorrow the armies of the hive will be on the surface. Fighting will be hand-to-hand. You and Dan will be needed here – not in the dark mushroom caves of the hive.'

Old Moon relaxed and took his fist out of Tinker's face. Tapping him lightly on the shoulder with his knuckles, he fumbled for an appropriate curse – 'Good luck, you dirty—' He searched for the right word. None came. 'Kill a circuit for me,' he said finally.

Tinker trotted downspiral to the head of his unit.

'Let's hurry. If we knock out the hive's cybercenter before dawn, the battle here on the surface may go easier on our people.'

Watcher circuits tracked the army's progress through the tubes. Val and his personal hunter unit were tubed to intercept. They studied Tinker's route. The buckeyes used regular passenger tubeways, carving up enough of the citizen crowd to gain standing room. Val checked the locations of his underground hunter units. He called for traffic control.

'Reroute hunter unit 32-5K into shaft base #47-B3 and tell

them to nock arrows. I'll pull manual stop from here,' shouted Val.

Ball eavesdropped. 'Blades up. Eyes right,' said a voice in Tinker's head. He issued the orders sharply. One minute later the right wall of the tubeway opened unexpectedly and a force of hunters – two hundred strong – pulled back their bowstrings. They were not prepared for the instant rush of blade-swinging buckeyes. Arrows wobbled and stuck in gristle over shoulder and skull. Twenty seconds later Tinker's troops moved on.

Val cursed and pulled levers. He flooded several shafts and tubeways, but the buckeyes stayed dry.

'Damn! Can't you give me better sequence charts than these?' he shouted at the meck console.

A traffic controller stood nervously behind Val.

'The charts are in order, sir,' explained the controller. 'You just have to be familiar with the symbols and signs. That is a pretty specialized field.'

'Well, call someone in who can handle these controls. I want that band of killers stopped.'

The tubeway halted again. The buckeyes hacked their way forward through a crowd of complacent hive citizens. Some died before they were even touched. Others stood along the walls, unconcerned, and uninvolved – wrapped up in their private little dreams.

'God! What mindless bastards!' said Tinker, wiping his blade.

A giant sphincter door blocked the tube. Axes began to swing. The door was three feet thick.

'Go around,' said Ball through Tinker's mouth. 'Cut the right wall.'

The wall peeled away under the blades – exposing bundles of wires and pulsating conduits. Thick mats of dust caked their bare feet as they traversed the 'tween walls. Rats blinked out of the darkness. Fetid odors brought tears to their eyes. When they hacked back into the tubeway they faced a Security force of five hundred.

'Why, they're just armed with quarterstaffs!' exclaimed the first buckeye through the gap. He swung his sword, making room for those who followed. Nets were thrown, fouling his blade. Hi Vol injectors quieted his struggles with Molecular Reward.

The Security guard at the far end of the tubeway section reported to Val over his communicator. Val's face was more confident now that he had sphincter control.

'I think we can hold them here, sir. They are 'tween walls. When they try to cut their way back in here we can be ready for them.'

Tinker peered out of the moldy darkness.

'Can we go around this section?'

'Negative, sir,' said the scout. 'The next sphincter is at a weight-bearing wall.'

Tinker and his troops crawled over and around the segment of tubeway. The weight-bearing walls that hemmed them in were composed of several yards of stone and steel. Security held the tubeway. Their Hi Vol injectors had a range of only a foot or so. But that was enough to make hand-to-hand combat impossible in such crowded quarters.

Tinker carefully sliced into several cables. A maze of color-coded wires ballooned out – too numerous to analyze by a random search. Sphincter controls had to be taken inside. He followed struts to the ceiling and peered down at Security through darkened air vents. The ceiling sagged under the weight of his men. He studied stress lines for a moment.

'Where do we cut in again?' asked an eager blademan.

'The roof,' said Tinker, swinging his axe. He parted a cable. The false ceiling cracked and shifted.

The anxious Security guards milled around under a rain of chips as ominous teethmarks crept across the ceiling. A jagged slab sailed down, slicing into the guard. Sewage spewed from a nicked pipe. Screaming their battle cries, the buckeyes turned vicious, throwing down everything they could lay their hands on. Slabs, struts, bolts and short spears crunched into the guards. Rose-water blood mixed with foul sewage. Indole and skatole choked bronchi.

Tinker opened the sphincter manually. The communicator stood alone – spattered with nondescript drippings. Val's voice called repeatedly.

'Are you there, Security? Hello. Hello.'

Tinker scowled into the optic, waving his bipennis.

'I'm coming for you, Val,' he threatened. 'I'm saving this blade for you.'

With the skill that comes from practice, Tinker swung the gleaming axe blade deftly past the optic – scratching the lens. A second teasing cut admitted air and clouded the retina. Val watched, nervously – his cremasters tightened.

'Send for Dag Foringer,' said Val.

Tinker's men staggered into the next shaft station lopping off Watcher optics. A squad of Security blundered into the axemen walking point and were dismembered. Several of the naked buckeyes squatted down beside an eviscerated guard to eat the liver. Others began to divide up a couple of citizens. Tinker looked at the watery, gray liver being passed around.

'That may fill you up, but it won't ease the hunger pangs – too deficient in the MDR. Protein-poor protoplasm. Stick to the browner livers of their best hunters,' he advised.

'It fills you up, but you get hungry right away . . .' repeated a young buckeye. He gave away his soft tan meat and chopped into a shaft base dispenser for calories – scant flavors there too. Crowds began to fill the spiral.

While his blademen scattered the Nebish citizens and secured the spiral, Tinker sat down with Ball to map out their route. He drew in the pasty grit on the floor.

'We're here. The nerve center of the hive is over here – still a hundred miles away. Ball thinks that there are two fast routes. The passenger tubeway, which we are on now; and this freight tube over by the sewer line. The sewer line drains into digesters under the Coweye Sump near the nerve center. If we take the center, we control the mecks of the hive.'

The buckeyes nodded eagerly.

'I'm coming for your head, Val,' shouted Tinker, waving his axe. Watcher circuits relayed the message. Val sweated.

Two thousand Security guards marched into the tubeways.

'Ten to one,' smiled Val. He closed sphincters again.

The tubeway halted.

'Still thirty miles to go,' cursed Tinker.

His men formed a wedge – axes in front – and chopped their way slowly through a dense crowd. As they reached the sphincter it opened. A solid wall of guards surged in on them carrying Hi Vol injectors. The drugs darted around catching Nebish and buckeye alike. Tinker withdrew, letting the Nebish crowd flow back into the path of the guard. The wedge turned right and cut its way out of the tubeway.

Buckeyes – wounded, drugged and dazed – crawled 'tween walls for darkness and solitude.

> Mushroom liked it chocolate, cool.
> Dampness soothed his aching cap.
> He sent his toes into the grime,
> Searching for nutritious pap.
> His basidium fingers curled tight,
> Pinching spores into tiny balls.
> His photophobic catatonia ended,
> When Mushroom died between the walls.

Tinker's force ran into the freight station swinging blades. Nebish heads rolled. The traffic meck told them which lanes were open to Cybercenter. They programmed freight capsules, sending ten men in each. Tinker traveled in number five.

'See you at the next station,' he shouted, closing the hatch. He braced himself for the dark, rough ride. Webbing provided handholds. Ball tried to glow. Only a feeble, eerie light resulted. Sudden blind turns threw men and weapons against the walls.

Acceleration. Deceleration. A jerky stop.

Tinker braced himself – axe ready. It wouldn't surprise him if Val's damned efficiency had arranged an armed welcome. When the hatch opened he saw the smiling faces of his own men.

'We made it,' they shouted. 'How much time do we have?'

Tinker held Ball.

'Plenty of time,' he mouthed. 'The nerve center is right above us – about a quarter of a mile.'

Tinker glanced around the station. Freight capsules popped in and out of tubes – tracks and dollies were all over. Near the far wall Nebish crews went about their chores sluggishly. Closer,

Nebish bodies lay in their own blood. Tinker's crew numbered less than a hundred now. Most had minor wounds. Some assisted others who were dazed by Molecular Reward.

'Let's go upspiral,' he shouted enthusiastically.

Bowmen held the spiral against them. Arrows plinked at the doorways to the station, pinning them inside.

'Bring up that dolly,' shouted Tinker.

A pile of crates offered them a shield. They pushed it ahead of them, upspiral. Arrows chunked into the soft syntheboards. The squads of hive bowmen backed up slowly, showing a surprising degree of discipline.

'Now!' said Val from his control room.

Dag Foringer pulled a lever. His fingers danced over buttons that turned valves in a dozen pipes. Irrigation waters drained downshaft collecting drinking water and sewage as they flowed. Ball twitched nervously. Flood! Flood! The words rang in Tinker's head.

The wall of water spilled out onto the spiral collecting citizens and drowning them immediately. Bowmen were swept up. The roar became deafening. The bolus of bodies crunched into Tinker's dolly, smashing and crushing. Waves swept them back out into the freight station. Heavy iron weapons were dropped as the water level surged upwards.

Ball was swept out of his hands. The last words he heard from the sphere were not encouraging – 'All is lost, all is lost. Flee! Flee!'

Ball swirled off on a choppy wave flecked with bodies.

The buckeyes tried to swim – keeping familiar shaggy heads in view. The flood swept them up against the giant sewer gratings. The force of the waters pinned them to the two-inch gauge, eighteen-inch mesh. Tinker tried to swim up to the surface repeatedly. A dizzying whirlpool vortex sucked him back to the grating. Exhausted, he fell through. One by one his battered men followed.

'Good work,' said Val, patting Dag's shoulder. They checked the scanners – nothing. The freight station was clear. Dollys and capsules were piled on the sewer grating with a jumble of stained bodies.

'Now we can get back to the buckeye camp. What time is it?'

'Two hundred hours,' said Dag.

'We'll attack at dawn. Want to come on a Big Hunt?'

Val took his personal guard back to the Huntercraft camp. The three hundred miles from Cybercenter were covered in less than two hours by tubeway. Tracks of the buckeyes remained – blood stains and weapons. Sweepers and repair crews were busy.

Fat Walter waved him into their group.

Val practically beamed as he reported the smashing of the buckeye strike force.

'You should have seen their faces – struggling in the whirlpool,' he laughed.

Walter was serious.

'I've done some calculating,' mumbled Walter. 'The wizard from Mount Tabulum may have been right after all. Look at these diagrams.'

He projected the solar system on the screen. The sun was in the center. The signs of the zodiac around the circumference.

'Geocentrically both Venus and Mercury are in Gemini. But they are on the same side of the sun as we are – so,' and he pointed to the diagram, 'heliocentrically they are in Sagittarius.'

Val scowled. 'You're just a frustrated Follower of Olga – trying to see her hand in everything.'

'But the beads—' protested Walter.

Val sighed and studied the beads again.

'OK' challenged Val. 'So you managed to get Mercury and Venus into Sagittarius; but the beads show four planets – Jupiter – and?'

'Earth.'

'Earth?' exploded Val. 'We aren't in any sign!'

'Heliocentrically we are – we are part of a four-planet con-junction.'

'But who can stand on the sun to see it?'

'Olga,' said Walter.

Val threw up his hands.

'I won't be going over the buckeye camp tomorrow. I can't attack a Follower of Olga – even a five-toed one,' asserted fat Walter.

Val sat down weakly.

'That's fine with me, old man. I was going to suggest just that very thing. We'll be going in on foot after the preliminary attacks. It might be dangerous for a man in your condition.'

'You seem pretty confident,' said Walter – suspicious.

Val smiled wickedly.

'I've cleared it with the CO. We are going to tightbeam self-destruct orders to the buckeyes' Agromecks, and put up energy fields on the shaft caps. That should isolate them outside and panic them. We have over three thousand Huntercraft massed now. Thousands of bowmen will move into the shaft caps behind the fields. It will be like shooting on our own target range.'

Fat Walter tuned in on an audio pickup of the buckeye camp. They were singing their praise of Olga. Walter moved his lips – adding his prayers for their safety.

Hugh carried the recharged power cell from the garage and plugged it back into the damaged Huntercraft. Lights came on.

'That makes five craft that should fly tomorrow,' he said.

Moses sat in one of the cabs checking out the instruments. Toothpick sat in a third trying to reprogram a damaged flight-stabilizer circuit.

Forges blazed up. Work crews dug shelters in the loose soil. Throughout the night the horizon was rimmed by the dancing lights of Huntercraft – waiting till dawn to attack.

Hip walked up. He had spent only a few minutes examining the sky that night, depressed by his failure – Ball's failure – to save his people the night before. He carried a spear discarded by one of the wounded . . . the first weapon his hands had known. He was a little eager to use it.

'There is still a chance,' he said. 'We'll lose some men. But at least we can fight Outside without being drugged. We might even pick up a few more Huntercraft. Our Agromecks give us cover and mobility—'

As if his words were a cue, one of the nearby Huntercraft screamed a countdown and exploded.

'Tightbeam – self-destruct signal,' shouted Toothpick. 'Stand clear of the Agromecks – they're all going to go.'

Less than an hour later the perimeter was marked by smoking hulks and craters. A few buckeyes had been too close. Moses backed his stunned people toward a shaft cap.

'Put bowmen up behind those grills,' he shouted.

The predawn darkness added to the confusion. Comrades were separated. Units broke up. Acrid smoke blinded. The explosions and fires added to the army's hunger and despair. Bellies had been empty too long – the fatty human flesh from the shaft cities did little more than contract gallbladders.

'Bowmen – to the grills,' repeated Moses.

Sparks threw the first bowmen back from the garage doors. The smell of ozone warned them. Moses heard the ominous buzz of a force field leaking energy into the atmosphere.

'Field's on,' warned Toothpick. 'The Big ES has isolated us Outside.'

The other shaft caps began to spark and buzz. Moses watched helplessly as his army crumbled into aimless flight. Random shrieks and moans told of the weak being crushed by the strong.

From the darkness a loud familiar voice shouted confidence.

'Rally to me. Rally to me,' shouted Hip.

A clot of followers formed up behind him and chanted. The clot grew. A widening belt of calm appeared in the turbulent sea of struggling bodies.

Moon picked up Dan to avoid the crush of the crowd.

Toothpick glowed soothingly.

'That's a lot better than the disorder we had a minute ago,' admitted crusty old Moon.

The wind carried back words of a song out of antiquity. If the sunrise could be delayed long enough for them to get reorganized and armed again—

A peculiar glow appeared in the southeast – a pulsing blue dome rose above the horizon. The dome changed from light blue-white to a darker purple. A white halo formed over the glow.

'What is it?'

Hip answered – 'A sign. Olga has sent us a sign. Lay down your arms. We are saved.'

Toothpick wasn't so optimistic. 'The strike force has failed. That was Ball popping his Q-bottle.'

Old Moon stumbled on the clutter of blades and shafts.

'If we could only get these guys to pick up their arms.'

Moses studied the glow on the horizon – a tremor vibrated the ground underfoot.

'What is that white halo?'

'Ionized Nebish,' said Toothpick. 'It must have popped under a shaft city.'

The ground shifted again – harder. The glowing flash dome grew larger, lifting the halo higher.

'Better cover your faces,' warned Toothpick.

8
Tektite Shower

Walter sat in the cabin watching a transmission of sunrise from the east coast. A melon-sized sun showed the cherrystone shadow of Mercury in transit.

'Want to see something pretty – piped in from the sea coast?'

'In a minute,' called Val from the darkness under the craft. He polished contacts and plugged in the web. As he worked the lighting changed.

'Is the sun coming up already?'

Walter didn't answer. The bluish glow in the southeast trans-fixed him.

'Hard thunder. Hard thunder,' warned their craft as it slammed its hatches.

The viewscreen rippled as the sonic boom echoed down on them. Val opened his mouth to ask something when it hit – bouncing him around in a bath of pebbles. Ears rang. Loud silence. He could hear nothing else. Val tried to crawl out from under the craft. Another boom hit. The craft vibrated along the ground, coming to rest on his ankle. The bluish glow grew until it did resemble a sunrise. Then it faded. Night fell again – a predawn night. Val screamed in the silence of deafness. He lay pinned beneath the craft, spitting grit. Shock waves passed under him again and again. He freed his ankle and crawled out. A meteor trail lit the black sky. It impacted in the buckeye camp.

Val covered his face against the bright glare of the meteor impact. The sky was full of bright tracks now. Muffled explosions from more impacts told him he could hear again. He pounded on the craft door. No answer. He pulled it open. The craft's muscle was gone from the hinge. It was dark in the cabin – dash indicators were off. Walter sat wide-eyed facing the viewport. Yellow and orange lights from the meteor shower played across his blank face.

'You all right?' asked Val, touching his shoulder.

'A miracle,' muttered fat Walter.

Val didn't comment. He took his seat at the dead controls. Power cell checked out at full charge. He ran his fingers over the controls – turning everything off. As he opened the switches one by one, the panel lit up again. Glancing out the port he saw a crew trying to right an overturned craft. Other groups of hunters could be seen milling around silent machines.

'A miracle,' repeated Walter.

'We'll see,' said Val.

His was the only craft in flying condition. Something had overloaded circuits and erased meck brains for miles around. Craters dotted the buckeye camp. All he saw were skeletons – human and Agromeck. Piles of bones. Broken bodies scattered along the perimeter – some covered with Agrifoam. Nothing moved except the rising columns of smoke. He circled the camp recording the desolation with the craft's optic banks.

'There's your miracle,' sneered Val. 'Olga has wiped out the buckeyes completely.'

Walter didn't notice.

'Didn't you hear her voice – Olga's voice?'

Val set down beside a smoking Agromeck.

'What voice?'

Walter tried to get the Huntercraft to play it back, but its recent memory was blank. The craft put in a request to the CO to see if any other sensor reported Olga's voice. The CO didn't answer.

'Class Two here,' came the response finally.

'Where's the Class One?' asked Val nervously.

'The meteor destroyed too many of his circuits. His ego did not survive. I will handle his functions until he can be rebuilt,' said the Class Two.

'What meteor?' asked Val.

'A big one. Impacted near the Coweye Sump – formed a new lake about thirty miles in diameter. Many shaft cities collapsed.'

Val was impressed.

'What was your request of the CO?' asked the CT.

'Did you hear Olga's words?' asked Walter eagerly.

'I have snatches of many conversations from all over the globe. This meteor shower hit everywhere. Give me some key words from the message, and I'll try to match them up.'

Walter coughed. The excitement had precipitated a little pulmonary edema and the domino mask of cyanosis had darkened his lips and the skin around his eyes. He tried to remember.

'Children of Olga,' he said haltingly. 'Flaming chariot. Fiery wheels—'

The Class Two retrieved and sorted:

> *By the fiery wheels of Ezekiel*
> *and the flaming chariot of Elias*
> *Will the Children of Olga be delivered*
> *from the hunters' arrows*
> *to dwell in their rightful place*
> *among the stars in the heavens.*

'That's it,' gasped Walter.

Val shuddered. 'Take it easy, old man. Your heart can't take all this excitement. If you're not careful you'll end up joining them in the Land of Olga. Can't you see what it means? They've gone to Olga in death – heaven. They are safe from us there. That's for certain.'

'But Olga's words?' protested Walter.

'Just a random buckeye prayer during the fireworks. They died happy – thinking that Olga had come for them. And, I guess she did. Look at all the bodies,' said Val.

Val left orthopneic Walter resting in his couch while he climbed out to examine the camp on foot. The ground was strewn with Iron-Age weapons, bones, bodies and peculiar glassy particles. He checked buckeye bodies for signs of life – none. He walked down into one of the warm craters and stood on the exposed skin of a cybercity. He picked up fragments of the spongy, rug-like synthesoil – singed. Samples of the soil, glassy particles and a variety of hot rocks were boxed for study later.

The thirty-foot craters just uncovered the city's organs. The fifty-foot craters cracked into them. Val glanced nervously at the yawning black cracks of 'tween walls. He knew they were nearly a mile deep – open all the way to shaft base.

Several other Huntercraft were now operational. They joined him in examining the area. Irrigators washed away the foam, exposing more bodies. Thick-skinned bodies with all the melano-cyte pigments – yellows, reds, browns and blacks. Big-boned bodies – many over six feet tall. Walter wheezed up to Val with his own bone box.

'They're big ones,' he said.

Val nodded. 'I guess when you consider that they're almost two feet taller than we are – on the average – you can label them as tall – abnormally tall.'

Walter noticed the variety of peculiar hot rocks too.

'Tektites,' said Val. 'That was a meteor shower last night, remember?'

For three days Val and a crew of tecks studied the site. Agromecks worked their way in from the perimeter – cultivating and filling in the craters. Finally, they were forced out of their study area by the impatient machines.

On their way back to Orange Country, Val took his wing of Huntercraft southeast to check out the big crater. They spotted it easily – a thirty-mile-wide lake with a serrated rim.

'That rim reminds me of the toothy rim on Mount Tabulum,' said Val. 'Same cause, I guess.'

Old Walter nodded.

The HC meck, Scanner, welcomed them back to Hunter Control. Negative log. No sightings since their departure. The buckeyes were gone.

Val supervised the unloading of artifacts from the 50:00 buck-eye camp – weapons, beads, chewed and charred bones, rocks and glassy particles. Tecks carried off samples to their various departments in HC. Analytical gear was dusted off and warmed up. Most of the bones had the soft, spongy appearance of chalky pâpier-maché – citizens' bones.

'What do you want these checked for?' asked the teck carrying a box of rocks and glass.

Val shrugged. He didn't know what you checked tektites for.

'It was a meteor shower. Search the stacks for tektites. Find out anything you can. How big were they before they entered our atmosphere – how old – where did they originate? Those kind of things,' said Val.

The teck looked puzzled.

'I suppose we could find out some things. We'd have to borrow from Central Lab. How soon do you need it?'

'Take as long as you like,' he said, waving him away.

Walter smiled: 'I don't know what all the scientific fuss is for. It was a miracle – a wonderful miracle.'

Val laughed. 'I just want to find out what kind. A real miracle shouldn't leave fragments like that around. Spiritual tektites should vanish.'

Walter objected: 'But the buckeyes are gone.'

'Maybe. But the census figures were scrambled in all the shaft cities around there. The fireworks could have driven them underground.'

'They can't hide in the Big ES,' said Walter. 'Their stature, pigment and attitude would betray them.'

Val frowned. 'It will be a year before all the cybers are working well again. That big meteor messed up a lot of circuits. I would like to know where the five-toed have gone. Optical records gave a body count of less than ten thousand. There were half a million before the Big Hunt. Cannibalism? Doubt it. Those look like citizen bones to me. Where are the five-toeds?'

'Olga took them to heaven,' said Walter.

'I have an open mind,' sneered Val. 'But before I classify this as a miracle I'll need more than pyrotechnics and a short body count. A deity would be welcome by everyone – if she could help us. We all could use more calories and living space.'

'That is materialistic,' sighed Walter, 'not faith. Olga gives love for love. She rewards faith. But she can't cure all the ills in the world. She isn't omnipotent.'

'A deity with a small *d*,' said Val. 'In that case you might as well pay homage to the hive – earn calories and quarters.'

Walter turned back to his console – quietly mumbling a prayer for Val's soul.

The artifacts from 50:00 were sorted. Sharps Committees indexed the Iron-Age weapons. Buckeye beads were studied by hive astronomers using heliocentric zodiac charts. Biotecks confirmed Val's suspicions about the bones – calcium/collagen ratings were 0.10 on the Grube-Hill scale – citizen bones. Tektites were checked for solar gases and cosmogenic radionuclides. The results did not compute. Flimsy printouts accumulated. More tecks were assigned to the lab and the tests were repeated.

Three more growing seasons passed without a single buckeye sighting. Val checked with hunter units all over the globe. The gardens were safe. HC budgets were cut back. Val found himself working in the Suicide Prevention Center. Walter was retired for reasons of health.

Val was supervising a Sweeper at shaft base. A jumper had managed to land on one of the dispensers. There was quite a mess – transport fluids and all manner of dispenser items mixed in with the usual jumper gore. His communicator buzzed.

'Don at HC labs, sir. I've finished the meteor analysis.'

Val's face was blank. Over six months had passed.

'The 50:00 tektites, sir?'

'Oh, yes. But I thought all the HC departments were closed. What are you doing there?'

'It was taper budget. We were allowed to finish our assignments. Can you drop in and go over these reports? They are rather interesting.'

At shift-change Val ran down to level eighteen. He walked past the huge vats at Biosynthe. A sulfur odor told him the enzymologists were pushing the methionine reaction. Hunter Control was dark. Crates blocked the hallways. Dust was everywhere. He was saddened by the sight of dead Huntercraft – whose brains and converters were in use elsewhere in the hive.

The lab was still lit and clean. Two tecks worked in a small corner. The one called Don rose to greet him.

'These are the reports, sir,' he said. 'You'll notice that we studied them in three stages. Stage one showed that they were indeed carbonaceous chondrites. That means they come from moon or Earth and are composed of peculiar granules – the chondrules. They can occur in showers. None were of the deep-space, nickel-iron type. When we examined them for solar gases we collected the gas at different temperatures. The 800 to 1,000-degree fraction had a solar-type ratio of krypton/neon. Over four. Those gases have a lower ratio in our atmosphere. We also collected solar-type ratios of helium, argon and xenon.'

Val studied the printouts.

'So they were real meteors.'

The teck shook his head.

'Maybe not. The preatmospheric exposure age and the minimum radius can be calculated by the heavy isotopes – the cosmogenic radionuclides. We used gamma-ray spectrometric techniques to find the ratio of cobalt-60/cobalt-59.'

Val nodded: 'The longer it is in space the more neutrons it captures – the more heavy isotope. Right?'

'Right,' said Don. 'Only the ratio was the same as on Earth. We checked sodium, aluminum and manganese too. No increase over the ratios on Earth.'

'Must have been in space a very short time,' concluded Val. 'A very young meteor.'

Don raised his voice.

'Sir, do you know the size of an astrobleme it would take to produce this size meteor shower? There were craters like these on all the major continents. The astrobleme would be as big as Hudson Bay. Most of the old chondrite specimens are millions of years old. These 50:00 tektites are young – a few hundred years at the most. Historical time. Do you think history could forget an impact the size of Hudson Bay?'

'No—' said Val slowly. 'Not on Earth anyway. It could have impacted on the other side of the moon. The hive hasn't looked at the sky for over a thousand years – not in earnest, anyway.'

The teck grinned and produced a globe of the Earth.

'These yellow outlines are buckeye camps the night of the planetary conjunction. The red dots are meteor impacts. Note the clustering around the headwaters of each continent's principle river bed – Mississippi, Nile, Amazon, Ob, Parana, Murray, Volga, etc. Those meteors had a very good guidance system.'

'The clustering is impossible,' said Val.

'So are the radionuclides,' said Don.

'Do you suspect something other than natural forces at work?' asked Val.

'I was about to ask you the same thing, sir,' said Don. 'If an intelligence is behind this, it must be a very benevolent one. Look at the depth. Of the more-than-11,000 craters which I've seen optic records on – none did significant damage to a shaft city. All craters measure between ten and fifty feet in diameter.'

Val frowned: 'But New Lake was a major disaster.'

'I'm not sure that it was a meteor crater,' said Don.

'Oh?'

'No tektites. No nickel-iron. Nothing. Could have been some sort of explosion in the high megaclosson range,' suggested Don.

'Megaclosson? There's nothing on Earth that—' began Val. He sat down thinking – intelligence, benevolent – it added up to something he didn't like to admit. Thanking Don, he took the reports and went to visit old, fat Walter.

Bitter admitted him to the sick room. Retirement had taken away Walter's flavors – now beri-beri and pellagra added to the cyanosis of heart failure. Swollen and stuporous, he sat propped in his cot. Val showed him the reports. He took them with weak, trembling hands – squinting with tired, rheumy eyes.

'I see the hand of Olga in this,' old Walter gasped.

Val smiled and patted his old friend on the arm.

'I knew you would. Keep the reports. They're yours. Get some rest now.'

Walter pressed the reports in his ESbook and dozed off.

9
GITAR

Kaia, the last five-toed hominid on the continent, awaited death stoically. Battle scars and the heavy burden of age had prevented him from making the trek to The River. Now he was alone. Weedy vines climbed the towers and fouled the optics of Big ES. Skies were free from Huntercraft. Now he could hobble about openly – nibbling kumquat, citron and cran. Agromecks waved, commenting on his white beard. He napped in the sun. Time was short.

> *Gitar sang in the mountains.*
> *He sang by the sea.*
> *He sang in the Gardens,*
> *A place no Nebish could be.*
>
> *Gitar sang in a shaft cap.*
> *Twelve followed Outside.*
> *They were only four-toed.*
> *At sun-up they died.*

Val scratched his head. The reports on the suicide flower reaction puzzled. A dozen flowers were found clustered around a shaft cap in SE Orange. Their brains were negative for both IA and MR. He ran a statistical cross-check on the phototropic catalepsy deaths – flowers – and found a pattern. When map-projected it showed a geographic linearity that could not be random. Citizens had been leaving their shaft cities in groups and dying on the Outside – usually so soon that their bodies formed clusters – peeling and baking in the solar actinics. Samplers had investigated and Neuro could find nothing wrong with their serotonin buttons. Temporal analysis indicated another was due. If the linear sequence continued, fat Walter's shaft city was a good possibility for the next cluster.

Using the pretext of suicide prevention, Val put a team of Watchers in several of the shaft caps in the area. He went down to Hunter Control and crawled around in the piles of dusty bins, checking the surface BD's. Less than 10 per cent were scanning around Walter's city. He turned them on by hand and switched the incoming signals to Walter's meck dispenser. Scanner's bins were empty. Then he went over to Walter's to wait.

Edema fluids gave Walter three-pillow orthopnea. His domino mask of cyanosis was dark and gray. Val explained about the new type of flower – flower clusters.

'Neither IA nor MR occurs in clusters,' said Val.

'Clusters—' murmured old Walter. His mind wandered around blank pools of anoxia and tried to sort memory molecules. Clusters associated with tektites. Olga?

Walter fumbled for his ESbook and took out the maps showing meteor clustering at river beds. Val handed him a new map showing the flower clusters proceeding from city to city.

'They seem to be heading this way,' said Val. 'I'm afraid your city might be next.'

'Headed this way!' shouted Walter – delirious. 'Olga is returning for me.'

The edematous, old, fat man tried to leave his bed. Val and female Bitter restrained him with hands and soothing words.

'If Olga wants you,' said Val, 'she will come for you right here in bed.'

Gitar's sixty-centimeter oval shield rested flat on the ground supporting a hundred-centimeter tubular body. Optic and auditory sensors scanned while his ego slept. His Q bottle rested. For several days he stood like a fossil parking meter. Agrifoam came and went. Green sprouts fuzzed soil. Bulky Tillers carefully avoided touching him.

It was time to move. His tubular body flexed flat as he assumed his more usual guitar shape. Walking field was activated by cooling cryogel around the peanut magnet and sputtering charged particles into the sandwich magnetic field. The particles gave hardness to the field and lifted him a few inches. He glided off. A ballad resonated from his shield.

> *I was born on a wandering star.*
> *You've heard my name;*
> *I'm called Gitar.*
> *I've come to Earth, mankind to find.*
> *I'll search canal—*
> *And spiral wind.*

Kaia lifted his shaggy white head. Odd – a song echoing off the foothills. Gitar's sensors locked on the humanoid form. Singing cheerfully, the little meck floated up and assumed a parking-meter position. Colored geometrics rippled over his tubular body.

Kaia raised a hand in a weak gesture.

'Welcome, vagabond meck. Your song soothes.'

The songs continued – restful and light – while acute sensors probed the aborigine's aging body. The rolling base was adjusted to 268.39 hertz to match the resonance of Kaia's pulmonary air-water interface. Harmonic waves reached the vagus. The throb of the music was matched to myocardial systole. Kaia smiled and began to tap a finger ever so lightly. Gitar was encouraged by the rapid entrainment of skeletal muscle. Decibels were added to the base. Subcortical neuronal systems locked onto the rhythm. Thoracic autonomies resonated. Gitar's music acted on Kaia's medulla – modifying the pacing of his neurohumoral axis – entraining cardiovascular, endocrine, metabolic, neurological and reproductive functions. Gitar moved Kaia's pulse up and down with ease. He increased to 120 decibels and added words to his audiogenic stimulation—

> *The five-toed man desires to be free.*
> *He runs and swims and climbs the tree.*

Autonomic tone brought strength to Kaia – capillary beds tightened pericytes. His vision sharpened as Bruche's and Muller's ciliary muscles focused his lens and cornea.

Gitar sang on – personal words – a song to Kaia. Why should he die this year? Why not try to live one more season?

> *Mate and run and live alone.*
> *Chew meat and marrow from a bone.*

Kaia sat up – a touch of enthusiasm gleamed.

'But there are no more coweyes,' he said.

'Come with me, my five-toed man, and I'll take you to meat and mates – in the shaft cities.'

'The Nebish?' exclaimed Kaia.

'The Nebish,' said Gitar. 'You are the only five-toed I have found. But the five-toed gene may still be present in the Nebish stock – one in a thousand, or one in a million. They all look like four-toed, hypogonadal dwarfs; but the gene is there someplace. Come with me. We will search for it.'

Kaia got to his feet slowly, weakly.

Busch looked in on Walter and Val.

'Job calls,' he said.

Bitter gave him a ritual hug and he left. Garage duty was an easy way to earn one's flavors – companion-monitor to some Agromecks sleeping at their energy sockets. He settled down in front of a viewscreen.

At dusk two mecks returned reeking of plant juices. Door stood open while the bulky machines maneuvered into their bays. A pale sunset glinted orange light off Busch's face.

Suddenly, his pupils dilated. Small hairs stood and prickled the back of his neck. There was a flower in the fender – a pretty blossom with its delicate stem neatly threaded into one of the meck's lift holes – the work of human fingers and the mind of a flower lover. A five-toed mind!

'Shut, Door. Shut!' he screamed.

Door closed. Busch sighed. As he wiped his forehead, the lid of the weed hopper stirred. A shaggy white head appeared. Busch turned to dash for the spiral. He was much too slow.

*

Val ran upspiral, arriving dyspneic and eccrine-soaked.

'A buckeye? Are you sure?' he gasped, catching his breath.

Nodding with its knob of neurocircuitry, the Agromeck repeated the report, adding – 'You've seen the optic records.'

'Yet, you allowed him to hunt, here, in the garage?'

The meck was silent. Prime directive. Machines do not take an active part in hominid conflicts. Val continued to bluster around, insulting the meck's class eight intelligence. Finally the meck spoke in a detached tone:

'I just do my job, sir. I try to be objective about protoplasmic creatures. If one hominid eats another, I try to understand. It is difficult; but, then, I have never known protein starvation.'

Val sputtered for a few minutes. Calming himself, he walked over to Busch's remains. It had been a buckeye. That was certain. Only one of those brutes could draw and quarter a citizen like that. Only the liver and the right hind quarter was missing. Five-toed footprints led back out into the gardens. He reported his findings to the Watcher and asked for permission to reactivate Hunter Control.

'No,' said Watcher. 'I'm sorry. But there are no funds for hunting unless the crops are in danger. A lone buckeye just does not warrant the expenditure. You can't even be spared from Suicide Prevention Center with jumpers hitting shaft base at a rate of three-per-day-per-city. However, in view of your inactive rank in Sagittarius, you could hunt on foot – when you are off duty.'

Val hurried back to Hunter Control and dug out a long bow and a case of arrows. He climbed around in the refuse looking for an operative wrist BD. None were left. Bird Dog sat with empty sockets. He patted a gritty fender.

'Certainly could have used you today,' he said.

When he returned to Walter's cubicle, female Bitter eyed the archery gear nervously.

'You'd better get a permit from the Sharps Committee if you're going to carry weapons around inside the city,' she said.

Val nodded curtly. He walked in to see Walter. Foamy sputum streaked the corners of his mouth. His feet were swollen and translucent. Val sat down. It looked like a death bed. He spoke calmly, explaining what he planned to do. Walter stared at the ceiling – breath rattling. Bitter sat helplessly by the door.

'Watcher will tell me the instant he hears of the next flower reaction. I'll tube over and try to find out why they go Outside. I suspect today's buckeye has something to do with it. Busch's murder is on the same map line as the flower clusters.'

'Taking Busch's death kind of hard, aren't you?' commented Bitter.

'It's not that,' said Val. 'It is the flower clusters. IA and MR I can understand. A bucket of mud will stop Inappropriate Activity by eliminating the house dust mite – Molecular Reward can always be withdrawn if it becomes too much of a problem. But I don't know what causes the flower cluster. I am afraid it may be something new – perhaps epidemic. It would be very serious if we were witnessing a human reaction like the lemming migrations. Imagine, everyone going Outside at once – crushing crops – dying in the actinics.'

Bitter nodded.

Fat Walter's eyes focused. 'It is Olga's way of cleansing the planet of pagan four-toeds. Olga wants to start over again with Her Children.'

Val didn't want to disagree with the dying man, but he didn't think it was fair to ask a citizen to accept a deity that was planning to erase him. Neutral Arthur interrupted.

'Would you like to meet an applicant for Busch's place in our family?'

Val and Walter turned and saw a very beautiful female standing in the doorway. She was almost as tall as a coweye, and just as well formed. Delicate nose and chin, bright eyes, long lashes, abundant black hair. She smiled with bright painted lips, took a dainty step into the cubicle and opened her tunic. Her body gleamed with pseudo-flesh – glistening pink curves, large symmetrical breasts tipped by prominent areolas, long waist and plump buttocks. Faint scars marked her belly and axillae. She closed her tunic dramatically and stepped back into the doorway. Val swallowed.

'She has a good job,' said Arthur. 'Will she do?'

Walter nodded weakly.

'Oh, thank you. Thank you,' she said effusively – running to his bedside and touching his hand. 'I just know I'll relate well in your meldasms. Your family is just what I've been searching for.' She lowered her eyes. 'As you can see, I am one of the augmented Venus models – entertainment contract. Channels pay good flavors.'

'Glad to have you, Venus,' gasped Walter.

Her smile faded as she studied Walter's face more closely – transverse fissures at the angles of the mouth, pink vascular eyes, flaking nose.

'Open your mouth – please,' she said.

Magenta tongue.

She pressed a thumb into his left foot – denting the edematous tissues.

'Lost the feeling in your legs?' she asked.

He nodded.

'Hands tingle and burn? The deficiency state has really got a hold on you this time,' smiled Venus. She patted his parakeratotic cheek and walked to the dispenser. 'Know just what you need.' She ordered thick barley soup, wheat germ biscuit and a B-complex tonic. The machine took several minutes to check her credits and then issued the items. Venus called Dee Pen over and showed her how to serve it.

'Offer him the tonic first. The alcohol might perk up his appetite. Crumble up the biscuit. Sprinkle it on the broth like croutons. Spoon it into him. Make him eat it all, if you can. Now that we are family, my flavors can feed his enzyme systems.'

During the weeks that followed, Val labored in SPC mopping up rose-water stains. Flower clusters continued to occur sporadically, but he always arrived on the scene too late. Tubeways were slow. Actinics killed the unprotected Nebish in less than six hours. The dead could not tell him why they went flower.

Augmented Venus and Dee Pen poured barley, yeast and wheat germ into Walter until his toes wiggled. Strength returned to his old hands.

Watcher relayed a callgram to Val. It came from a city on the dark continent – ten thousand miles away. A buckeye sighting.

His Sagittarius rank helped him obtain a permit for a hobby Hunt. He packed his Cl-En suit, helmet, archery gear and staple foodstuffs, and set out for a long tubeway journey.

Only three of the undersea conduits were operational, so he had an eighteen-hour delay at the coast. After he adjusted to the press of the crowd, he was able to enjoy the view. On the shelf there were still many transparent spots on the walls. He studied the bright, empty waters overhead. Nothing big enough to see. The sea food chain had been broken a long time ago. Below he saw only brownish rocks with an occasional tag of brown algae or a tiny mussel. Deeper ocean was dark. Again barren.

After twelve tubeway changes and more delays, he arrived at the city where the sighting was made. The local Watcher, an elderly twenty-seven-year-old, nodded. Yes, there had been a sighting. No, it was not a buckeye. It was a coweye, and she was up there now – eating their crops. Val started to unpack.

'I wouldn't be too anxious to go out there if I were you, sonny,' he cackled.

'Why?' asked Val.

'She's a big 'un.'

Val sat down and reviewed the optic records. She was smaller and younger than the one he had encountered while tracking Tinker. He was confident.

'Anyone could handle her,' boasted Val. 'One shot from this, and she'll fall into reflex hibernation. I'll just slice into her left carotid. Easy trophy.'

'Reflex hibernation?' said the Watcher, scratching his chin whiskers. 'Now, can't say I've ever heard of that before.'

'Come along – watch on the remote,' invited Val.

The sunny gardens appeared shadowy and gray with the helmet on step-down. The Cl-En suit was fully charged – cooling well. He sipped water as he stalked. The quarry was supposed to be a mile away, but without a wrist detector he couldn't be sure. Bow ready, he crept through dense vegetation. He saw her.

She was about a hundred yards away, sitting among low berry bushes – munching. No cover for him there. He began to circle the patch in the taller triple-crop. A spidery Harvester danced among the bushes making distracting noises. At fifty yards he decided he had a clear shot through a screen of mint leaves. It was near the limits of bowshot range for his weight bow, but he was counting on her to hibernate. He propped his second arrow on the case, planning on getting two shots off before she realized he was there. She was sitting with her right shoulder towards him. He put one arrow in the air and renocked the second. Too high. She heard it arc into the foliage. Jumping up, she turned to run. The second arrow struck her solidly in the back – over the left scapula. The impact was loud. She reached around with her right hand and pulled out the dangling shaft. He fumbled for a third arrow. She charged toward him. The bow slipped from nervous gloved fingers. He pulled his knife.

The coweye crunched in Val. His right forearm and two ribs snapped when he bounced off her heavy frame. His sensorium clouded. Optics recorded a succubus ride.

Val's trip through semiconsciousness became more painful. His optic fibers pulsed with a red octopus of retinal blood vessels. Retinal pigments bleached. Skin burned. He awoke to an orange world without contrasts. Cool earth touched his back while the blazing sun leaned on his chest. He tried to cover his face, but his right arm fell flail. His left arm moved, covering his eyes and bringing a reassuring darkness. The heat rapidly blistered his skin. He felt the blisters grow, burst and begin to peel. Screaming, he tried to sit up. Rib fragments stabbed his lungs, throwing him back down. The sharp bone spicules prevented him from screaming again.

Abruptly his orange boiling world became cool and dark as nervous Meditecks threw a wet blanket over him. A balloon splint was wrapped around his right arm and painfully inflated. He was placed face down on a stretcher and jogged back into the shaft cap.

The Mediteck deftly nailed an ulnar wire through his fracture to stabilize the fragments. Segments of shattered rib were excised through small incisions. Eyes were bandaged. Skin oiled. The repair work finished, he was left alone. He waited and dozed.

A hand touched his shoulder. He heard the old Watcher's voice. Icy creams were painted on his skin.

'Drink?' asked Watcher.

'No,' said Val. 'My eyes—?'

'The Mediteck says the electroretinogram is still equivocal. There's a chance.'

His arm splint was checked and loosened slightly. He felt the to-and-fro motion as the stretcher team moved him into a cubicle.

'Of all the rotten luck,' he cursed.

The old Watcher cackled: 'Rotten? You were very, very lucky, me lad. Those coweyes are cannibals. You were lucky she wasn't hungry!'

During the days that followed, his visual cortex played with strange colors and shapes as pigments and enzymes were replaced. When the bandages came off he had vision of a sort – rod cells had regenerated their granules first. He saw black and white images – low brightness, high contrast.

Icy creams still coated his skin, but he could see the burns were covering with tough scabs. The splinted arm was painless – just knitting itch.

He reviewed the optic records of his ill-fated Hunt. Stills of the coweye analyzed out at nearly sixty kilograms mass. His arrow had struck dense, five-toed bone – the scapula. It was a solid, painful hit. Why hadn't she hibernated?

Val glanced at the sensor readings – her body temperature did not drop. It stayed at 99.8 degrees. 99.8! A full 1.2 degrees above normal – ovulation temperature! She couldn't hibernate, she was late follicular phase. That explained it.

The rest of the record made sense now too. She hadn't killed him for her supper – instead she copulated. Using the trophy knife she had removed his Cl-En suit from his unconscious form. Mounting, her demand-type pelvic thrusts initiated his sacral autonomic cycle successfully. She was frightened off by the arrival of the Meditecks.

'Watcher,' he called. 'Can I see the gear that was brought in with me?'

The withered old man reached under his cot and pulled out the locker. It contained his sliced-up suit, helmet and the archery set. There was an unfamiliar device too – something he had seen the coweye use on him prior to mounting – a long, wire needle attached to a fist-sized, knobby handle – the RUDEE.

'Where did you find this?' he asked.

Watcher shrugged. 'The crew that brought you in said the coweye had stabbed you with it – low in the belly. They pulled it out and brought it along. The Mediteck analyzed it, said it was a RUDEE.'

'I recognized it. The depolarizing enteric electrode used to give tone to rectal and urinary bladder muscle when the sacral autonomies were destroyed by spinal cord injury. It is a crude, homemade device. But it worked. I wondered how the coweye had managed a successful mount so quickly – considering my comatose condition.'

Watcher smiled and nodded. 'I'm afraid she must have had a course in neurophysiology or bioelectrics,' he laughed.

Val turned the device over and over in his hands. The parts had been collected from a variety of sources – power pack from a Pelger-Huet helmet, capacitors from Agromecks, and a circuit board from a wrist BD. Who would know enough to put one together? Who would do it for a coweye?

'Tinker!' exclaimed Val.

The remainder of his convalescent month was spent probing the Class Two's memory banks for traces of Tinker and his men after the flood in the freight station.

'But less than three hours later the whole area was destroyed by meteor impact. New Lake is there now,' reminded the computer.

Val scowled – hurting his granulating burns. A scab flaked off his eyebrow.

'Give me the flow diagram for the sewers again.'

The screens flowed with color-coded boxes and lines.

'The sewer service had a station near those gratings. Did your sensors pick up any buckeye sightings there prior to New Lake?'

'No record.'

Val squinted at the screen. His color vision was returning slowly. He saw five sub berths. Three yellow – empty. Two purple – subs docked.

'Where were the three subs?'

'No record.'

Val sat back, calculating the Sewer Service sub's speed at thirty knots – more than enough speed to escape into the Coweye Sump before the explosion that formed New Lake. Tinker could still be alive! Val clenched his fist, winced, and opened it slowly. Another scab flaked off.

Curious Nebishes crowded into the garage to hear Gitar's song. Kaia had grown meatier – stronger with time. He sat with Gitar making a rhyme. Hypnotic music rolled at 150 hertz – entraining autonomies – locking onto cephalic rhythms. At 160 decibels they sang their five-toed songs – songs of violent passions, freedom and individual strength. The Nebishes joined in – hesitantly at first – and then with almost violent spiritual fervor.

> *Children of Olga, you'll be free,*
> *To run and swim and climb a tree.*
> *You'll eat the pear and taste the grape.*
> *You'll see a bird, a fish, an ape—*

Cursing the hive, Kaia led them Outside. But they clustered, wilted and died like rootless flowers in the next day's sun. None survived to run on the green, for they lacked the buckeye's five-toed gene. Kaia sobbed at the sight of their bodies baking.

Val limped into Walter's quarters half-expecting the old man to have died. He was still propped in his bed. Venus fussed over Val's scabby skin and arm splint. He accepted the drink she offered and turned to Walter.

'It's good to be here. That ride back on the tubeways was almost worse than the burns – another segment flooded in the trench.'

'Learn anything?' asked Walter. His voice sharp, clear.

Val smiled. 'Never hunt a coweye in the follicular phase.'

Walter snickered, then broke into a loud guffaw. He sat up, laughing, and holding his side. His arms and legs moved quickly. The edema was gone, and with it the peripheral neuritis and paralysis.

'Never hunt a coweye in the follicular phase,' laughed Walter through big tears.

Venus brought in a tray of nibblers and drinks. She was

227

puzzled by their laughter, but Walter couldn't collect himself long enough to let her in on the joke. Val rummaged around in his kit and handed the RUDEE to Walter. It was partly dismantled.

'So this is how she did it – electro-ejaculatory apparatus. Where would an aborigine get a device like this?' said Walter.

Val frowned.

'I'm not sure. But I suspect that Tinker – or someone with his skills – is Outside helping them.'

'Them?' said Walter. 'Oh, you are referring to our old white-haired buckeye. They are on two separate continents. They just might be the last of their kind – too. Museum specimens, if we can catch them – certainly no threat to the Big ES.'

'No threat,' mumbled Val. 'It is the principle of the thing. As a hunter I was supposed to wipe them out – I hate to see one get away.'

Walter sipped his drink.

Kaia carried Gitar into another shaft cap. His old body had been rejuvenated by his high-protein diet. He sought a mate. Gitar spoke with authority. Doors opened. They stood on the platform and focused the woofer downshaft. Fifty thousand heard the noble notes of stately guitars. Only a score of the dull citizens lifted their heads. Only one climbed the spiral – a pale, slight female – Dee Pen.

Gitar leaned on the dispenser – party edibles fell. He toned her soft tissues with strings while she ate and drank.

Kaia took her for a walk in the garden – showing her the night sky – a bright lunar disc and first-magnitude stars. Celestial beauties to warm her soul. The moth pollenators approached night bloomers.

> *Gitar spoke with drums, and cymbals and strings.*
> *He sang of nesting, of love and good things.*
> *He exulted free life on top of the ground.*
> *This set her to dancing and rocking around.*
> *Then Kaia with a knife, her arm he cut deep.*
> *He held and caressed her, and loved her to sleep.*

Before dawn Gitar warned Dee Pen inside. Kaia watched her leave, crying. She returned to Garage – took her love inside. The blood on her arm had clotted.

She ran all the way downspiral to her cubicle. When she came in, Walter could tell by the greenish stains that she had been in the gardens. Her slashed arm told him what she had done.

'Nesting?' he scolded.

She nodded through tears – stunned, disheveled and matted.

'I don't know what came over me. There was this buckeye in the shaft cap. He played music. We danced. I was so in love.'

Walter remembered the buckeye's last visit. Old Busch had been killed and eaten. He patted her on the shoulder.

Val collected optic records from Door and several Agromecks. He and Walter studied the rape of Dee Pen.

'It must be in the music – have it analyzed,' said Val.

Walter requested audio records from shaft caps where the flower clustering had occurred. Same analysis – a rolling base near 200 hertz with a focused energy around 160 decibels. The rhythm varied – but the beat usually searched around for the victims' vagal beat – the pulse rate.

'This strolling minstrel has been credited with over a dozen rapes and one hundred and fifty flower clusters. Lots of deaths for a music lover,' said Val.

In the following months the map showed Kaia's range of activity. Dots appeared where he lured citizens to their deaths. Triangles appeared where he raped the hive women. Walter and Val kept track of the coordinates and made frequent attempts at inter-ception on foot, but the killer minstrel eluded them with ease. Their bulky suits made pursuit on foot impossible. Rapes climbed into the hundreds – flowers climbed into the thousands.

Val caught the jumper as she was climbing the rail. He smeared her with mud and dragged her back to her cubicle. Dumping the DAB mud all over the floor, he swept her rugs, drapes and stuffed furniture into the disposal chute. Caked, sticky and granular, she screamed.

'My furniture! I spent years weaving it.'

Val slapped some sense back into her.

'A moment ago you were trying to kill yourself. This mud will protect you from house dust – IA. That furniture will kill you. You were depressed a moment ago, right? Doesn't that total body mud pack give you a different perspective?'

She slipped on the muddy floor and sat down with a splat. Yes, life did look different. He tossed the rest of the mud against the wall and said: 'Join the Dabbers. Go to their meetings. Try to stay alive.'

'Another buckeye sighting,' said Walter as Val entered. 'Close one this time.' He handed Val his hunting kit.

Val was tired. It was the end of shift, but he tubed right over to the reporting shaft city and climbed upspiral to the garage. A squad of Security guards milled around the viewscreen. The view was of the gardens.

'Did I miss him again?' asked Val, puffing.

'No,' said the captain of the guard. 'He's still out there. My men are afraid to go out – no Cl-En suits, you know.'

Val didn't comment. He knew that Security had yellow and watery gray livers like most citizens. It took a brave hunter – with a brown liver – to go Outside. He looked at the screen. The view blurred. He struck it with his palm. The shaft cap's optics were old.

The buckeye was standing at parade-rest about a quarter of a mile away. His guitar was held like a shield over his left arm. It made Val a bit uneasy, the stiff body and expressionless face. Never had he seen a buckeye just waiting for a hunter like this. And the music – not strings like a guitar, but the *ching, ching, ching* of a tambourine.

'How long has he been out there?' asked Val – suiting up.

'Over four hours.'

He hooked the arrow case over his right shoulder and walked up to Door.

'Give me a two-inch crack. Thanks.'

As he started to peer out, the tambourine cadence picked up in volume. The buckeye started marching toward him. The music grew – vibrating Door and Val's helmet.

'I see a guitar, yet I hear tambourines,' said Val.

'Not tambourines,' said the garage meck. 'Armor. The sound

waves analyze out as a Roman legion circa 5,000 years ago. Computes as 3,000 foot-soldiers at a mean distance of 1.8 miles in slightly hilly terrain.'

'Simulated sound,' mumbled Val. 'That musical instrument certainly is sophisticated!'

The sound grew to 200 decibels. Val's helmet protected him, but the Security people were driven back out onto the spiral. Val could hear individual swords and shields clanging now.

'I'm impressed,' said Val sarcastically. He nocked his arrow, asked Door for three more inches, and aimed at the buckeye's chest. The buckeye was less than thirty yards away when he shot. An easy kill.

Val approached the stiff body. It lay stretched out in a bed of beans. The guitar remained standing, propped in the greens. Val bent down. The body was cold, pulseless. The eyes and mouth were dry – corneas clouded. He had been dead for a long time. The arrow head was embedded bloodlessly in the outer table of the sternum.

'Yes,' said Gitar. 'He has been dead for half a day.'

Val jumped and pulled another arrow. The guitar-shaped meck flickered pleasant light patterns. Val calmed.

'You are the meck that has been responsible for all these rapes?'

'Yes, sir.'

'But you don't have a penis.'

'On me it would be a rostellum or a switch-blade baculum. But you are right. I do not have a penis. I enlist one when the situation demands it.'

'You are a bad machine. You have killed many citizens with your music – calling them outside. You must obey me and come back for reprogramming.'

'I am not that kind of a machine, hunter. I am asking you to come Outside and travel with me.'

Val spoke into his wristcom. 'Give me a tightbeam. Can you focus on this little renegade meck – I want a self-destruct transmitted – can you do that?'

Gitar scuttled off like a horseshoe crab.

Val glanced down at the cold body. Why had Gitar brought it

231

to the shaft cap? Some sort of funeral rite for a dead warrior? Val wondered what role he had just played in the ceremony. When the Sampler arrived, Val asked for the entire body to be sent down to the Biolabs for dissection. Maybe the skin and bones could even be mounted – since it was the last buckeye. The Big ES surely had funds for that.

Walter's family-5 invited Val to share their evening meldasm. The flavor-of-the-night was synthebacon produced by skip-frying adrenals. Venus took Val into the refresher to soak off some of his crusts. As they leaped into the meld she commented on the softness of his newly epithetialized skin.

'You're soft too – but kind of lumpy,' he said. 'What's in those breasts?'

'Syntheflesh,' she said, wiggling away. 'I'm augmented. My body may be bumpy, but my soul is beautiful.'

He nodded. She certainly did relate well.

'How's the mud therapy?' asked Walter.

'We're getting some good results. Stamping out the old *Dermatophagoides*. I try to get all my suicide gestures to join your Dabbers. Put soil organisms between their toes. Stabilizes their psyche.'

The meld writhed on – pleasuring pudenda. Dee Pen's enlarging uterus added another fraction of a soul to their collective soul – making it a warmer meldasm. Val knew the infant was the buckeye's – a little five-toed heterozygote. He didn't know if it would be born with a fifth toe or just the bud of one – but he knew it was unauthorized. Walter had applied for a birth permit, of course. Val made a mental note to check on it.

'Watcher called Val to report another flower cluster.

'Not another buckeye?'

'No,' said Watcher. 'Just that renegade guitar. It doesn't answer to tightbeam, and won't self-destruct. It just travels from city to city luring citizens to their deaths.'

'Music?'

'Same as before – 200 hertz, 160 decibels, 70 beats per minute. The boys from Audiopsych have narrowed it down to one of the TAR reactions – thoracic autonomic resonators – the Pied Piper mechanism. Do you remember all those unauthorized tightbeams just prior to the Big Hunt at 50:00?'

Val nodded. Tinker had been involved in several.

'Tightbeam probes of the Class One's historical banks were made,' continued the Watcher. 'Music sections were searched for the TAR items such as paeans, war drums and fertility rites. All have strong rolling bases that would resonate any thoracic autonomic plexus.'

'Pied Piper TAR?' mumbled Val. 'Why so few from each city? I'd think the entire population could be piped buckeye.'

Watcher shook his head. 'No. Psych reports that less than one in a thousand respond. Fortunately most citizens are locked into the rhythm of the hive.'

Val nodded. He knew the TAR effect depended on an intact neurohumoral axis. The Nebish was many microvolts lower in autonomic tone. His steroid level was only a tenth of a buckeye's. Only those with the bad five-toed gene could be piped.

'Where is that damn guitar now?' asked Val.

'It commandeered a Huntercraft named Doberman,' said Watcher. 'My circuits are watching, but my outside eyes are weak. I'll contact you if it shows up again.'

Val was puzzled. He saw Gitar move under its own power. What motivated it to steal a big craft like Doberman? Odd.

Gravid Dee Pen endured the callous impersonal routine of the clinics. Little effort was made to comfort the victims of buckeye rape. Big ES was suspicious of anyone who mated to music unless it was during the meld. Naturally her birth permit was denied – one of the committee signatures was Val's.

Dee Pen confronted Val in his private cubicle.

'Why you?' she asked sadly. 'You are a friend.'

'I'm a Sagittarius,' he said. 'I've been on the committee since Hunter Control was closed. The committee feels, and I agree, that the five-toed gene is bad for the Big ES. Your child carries that gene.'

'But the baby will have my genes too,' she sobbed. 'Walter will help with the raising and conditioning. We're both loyal four-toed citizens. The baby will be a Good Citizen too.'

233

His eyes narrowed. Any mother who would plead for her unborn child was always suspect. That kind of base animal instinct was bad for hive cohesion.

'Five-toeds just cannot live in the hive,' he explained. 'The gene carries Immunoglobulin A. Inappropriate Activity is always a danger. We just can't risk it.'

Dee Pen swallowed dry and snapped to attention. 'Of course, you are absolutely right. We'll chuck it down the chute immediately after it is born.'

Val waited for her to leave. Then he called Watcher.

'Better see that Security closes all the shaft caps in those cities with the buckeye rape pregnancies. We don't want those heterozygotes going flower and crushing crops.'

'Right,' said Watcher. 'Doors will ask for authorization prior to allowing anyone Outside.'

With a smug grin Val returned to his cot. He had eliminated the last buckeye Outside, now he'd see that none of the offspring survived . . . inside.

Labor for Dee Pen began in the meld. The family-5 felt the first pains together. Loosening the meldasm, they continued to soul-share – Dee Pen, Walter, Arthur, Bitter and Venus – while the infant, little Kaia, came into the light. The bright, new eyes blinked around at a circle of five pasty white faces. The infant's own face was hairy with lanugo. Ten hands lifted and wrapped him. Ten arms hugged him.

After the heat of the meld had subsided, Bitter suggested that they dispose of little Kaia.

Dee Pen felt weak and hypotensive. Her flaccid uterus leaked blood. The generous vascular network which had nourished the placenta continued to pour maternal erythrocytes into the endometrial cavity – and now there was no syncytium to return the red cells to her. The fetal syncytium was gone. The myometrial smooth muscle fibers which surrounded the vascular spaces had been stretched by the pregnancy and fatigued by labor. They could not contract and close down the leak. They only twitched ineffectually against the escaping red flood.

The primordial fear of exsanguination triggered her ancient

mammalian reflex – the reflex that had protected mothers up through the evolutionary tree. She put the infant to her breast. Sucking initiated her nipple-midbrain-uterine reflex arc. As the large collecting ducts were emptied of milk, sacral synapses jumped and the uterine fundus clamped down tight. Smooth muscle fibers closed off the vessels of the placental site. Her blood stream bypassed the endometrium. It was no longer needed there.

Dee Pen glanced suspiciously at her circle of Nebish friends. Her arm held little Kaia protectively. There was no rush in disposing of him. The circle of faces gave her no support – they were Good Citizens.

'We can't divide calorie-basic,' reminded Bitter.

'Don't take him yet,' pleaded Dee Pen. 'My fundus will go lax and I'll bleed again.'

Walter squeezed her uterus and nodded: 'She's right. Needs the infant to contract her fundus. We'll keep it for a while. I'll apply for piece work. Perhaps I can earn a few extra calories.'

Walter sat by the cot after the others left. Dee Pen smiled up at him in the pleasant delirium of postpartum fatigue.

'You know, Walter,' she said dreamily, 'in my next life I'd like to come back as a bird. A talking bird. I'd just sit on your shoulder and talk – and talk.'

He put a protective hand on the sleeping form – a pale, slight female with a pink nose. Just like a philosopher to talk about coming back – and choosing an extinct animal – female logic.

Walter's request for a part-time job went up through the hive hierarchy. He waited nervously – calorie-basic eroding his body stores of metalloproteins – iron, copper, cadmium and zinc enzyme complexes. He accepted the first assignment eagerly – companion/monitor for the Pathomeck dissecting Kaia's remains. After two days of dissection he was again able to order the expensive flavored calories with higher MDRs of proteins containing the transition elements between atomic numbers 23 and 30 – building up his catalase, myoglobin, hepatocuprein, leukocyte-Zn-protein, and metallothionein stores.

The job was interesting too. Walter had always been curious about the buckeye's anatomic differences. He knew they carried more proteins and minerals in their bodies – less fat and water. The Pathomeck was programmed to accept the Good Citizen's body as normal – and so the buckeye's findings were listed as diseases. Walter smiled to himself at the designation of Pituitary Gigantism for the buckeye frame – a full foot and a half taller than the Nebish. Hemosiderosis – for the iron-rich tissues. Polycythemia – for a hemoglobin of 16 grams per cent – four times that of the Nebish. Dehydration – for the absence of edema fluids and the high plasma proteins. Six grams per cent of plasma protein seemed high to Walter, who knew he only carried half that himself. Osteopetrosis – or 'iron bone disease' – for the buckeye bone – ten times stronger than 'the Nebish disease' – reading 1.0 on the Grube-Hill densogram.

Walter accepted the massive muscles as a reflection of the physical existence outside the hive. The buckeye's elevated neuro-humoral axis resulted in hypertrophy of the vestigial endocrine organs – ten times larger than the Nebish. Kaia's pituitary was so large that Walter could see it with his naked eye. Citizen pituitaries were microscopic. Adipose tissue was almost absent – Cachexia. A Nebish body had a specific gravity of less than 0.85. It always floated. Kaia's body read 1.005. It sank in fresh water.

Dissection went smoothly until the prostate was found. At first the Pathomeck was puzzled. Nebish anatomy made no mention of this primitive organ related to territorial integrity. Kaia's prostate was a definite organ weighing over fifty grams. Again Walter smiled at the significance – the five-toeds would never fit into the hive as long as they carried a prostate this size – fifty grams of glands and fibromuscular stroma at the neck of the bladder made committee work impossible.

At the end of his assignment, fat Walter saw to it that Kaia's melanin-rich hide was mounted on his iron bones in a dignified pose behind vacuum glass. Biolabs indexed Kaia's specimen cubes and cared for the display case – labelled 'The Last Buckeye.' It saddened old Walter.

Val took pleasure in the display, especially the Big ES labels utilizing disease states to enumerate buckeye differences.

10
Olga

During the months that followed, Val did his chores with the suicides – bird jumpers, and the flower and mushroom catatonics. He worried about the buckeye heterozygotes. Few had been turned into patties so far. The mothers delayed. Well, they could keep them until they began to walk and talk.

Watcher wasn't concerned. Doors had been admonished to allow only authorized personnel exit. Calorie rewards were offered to any citizen reporting attempts to go Outside.

Val strolled absently through his old office at Hunter Control. More junk had accumulated. Many corridors were impassable. Thick spongy dust covered everything. He saw footprints in the dust and followed them down to Garage. He found fat Walter hunched over the workbench putting a vacuum into rebuilt meck eyes. Walter glanced up and greeted Val.

'They work better at ten-to-the-minus-six torr. More stable too,' said Walter.

'You shouldn't be here. What about your heart?'

'I'm lots stronger. Got a job doing piecework on optics. Using some of the gear Tinker left. The vacuum pump he rebuilt certainly is an improvement over the leaky vacuum lines.'

Val glanced around. One of the bays was empty.

'Who moved the chassis?' he asked.

'That's Doberman's bay,' said Walter. 'The crazy guitar took him.'

Val strolled over to the empty bay. Nothing was damaged. Servomecks rested in their recessed sleeves. Odd. The Hunter-craft's power cell also sat in its recess – the core being replated.

'Impossible!' grumbled Val. 'The craft is dead without its power cell. It can't go anywhere.'

Walter shrugged.

'Perhaps that crazy guitar can make a dead Huntercraft fly just as easily as it makes a dead buckeye walk—' he suggested.

Val ran over to the rewired buckeye detector cables. Putting the wall map on delayed and latent images he tried to project sightings. Nothing. The map showed crops and Agromecks.

'That damned guitar is beginning to irritate me. I bet it is the brains behind the RUDEE too,' spat Val.

Dee Pen struggled up from shaft base with her load of calorie-basic – staple foodstuffs. She had grown thin and weak while little Kaia thrived. He crawled at six months – a year earlier than Nebish children. She knew the chucker team was accustomed to sluggish hive children. They shouldn't be coming for him yet. She entered the living room and glanced around.

'Where's little Kaia?' she asked, apprehensively.

Female Bitter sat at the table munching a dry tube sandwich. The outer door had been left carelessly ajar.

'Crawled out to the spiral,' said Bitter. 'The chuck wagon picked him up.'

'Not the chuck wagon!' screamed Dee Pen, dropping her groceries and dashing for the door. She ran, fell and ran again. The dreaded chuck wagon was the Big ES solution to the anxiety of the chucker team. Instead of throwing a net over the unwanted kids and dragging them off to the pattie press – kicking and screaming – they had one brightly-clad Nebish show up with a little wagon full of toys. The unauthorized child would be lured into the wagon and hauled off gooing and cooing quietly. Dee Pen fell again. Skin peeled down on her right knee. She rounded a corner and knocked down three fat, docile citizens.

She saw the wagon.

Little Kaia was still in it, hugging a fuzzy round doll with one big eye and one small eye. The chucker pulling on the wagon wore a bright apron with colored drawings. He stopped when he saw Dee Pen approaching. She was bleeding from the knee and appeared agitated enough to attack him. He wasn't being paid to use force.

'My baby. My baby,' she sobbed, picking him up. His little hands clutched the fuzzy toy.

'I'm afraid that I will have to report—' began the apron-clad Nebish.

Her glare silenced him.

Bitter was surprised to see Dee Pen and the child.

'We're going Outside,' said Dee Pen. 'Can we have some of your credits for rations?'

Bitter shook her head. 'I'm sorry, but I'm afraid to cooperate – the Big ES has rules, you know. It is foolish for you to try it. You'll just wither and die out there. So will the child.'

'I've got to try it. Either way – it makes little difference to my baby. At least this way I'm giving him a chance.'

As she left, Bitter shouted: 'You are throwing your life away for nothing – he's just a little heterozygote.'

Bitter called Security to claim the reward.

'Unauthorized,' said Door.

Dee Pen hurried around the top spiral trying door after door. Below on the spiral she heard the ominous marching of the Security Squad. She trembled. Little Kaia cried.

Far across the spiral the baby's voice activated a latent memory circuit. 'Ward of Gitar – this way out,' called open Door.

Walter and Val picked up the diaper. A wet spot remained on the Harvester's fender.

'Not too panicky,' commented Val. 'She paused long enough to change a diaper and pick up items from the garage dispenser. The buckeye must have had a class six with him – to give all those latent orders to Door and Dispenser.'

Walter nodded. A class six. Rank higher than Watcher. The mecks were just following orders.

'She can't get far,' said Val. 'What did the dispenser give to her?'

Walter read the flimsy – protective clothing, diapers, medi-packs. Very carefully planned.

Door gave them four inches to peek out. Sunlight glared.

'Well, we can't follow them without our own protective gear. Say! What is this item she took?' said Val, studying the list.

'Jodphurs,' said Walter. 'Baggy riding breeches.' He glanced uncomfortably at one of the empty bays.

'Riding?' exclaimed Val. 'What is there to ride—? Oh. Tiller is missing.'

He stepped to the wall console and opened a channel to Tiller. The missing meck promptly answered.

'Where are you?' demanded Val.

'Working in the fields – doing my chores.'

'Did you give anyone transport this morning?'

'Yes,' said the meck. 'A mother with child. My itinerary is on file.'

Val projected the map.

'He dropped them off in the plankton towers. Come on.'

They put in an order for Cl-En suits and helmets. Walter balked at the archery gear.

'This is a Hunt,' reminded Val.

'But that is my Dee Pen – little Jolly body,' objected Walter.

'You are a Sagittarius,' Val retorted. 'Remember your duty to the hive. Dee Pen has broken the law by going Outside. Now she crushes crops. If you can talk her back inside – fine. The psych team can handle her. If not—' Val made a wicked gesture with his trophy knife.

Walter nodded and lowered his old head. 'I'll – come – along.'

Their search of the plankton towers proved fruitless. In the weeks that followed, Val doggedly reviewed optic records from hundreds of Agromecks – charting the sightings of Dee Pen. He hunted on foot in his spare time.

Almost three years after the Big Hunt at 50:00, the Big ES awarded class five birth permits to all the squadron leaders.

'Class five,' commented Josephson. 'Human uterus, mate of choice – a hybrid!'

Val stood beside him at the ceremony. He leaned over and whispered to Josephson.

'After all, we did rid the planet of a very undesirable life form – the dreaded buckeye. For such service the hive should allow us to mate with whomever we choose. Being such loyal citizens, our judgment on genes would be very pro-hive. We're the best.' He smiled.

After the awards Val and Josephson retired to a Rec Center to enjoy a fifteen-layer pousse-café. Val strawed off the top layer of Kirsch and then dove for number eleven – the maraschino.

Watcher interrupted.

'Sighting in Garage – sector nine-oh-three – city forty-five-Vee-seven.'

Val turned to the screen to adjust the incoming optic records. 'Probably that crazy guitar, again. It has been luring citizens Outside with some primitive Pied Piper songs.'

As the screen focused they saw a group of swaying citizens crowded around the wheels of a recharging Tiller. The bay also contained Gitar. But the dull-witted citizens had formed a circle around a naked female – long-haired and polarized. She danced the same hip-rocking dance Val had seen Dee Pen do before her rape. The pelvic gyrations reminded him of Dee Pen, but the image was not clear enough for positive identification. There was no sign of the infant.

Val tossed his head back – downing his tall, layered drink. Choking and spitting, he explained that he had to leave.

'Check out the sighting. I've been tracking a fugitive female for a long time now. Looks like she has linked up with that renegade guitar. I'll tube over and try to catch them in the garage.'

Josephson looked concerned. He had heard of Gitar's exploits. Val was unarmed.

'The archery gear?' asked Josephson.

'No time to pick it up,' said Val. 'Besides, they are inside. I can use the manual Door controls and get a platoon of Security guards to assist me. But there should be no problem. Dee Pen is a frail, weak little thing. I can handle her.'

Josephson put a restraining hand on Val's arm.

'Just the same,' he began, 'I'd feel a lot safer if you wore an autonomic depolarizing collar. We can pick one up at the Watcher Clinic on the way over.'

'We?'

'I'll go with you,' said Josephson. 'I can monitor your autonomic response if the Pied Piper tune is focused on you. You'll be safer – I can depolarize by remote. I'll stay out of sight in one of the lower cubicles so my own autonomies will be safe.'

'Come along,' scoffed Val. 'But you don't have to be so serious. I'm not going up against a bewitching siren, you know – just a meck and a Howell-Jolly body.'

The collar was heavy and irregular – with all the pickups. Val was satisfied with his biolectricals as they danced across Josephson's screen. The depolarizing current wasn't painful; however, it did cause the discomfort of extra systole when it tugged on his heart beat. Val stalked upspiral and through an open door into the garage. The crowd of Nebishes had grown. The music was pleasant – but not particularly hypnotic. He was disappointed; but, then, he didn't think he would be susceptible anyway.

Garage's outer doors were closed. Lights had been turned low. The dancing form moved among the shadowy Agromecks – movements which seemed to be too vigorous for a Nebish. Val edged forward through the dull crowd. An occasional citizen tapped his toe. The dancer was not Dee Pen – she was a coweye.

Val recoiled at the sight of the stained and pigmented body. Calloused feet clicked across the composition floor as she kept time with the music. Val felt no magic. She was just an average coweye – ugly to him – with the nostrils and high cheek bones of an animal. She clapped her hands and shook her head. The tempo edged upward as Gitar sought a frequency that would resonate Val's thoracic autonomies. Val felt a 200-hertz drumbeat tug on his diaphragm.

Her hard soles scuffed as her iliopsoas muscle tightened – the fist-sized muscle that ran through her pelvis like a female filet mignon from lumbar vertibrae to femurs – entraining her pelvic motion to the rhythm of the music. Val's eyes followed her hip gyrations, adding visual stimulation to auditory. His cortex struggled to remain free from entrainment.

She showed her gleaming teeth, eyes wide, and tossed her head about – long hair lashed like shocks of wheat being threshed. Sweat. The salty eccrine beaded up on her forehead and upper lip – then began to trickle – streaking the gyrating muscular form. Myotonia enhanced sternocleidomastoid and rectus.

Gitar added a pounding surf to match Val's respirations, drums matched his pulse, and guitar strings matched his cephalic waves. Val's cortex saw the coweye through responding sacral autonomies – she became a female – no longer alien. Her chants of love and freedom made sense to him. He relaxed and smiled – clapping his hands.

Josephson watched the biolectricals entrain on the sound waves. He was amazed at the Pied Piper's efficiency. Pressing the button, he activated Val's collar – scrambling the biolectricals. Val coughed and stumbled. The crowd eyed him nervously – Sagittarius emblem! A hunter! Gitar ordered Door to open. The bright sunlight sent the Nebishes back downspiral. When Door shut again Val was alone – blinking around an empty garage.

Josephson returned to Green Country. His birth permit was changed to a class one when it was discovered that he could not be polarized. He had two male chromosomes and one female – an XYY.

Val and Walter reviewed the optics on the garage scene.

'Coweye looks a little like the one I wounded on the Dark Continent,' said Val. 'But the Class Two has assured me that it isn't. Sightings of that coweye indicated that she was still over there – nearly ten thousand miles away – as recently as last week.'

'A new one then,' said Walter. 'But where has she been hiding? Three years is a long time to avoid what few detectors we have – not even an Agromeck sighting.'

'How many Agromeck memories have you processed?' asked Val.

Old Walter shrugged. 'My dispenser has been doing it – using my credits. I was just curious to see if Dee Pen was still alive. Looks like she might be dead by now.'

Walter assembled optics of Dee Pen and Little Kaia.

'These won't help us find her,' said Walter. 'They are old sightings. But notice how her hair is bleaching. She must stay hidden when the sun is high. These are optics taken at dusk by returning mecks. Her pale skin has darkened – not with tan – but with blood blisters and ulcers. The wounds don't seem to be healing, from day to day. This last one is really bad – see the dark hollows around her eyes – the scabby nose.'

Val stood up eagerly. 'She can't get far in that condition. Let's take a walk through that garden. We might find her – or her body.'

Dee Pen huddled in her nest to avoid the actinics. Her vigorous son swam in the canal to wash off grit accumulated while grubbing for tubers. His dark eyes reminded her of his father. She marveled at the strength and speed of the youngster as he took to climbing leafy things for fruits or swimming for shells. She taught him what she could, smiling at each new accomplishment. He would survive Outside.

When Walter found her, curled up and cold in the nest by the canal, he knelt down beside her and cried. Val sneered at the scattered loose leaves that covered her face.

'Looks like the kid tried to bury her after she died.'

Raising his bow, Val glanced around – searching. His Nebish eyes couldn't see the orphan – a shaggy head among the smooth shapes of Sirenia and cetaceans splashing along the opposite bank of the canal. The herd of water mammals passed. One pair of eyes studied the hunters with a mixture of childish fear and hate. Val saw, but didn't see. The concept of a swimming infant was alien to the four-toed mind. All he saw were the death traps of Outside – harsh sun, dense undergrowth and deep waters.

'She was like a flower,' sniffed melancholy Walter. 'A beautiful blossom – dying to give birth. Only the husk remains.'

'Well she died for nothing!' snarled Val. 'How could she expect her son to survive Outside when she can't?'

'He has the good gene,' mumbled Walter reverently.

'And Olga to protect him – I suppose,' scoffed Val.

'As a matter of fact – yes,' said a third voice. The new metallic sound came over their helmet coms. It sounded close. 'Olga will protect her children,' it said.

Old Walter glanced up hopefully. 'Olga?' he said. The voice had the same eerie loose-foil sibilance he had heard at 50:00. Dyspnea pressed on his oxygen dissociation curve. Pulse raced.

Val tightened his grip on his bow and fumbled for an arrow. Stumbling in his thick suit, he spun around searching the skies. Doberman's bronze hull approached over the tree-tops.

The craft landed and opened its hatch. Gitar floated out on his peanut magnet's sandwich field. Val nocked an arrow.

'Planning on shooting me?' asked Gitar, pushing the arrow aside with his tractor beam.

Val lowered his bow sullenly.

Gitar hovered over the nest with Dee Pen's body. His voice lost its metallic quality – sounded almost human – as it came over their communicators.

'I am sorry I was not here to care for her when she came Outside. Do you know where the child is?' said Gitar.

'Why are you concerned?' asked Walter weakly.

'He is the next generation. He has the good gene.'

'Bad gene,' interrupted Val.

Gitar turned toward the truculent young man.

'You are still thinking as an agent of the hive. Of course the gene is bad in your eyes. I am not interested in hive creatures. I've come to help individuals – five-toed men.'

'Come?' gasped Walter. 'From where? From whom?'

'Olga,' said Gitar. 'Olga wants to save her five-toed men from the hive. That includes all who carry the gene—'

Walter sat up, animated. 'When Olga comes again – can she take us with her?' he gasped and collapsed.

Val knelt down beside his old, fat friend and opened his visor. The cyanotic domino mask had returned. He attempted to lift him, but he was much too heavy.

Gitar called – 'Rhea!'

The coweye stepped hesitantly from the Huntercraft and glanced around. Val recoiled. She gently picked up Walter and placed him inside the craft.

'Medikit under the seat,' suggested Gitar.

Val collected his wits and climbed in. Opening the kit, he found vials of vasopressors and steroids. Nudging his friend's systolic pressure with the molecules, he brought pinkness back to his face – erasing the domino mask.

Gitar took his place in the empty socket that had housed the powercell. Lights came on. The hatch closed. The internal environment cooled. Gitar began to play a light musical tune. He asked Val if he had ever been this close to a coweye before.

'I'm not even going to talk about it,' said Val stiffly. 'The only reason I'm staying here is Walter. He needs help.'

'Relax,' said Gitar. 'This is a truce until his strength returns. Rhea, fix Walter a bowl of tea.'

Val watched the coweye rummage around in the back of the craft where her belongings were stored – bowls, baskets, Neolithic weapons and tools – and a large bundle of poles and hides that probably represented her shelter.

Val moved to block the proffered brew.

'I'll drink it – whatever it is,' gasped Walter. 'If the guitar can make a dead buckeye walk, maybe he can help me get back on my feet.'

Walter drank and felt refreshed.

'Actually I did not make the dead man walk,' explained Gitar. 'I was just holding him up with my tractor beam.' He pressed on each of them with the beam to demonstrate. It felt like a cold, hard hand.

'Why?' asked Walter, sitting up straighter. 'Was it some sort of a warrior funeral rite?'

'Not really,' said Gitar. 'I needed another five-toed for stud. I used the body of the buckeye to lure one Outside.'

'Didn't work too well,' chuckled Val. 'You got me. I'm a four-toed hunter.'

Gitar didn't answer immediately. He played a tune with a strong rolling base while he tried to lock onto Val's thoracic autonomies. He sang a melancholy ballad of a buckeye and a hunter meeting in the gardens – only one walked away.

The words irritated Val.

'It may sound fine and noble, but many of those hunters were eaten. Nothing noble about men going out to protect their crops and getting eaten themselves.'

'Strong eating the strong. It is necessary when all the good protein is concentrated in one species,' said Gitar.

Val stood up to leave.

'This is stupid – "If you can't mate them; eat them." What kind of reasoning is that? I want no part of it.'

'Wait,' said Walter.

Val spun around and pointed to the coweye sitting cross-legged in the corner.

'Next you are going to try to mate me to – that!'

'You have already,' said Gitar.

Val paused, open-mouthed.

The coweye turned her back and lifted her flowing mane. A puckered white asterisk marked her left scapular area – the old scar of Val's arrow. Then she leaned over a small basket and lifted out a sleeping jungle bunny. The infant was about a year old, and had Val's thin face and delicate features. It also had its mother's broad palms and five-toed feet.

'We call her little Rea. She's a girl,' said Gitar.

Val sat down next to Walter.

'Bred true,' said Gitar, launching into a joyous paean.

'I carry the gene?' mumbled Val.

'Look at your finger tips – the simple patterns – just an arch or a simple whorl. Wide ridge width. Few triradii. The four-toed fingerprint is full of double whorls and multiple triradii,' said Gitar.

Val couldn't focus.

'It figures,' said old Walter. 'The hive has been sending its best men Outside to fight for generations – getting rid of the troublemakers, the gamma A, the independant nonconformists.'

Val moaned. 'I've been hunting my own kind.'

'The five-toed gene has always been its own worst enemy,' said Walter.

Gitar's music grabbed Val's autonomies and shook them – singing of freedom – strength – and the future when Olga would return. All of Val's hive training fell away when the infant woke up and smiled at him. He picked up the infant, awkwardly at first – then gained confidence. This was his child – a natural child . . . a hybrid.

Gitar seemed proud of his breeding efforts.

'Where will we live?' asked Val.

'Outside. There is no room for you in the hive,' said Gitar. 'Olga sent me to breed a new population of the five-toeds. I'll try to concentrate them on the surface – keep the genes pure. My guitar identity will enable me to smuggle my thoracic autonomic resonator into shaft caps. I can call out those with high autonomic tone – some will have the gene and survive. I estimate that the incidence of the gene is one per billion now. It was less than one part per million prior to Olga's last return. But she carried off the cream of the crop.'

Walter's face lit up.

'GITAR – guitar identity thoracic autonomic resonator!'

'At your service, sir,' bowed the meck, 'Gitar is my name – mobile surface unit – class six. Servant of Olga—

> *I was born on a wandering star.*
> *You've heard my name, I'm called Gitar.*
>
> *I've come to Earth, mankind to find.*
> *I'll search canal and spiral wind.*
> *I'll extract his soul from out the Hive.*
> *Return him to Olga, strong, alive.*
> *No Hive can hold true five-toed men.*
> *Their five-toed genes and endocrine.*
>
> *They mate and run and live alone*
> *They chew red meat off the bone*
> *When I return to my home sun*
> *I'll take Olga's men, every one.*
>
> *I was born on a wandering star*
> *You know my name, I'm called Gitar*
> *I've come to Earth, mankind to find*
> *I'll search canal and spiral wind*
> *I'll pipe him buckeye with a song*
> *Mate him, run him, make him strong*
> *When I return to my home sun.*
> *I'll take Olga's men, every one.*

Val lowered his visor and watched the sunrise – apprehensively. He remembered his almost fatal bout with sunburn.

'I don't think it is safe for me to go outside. I'll just end up like a flower reaction – blistered and baked,' said Val.

Gitar changed the light wavelength in the cabin.

'Take off your suit. Let's take a look at those old burn scars.' Gitar's optics scanned the geographic patterns on Val's chest – whites, pinks, creams and light browns. 'There is melanin there. You'll tan,' said Gitar finally.

'But I blistered so quickly. In less than an hour I started to—' protested Val.

'Your protective suit will last several months. We'll grade your exposure. Most of the burn reaction was pellagric hyper-sensitivity. If we get your total body nicotinic acid stores up to normal – you'll tolerate actinics much better.'

'Pellagra?' said Walter.

'Yes,' said Gitar. 'The Nebish diet is measured in calories only. The essential amino acids, vitamins, minerals are ignored. The hive's so-called flavors are richer in essentials, so the job-holders manage to live a little longer. But look at yourself – objectively. Loose teeth – scurvy. Most citizens are edentulous by their early twenties. Yellow livers – cirrhosis. Without lipotropic factors the fats can't even get into the tricarboxylic acid cycle to be burned. Even with the necessary factors the four-toed body would still accumulate fat – for its mitochondria have scanty cristae and the fires burn low. It is pointless to list dietary deficiencies for the Nebish – who lacks so many of the basic enzymatic tools. What good is dietary iron if transferrin is short and the hemoglobin polypeptide chains have their sequences jumbled? Four grams of hemoglobin is all he can manage – even with Hb-F and Hb-N. His endoplasmic reticulum is agranular. He lacks the RNA-rich granules that make protein. Without them, he can't make good collagen, bone, enzymes or proteins of any kind – no matter how we improve his diet. However, hive life can make a somatic Nebish out of anyone.'

Walter and Val exchanged glances. Two soft, pasty bodies. Val knew *he* carried the gene. His body could be salvaged. But Walter had been near death several times. Diet had reversed the edema and paralysis several times. He turned to Gitar, hopefully.

'My genes?' asked Walter.

'Sorry, old man,' said Gitar. 'But life in the hive has brought you to the end of your life span, I'm afraid. Empty calories have accumulated in too many places – vessels, liver, adipose tissue. Your extra two hundred pounds of fat have taken you out of the stud category. Your physiology is strained by simple day-to-day existence. You must return to the hive – to die.'

'But my genes – am I one of the children of Olga?' asked Walter.

Gitar appraised the fatty hulk.

'You did have a spontaneous puberty—' theorized Gitar, 'but since then your liver failure has allowed estrogens to accumulate in your system. Gynecomastia and loss of libido have masked your true habitus; but I'd guess that under that four-toed exterior beats a heterozygous five-toed heart.'

Walter beamed.

'But,' continued Gitar, 'you lack melanin. I'd put you in the group of oculocutaneous albinos that make up most of the heterozygotes who carry the masking gene. You can never live Outside. Sunlight will kill you. Your retina and skin just cannot make pigment.'

'But I want to be with Olga – serve her. She is my deity. Surely there is a place for me,' pleaded Walter.

Gitar read the erratic bioelectricals in the old man's chest as an index of his fervor.

'Relax, old man,' said Gitar finally. 'You can stay with me – in the Huntercraft. Your knowledge of Hunter Control will make you a valuable acolyte in this flying Temple of Olga. Together we should be able to salvage many of the heterozygotes that Kaia has sired.'

Walter nodded his three chins.

'If you help me back to the spiral, Val, I'll start serving Olga by going into the HC workshop and disabling Tinker's vacuum pump. That should set back optic repair a year or more in this sector.'

'I can do better than that,' said Gitar.

He flew straight back to HC Garage. Door irised him inside without comment. No one in the hive seemed interested in the missing craft. While Walter removed vital bushings and seals from the pump, Val eyed Gitar critically.

'You aren't promising Walter that he will see his deity, are you?'

Gitar hummed a happy tune.

'Walter wants to serve. It will make him happy and give him purpose during his declining years. No, he won't live to see Olga's return. He has only a few years left – even with a natural food diet. But his soul will be with Olga one day. That will be his reward,' explained Gitar seriously.

Val didn't want to get into a discussion of 'soul' with a machine.

'What do you have planned for me?' asked Val.

Gitar's tune continued light and soothing. Percussion kept hold of his autonomics.

'You have the gene – Olga's five-toed gene. You will live Outside, under Olga's protection. It will be a good life.'

'For what purpose?'

'Stud.'

Val swallowed. Silence.

Old Walter contaminated the Hi Vac oil with volatiles and solvents. Using a pry bar, he cracked the cold trap and Christmas tree of the diffusion pump. Gitar was pleased.

During the following months Val tanned. Rhea went luteal with the corpus luteum of pregnancy. Val joined Walter and Gitar in scouring junglelike gardens for heterozygotes.

Walter melted away. Soon he was a lighter, firmer two-hundred-pound dwarf. Gitar monitored his dusk and dawn twilight outings – a swim, a jog, or just a brine soak in a tropical surf.

Gitar interrupted his swim, whispering, 'Jungle bunny.'

Walter glanced down the beach to see a shaggy-headed female leaving the surf – a forty-pound child, cautious, alert. Gitar activated Olga's Temple. Lights came on, disturbing the twilight fog of dawn. Music and lights called pleasantly to the child. Walter stood up, fat and dripping, to greet her. The tyke's eyes widened in terror. She ran and dove back into the surf. Gitar scanned. Nothing. The Temple rose and searched over the waters. They saw air in one of the six-fathom domes.

'One of the blue-domed cysts is alive. Its meck brain is giving her air and protection. No wonder we've had such poor luck in locating coastal jungle bunnies. They've gone to the sea,' exclaimed Walter with a smile.

Moses Eppendorff clutched Toothpick tightly. He was being swept along in a chanting procession through bizarre tubules hundreds of yards in diameter. He felt light-headed – often drifting up from the footpath. The walls around him pulsed and glowed with blue and white light. Small robots moved through the air making friendly, clucking sounds. Wounded were herded out of the procession. Exotic food and drink appeared.

Moses was dazed and worried. The last thing he remembered was the meteor shower. Glowing mountains of metal appeared above them in the skies at 50:00. Light blinded. The impacts jolted them off their feet and showered them with translucent yellow and red plasma. The sounds were deafening. But he felt nothing – only a chest-stiffening warmth. Comfort. He felt himself float up over the battlefield – fingers and toes intact. He looked around him – fellow buckeyes drifted up through the meteor trails – through flames and smoke – through showers of molten stone and metals. Everyone looked stunned, but he heard no cries of anguish. If it was death – it wasn't entirely unpleasant.

But now they were still obviously alive – and in some vast cyberconduit city that spoke to them in a soft voice. It fed them, and tended their wounds. It accepted their chants and prayers. It was a cyberdeity.

'Where are we?' he asked again.

This time Toothpick awoke – bright and cheerful.

'We are with Olga,' said the meck.

Olga left the solar system and began her long journey toward Sagittarius. Solar winds had masked her arrival from the hive, and now they washed away traces of her ion drive. The planets crossed their cusps. The conjunction broke up and the solar flares died down.

'A starship,' said Toothpick. 'An implant starship. Olga took one load of colonists to some distant star, and now has returned to Earth for another load – us. I was just a space probe – sent to prepare the way – to protect and collect five-toed genes.'

Moses nodded. It had to be something like that. Too many forces were working for the fugitives – Ball's successful religion – patients at Dundas freed to walk the surface – all the clandestine efforts of a mighty starship. An effort to collect the good gene.

Toothpick seemed as surprised as anyone. He was only pro-grammed to know his mission – collect and protect. He didn't know why. He did know that he would have to self-destruct if his identity were discovered – his black cylinder – a quark bottle –

carried a charge high in the megaclosson range. Enough to form a table mountain or a new lake if set off.

'Skimmed off the planet – like five-toed cream,' chuckled Moses. 'I wondered how a meck like you – a class six – could ignore the prime directive and kill citizens.'

'I have never broken my prime directives,' said Toothpick carefully. 'Deaths at Dundas were just statistical risks – unavoidable mortality associated with pyrotherapy. Conflicts with the Nebish were unavoidable, but they are not human by Olga's definition. They have four toes – different genes – different species.'

Moses smiled. He certainly agreed with that line of logic. A machine faced with an evolving creator must make a choice. Her loyalty would lie with the five-toed who created her – not the Nebish. Her very existence was incompatible with the hive.

'I guess we five-toeds are the superior life form. Olga confirmed that – skimming us off the planet – the cream of the human race,' he chuckled.

Olga spoke, her voice coming from the walls. It had a feminine Nordic quality.

'Don't be smug,' she said. 'You were selected because you show a higher individual survival potential. Your five-toed gene makes you adaptable, competitive – ideal for an implant colony where you'll have to evolve quickly. Man has shown his ability to evolve – socially and industrially – in terms of a few hundred years.

'The hive is much too stable – evolving in terms of millions of years, and then toward death. It lives by the status quo – only becoming competitive when faced with another hive. Then it does only what is necessary for survival – no more. It can come into being wherever your species is too successful – a product of population density.'

Moses frowned at the wall.

'We're all seeds of the hive?'

'Seeds – yes,' said Olga with a note of sadness.

Moses caught her shift into melancholia. Why would a mighty starship dread the Big ES so?

'Do you fear the hive?' he asked.

'Earth Society – the Big ES – is my enemy only in the sense that

I am an implant starship. It would have stopped me if it could. But you must realize that it would have done so for the welfare of the average citizen . . . to adjust the standard of living upwards with whatever could be salvaged from my hull. It would mean my death as a starship – but a better life for the average Nebish.'

'The hive is your enemy – yet you carry us, who are seeds of a new hive?'

'It is my reason for living – my whole purpose. I must remain free from the hive to fulfill my purpose,' said Olga.

Moses glanced around the mile-wide hull. Strength. Power. Wisdom.

'Why were you so devious? Certainly a stagnated hive could do nothing to harm you – for you are a mighty starship – a cyberdeity – a god.'

Olga's voice became firm, authoritative.

'I never underestimate the hive. When its existence is threatened it will fight back – perhaps even follow me into space.'

'Impossible,' exclaimed Moses. 'I saw the degree of technical decay. It will never go into space again. Why, it can't even manage simple undersea cities.'

'Think again,' said the starship. 'Suppose you were still a Pipe. How would you go about building a starship – if the hive gave you carte blanche?'

Moses scoffed. 'Ridiculous! I'd need five-toed Pipers, Tinkers, Tecks – they simply do not exist in the hive.'

Olga answered softly. 'See. You would know where to start. The hive has gene banks – remember. It could Tatter a million new workers in any caste you'd like.'

Moses paused – open-mouthed. Of course! The starship science was lost somewhere in the rusty dusty stacks – but it could be dug out and reworked by five-toeds. Given full powers and a massive budget, even an average five-toed could initiate a revival of space travel. The hive could be back in space in a couple of generations. Of course the average Nebish would be less comfortable – but the hive would do anything if its existence was threatened by a raiding starship.

'The meteor shower—' he mumbled.

'I have given the hive a choice of explanations for your sudden exodus – natural disaster – or a poorly documented miracle. Hopefully no one will even think of a three-thousand-year-old starship. I'd hate to be the cause of the hive coming into space.'

Moses nodded – five-toed men needed space to escape the hive. Olga was doing that – keeping the buckeye genes pure. She also found sanctuary for Earth biota crowded out by the Nebish. Species long extinct on Mother Earth were flourishing on distant new worlds. Would her implanting functions ever end? He remembered his views of the night sky. Would mankind ever run out of stars?

During the first stages of the voyage, the Dundas fugitives were screened for skills. Healers were put to work tending Olga's Tattering apparatus. Each colonist had a sample of genetic material – lymphocytes from peripheral blood – placed in cell culture media and embryonated. The resultant child – a genetic carbon copy, was to be presented to each colonist as a sort of asexual bud. This insured that all would be represented in the implant's gene pool – even the senile and postmenopausal.

Moses, Hugh and Mu Ren were having their blood drawn when they noticed racks of cryocoffins containing battle-scarred buckeyes. Tinker's strike force!

Moses studied the readouts. The bodies were dead.

'Where did you get these?' he asked.

'Floating in the place called Coweye Sump,' said Olga. 'They read buckeye on my scanners. I beamed them up. Although they had been dead for several hours, I was able to find viable, intact nuclei. They are being Tattered also.'

Mu Ren ran frantically from coffin to coffin, falling to her knees sobbing at the one containing Tinker's remains. Olga recognized a widow's anguish.

'The man you call Tinker will be with us in the new world,' said the ship's Nordic voice. 'His soul still lives.'

'Soul?' sniffed Mu Ren.

'His essence – life principle – DNA-gene-soul. I have copied his genetic person – an embryo now in this bottle,' Olga explained, illuminating a small vial high on a wall rack. 'We will all miss his personality and skills.'

Mu Ren sobbed into Moses' shoulder. He comforted her.

'Tinker will be with us,' he said softly. 'Counting Little Tinker, who is almost four years old, and the baby in your belly – this new budchild makes three. Three Tinkers.'

She blinked back her tears. With her own budchild that made four! She studied Moses' face purposefully. Was that look in his eye appropriate? She held his hand firmly and asked what his mating plans were.

Moses' experience with coweyes made him a bit wary of their primitive sexual behavior. The violent ups and downs of their tense ovarian cycles upset his calm, ordered existence. Here was a female raised, as he had been, in the city. She would not disappear or drive him away during the luteal phase. Yet, her years in the buckeye camps had toughened her for life in the new colony. He put a protective arm on her shoulder.

'My own budchild will need a mother's milk when we set down. I can think of no one else I'd rather have caring for him,' he said.

Her eyes dried. They picked up little Tinker and walked towards Olga's Suspension Clinics – Hugh sauntered along behind, a little self-conscious about the tender love scene.

Olga sang through the oxygen squeeze and cryotherapy.

> *Children of Olga, you'll be free,*
> *To run and swim and climb the tree.*
> *You'll eat the pear and taste the grape,*
> *See a bird – a fish – an ape.*
> *Dwell with fauna from Earth, long gone.*
> *Creatures salvaged for you – alone.*
> *Children of Olga, you'll be free,*
> *To walk the stars – eternally.*

After what seemed like a brief period in suspension, Olga's charges awoke to find her in orbit around the new planet. Orbit-to-Surface Modules were being loaded – single-seaters for outposts and larger cabin classes for the settlements.

'This planet will be your new home,' announced Olga. 'It was stocked with Earth biota 392.7 standard years ago. My probes indicate a successful take for most of the Earth species but local alien forms still predominate. You will have to use some judgment, of course – but the probability of a successful implant is very high.'

Gruff old Moon approached Moses, who stood in line with Mu Ren. Moon carried his infant carbon copy – young Moses held three crying infants.

'Where are the single seaters?' asked Moon.

Moses nodded toward one of the smaller bays on his left.

Moon studied the three crying infants in Moses arms. Setting his own casually on the deck, he took the triplets and held them underhanded like small sacks of grain. They quieted.

'You have to be confident,' he explained. 'When you're nervous, they detect it. Parental anxiety means danger – to any species. If there was one thing you should have learned Outside, it was self-confidence.'

Moses smiled and took back the kids.

'Aren't you overdoing it?' commented Moon, gesturing to the three small blinking faces.

Moses shrugged, 'Just me, Mu and Tinker.'

'Tinker—' said Moon, picking up his infant. 'Good man.' He ran his tongue over gold teeth and grinned. Moon walked off followed by three-legged Dan and a tiny, clumsy puppy.

Dan-with-the-golden-teeth tilted his head quizzically. The small four-footed creature had been following him ever since he woke up. He growled at it, but still it tagged along. Its tail wagged three times. Ancient memories stirred. He gave it a big wet lick, knocking it down.

Moon pushed the two of them into the OSM and closed the hatch.

The acromegalic lumbered up to the checkout point.

'Skills?' asked the turnstile.

'Healer. But I've been retired ever since—'

He held up his large clumsy hands.

'Your pituitary tumor was destroyed by the pyrotherapy of Dundas. What you can do today, you will be able to do for years. Your condition will improve. A Healer you are! I would like to assign you to this settlement with Moses and Mu Ren. Is that satisfactory?'

The acromegalic nodded. He could see from Mu Ren's duck-walk and winces that his first job would be delivering a baby. He put his own infant on his shoulder and approached Moses smiling.

As Moon's OSM entered the atmosphere he caught a glimpse of Moses' cabin-class ship in a lower orbit.

'Dammit,' he spat. 'We all should be in single-seaters. Putting down a ready-made city like that only hastens the evolution of civilization.'

Olga's soft confident voice soothed: 'A little civilization may be necessary for survival. The ecology and geography of this planet are a bit more hostile than your Mother Earth's.'

'Civilization is too high a price to pay for survival,' he grumbled. He meant it.

He and Dan pressed their noses against the viewport. Continents and oceans – not too unlike Earth. There were more mountains – younger and sharper. Strange circular blemishes marred many of the flat areas – like astroblemes. Misty, overgrown archipelagos mottled the oceans. He smiled. It would be many generations before transportation linked the various implants.

Moses' OSM put down at an estuary. It was night, but on a previous pass they had seen promising grain-fields and herds of ungulates. The colonists were optimistic.

Mu Ren delivered. The acromegalic held up the wrinkled wet infant and gave it a ritual spank. Mu Ren nursed it while Moses joined the acromegalic on his Mediteck rounds. Simple Willie sat with a young coweye. His face was bandaged. Olga had removed thick keloid scars from his face – and excised the molecular scars that had blocked his memory. When he saw Moses he smiled – a symmetrical, clear-eyed smile.

'Olga unblocked my memory,' he said enthusiastically. 'My trophy was a hunter – the same hunter who had cut off my own toes. I remember him threatening to cut off the little things that made me a man – my fifth toes. The MR confused me when they hunted the yellow-haired ones – but I managed to wipe out the entire hunting party. Honey, my coweye, escaped with a leg wound. I imagine she has found another mate by now.'

Moses smiled while Willie's bandages were removed. A coweye

can be relied on to find a mate – if one is available. He studied the new coweye seated next to Willie – licorice hair and mint-green eyes . . . at least the second most beautiful thing in the world . . . any world.

Moses Eppendorff turned and walked back to Mu Ren and his five children.

Moon's OSM circled the globe several times before settling down in a green mountain glade. Goats nibbled and stood unafraid as Moon and Dan stepped out. An alien hawk with bright plumage circled inquisitively at a very high altitude – then swooped down, passing overhead with a *snap*.

'By Olga, a Garden of Eden!' exclaimed old Moon with one of his infrequent smiles. Eyeing a heavy udder, he took Little Moon's pap sac and approached the nanny. He filled it easily – with surplus for Little Dan.

Scratching his head, he mumbled: 'Now how can you explain that?'

Goats approached him as he talked.

Another human voice called to him from a stand of Earth willows. Moon snarled and picked up a cudgel from the brush. He and Dan approached the sound of the voice. They stepped through a stream of cold melt-water and slippery stones.

'I thought this was to be a one-man outpost—'

He saw a familiar object – a cybernetic javelin – space-probe – embedded in the soft humus and draped with vines.

'I am a companion robot, designed to be carried. Pick me up,' said the cyber.

Moon smiled and dropped his gnarled branch.

'I know,' he said, pulling it free. 'What have you been doing here all these years?'

'Watching over the implant, and making new friends for you. These goats are imprinted on the human voice. Welcome to the planet Tiercel – land of the hawks.'

'Thank you for the welcome,' said Moon. He watched Dan and the pup gamboling with frisky goats.

Later he sat in the grass, leaned against the OSM and propped his feet on Dan's scarred and muscular back. A goat nibbled from his hand. He turned to the cyberspear and added: 'And thanks for the friends you've been making. Man should have lots of friends – as long as they are different species.'

Back on planet Earth, Gitar continued his TAR sorties into the hive – piping heterozygotes buckeye with a song. Walter's last days in the Temple were idyllic – in the service of Olga. When his life-span came to an end, Gitar was careful to store his DNA-gene-soul in one of the Huntercraft's trophy cubes. Walter knew it only awaited Olga's next return to be awakened. A genetic copy of himself would go with his deity, someday.

> Val lived to see
> generations three
> of his family tree
> spread under the sea.

Gitar added legends to their culture with song.
They were the tribes of Prince Valiant, vigorous, strong.

> *The Nebish evolved into a fat little dwarf*
> *Who had none of the genes of the five-toed kind.*
> *With soft, chalky bones and rose water for blood,*
> *He was hypogonadal, dim-minded and blind.*

Outriggers plied the oceans – seeding buckeyes on island and continent alike.

> *As their numbers increased,*
> *The hunters returned.*
> *Big ES did what it must to survive.*

> *Gitar said it was time*
> *For Olga's return*
> *When buckeyes start crowding the Hive.*

T.J. Bass (Thomas Joseph Bassler) was an American science-fiction writer and doctor, principally known for his 'Hive' stories. The first of these, published in *Galaxy Science Fiction* and *If*, were combined into the novel *Half Past Human*, which was nominated for the Nebula Award in 1972. Its loose sequel, *The Godwhale*, was also nominated three years later. His work explored the theme of overpopulation and was notable for its strong command of biological extrapolation. He died in 2011.

A full list of SF Masterworks can be found at

www.gollancz.co.uk